OUR SONG (THE WILDER BOOKS #1)

SAVANNAH KADE

GRIFFYN INK

For Jarett and January who keep me smiling and laughing.

CHAPTER 1

The screams tore the air. High pitched and long, they sounded like someone was being stabbed.

Kelsey's head swiveled, like every other head in the store, until she found the source of the wail. Then she relaxed.

It was just a normal little girl, maybe five years old, screaming her head off, but looking quite unharmed. Her head tipped back to make sure that the sounds radiated in every direction. Her straight dark hair slid down her back, looking as if it hadn't made friends with a brush in a few too many days.

"She's upset." Daniel commented in soft tones. He looked up at her from the basket of the shopping cart, his widened eyes and slightly opened bow mouth told what he thought. He watched, but that was all. Daniel had never been one to participate in anything resembling a tantrum, for which Kelsey was supremely grateful.

Her eyes flicked back to the girl, as she let loose another wail. A store employee was rapidly making her way over to help, hands wringing nervously as she gamely pushed her way through the racks.

As the girl took another gulp, Kelsey mentally closed her

ears. She wanted to push her cart and her kids away, but something held her there. She needed little girls' clothes for her own daughter, and she wasn't about to let a screaming kid rule her decisions.

This time the wail got through to Kelsey's shut-off brain. Just as she had picked up the leg of a pair of bright blue jeans, the little voice spoke, "He is *not* my Daddy!"

Well, that made her head snap around again. She barely registered the employee looking between the child and the father, but she saw that the little girl's pants were too short and too tight. Her shirt didn't cover her belly when she tipped her head back to scream. She was unkempt, upset, and glaring daggers.

The father instantly earned Kelsey's sympathy. She wasn't sure why she never believed that the little girl had been kidnapped. But she didn't. And a father didn't deserve to have his kid pull any of this on him—certainly not in public.

She also felt supreme pity for his total lack of parenting skills. Otherwise, he looked strong and capable in fitted jeans and a t-shirt that showed off what he'd worked for. His deep brown eyes and straight nose looked like they belonged on a man who stood his ground. Her heart turned over for him as he stood with feet apart and shoulders straight as he held up a sweet little outfit that was totally dwarfed by the sheer size of him. His dark hair slipped over one eye, only partially obscuring the red that crept across his face and appeared to be setting up permanent residence.

Even though he was facing her down, the child had clearly won.

"Look!" Allie held up a small doll. "Look!" Kelsey blinked for a moment. Only when her eyes landed on a nearby display did she realize that her pigtailed three-year-old had filched it as they passed. With a frown, she looked down and saw the shredded cardboard blister-pack. *Well, that would have to get purchased.*

Now she needed to take the doll away, or get something comparable for Daniel, who had been an angel. There was no good way around that one. Except, maybe . . .

"I don't want new clothes!" The voice was rude, sharp, and tiny. At least the little girl wasn't shrieking anymore.

"Honey, those clothes are too small." The father stood over her, his voice steady, although Kelsey wasn't sure how he managed that.

"My *mommy* bought me these clothes." The little girl's arms crossed over her chest and she clamped her jaw so tight Kelsey was certain that she'd hear little teeth grinding.

Again his voice was soft, and this time full of defeat. "I know." He absently hung up the outfit on the nearest rack and sighed.

The store employee had disappeared, but Kelsey pushed her way through to them. They probably didn't need her help, but she felt drawn in. Besides, there was that cute doll that she had to pay for and couldn't let her daughter keep. "Allie, give me the dolly."

With a small pout that had Kelsey pressing her lips together, Allie handed over the doll and assumed her own cross-armed position. Kelsey ignored her.

"Would she like this doll?" She was grateful that her voice didn't shake like it wanted to.

The father looked her square in the face, the first time he'd looked *at* someone since his daughter had started wailing in the middle of Target. Kelsey felt something tug inside. His eyes were a combination of grateful and exhausted, the deep brown riddled with shadows and regret. His voice sounded the way he looked. "You are more than welcome to try."

Daniel and Allie looked on with avid curiosity, while she

leaned down to the little girl and held up the doll as bait. "Do you think you could help me out?"

There was only a pout and glare as response.

"I'm buying some clothes for Allie and maybe you could try on some of the same things." Kelsey wiggled the doll, watching its pink nylon hair sway, and she got a great idea. Quickly, she stood and searched the cart, certain that the doll had come with a little plastic hairbrush.

Grabbing it, she began brushing the doll's hair as she walked back to the little girl. Brown eyes were watching her with interest although no other part of the small body had abandoned the furious stance. "This dolly really needs her hair brushed, can you help her?"

Kelsey didn't wait for an answer, just shoved the doll and brush into the little girl's hands and turned past the father, offering a small smile. Grabbing the abandoned outfit from the rack she turned and carefully picked out the same clothes in Allie's size.

"Allie?" She held them up. "Do you like these?"

Allie nodded vigorously and attempted to stand up in the cart. Kelsey held out a hand and shook her head. Allie promptly sat back down, but held her hands out for the clothes.

Kelsey turned back to the little dark-haired girl. "Would you like to try some on, too?"

She didn't say 'yes', but neither did she protest, and Kelsey led the bunch through to the fitting rooms. Only as she walked in did she realize the father wasn't allowed in the ladies' fitting rooms. Kelsey started to explain, but he just shook his head.

"If you can find out if they fit, then you are light years beyond me."

"Okay." Kelsey felt as small as the word, but she plucked Allie then Daniel from the cart and reached out for the little girl's hand. After a moment, there it was in her own. The little face was a little dirty, she noticed from up close, but she didn't say anything. "What's your name, honey?"

The answer came from behind her in a masculine voice lined with a deep sigh, "Andie."

Kelsey felt her back stiffen. *Not another Andy.*

Her hand must have jerked, because the little hand belonging to little Andie grasped a little tighter.

With some resolve, she marched the three of them into the changing room and tried the clothes on the girls. As she had expected, little Andie bore no marks of abuse, just a need for a bath and new underwear. But she tried on the new clothes without much fuss, and Kelsey was pleased to see that the 5T size fit her perfectly.

"Look!" Allie jumped exuberantly in the new outfit, eyeing Andie and smiling that they were dressed alike.

"Let's go show your Daddy." Kelsey stood and walked out, three small children trailing her like ducks. Daniel solemn and sweet, Allie bubbly and charming, and Andie defiant as ever.

Her father stood outside the doors, his head leaned back against a mirrored column, looking like the day had worn him down. He snapped up at the sight of his daughter wearing clothes that fit. He gave an obvious sigh of relief. "They're great."

Kelsey smiled. One screaming fit averted for the day.

"Andie," She choked the name out and then pushed through the rest pleasantly, "I think Allie is going to just wear her new outfit." She reached down and pulled the tags off to ring them up when they left.

Andie motioned for her to do the same, but Kelsey pawned the job off on Daddy. "Can you stay out here with them? I'm going to go grab their old clothes." She didn't really wait for a reply. The pained expression on his face told her he was going to say 'no'. So she simply smiled and didn't let him.

Kelsey gathered small clothes in her arms, and then stepped back out, handing Andie's dad the too-small clothes, and wadding up Allie's. She helped her own kids back in the cart and turned to speak over her shoulder. "She needs new underwear, too."

He panicked. "What size?"

"She was in fours, so sixes should do it. They're right over there." She shrugged and pointed. "The size 5T fit her great, so you can pretty much pick up anything else that size and not worry about trying it on."

Again his shoulders worked through a sigh, and Kelsey felt a pang of pity for both of them. "Thank you." He stuck out his hand, and gave her an odd look before shaking his head as though to clear the thought. "I'm JD. And I can't tell you what a help you've been. How did you do it?"

She shook his hand hoping she looked nonchalant. She wasn't getting into any of that with a perfect stranger. "I'm Kelsey. Good luck."

She wheeled away thinking she needed a new seat cover in the car. She needed to replace one Daniel had ripped accidentally, and do it without upsetting him about the one he had ruined. He was sensitive that way, but no wonder.

She browsed the automotive aisle a few minutes before trying to furtively place the blue Hawaiian slip cover under the cart. But Daniel saw it and his lip began to tremble. At moments like these she prayed that she wasn't seeing vestiges of his father. But the problem was either there or it wasn't; she knew that from experience. No amount of hope or help could change those facts. So she smiled and made the best of it.

"I think we need to re-do the whole car. Maybe these ones with the frogs on them?" She pointed. At twenty bucks a pop they weren't what she was planning on spending. But she could afford it. Just.

Daniel smiled. "They have lizards, too, can we get some of each?"

Allie spotted ladybugs and Kelsey smiled. So the car

wouldn't match. Those smiles were worth every penny. The four different covers were all black velvet, so Kelsey figured they wouldn't embarrass her when she went to meetings.

Just before she buried it, she pulled out the shred of cardboard with the barcode for the doll and put it with the tags from Allie's clothes. This trip had turned far more expensive than she planned.

Pushing the cart to the register, she mentally tallied how much they had spent and tried not to grimace. At least her kids were being well behaved.

What the hell. "Who wants to get pizzas?"

"Me!"

"Me, too!"

Allie jiggled like Jell-O with the prospect, and Kelsey made a mental note to strip off the new clothes before she handed over any pizza.

A few minutes later, Kelsey had tucked the bags and the pizzas into the cart, filled up the drinks, and headed out to the car. Once she had everyone buckled, she pulled out of the parking lot, the passenger seat loaded down with bags. It made her sad the seat didn't have her own Andy in it.

"Mommy! My new shirt is pink."

"Yes, baby, it's pretty." She answered Allie with a pre-packaged smile, grateful to be distracted from memories of Andrew.

"When we get home, can we put the new covers on the car seats?"

"Well, Daniel, I think we need to eat dinner first."

Kelsey went back and forth with Daniel, trying to work out *exactly* when they could put the new covers on. She wasn't sure quite when, but sometime during the conversation she noticed an old grey sedan following them. Andrew's phrasing came to mind: an old Honda P.O.S. he'd always called them. Piece of shit. Kelsey had always argued in favor of any car that stayed on the road, functioning, for that long. But it figured—Andrew had never worried about money. He'd never understood it.

The Honda followed them through the next few turns, ratcheting Kelsey's anxiety up a notch every time it stayed close behind. She had her kids with her. She wouldn't lead someone to her house. She considered driving on to the police station and made the decision just as she drove past her own garage.

They lived in the corner house, so she swung to the right, ready to head around the block, when she noticed that the Honda had pulled into the condos that stood on the corner just behind her house.

With a hiss of breath and a shake of her head, Kelsey cursed her own paranoia. It was only one of her neighbors. If she'd made any effort to get to know them better, she might very well have recognized the car and driver and never thought anything of it. Wasn't that part of the reason she had moved here?

"Okay kids! Out!" She unlocked all the doors and helped Allie down and over to the sidewalk before grabbing the pizza.

"Why are we parked over here?" Daniel looked up with glassy eyes, worry shining bright.

"Oh, I just felt like it."

He nodded, and traipsed off after Allie, only to both be called back. "Daniel, you can close your door, and everybody carries something." The kids grumbled, but they knew the routine, and each picked up a bag and lugged it to the front door.

Kelsey juggled what she was holding and got the front door unlocked. Just as she was marching the kids inside, she heard her name.

She looked up to see JD from Target round the corner, wearing a true grin for the first time. "Kelsey? I thought you looked familiar."

She shooed the kids inside, and set down the groceries before stepping to the front porch and easing the door closed behind her. "You live there?" She pointed to the condos just behind her house.

"Yeah, we just moved in."

He shook his head as if he didn't know what to say, and she realized for the first time that he was younger than she had first taken him for, maybe mid-twenties. He looked nervous there with his hands shoved into the pockets of the jeans she now saw were a bit worn. His sneakers, too, had seen better days. He smiled and nodded, "Well, I'll let you get to your dinner. Thanks again for all your help."

With that, he headed back to the condos and missed the vague, overly-polite smile that passed across her face.

For a moment Kelsey tried to remember the last time she'd had a real smile.

CHAPTER 2

K elsey sat to one side of the table, with papers spread
out across the blue plaid cloth. Two dirty Curious
George placemats held place at the opposite end, but her work
didn't migrate that far. She had a headset perched over her
ears.

She let a sigh slip out as she punched the 'Off' button on the
phone. She'd worked her butt off, but finally got a second
appraiser to come in another ten thousand higher on the house.
That meant her latest clients could close out their re-finance at
a lower rate, because the equity in their house was now at
twenty percent.

She was glad the kids were out today. Their babysitter was
going to be a high-school senior this coming fall, and was a gift
from the angels. When Bethany went off to college, Kelsey had
no idea where she'd turn. Bethany had taken the kids out of the
house all day today, and after fighting for that estimate Kelsey
was supremely thankful.

She stood, stretching out her shoulders and rolling her neck.
It was all coming together, and that was a good feeling. It meant
an infusion of cash into her account soon. They could use it—

they always could. She almost had enough saved up for a week at the beach.

"Andie!" The angry, male voice punched through her senses. Though her brain registered that it wasn't her own father yelling, it didn't take the snap out of her spine.

Out the window she saw little Andie from Target go running by, her long dark hair trailing behind her like a banner.

Kelsey almost laughed out loud that she was still so programmed to jump when she heard that name. But she was on her feet and halfway to the sidewalk before she saw JD go running past, yelling Andie's name again, his lean body in perfect form as his feet ate up pavement.

"Wait!" She caught up to him, grabbing his arm and stopping his mad flight.

"What?" He was breathing heavily, and clearly angry judging from the look on his face. But to his credit it slid behind a curtain of sheer fatigue. "She won't brush her hair."

Just then, he noticed that Andie was nowhere in sight. His first response was to panic, but Kelsey's fingers tightened around his arm, stopping him by her calm demeanor. Because it certainly wasn't her strength that kept him there. "Don't. She'll just run further. She's pretty safe here."

He still looked worried, so she tried again. "I saw her duck into the Hendersons' yard. The worst that can happen is the yorkie will bark and Mrs. Henderson will feed her too many cookies."

"Okay." His breath came in great gulps as he lowered himself to the curb. He planted his feet and let his arms rest across his knees. Only then did she realize that he was clenching a hairbrush hard enough to turn the knuckles of his left hand a vibrant white.

For a moment Kelsey almost feared for little Andie's safety. The words just fell out of her mouth. "Do I need to do a background check on you?"

He gave a bark of laughter. "No." But his head didn't come up until a minute later when he asked if there was any way she could watch Andie for an hour or so while he went out.

She didn't mind, but . . . "Are you coming back?"

He gave another long pause, scaring Kelsey. But when he finally answered, it wasn't what she'd expected. "I'll come back. I have to. But I could really use enough time to get shit-faced drunk and then sober up." He gave a wan smile, letting her know this wasn't his usual afternoon activity. Still Kelsey wondered what the hell she had gotten herself into.

Before she could say anything, two little pairs of feet came pounding up to where she and JD sat on the edge of the sidewalk.

"Mommy!" Allie's voice broke the layer of despair that JD had brought with him and Kelsey looked up in time to see Daniel put an arm out, blocking his sister from running to Mom with the latest news of a day with Bethany.

"Hey, Kelsey! They were great." Bethany knew that the first thing Kelsey wanted was a report. "They both ate a good lunch."

"Is there any chance you can keep them a few hours longer?" Kelsey stood up and brushed off the backside of her jeans, looking at JD where his broad back still showed strength even through the cloak of exhaustion.

Kelsey knew Bethany was saving to go to cheerleading camp over spring break, and that was a powerful incentive. But Kelsey had to be completely honest. "Let me tell you what you're getting into first. You see the little girl peeking out from the hedge down there?"

Bethany nodded, looking a little warier, and Kelsey thought that was a smart expression.

"You'll have her, too." She turned to JD, "That is, if you want some company and to tell me the whole story."

"That sounds good." His chocolate gaze shifted to Bethany, landing first on her sneakers and traveling up her longs legs and finally settling on her face, looking young and fresh and all the things Kelsey didn't feel. His voice was calm but strong, "Let me warn you, she can be a handful."

Bethany looked back and forth between the two of them until she came to some kind of decision. "I'll call my mom."

It was only after she'd shoved the phone back in her pocket, saying everything was fine, she could stay as late as she was needed, that Kelsey realized Bethany thought this was going to be a date.

Kelsey shoved down the laugh trying to burble up. It was a date to find out if this man had kidnapped this little girl, and what the hell was going on. Kelsey didn't remember what a real 'date' was, but she didn't tell Bethany.

JD was content to let Bethany and the now ecstatic Daniel and Allie go fetch little Andie. He handed over a few bills to cover the kids' dinner and agreed to wait while Kelsey changed out of her T-shirt. After slinging on a light button-down blouse she followed him back to his place.

They walked past her closed garage door and around the cinderblock wall that was just barely higher than the top of her head. His unit was on the end, and she followed him up the back stairs calling herself all kinds of fool as she did it. What if he was one of those incredibly handsome men who turned out to be a murderer or worse? While she didn't believe it, what she'd seen led her to believe that things weren't right.

He pushed the back door open without bothering with a key, and only then did Kelsey remember that he had come bolting by after Andie, he probably hadn't stopped to lock up. Sure enough, he still held the powder pink hairbrush in his grip.

The house looked spotless. And nearly empty. An old blue couch sat on one side of the room opposite a large black TV. Every room she could see was done in décor she and her friends had always referred to as 'early college'. He stopped in the middle of the room, his hands on his hips, as if challenging her to find faults. "We can order pizza or go out. Your choice."

She tilted her head, trying to read him. He truly seemed too tired to be dangerous. "Are you going to tell me what's going on?"

"If you promise to help me until they take her back."

"Take her back?" That sent a shiver through her like bad lightning.

He looked worse for wear than he had even a few minutes before, although Kelsey wouldn't have thought that was possible. So she took a deep breath and didn't say anything.

Without a word—he didn't look like he could really form one—JD wandered into the kitchen and opened the fridge to offer her a drink. But the fridge lit up like a bright beacon, illuminating the single bottle of beer and leftover McDonald's boxes.

Her voice cut through the darkness that existed inside the house even though it was bright day outside. "Oh, no. We're going out. You look like you could use a decent meal."

"Okay." He didn't argue, just trudged upstairs saying something about changing. Kelsey looked around, feeling like such a mom. Here she was with a good-looking man and she was worried about his eating habits. Oh well, she had to be older than he was, and she couldn't remember a time when she hadn't been a mom in some way. Maybe that's why she had never become a wife.

Just a few minutes later JD trotted back down the stairs looking much more presentable in khakis and a ribbed shirt. He had even traded up the dead Converse sneakers for Doc Martens. A half grin crinkled the corners of his eyes, "Yes, I do own clothing other than sneakers and jeans."

It added a handful of years to her estimate of his age. "Just how old are you?"

Well, that just fell out of her mouth. Words and phrases and odd questions were coming out of her with no control lately. Every time they did, her spine stiffened just a little, waiting for the yell or the snap.

But JD did neither. "I'll be twenty-nine next month."

It was like her subconscious was searching for his break point and the words just fell out again, "The real twenty-nine or are you holding there?"

He laughed. "The real twenty-nine. I promise next year I'll turn thirty."

The laugh was the first sound of true enjoyment she had heard from him. His face lit up, his smile transforming him from simply good-looking to heart-breaking. It was certainly unexpected given the hangdog expression he had been wearing before.

Just then the doorbell rang, immediately followed by a pounding noise, then a muffled yell. "JD! Open up!"

Kelsey's eyebrows rose right about the same time JD said, "Shit!" He turned to her. "What day is it?"

"Tuesday." She shied back a few feet.

He threw open the door to reveal three guys who were the lifestyle brothers of the earlier JD. They all wore faded jeans, one with intricate tribal markings in black across the nearly white denim. Hair was in eyes and t-shirts ranged from old to mildly vulgar to muscle-baring.

JD's voice stopped her musings, "Guys, no practice tonight. But come in." He held the door wide and ushered the now disgruntled looking band inside.

And that, Kelsey realized, was exactly what they were: a band. She hadn't noticed before, but there were guitars and cases slung over shoulders and hauled in tight fists.

"You're ditching practice for a chick?" The blond with the lip ring and tribalized jeans looked pissed. And, on him, pissed was a whole other level, Kelsey thought.

JD shook his head. "The homeowner's association called

after last week. I told you we wouldn't be able to practice here. We have to find somewhere new."

There was a chorus of "damn" and a few other choice words, followed by, "That kid has screwed with all our lives. Makes me want to keep it in my pants."

"I appreciate your support." JD was getting angry, "But you don't know the half of it."

"You're leaving the band, aren't you?" This from a blue-eyed younger version of JD; the guy *had* to be his brother.

Not a one of them apologized to her for their language or even tried to introduce themselves, but she didn't care. None of them was swearing *at* her, and polite introductions existed in a world her family had been forced to abandon a long time ago.

"JD can't leave the band. None of us can. We're screwed without all four of us." That was the blonde with the lip ring again.

JD shook his head. "I'm not leaving the band. At least I don't think I am." That was met with groans and a few, *'yeah, right's.* "I'm not practicing tonight because I am about two minutes from total meltdown. And because we don't have anywhere to practice. Find a place for next week and I'll find a way to be there."

At least now they looked disgruntled, which was a full phase better than pissed off. The counselors had always said disgruntled was very much in the realm of acceptable.

Now that the group was generally calm, JD turned back to her. "Gentlemen, this is my neighbor Kelsey. She's going to help me figure out how to deal with Andie."

Hadn't she heard that phrase before? And wasn't she always the best at 'dealing with Andy'?

His voice broke her thoughts. "This is Craig. He's our bass, and one of our songwriters." The blonde simply nodded at her, clearly still scoping out the situation and wondering if she was going to break up the band. Kelsey almost laughed out loud.

"Alex, our drums."

Alex shook her hand and withheld judgment, just as he had withheld any words during the exchange.

"And my little brother TJ. Lead vocals."

TJ smiled like a charm-shark, "Kelsey, nice to meet you. What are you doing with my brother here?"

She started to reply, *'feeding him'* but JD glared. "She's my neighbor, so back off TJ."

Kelsey mentally inserted her own little cat growl into the conversation, then stifled a laugh.

Inside a minute, he had them all ushered back out the door, and he turned to her as though trying to read her. Not that she thought that was going to happen anytime soon. He asked, "So, where are we going?"

She pulled her keys out of her purse, "Somewhere with vegetables."

He winced, reminding her of the kid he was.

"I promise I won't feed you just squash for dinner." She pulled his back door open, figuring to lead the way, "How does Italian sound?"

"Actually, that sounds really good. I was afraid you were going to go vegan on me."

There wasn't any conversation as she led him back around the cinderblock wall and to her garage door. He stepped in front of her and lifted the handle, swinging the door high without any of the effort it usually cost her. He even held her car door, which she added to his list of good qualities. Now if she could just figure out what was up with his daughter . . .

He bounced a little in the passenger seat. "It's comfier than I expected. What made you get a mini-van?"

"Family of five to haul around."

He nodded absently and asked a little too casually, "Your husband willing to drive this?"

She almost laughed, at him and at the question. "There's no husband."

He smiled. "Good, you just never know what a guy might think if his wife was out in the mini-van with another man."

This time she did laugh. For the briefest of moments, she wondered why it felt so strange, then she realized it was because she hadn't done that in over a year. She should thank JD, but then she'd have to explain, and she still wasn't up to that. "Okay, dinner, and then you're going to explain about your daughter."

He nodded. "And you're going to tell me what you did the other day to get her to function. I really need help."

"I can see that." She took a corner and waited at a light. All the while staying silent, hoping he would fill in the space.

Finally, he did, but with another question of his own. "So, I only saw a family of three. Where are the other two?"

It was casual enough that she knew he didn't understand what he was asking. So she gave an honest response but told none of the real issues. "They aren't here anymore."

She pulled up in front of the restaurant just as he commented. "Oh, but I'm supposed to spill my guts."

"If you want help with Andie." She popped out of her side of the car and bee-lined for the front doors, not certain why that made her so upset. But it did.

She'd have to be a good girl and examine those thoughts later, but right now she owed JD an apology. Stopping on a dime, she spun around to see him approaching with something akin to irritation on his face, although she couldn't quite place the feeling she was reading. "I'm sorry, that was rude of me. I just can't talk about it yet. When I can, I'll tell you."

"Fair enough." He reached behind her then and pulled the door open, letting the cool air blast over her, and she turned to go inside.

They were seated and before she had time to think, the

server was setting down a rum and coke for JD and a tea for her. JD questioned her about what she liked then chose an appetizer.

He took a drink of the rum and coke, and, to Kelsey's surprise, when he set it back down it was empty.

He eyed her. "Don't worry, I'll stop at two. Okay three. I *do* have a designated driver, right?"

"Yes, you do."

He motioned to the server to get him another one, and turned back to her. "I'm worried all the time. About Andie, about money, about me."

"Well," she tried her best to be soothing. "You don't have to worry about Andie right now. Bethany's great."

"Of course Andie's fine." He gave a harsh laugh, "Now it's Bethany I'm worried about." And before she could ask, he filled in the blank. "Andie can be a devil child."

Kelsey just shook her head. Didn't she know that one from her own Andy?

"Bethany will be fine. It seems Andie just has some issues."

"Some *issues*?" He almost snorted as he picked up the fresh drink the server had just quietly set down. "Andy *is* issues. That seems to be all that exists in her. And with good reason."

He drained the glass and motioned for a third.

Her face must have told the story, because he immediately reassured her that he was slowing down now.

Kelsey rested her elbow on the table and tucked her chin into her hand. She had been raised with all sorts of manners, but they had been abandoned as a way of life a long time ago. "So, explain all this to me."

It took all of ten seconds before the story started pouring out, punctuated by her questions.

"I only got Andie three weeks ago. I only found out she existed four weeks ago."

"Wow." That was big. "So do you have sole custody? Was there a problem?"

He made that same harsh sound that wasn't laughter, "Yes, there was a problem. Her mother died of cancer, and her birth certificate says she's mine, not that I was ever made aware of that. So Child Protective Services just calls up one day and tells me I have a daughter and I need to come get her." He paused for breath and pushed a hand through his hair.

Wanting desperately to jump in, Kelsey held back. Years of therapy had taught her that the good stuff came when you tamped down your own feelings and waited the other person out. JD proved her decision wise.

"Well, she was in Texas, where I'm from, and so it took a week to get ready and go get her. I did all of it myself." He took a gulp of air, as the waiter showed up again with a loaf of bread that JD tore into.

Kelsey waited her turn, still staying silent, taking a hunk of bread when JD offered it to her. This was getting interesting.

"I told TJ about it because he was going to see the kid. But my folks would not understand having a child out of wedlock and they had never understood why I dated Stephanie in the first place. By the end of it I could see why. Stephanie was totally psycho, which explains a lot of this mess."

Kelsey winced at his terminology. She'd heard Andrew referred to as 'psycho' too many times, and she feared for this little Andie whose father had termed her mother that. But again she stayed quiet, munching on bread as much for an excuse to not participate in the conversation as for food.

"So I drive to within an hour of where my folks live, and pick up this little girl who just lost her Mother, and that I didn't even know existed. CPS warned me that she had issues. Which makes perfect sense: she's been handed off to strangers and her Mom died of cancer, so she wasn't doing a very good job there at the end. I couldn't figure out why Stephanie didn't just call me."

At that moment their food showed up, and the story stopped

for plates to get settled. JD dug in, fork first, ignoring the broccoli that came on the side of his chicken parmesan. Kelsey eyed her asparagus and wondered if JD ever ate vegetables. Probably not, after all he was in his twenties and clearly stuck in the college phase. The guy even had a band, for crying out loud.

Picking up the thread of the story, she held it out to him. "Of course Andie has issues. She's been abandoned and kidnapped."

That got him. "She has not!"

"Well, of course not. But that's the way a five-year-old would see it."

He went back to his dinner, his eyes moving with his thoughts. "That makes sense. That does explain why she's so stubborn. She doesn't want to do anything I ask, and she won't stay still or quiet to let me work." He sighed, sounding much older and very worn out.

"Have you tried working with her?"

"Of course I've tried working with her. She doesn't do her share. Even for a five-year-old."

Kelsey twirled her fork in her linguini just to keep her hands busy. "What I mean is make it look fun. If you need her hair brushed, then you brush her doll's hair. Get her to do it herself if she won't let you. When you have to work, give her something to do that looks like your work. My kids love filling out old forms while I write loans. It isn't perfect but it's better than the alternative."

"Okay, June Cleaver, tell me more." He sat back and eyed her. At first she laughed at being called June Cleaver, but then she gasped.

"Where did your food go?"

"I ate it. Have you never had a guy around before?"

She gulped. For years she'd had Andrew. "Not one that ate that fast."

JD smiled. "I guess he didn't have competition. Between me and TJ, it was eat fast or don't get seconds."

In her mother's house 'sedate' was the key word. Though, the Lord knew Andy had never fit that.

JD motioned for her to eat again, then ruined it. "In another eight to ten years, you're going to have a teenage boy in your house, so watch out. . . Now, tell me more about how to tame the shrew."

That put a damper on the eating. But getting this poor guy help with his daughter was the priority. "Figure out what's bothering her and address it. Ask her what she wants to do. When you talk to her crouch down to her level. Give her choices. Ask her which veggie she wants with dinner, and give her a few options. Maybe you get her new clothes but let her pick from a few things you've already chosen."

"Okay, is there any way to do this on a shoestring budget?"

"Oh, yes." She ticked off her points on her fingers. "Buy generic at the grocery store, eat at home, trade babysitting instead of paying for it, rent movies, play board games, spend time at the park, it's free."

"So, it can be done."

Kelsey smiled. "I'm living proof."

"I've been living poor for two and a half years. We're trying to get this band up and making a profit. Alex lives with his folks, Craig's girlfriend paid their rent. At least she did until she walked out on him two months ago. Then TJ moved in with him last month because I had to move out of our apartment and get a room for my six-year-old. So I don't have anything left to help TJ out either.

"I'm renting the condo because CPS wants her to have her own bedroom and bathroom and no other adults living there. I signed a year lease, then left for Texas. I was so close to my Mom and Dad's, but I turned right around and drove back. It's costing a fortune, and this little girl doesn't have anything but a bed and sheets and a few teddy bears. All her shoes are too small, her clothes are too small. She didn't know where her toothbrush is . . . I've had to replace all of it."

His head slipped into his hands again, frustration rolling off him in waves.

Kelsey reached her hand out to rest against his arm. It was all she could think of to do. The heat of him radiated through her skin and reminded her that he was probably the first adult she'd touched in a year. "It is tough replacing everything, but you'll only do it this once, and after that it will only be small things one at a time. Kids aren't cheap, but they don't have to cost as much as most people pay."

"The kicker is, she doesn't even want me. She wants her mom, and she just hates me." He kept his head in his hands, but didn't shrug off her touch.

"She'll get through it. It will take a while to see how much you care, but she'll see it."

He lifted his head and looked her square in the eyes. "I've been thinking of calling CPS and having them take her back. Put her up for adoption."

That hit her like a shove to the chest. She hadn't seen that coming from a guy who seemed to be doing everything he could to help this little stranger.

"Why!?" She wished she could swallow the accusing tone that had flown out with it. But she couldn't.

JD, true to his laid-back self, didn't take offense. "Because she doesn't want to be with me. She's cute, she's bright, someone will adopt her, won't they?"

"Not necessarily." Kelsey hardly knew this child but she briefly toyed with the idea of adopting Andie herself. "Older kids don't always get good homes. Especially if the foster homes in between aren't good, or if she feels abandoned again and her behavior gets worse." She knew she was painting a bad picture for him. But there was no guarantee that a kid would get adopted.

Even from across the table she could see his back teeth grind. "I think there's every possibility that they'll take her back anyway when they figure it out."

"No, they won't." Kelsey shook her head at him. He was in a horrible spot. "Look, I don't think people should have kids they don't want, but you didn't even know about her. If there was a better alternative for her, I'd recommend it. But shouldn't it be best to be with her father? It'll just take time."

"Well, see, it just gets better. Her paperwork arrived yesterday. I saw her birth certificate. Never mind that Stephanie named her Anderson. Anderson Winslow Hewlitt—my last name." He stopped and took a breath. "This is why I had to get away from her. Aside from the fact that I haven't had any sleep, I can't talk about this in front of her. Who knows what she'll think?"

It sounded like some grand conspiracy theory, but Kelsey was a trained wait-and-see-what-you-get kind of girl. Through hard earned skill, she kept her face neutral.

JD leaned forward. "She's five. Barely five—not almost six."

Okay?

She waited.

"I haven't even seen Stephanie in almost seven years."

Kelsey frowned. Of course he hadn't. That was how he didn't know he had a daughter. Then the math clicked, and her mouth fell open.

JD saw that. "Yeah, she's not mine."

"But she looks just like you!" *Where had wait-and-see-what-you-get Kelsey gone?*

"That's because Stephanie had a type." He pointed to himself. "Dark hair, dark eyes." He leaned back, having grandly let the cat out of the bag. "I found out that she cheated on me while we were together—with a guy who could have been my brother."

"It wasn't TJ!?"

"No. TJ wouldn't do that to me."

24

Kelsey sucked in a lungful of relief. It was like a bad soap opera.

JD picked up the thread. "I knew there was every possibility that Andie wasn't mine. Stephanie had been sleeping around. But this . . . it's, . . . I don't know what."

Kelsey started doing some fast math. "So you two split ways and a year and a half later she has a baby and puts your name on the birth certificate."

"The only thing I can figure is that she didn't even know the names of the guys she threw herself at."

"Was she like that?" For some reason, this other woman piqued Kelsey's curiosity like nothing had in a long time.

JD's face turned sad and thoughtful for a moment. "She was not right in the head, and I didn't know it at the time. I just didn't put the pieces together."

Kelsey chewed her asparagus.

"I'm ashamed to admit that I watched one of those self-help talk shows even once . . . and even more ashamed to admit that I learned a few things." Half his mouth pulled up in a wry smile.

"Oprah, huh?"

He held his hands up, as if proclaiming some sort of innocence. "It was a re-run one night a few years ago. I couldn't sleep, and I haven't touched the stuff since."

She laughed. "So what did you learn?"

JD turned serious. "But they were talking with survivors of sexual abuse and it all sounded just like Stephanie. She grew up with her father and her uncle. She moved out the moment she could and wouldn't set foot back in that house. Hated men in general, but slept around like there was no tomorrow. I thought she was just a slut. I broke up with her for it." There was a slight pause, then he raised one eyebrow. "This may be some sick revenge."

Setting her fork down, Kelsey waited until she got JD's full attention. "Did it ever occur to you that this wasn't about you, but about Andy?"

A frown marred his otherwise perfect features.

"That maybe when the time came to assign her child a father, this woman, who hated all men, wrote down the father she would have wanted her child to have. Andy isn't revenge on you. *You* are a gift to *Andy*."

CHAPTER 3

JD bit down on his tongue, to stop himself from what he'd been about to say. He'd always wanted to be a parent someday, but not like this. His kid had a major behavior problem. He hadn't expected to always say "we can't afford it." Of course, he'd also thought he'd be older and have a wife and . . . well, he'd thought a whole bunch of things that weren't turning out that way.

Child Protective Services was supposed to come and counsel him. But the regular visits they promised dwindled to a single phone call before the first visit had even occurred. That call had been from Andie's caseworker stating that she wasn't going to be able to make it. JD wasn't holding his breath for a second call. CPS was overloaded and under-budgeted and he was small potatoes. He didn't even have to worry about adopting. Thanks to that erroneous birth certificate, Andie was all his.

"Andie," He squatted down in front of her, giving her the advantage of height. Kelsey was right: that part had worked. Andie still always disagreed, but now she stayed and listened. "We have to brush your hair, honey. It has tangles."

This was one of the many battlegrounds Andie had chosen.

He made it happen every other day, or else her hair got too tangled to do anything with. Mentally, he cycled through the advice Kelsey had given him. "We can get rid of the tangles entirely."

That got Andie's attention.

"We can cut it short, or we can brush it every night. Which do you want?"

Andie's eyes had gone round at the mention of cutting it. That clearly was not going to be her choice. He hid his smile from her, knowing that he would win.

But he didn't.

Andie shrieked. "You will not cut my hair! You don't touch me!"

His teeth clenched even as he fought to keep his outward appearance calm. He rotated away and stood to his full height, no longer caring if Andie felt reassured.

Twice this last week he'd taken her over to see Kelsey and her two kids. When Kelsey was there, Andie always did what she was told and agreed to things. She helped Daniel put away the lawn toys. She let Kelsey brush her hair that night. She ate vegetables.

But once they were home, and the magic that was Kelsey was gone, Andie turned into this demon again.

JD felt his anger fade to utter despair. Andie simply hated him. It wasn't getting better as Kelsey promised. And Kelsey didn't see it, because Andie was improving when Kelsey and her kids were around. Just none of the improvements were sticking when he got her back home.

Or maybe he wasn't doing it right.

Regardless, it was Tuesday and he still didn't have a sitter lined up for tonight. He needed one fast. So he simply walked away from Andie, clutching the hairbrush in his hand, afraid to let her hold the thing. He was certain that if he did, it would hit him square in the back when he wasn't looking.

His fingers punched Kelsey's number by memory, he'd pestered her so much this past week. But she'd seemed glad to help every time he had needed it, and he hoped that she would feel that way again.

"Hey JD, what do you need?" Her caller ID told her it was him, and the fact that it was him told her he was in need of something. He winced.

He wanted to say, *I'm just calling to chat* or *I'd like to pay you back for all your help*, but neither of those was going to come out of his mouth tonight. "I need a babysitter tonight. Do you mind if I call Bethany?"

"I don't mind if you call Bethany, but you have to pay her."

That set him back. He was pushing the envelope of his bank account these days, but he wasn't going to write a rubber check to the sitter.

Kelsey's voice in his ear took away his concern that she thought so low of him. "I'll trade you if you want to bring her here tonight."

"How does trading work?" Trading scared the crap out of him. He was doing so poorly with one child that the thought of all three kids was enough to make him go after the kitchen knives and try to expose some veins. At least Kelsey's kids seemed as angelic as their mother.

"When do you need to leave tonight?"

"About five." He turned and saw Andie brushing her doll's hair. The pink nylon threads gleamed while her own tangled mess was untouched.

"Why don't you both show up an hour early and I'll feed the kids and we can work out the details?"

Just then he knew.

Somehow she must be able to see into his living room—into his life. She could see that he was failing miserably. Kelsey was taking pity on him.

Well, while he would have liked to be getting something else, pity it was. "Okay. So we'll show up around four. Thank you."

They hung up and he refrained from a victory dance. He was certain Kelsey was watching.

For the next half hour, he worked on sheet music while Andie watched some cartoon on TV. It was a Kelsey-approved cartoon, and that meant it had some redeeming qualities. He had followed Kelsey's advice in this, like many things. She seemed to have the whole single-parent thing worked out, and he was just floundering. He'd start making his own decisions just as soon as he could figure out what the hell choices he had.

He scribbled notes and tried to upgrade the lyrics he'd written. He heard all of it in his head, but instead of playing it out loud he kept it to himself. JD wanted to pick up the guitar sitting in the corner and put sound to thought. But he didn't dare put reality to the music in his head in front of his daughter who hated everything.

Having Andie know the guitar was something he cared about was not anything he was anxious to have happen soon. She left towels and new clothes on the floor, stomping on them as a way of showing him how she felt about the things he cared for. The few toys he'd bought her always wound up irreparably broken within a few hours.

Aside from giving away the value of his music to the small demon, he figured he couldn't pull off the song tonight anyway. He was more in the mood for revenge, and the lyrics that popped into his head were altering the tone from romantic to evil. One of the other guys was going to have to change his trite wording to something better. It wouldn't be him, not today.

He looked at her again, noting that she seemed content now, brushing the doll's hair.

I'm doing the right thing.

He was certain he wasn't doing it the right way, but Andie needed him far more than she knew. Kelsey had galvanized him with those words about Stephanie choosing him as the father of her child, even if he wasn't actually the father.

Well, he was Andie's father now. He had flat out told the CPS caseworker that he hadn't even seen Stephanie in seven years. If they hadn't done the math yet, they weren't going to. The little girl was his to keep.

It soothed his conscience a little to raise Stephanie's child. After that overly-enlightening Oprah show, he'd tried to find out where she'd gone, but he hadn't been successful at locating her. It had hurt to know she'd been just an hour down the road all that time and he hadn't followed through enough get the address or phone number.

Kelsey suggested that Stephanie didn't want to be found. That she wouldn't want him to know what she'd done. Which was probably why she hadn't called when she was sick either.

Kelsey, Kelsey, Kelsey.

He placed all his eggs in the basket she'd advised. After all she was living proof that it could be done. She had *two* kids she was raising on her own. Plus, she'd had them since they were babies, and that meant she'd been a mom since she was probably around twenty-one, he figured.

If she could do it, so could he.

It didn't help that she was hot with those wide hazel eyes and lush lips that she chewed on occasionally.

He attempted to push the thought away, just as the timer dinged at him—the timer Kelsey had loaned him to help out with setting limits for Andie.

He gathered up his papers, shoving them all down into the pocket on his guitar case. The four of them had been at this for a full year now, with no real success at it. Just enough money came in here and there to keep them thinking they stood a shot.

Now he questioned that. Now he had a kid to think about.

"Come on Andie, your show's finished. Let's go over to Kelsey's."

Andie popped right up, still clutching her doll and the tiny hairbrush. That was his only offer that she'd ever truly accepted —going to Kelsey's.

Andie didn't speak, so he filled in the empty spaces. "You can play with Daniel and Allie tonight, and I expect you to go to bed when Kelsey tells you."

Yeah, that was a laugh riot. Of course, Andie would do what Kelsey told her to, with no fuss whatsoever. Kelsey could tell her to eat a bucket full of worms, and JD didn't doubt that they'd all go down without a single complaint. If Andie wanted ketchup to dip them in, she'd say 'please' and 'thank you' to boot.

CHAPTER 4

He slung the guitar over his shoulder and let Andie out the back door. He tried casually brushing his fingertips across her head in a show of affection, but Andie must have seen it coming. She ducked.

He ate the sigh that threatened to escape. As much trouble as Andie was, he was certain that she felt far worse than he. He was trying hard to be the adult here.

Andie skipped the thirty yards to Kelsey's front door. *For these small things, Lord, we are grateful.*

Kelsey opened the door at Andie's light, polite knock. His daughter held the pink-haired doll up for inspection. "Look! I gave her pony-tails like Allie's."

JD looked at the doll. Sure she had. *Oh, the irony.*

"Ooooh!" Andie squealed in pure delight. "Just like you!"

That popped his head up. Sure enough, Kelsey looked like serious jailbait, her caramel hair gathered into Ellie-May pigtails. Her outfit reflected the day's heat—a tank top that didn't quite reach the waist of low slung jeans that had been sheared almost indecently short. Ellie-May meets Playboy.

Luckily, she started speaking and that helped stop his mind

from the track it had wandered onto. "Kids! You guys go play for a while. JD and I are going to talk. Then after JD leaves I'll give you guys hot dogs."

He started to speak, but Andie beat him to it. "Will you make me pony-tails like that?" She pointed one small finger to Kelsey's own hair.

"After your Daddy and I talk." Kelsey turned back to JD as though that was that. He would have to remember that: just speak his mind and declare the conversation over.

Kelsey walked herself into the living room, unconcerned that the kids were going off into another room to play. A place where no adult eyes would be on them. Then again, while Andie broke things and wreaked havoc at his house, she didn't damage a single thing here. Which just proved that Andie was capable of being good—and added fuel to the Andie-hates-me fire.

His nerves settled as surely as he settled himself into the comfy couch. The furniture made him think of families with sweet moms and dads that came home after work. But no dad came in for dinner here, and he didn't remember any of the moms from his childhood looking like that.

He switched the topic to the only thing that was keeping him from being completely at ease. "So tell me about 'trading.'"

She shrugged. "It's free. We just keep track of hours, and try not to let one of us get too far ahead of the other."

"How do I pay it back?"

She laughed out loud at him. She had to see that he was terrified. "You watch the kids and I go out for a while."

"Yeah, that's what I was afraid of." That was the only downside to this trading business.

"It's not that bad. I actually think it's easier with all of them here. Andie is new, and she keeps them occupied. Aside from the usual policing, she isn't much extra trouble." Her finger found its way into one of her pig-tails and her lean legs tucked up under her on the couch. Yup—jailbait. But Kelsey kept speaking, "I think you'll discover you like having them over. You'll get more done."

"Yes, because your children are angels." JD decided to confess his troubles. Kelsey may be jailbait, but she was his lifeline, in a way CPS never could have been. "Andie is still terrorizing me. She's a different kid here. At home she breaks things, screams, throws tantrums. She took her dinner plate off the table and threw it on the floor last night. Thank god it was plastic."

He felt lighter telling her that. And lower.

"So there's something there specifically directed at you."

He nodded. He'd already figured that one out.

"Can you get her to counseling?"

"The state's supposed to send somebody, but they called and canceled." Kelsey's eyebrows raised at that, but he kept speaking. "Our insurance doesn't cover therapy."

He couldn't believe he was saying these things. His money situation hadn't bothered him before. He'd chosen it. But he'd chosen it for himself. Now he was putting Andie into it too. And confessing it to Kelsey.

"Well, I'm no professional, but she does talk to me. I'll see what I can get out of her until we come up with a better solution."

He changed the topic back. "So you'll watch them tonight and I'll owe you about five or six hours of baby-sitting. When do you want me to watch them?"

Kelsey shrugged. "I don't know, is that okay?"

He didn't respond.

She smiled. "You can always say 'no' if I need a sitter and you can't do it."

"Okay."

"Oh!" Her mouth flew into a perfect 'o'. "You won't owe me the whole six hours. Only . . . two thirds. I have two kids and you only have one."

JD snapped back a little at that thought. That did make the whole trading thing better.

"Are you available any daytimes?"

He nodded. "Yeah, I'm home during the day."

Kelsey frowned at him. "Are you home with her all day every day?"

He nodded and watched as Kelsey's eyes grew two sizes. "No wonder you're crazy. Mine go to day-care two days a week in the summer."

"I asked TJ to take her one day, but he brought her back within the hour. She'd kicked him in the shin. Twice" JD almost laughed. "He said he wore condoms so it wasn't his problem. I wanted to tell him, *so did I.*"

Her face froze.

Oh shit. He'd said the wrong thing. He'd just been talking and he'd offended-

She laughed hysterically, her hands flying to her mouth to try to keep the sound in. "You didn't tell him?"

"No, I haven't." Thank god she hadn't been offended.

After a moment she calmed down, and changed the topic. "You do need to find a spare babysitter in case I'm not available. I suppose you could use Bethany, but I may have her, and she's already busy Tuesday nights."

"Where does a person find a babysitter? There isn't a secret directory somewhere, is there?"

"No." But she smiled at the thought, a wide, teeth-revealing grin. For the first time he understood what he was seeing in her eyes all the time. She looked like there was a core of sadness that no laughter could quite penetrate. He fought the urge to ask her about it, and when she spoke again something in her tone let him know he'd been scrutinizing her a little too closely. "You find babysitters at church."

"Church?" The word rolled off his tongue like it belonged to a foreign language.

"Do you go?"

He shook his head.

"Well then, there are babysitting clubs, where you log hours with anyone and a central member keeps tabs for the whole group." Her finger crept back into the pig-tail again, winding it around, as though her brain had no idea it was there. "But I'll be honest, when I checked it out, they were all homemakers and career moms who compared the size of their SUVs and talked about their kids' test results and soccer teams. I didn't fit in very well. I imagine you'd fit in even less. But . . ."

He just shook his head. That sounded way too close to his definition of hell.

"Then church is the best place." She nodded at him. "I didn't go again until after my mom died, but it was a great place for support and even just some peace of mind on a Sunday morning. It's not like I was getting to sleep in anyway."

That erupted a bitter laugh from him. He hadn't slept a full night since Andie had arrived in his life. She woke up screaming like a banshee, or worse, he'd awaken to muffled sobs. At times it was the only reminder that she was a scared little kid and not an actual hell-child.

Church it was then. He'd been raised Catholic, and he'd find a nice place around here. Maybe he could sleep through the service.

Two problems solved in one night was about more than he could handle. He stretched and closed his eyes for a short second, only to have Kelsey jostle him.

She stood over him, her legs straddling his for balance, and nudged him. "Hey sleepyhead, time to wake up."

"What?" He blinked. He hadn't fallen asleep, had he?

She pointed to a clock. "It's five already. You were out for about forty minutes."

He blinked up at her smile, wide and friendly.

He had to go.

She stepped away, now that she knew he was awake, and he bolted for the bathroom. He ran his fingers through his hair, and rinsed out his mouth. He splashed water on his face and wondered how he could have just passed out on her couch like that.

He used the hand towel that was hanging perfectly beside the sink to dry himself. The whole bathroom said a woman lived here. That someone had made a home for the people here.

He ran for the front door, and grabbed his guitar. Kelsey waited to lock up after him. And he felt bad for saying it. "I might be late."

She shrugged. "Be as late as you need to be."

"Thank you."

He heard the lock click into place as he went down the front walk, followed by a faint sound that was surely her voice calling the kids to dinner.

Andie was safe and she'd behave. That meant Kelsey and her kids were safe, too.

JD moved on to his next worry: the band.

He walked the three blocks to Alex's parents' house. Alex was going to give him a lift. He was cutting every corner and saving every expense.

He was ruining the band. He considered bowing out. But then what? They had synergy. They just had to find their spot.

For two blocks he wondered how much he was lying to himself, if he was living his life on childish dreams, refusing to grow up. Thank god he hadn't actually had to say the words to Kelsey, *I have a band.* He might as well have just added *we're going to be famous someday.*

Not that he wanted to be famous. He didn't really. He'd been lead singer until he'd convinced TJ to join them. That had been the final piece; the point at which he'd become convinced that they had *it,* and they should keep at it until they made money.

Alex exited the basement door and walked up to meet him.

"You look a little worse for wear, dude."

"I am actually a lot worse for wear."

Alex shrugged as he undid the locks to his own old beater. "Well, if nothing else, it has really convinced me to wear my johnny hat, every time."

JD clenched his teeth. He so did not want to have this conversation. He was taking way too much heat about this, and if the guys found out that Andie wasn't even his child, he'd never hear the end of it. They weren't reacting well to the extra stress of his having a kid. They took it only because it seemed there was no other choice. They didn't realize that a quick blood-test would send Andie back from whence she came.

The problem remained: Andie was his child now. If not by blood, then in his heart?

Maybe.

Maybe he just couldn't stomach the thought of what might happen to an innocent kid if he sent her back. There just weren't any happy solutions here. So he was going to do his best.

When they got to Craig's, they honked and a minute later Craig's old Camaro pulled out of the parking structure. Alex followed to a row of old studios. They were crumbling. Not nearly as nice as the set-up they'd had at his and TJ's old apartment. But it was sure better than getting kicked out of his condo.

Craig hopped out of his car, grabbing equipment and slamming the door. "We can use unit three. It's already vacated. The land's been sold and the whole thing's getting demolished in three weeks. We can use it as much as we want in the meantime, every night if we want." He looked at each of them, making it clear that he thought that was what they should do.

There was no way JD could keep up that kind of schedule. He knew Craig was waiting for him to say so.

It was TJ who spoke up. "We can't practice Thursday night."

"Why?" Craig's voice was sharp to his roommate.

"Because we have a gig." TJ smiled.

Craig didn't. "Does it pay?"

JD stepped in. "It doesn't matter. It's better than rehearsal and we need the exposure." It had been ten months since he'd sold a song and that infusion of cash had more than disappeared on equipment and studio fees and the occasional pizza.

TJ smiled. "Yes. It pays."

Craig let his breath out. Deservedly so. He was working part time early mornings at Starbucks to make ends meet since his cushy ride had dumped him a few months earlier.

With the announcement, some of the bite left Craig, and no one commented on JD's lack of vigor. Maybe they simply expected that of him now.

They turned their attention to the Thursday night job they would play. After planning their set, JD spent hours pouring frustration after frustration into his guitar, until he was exhausted. But he couldn't just go home. Alex was his ride. He wasn't going to be the first to tap out for the night either. That was just a point of pride.

It was Craig who finally called off the dogs. Within a few minutes the room was silent and they had most everything packed away. With a borrowed studio like this, they couldn't really set up shop. But JD hoped soon they'd have their own place. He'd been hoping that for a while now.

At home, JD quickly stashed his guitar and headed over to Kelsey's, realizing only as he knocked that he should have showered first.

"Hey." She pulled the door open without checking, but he didn't chastise her for it. She looked thoroughly mussed, but simply ran her fingers through her hair and stifled a yawn.

"I'm so sorry I woke you." He practically fell over his own words and feet as he entered into the living room. "I won't stay out that late again. Let me pay you back at full time this time."

Her brows pulled together and she looked at him like he was nuts. "What are you, Catholic? What's with the guilt?"

He had to smile. "Yes, I am Catholic, and I'm sorry I woke you up."

"No big." She closed the door and walked away. She'd changed into a t-shirt and sweats, definitely ready for sleep. "Do you want a drink?"

"Oh, I don't want to keep you up." He'd just get Andie and—

"I'm going to pretend you didn't say that." She turned with her hands on her hips. "If you're tired and you want to get home, that's just fine. But I'm awake, I'm getting myself a drink, and if you want one I'll grab you one, too."

"Do you have a coke?"

"Ah, so you are wide awake, or at least you plan on being." She pulled two cold cans from the fridge and held his out to him before popping hers. She motioned to the sofa, but he refused.

"I should have showered. I shouldn't sit on your sofa."

She checked him out, and he was surprised that he was afraid she'd find him lacking.

"I thought you were going out for practice." She countered that statement right away. "Not that it's any business of mine, but you look like you've been to the gym."

He followed her to the kitchen, perching on a stool and setting his coke down on the counter. "Practice is a workout."

Kelsey propped her hip against the counter and continued to nurse her soda. Her hand pushed through a few papers that littered the counter, and she produced a little pink post-it. "Here, I got you the name and number of a possible sitter."

He was getting ready to thank her, when she shifted, looking a little uncomfortable.

"Listen," Her voice had an odd tone to it, and that made his brain perk up. "I'm just going to say this once. I've met Bethany, and she's gorgeous. She's twenty, and if you want to get involved with her that's one thing, but don't use her as a sitter if you want to date her. That's a cardinal rule: when you find a good babysitter you don't screw with it." She paused, then added, "figuratively or literally."

He laughed, even as he was unsure where the energy to do so came from. "I promise I won't screw the babysitter. Thank you."

She nodded absently. "I was thinking . . ."

"And?" This was it. He saw the other shoe, high over his head, poised to come crashing down.

"You said you had Andie all day, every day . . ."

"Yes?" The shoe came in a little closer.

"Well, my kids are at day care on Tuesdays and Thursdays. I could take Andie for part of the day on Mondays and Wednesdays." She clarified with the usual it's-no-trouble and I-have-my-kids-anyway and what's-one-more?

JD just stared.

How could he turn down free time? It wasn't free. That was it. "I'd love to, but I could never re-pay you in hours."

Her hand moved toward him, palm up. "You don't have to. Not for those days."

"Why not? I don't get it." He fiddled with the tab on his coke for a moment. "Why are you doing all this for us?"

"It's not just for you." She set down her own drink, and her hands made the beginnings of several different gestures before catching each other and sitting, calm in front of her. "My kids like Andie. I haven't been the best mother to them, and she's really—"

"You are shitting me." He stood up. "You're super-mom. You guys are all glued together. Your kids listen and speak politely and don't throw their dinner plates. So what else do you need? A plaque?"

She didn't answer. Her eyes found designs in the ceiling and the floor tiles, but she didn't answer. A full minute dragged by, and just as he was certain that she had decided that he should leave, she spoke. "The family of five that bought that mini-van is the one in the pictures in the living room."

He eyed her askance then went to check out the photos. He'd seen them, but not examined them. He didn't have to. They were of the happy, all-American family: mom Kelsey, blonde-haired blue-eyed dad, two happy kids, and a woman who had to be Kelsey's mother. On closer inspection all he saw was more of the same.

Kelsey just pointed. "That's my Mom. She died three years ago."

Kelsey pointed again, this time to Dad. "And that's my Andy. He died last year. We lived in D.C., in this little house my mother had bought. Andy died the day after I mailed the last house payment." He could see her head tilt as she thought. "All the shrinks told me it was the wrong thing to do, but I sold the house, packed the kids up, and moved here."

"Did you want to become a singer or something?"

She smiled, her hair sliding across her shoulders as she shook her head. "I was so sad that for a long time I was barely able to get food on the table on a regular basis. I've just been functioning, not being."

That sure explained the look in her eyes, and the way she laughed, almost like she felt bad about doing it. JD looked at the photo again. "I guess when you love someone like that it just holds you and doesn't let go."

A cloud slipped over her expression, as quick as if it had always been there. Then, as fast as it came, the cloud slipped away and the photo was forgotten. "Is that why you're here? Because it's music city?"

He laughed and turned back to the kitchen to toss his soda can in the trash. "I'm from Texas and I moved to Nashville and I'm in a band. Take your best guess."

"Are you guys country?"

He shrugged. "We're some sort of fusion. We're too country

to be pop, too pop to be punk, and too punk to be country."

"So you really have your own niche."

He wanted to laugh, then howl at the moon. That was the nicest way he had ever heard it put that, no matter how good they were, no one was going to take them.

Just like that, the caffeine expired on him, and he was dead tired on his feet. He wouldn't even get to sleep in. Andie would be up and breaking things with the sun. The clock read a quarter after one. Which meant he had maybe five hours to sleep, and that was if Andie didn't wake up howling.

Kelsey read him, she seemed very good at that, just watching what was going on around her and stepping in. "Tomorrow's Wednesday. We usually get started around nine. If you want to bring her by between nine and ten, I'll return her by three or four."

She didn't say anything else, just padded off in her bare feet and returned a few minutes later cradling a sleeping Andie. He took the weight from her, and thanked her again.

Softly, she closed the door behind him. As he watched, lights went off in the house, one by one, and he imagined her flipping each switch and looking in on her kids.

Andie slept even though the streetlights glared harsh on her features. They rounded the cinderblock wall, JD with his daughter heavy in his arms, as he wondered how he'd come to be here. Two months ago he would never have taken a bet that he would have a five-year-old who wasn't even his. Or that, in spite of that fact, he wouldn't be able to let her go.

He struggled to unlock the back door with the weight of her still precariously in his arms. But he got it done.

JD knew he was going to set Andie down and then be lucky if he made it to his own bed before he collapsed. He poured every last effort of the night into getting both of them up the stairs. Just before he got to her room, she turned, still sound asleep, and snuggled into him.

CHAPTER 5

Andie was making progress, Kelsey thought. But not for
JD, apparently. Which was a damn shame. It didn't really
matter in the end if Andie liked her and her kids. It mattered
how she liked JD and how they got along. Because one day JD
and Andie would pull up roots; they would stop renting that
condo and get a place of their own. Kelsey suppressed a sigh at
that thought.

The kids played together in the backyard, and she heard
snippets of conversations they had. They played 'death' far more
than was usual. But Kelsey wasn't going to haul the kids to a
shrink over that crap. The way she figured it, they needed to
play 'death': each of these kids had lost a parent, tragically, and
at a very young age. Any reasonable coping skills were fine by
her standards.

"Mom." Daniel protested, but only his mother would have
known he was upset. "Andie says we don't pull a sheet over her
head."

Kelsey wasn't getting in the middle of that one. "It happens
the way you all decide together. So wake Andie up and ask her
what she thinks, and the three of you all talk it out." She turned

her gaze back to Glamour magazine, in a constructed effort to force the kids to work out their own issues. She, on the other hand, would work out the issues of long-wearing blush. *5 Great Tricks to Try in Bed Tonight* sounded like fun, but about as useful as a white elephant.

It was close to three forty-five, and that meant JD would be here any minute to get Andie. If only there were articles in Glamour about how to get kids to connect with the parent they didn't know.

"Mom! We decided we need cookies!" Allie jumped in front of Kelsey, certain to get her attention. "Can I go get them?"

"Yes, but they stay closed until you get back out here if you want to have any." It was all she could do to stifle the simultaneous laugh and sigh of relief that wanted to force its way out. It would all be okay if the resolution to a game of 'mortuary' was that everyone needed cookies.

The chain link that ran along the side yard rattled behind her, startling her into early next week, and she almost dropped her soda.

"Can I come in?" JD stood on the other side of the fence, fingers grasping the links. His gaze darted from one kid to another.

"JD!" Allie shrieked as she bounded up to him. "We get to have cookies!"

"That sounds great. Can I come over?"

Allie nodded with a slow exaggerated lift of her head.

JD rattled the fence again until Kelsey looked up. He was in his usual uniform: old jeans, old sneakers, old t-shirt. He even had an old grown-out haircut that sometimes dipped over one eye and was starting to make ducktails at the back. Maybe it was a 'band thing'.

He should have looked like such a kid, but somehow he didn't really. At least he looked better rested than he had this morning. She suspected that he dropped Andie off most mornings and went back home and went to sleep. All he ever said was that he was 'working'. Not that she knew what an amateur band boy did for work.

"Can I come over, or should I walk around?"

She raised her eyebrow at him. "It's a seven-foot fence. You're just going to come over?"

"Sure," and with that he reached up, easily grabbing the top bar and wrapping his hand around it. While the kids stood watching with glee, he kicked over the top, then hopped effortlessly to the ground.

Kelsey told herself he was a kid. "Allie, I think that man deserves a cookie."

Allie peeled the bag open, handing an Oreo to JD, then eyeing her mother. "I deserve one, too."

She nodded. "I think we all do. Two each, maybe."

There were squeals all around. Allie handed out cookies, Daniel asked if JD would teach him how to do that, Kelsey intervened so that JD didn't say 'yes' and she didn't have to say 'no'. Only Andie didn't have anything to say to her father. She ate her cookies quietly, then headed up into the little fort atop the wooden jungle gym.

No, she definitely wasn't improving for JD.

He sat on the edge of the picnic table, looking after his daughter with a longing that he tried to keep hidden. Even so, Kelsey couldn't bear to look at him. Andie surely didn't know what a kind word from her would mean to this man who had turned his world upside down for her. Kids could be so casually cruel. It was a hard lesson she had had to learn repeatedly with her own Andy.

She was a master at cleaning it up, too. "So what did you do today?"

JD looked away from the fort as he polished off the last cookie. "Wrote some music, made some money."

"Can I ask, what is it you do to make money? Or should I

47

not?" She only at the last moment realized she might not like the answer.

He laughed. "I literally made some money today."

"You counterfeit?!"

"No!" He threw his head back and she could see the laughter as well as hear it. "I invest my savings and live off the proceeds. I spend a few hours each day watching the stock market."

"Then why . . .?" Why was he barely making ends meet? Why didn't he just get a real job?

The air left him. "Because I don't want to. I won't touch my principle investment, so I'm not making all that much." He looked himself up and down with new eyes. "I don't know what you see when you look at me. But I did that other life. I wore a suit every day,"

He had to see her eyebrows rise.

"I bought a high-rise condo in Dallas with chrome and granite, but I was too busy working to make the payments. Later I realized that I didn't enjoy what I was doing. And when I decided I might quit, I left work immediately to run the idea by my girlfriend. Only thing is, I arrived home to find she'd let herself in and was making use of the granite countertop for the first time. She was using it to run lines of coke."

Her eyebrows went higher.

"So I sold the place, took the meager profit, and headed to music city to try my hand at song writing. That was three years ago in December." He looked at her and waited while she digested.

That was not the story she had expected from JD. So she said the only thing that was still in her brain. "You wore a suit? Every day?"

He laughed again. "Yes, even most weekends."

She couldn't hide it. She tried, but the shock of it all had to be plain across her face.

"Close your mouth, Kelsey."

She did. Then she opened it. "So, if I gave you a wad of my cash you could make it grow?"

"I don't work in cash. It's all e-money." He looked uncomfortable, and her first instinct was to soothe. But her first instincts had gotten her here, and here didn't include Andy anymore. She didn't have to tiptoe around JD. He would weather it if she asked a question he didn't like. And it was time Daniel got over being so soft-spoken. She knew it was the remnants of having a father who flew off the handle at no provocation, and a surrogate mother who worked to keep the tantrums from happening.

"So, if I gave you e-money?"

"I could, but . . ."

Okay, that was it. That was the boundary of New Kelsey. Maybe tomorrow she'd push further.

He changed the subject, and not very deftly either, but she let him. "We went to church yesterday."

"Oh, how was it?"

The left side of his mouth pulled up, and for the first time she realized he hadn't shaved today. "I remembered why I quit going."

"Oh, no." She loved church, and for the life of her could only vaguely comprehend that other people didn't find it as soothing as she did. "Why was that?"

"The service was partially in Latin. The part I understood was mostly about how bad I was being. Although I did figure out why they stand up to sing so much—It's to keep me from falling asleep. Right as I would work up a good doze, I'd have to stand up and sing again."

"Don't you like singing?"

He shook his head. "I think I described my band as vaguely punk. So while I like singing, I don't think what they did is going to cut it for me. I won't be joining the choir anytime soon."

That gave her a fit of giggles. It was all she could do to contain the mental picture of JD, darkly handsome and equally wicked-looking in a choir robe, singing sweet hymns.

"Yeah, yeah, laugh it up."

He stood to stretch and called out for Andie to come, it was time to go home.

Kelsey could see on his face, even as he spoke, that he was bracing himself for the response.

It didn't come.

He tried again, and again Andie pretended deafness.

Kelsey fought her urge to jump in and help. It was like watching a baby colt learn to stand—necessary, but painful. Only this colt never seemed to get up.

"Andie!" He stood right behind his daughter, having looked in the entryway of the fort. But still she didn't respond. She put on quite a show and didn't even flinch at the sharp edge in his tone.

Kelsey couldn't stand it any longer. "Allie, Daniel, we're going inside now."

Her kids said good-bye to Andie and headed in the back door. They didn't tell him to have a good evening, or even anything so simple as 'good-bye'. Of course they wouldn't. She realized as she ushered them inside, they had lived under the shadow of Andy's disease. A little tension and they would jump when they were told, trying not to speak unless spoken to. And she suddenly felt like a horrible parent for letting Andy's illness take them all over like that.

Allie was starting to come out again, but Daniel had lived under it longer, and Andy was his father. In that moment, Kelsey realized that it wasn't just the kids, but her, too. She had to make the effort to bloom, she had to show her kids how it was done, so they could do it for themselves.

Andie's scream pierced her ears, and Kelsey could have

sworn that she heard the windows rattling. "You're not my Daddy."

Kelsey turned so cold inside at the thought—how much longer could JD hold out against that onslaught before he yelled back, *"That's right, I'm not"*? Not that she thought he'd do it, but she herself had said many just as harmful things when pushed to breaking.

He didn't say it. His voice was low and stern, though she couldn't hear the words.

Lord only knew what the neighbors were thinking as Andie screamed. "Kelsey will be my Mom! I don't need a Daddy."

Kelsey felt her eyes squeeze shut.

"Mom, what's wrong?" Daniel looked up at her, the small knit in his brows telling her he was afraid.

She was ready to brush him off, tell him it was all okay, before she realized he deserved more credit. "I'm scared about Andie and JD."

He nodded solemnly. "Me, too."

Allie had wandered off, happily oblivious to the turmoil around her. But it had always run deeper in Daniel. "What makes you scared?"

"She doesn't love him. She wants a Mommy. He's her Daddy, and she thinks Daddies are bad." He shrugged. "Are all Daddies bad?"

Kelsey was certain her heart broke into at least fifty pieces right then. "No baby. Your Daddy wasn't bad, he was sick."

"He didn't seem sick." Daniel eyed her that way every time she used the term to apply to Andy.

"He was sick in his brain." She sighed as she scooped him up, realizing even then just how heavy a six-year-old was. "It did make him seem pretty bad at times, though, didn't it?"

Daniel nodded. "Is JD a bad Daddy?"

"No, he's a really good one. He's trying really hard; he didn't even know he was a Daddy until a while ago."

He frowned. "How did he not know he was a Daddy?"

She smiled but she wasn't touching that one. "Pop Tart, that's a story for another day. Tell me, why does Andie think Daddies are bad?"

Daniel shrugged even as he squirmed to be put down. "She just does." Then the moment of lucidity was gone and he was six again. He ran off.

Kelsey stopped, her spine stilled in that sudden feeling that something isn't right. She breathed deeply, and listened to the house around her, Daniel yelling at Allie.

And that was it. That was what was wrong. Daniel had *yelled* at Allie. But really that was so right. He was six, his sister was almost four. They were supposed to yell at each other.

Maybe Andie's temper tantrums were having at least one good effect.

Kelsey looked out the window to see what had happened to Andie and JD, but they were gone.

CHAPTER 6

That Wednesday, When JD picked Andie up, Kelsey invited the two of them swimming with her and her kids on Friday. Andie accepted for herself, but graciously declined for JD.

"Andie, we can't go without JD."

"Yes, we can." At least it was stated factually and not rudely.

"No, we can't." Before Andie could protest, Kelsey put up her hand and explained. "Daniel and Allie and I usually go on Mondays, but we haven't been able to because there are now too many kids for one adult. So we need JD if we're going to go."

"Jesus, Kelsey." JD looked upset at her. "Then leave her with me on Mondays."

"No!"

They both ignored Andie's protest.

"It's truly not a big deal." She attempted to brush him off, but she should have known it wouldn't be so easy.

"It's altering your life. It's enough that it's altered mine. She's not your child."

"I am! I can be Kelsey's little girl!" Andie blossomed at the thought.

JDs cheeks clenched and a muscle in his jaw started to tic.

Kelsey had to actively remind herself that she was attempting to face confrontation head-on these days.

JD unclenched his jaw. "Why are you doing this?" He stepped away from the kids in a vain attempt to have a private conversation. "Are we your charity case?"

For a moment she didn't know how to respond. Then she felt the dam burst, and she remembered how it felt when she had been pushed to the edge.

"Do you see all my other friends around?" Her arms went out, gesturing into empty air. "I don't really know anyone here. My birthday's next week and I don't think anybody knows! The adults in my family are all gone. I don't date. I go to church, I work from home, and I'm a mom.

"I've been dead for a year! I've been in this fog since Andy died. I finally started seeing the world around me, and there was Andie, screaming her head off in the Target. You two need help, as anyone would in your situation, and I'm used to taking care of people. So pardon me."

"What do you mean, 'our situation'?" There was a threat in his voice, one that she was sure she'd never heard from JD. Her automatic first response was to read the faces around her and see if it was all going to blow up.

JDs face contained his anger, not the other way around.

"I meant that you just had a child dropped off on your doorstep. And there you were with no parenting skills and no place to go. That's all."

She wondered what he thought she'd meant.

"Kelsey, you flinched."

"What?" What the hell he was talking about?

"Just a minute ago, when I got upset, you flinched." He looked at her face as though he was looking for something. "Did you think I was going to hit you?"

Her mouth dropped open. She hadn't realized, but she probably had flinched.

His hand went into his hair as it always did when he was upset. "Jesus, Kelsey, I wouldn't-"

"I know. You wouldn't hit me. It's just an old reaction." She shrugged it off as casually as she could.

But that only upset JD more. "Did he hit you?"

She didn't have to ask who 'he' was, and she shook her head. "He didn't hit me, but I got hit."

"How the hell does that work?"

She didn't bother to correct him for swearing in front of the kids. At least they'd lost interest in the conversation a long time ago. If only JD would now.

But he didn't. He just stood there with his hands on his hips, in that moment reminding her of her own father, stern and sure of himself. He waited.

"Andy lashed out, but not at *me*. He threw things and I got in the way sometimes when I was stupid."

"I don't think that's-"

"Andy was sick. Mentally."

And JD was really listening. She wasn't sure anyone ever had. Even the shrinks had always seemed to be waiting for her to hand them the piece of information that would prove that they should shove their latest therapy down all their throats.

"Andrew had Schizophrenia with rages and poor impulse control, among other things. And I took care of him." That was nowhere near the full story of Andy, but it was more than she'd said to anyone in a year.

He looked across the yard to where his daughter was playing calmly, "That's why you're so good with Andie. How many years did you spend tiptoeing around and flinching?"

She couldn't even muster a shrug. "Seems like forever."

"Can you do me a favor?" He tucked his hands into his back

pockets. "Can you not flinch around me again? That worries the crap out of me."

She smiled. "Okay, but you stop swearing in front of my kids."

His hands flew to his mouth, looking far too masculine under his wide eyes and startled expression. "Oh, shit."

"Funny."

His eyes went wider, and she changed the subject. "So are you coming swimming on Friday? Three kids really is too many."

He snorted. "One kid is too many." Then he followed it with, "Sure."

Kelsey worked through Thursday, then dropped the kids off at JD's, even though Maggie had called saying her son Jason was sick and she wouldn't be able to make it. Kelsey contemplated sitting at home, and renting a movie, then realized that, from his condo, JD might very well be able to see that her lights were still on.

So she headed out to the mall by herself. Not the evening out she'd been going for, but two hours later, she had a pair of jeans and a two-piece bathing suit that made her look as good as she could. New swim suits hadn't been part of the budget while Andy was alive.

It wasn't like she was rich now, but it was the first time she ever had savings. Tomorrow morning, she was going out swimming with JD and the kids. JD was going to look like "young, hip, single dad" and she did *not* want to look like "tired-single-mom" next to that. The women would be draping themselves all over him. She'd need at least a few looks just to keep up.

She found a way-too-expensive sweater that she desperately

wanted. So she bought it, then hit the bookstore for a thriller before settling into a table for one at her favorite mall restaurant. She read and ate and tuned out the world.

After she headed home, she stashed her bags in the house before heading over to JD's.

She watched the pools of light from the streetlamps as she walked by. She should be more aware of her surroundings, she knew, but she was just content, for the first time in a long time. So she lazily walked up the back steps and knocked.

The door pulled open and she was greeted by four smiling faces. Andie jumped up and down in the background, while JD had Daniel on one leg and Allie on the other. "Mommy!"

"I thought you guys would be asleep by now!"

JD smiled over the tops of little heads. "After all you have done for us, I thought you might use the gift of sleeping in. So I wore them out."

"Ahhhh." That just might work.

Once shoes were on, Kelsey grabbed the bag they had brought, and ushered them out the door.

"So, how was the night out?" JD asked.

"It was good." Allie asked to be lifted up into Kelsey's arms and she obliged. She had to carry them as much as possible before they got too big. "Thank you."

He simply nodded and she started down the steps, only to realize a few moments later that JD was following her. She looked at him.

He looked back. "I'm walking you home."

"Thank you, but that's not necessary."

"This may feel like a small town in this neighborhood, but it's still a big city. Besides," It was soft-spoken but clear, "with everything else you've done for us, the least I can do is walk you home."

He crouched down and before she realized what he was doing, he had offered a piggyback ride to Andie, been turned down, and had Daniel up and was walking again and offering to carry her bag. Daniel was grinning. Andie tucked her hand in Kelsey's free one, and Kelsey couldn't remember the last time she'd given one of the kids a piggyback ride.

They were almost to her front door, and Allie was already sound asleep.

CHAPTER 7

Friday morning swimming had gone well, except for the part where JD had played with the kids and Andie had hung back. He had offered to teach her to swim, and she refused, instead asking Kelsey to teach her. Kelsey refused. She could have JD or no lessons. Andie chose no lessons.

They went to the pool again on Monday morning, with JD joining them at their usual time. Kelsey could almost see the summer slipping away. She sent JD to register Andie for kindergarten while she watched Andie.

They went shopping for school supplies that evening at Target, the same place where Andie had pitched the temper tantrum. JD seemed utterly relieved to have Kelsey there. No wonder, every time he tried on his own to get Andie to do something, she balked—when she was in a good mood that is. When she was in a bad mood she pitched a fit, the likes of which Kelsey hadn't seen since Andrew.

But with all of them there, she stayed calm. JD had swallowed the biggest bill, since Andie didn't have anything for school, practically nothing had come from her mother's. Kelsey made a mental note to ask Andie what it had been like when her mother was sick. It seemed the mysterious Stephanie had no help, and Kelsey wondered if the few incidents when Andie had climbed her counters to get something from a cupboard were indicative of how she'd lived with her sick mom.

Tuesday Kelsey closed another loan, picked up the kids, and took Daniel and Allie to the drive-thru for corndogs. Wednesday was her birthday, and she would simply have another day. She thought about asking JD to take the kids that evening, but she was afraid it would feel bad if she wound up spending the evening alone. So she decided that she wasn't going to do anything outwardly special to ring in thirty-two, but take the day off and spend it being grateful for all she had.

She started the next morning still in her pajamas when Andie and JD arrived. She invited him to stay for pancakes but he declined, saying he needed to make money. That made her laugh, and then she made dollar-sign pancakes for the kids.

She let the kids run through the sprinkler in the backyard. Then laughed and got wet when they hauled her in with them. She threw all the kids in the tub before letting them watch cartoons while she took a long hot shower and changed into dry clothes. She had Daniel read them Dr. Seuss, then the kids requested green eggs and ham for lunch and so she grabbed the food coloring and made it, even though she feared her skillet would never be the same. But it was just a skillet.

JD picked up Andie, and bowed out quickly, much to Andie's dislike, but she went with him. Andie always walked off with the look of a condemned man facing the gallows.

The kids begged to watch a movie, and she gave in. Then they cajoled her into watching with them. She'd probably seen Peter Pan a hundred times. When the movie was three-quarters over and she was half asleep, she heard her name from the back yard.

Allie and Daniel were right beside her. Her name had

sounded weird, and Allie looked confused, but Daniel was grinning like a used car salesman. "Daniel?"

Right then her name came from the back yard again. It was JD, she recognized it now, only it still didn't sound quite right. Making her way to the back of the house, she realized his voice sounded like it was coming over a PA system.

As she looked out into the back yard, she realized that she was right.

"JD!"

The place was festooned with helium balloons, the picnic table had a plastic party tablecloth on it, and was loaded with buckets of chicken and sides and—smack in the middle—a birthday cake. Her mouth opened.

She turned to say thank you to Andie, who was hopping up and down and holding about fifteen balloons, and yelling 'surprise', and to JD as well. But just as she realized that Craig and Alex and TJ were there, a heavily reverberated chord came out of the air, and she saw their instruments.

They burst into the Beatles' "You Say It's Your Birthday."

Her hands flew to her face, and remained there, as she stood on the edge of her patio, through the entire song.

Only as they finished the last chord, the synthesizer hanging on until it was just below threshold, did she move from her spot. "Oh my God, guys. Thank you."

JD leaned away from his mic, "Happy Birthday. We're taking requests."

"Um, all right, . . . how about *Should've Been A Cowboy*?"

TJ laughed. "We know that one." Before he was even finished saying it, she saw JDs foot reach out and touch something on the ground, and his fingers start to move over the strings. The chords were completely different this time, having lost the synthetic wail and now sounding acoustic in spite of the knobs and wires that adorned the instruments.

Daniel grabbed her hand and pulled her to the table,

pointing to what she had missed before in her surprise. "Look, Mom, we got you a whole pile of presents."

Every cell of her turned warm and something long dormant moved in her chest. She just hadn't expected this.

Her kids joined in at the chorus, but Andie held back. They'd have to teach her the words. Or clearly JD could if she'd just listen. For a brief moment Kelsey held out the false hope that in one of those brightly wrapped boxes was a smile from Andie for JD. But that wasn't going to happen.

Andie was having a great time, but she wasn't even looking at her father.

Kelsey was.

This was bad.

The entire band, still in their uniform of jeans and old tees and ratty sneakers, had transformed from slacker boys to sexy men. What was it about a man with a guitar? Kelsey was no sucker; it wasn't a band-boy thing. He was sexier with the guitar, certainly. But the guitar alone didn't do it. But each of these guys had easily upped the sexy quotient by picking up an instrument and shaking it with the band. Worst of all was JD. His muscles flexed while he was playing, his fingers flew in a serious demonstration of skill, and he smiled at her each time he stepped up to the mic to add back-up vocals to his brother.

This was bad.

It was bad to see JD this way. Because he was younger than she was. He was in her house all the time. He was Andie's father. Never mind that it had been niggling at the back of her brain for weeks that he had turned his whole life upside down for a child he legitimately could have given back to the state. It had been clear from the start that JD was just a good guy. If he was also a sexy one . . . well, that was bad bad bad bad bad.

She fought the red flush that threatened her cheeks.

"What's next?" It was JD's voice. She could tell it from TJ's even though they sounded remarkably similar.

So she blurted out whatever she thought of. "Copa Cabana."

That required a few minutes of shuffling before they started playing. The music started, and she swung Daniel around, laughing and accusing him of knowing about the party. He giggled that he had kept it a secret from her for three whole days.

The voice that started singing wasn't TJ's, but JD's.

Kelsey's head snapped up. It wasn't right. It wasn't fair. He was crooning about Lola and the Copa. It wasn't supposed to make him sexier. But he was having fun, and there was something about the way he held the stage, even if the stage was just a patch of grass in her back yard. And he'd thrown her a birthday party.

She pushed those thoughts away and got Andie into the next dance. Allie was always willing to be the center of attention, so she hopped around in little circles and shook her butt in a way that made the band laugh and Kelsey wonder what her daughter had been watching.

The kids kept dancing, but she stepped aside to sit out the next couple songs, and when they asked for requests she suggested they play something of their own. That only made them put their heads together and confer for a moment before TJ switched back to singing lead and JD slipped his guitar strap over his head, and toed his amp switches, sending the first chords softly into the air.

Kelsey could only sit and watch.

The kids played around, tugged some of the balloons out of their ties, and danced with them. But Kelsey was oblivious to anything in the world other than the band in her back yard. Even when Allie tripped and let go of her balloon, Kelsey let Daniel hand his sister another string and stop the wailing.

The song was a slow three-count about the one that got away.

She didn't say anything when the song ended, until it was

made clear that they were waiting for her. "You guys wrote that?"

TJ grinned that shark grin of his. "JD wrote that one."

"Wow."

They were simply *that* good. For a moment she wondered why she'd ever doubted them when they said they were waiting for their break. Then she wondered who the idiots were who weren't signing them. "Do another."

The second one was just as good, if highly different. It was about picking fights just for the make-up sex. It even had a funny line where the whole band pitched in their voices about going to bed mad and waking up glad. Kelsey was joining in by the third time it came around.

She rallied the kids to yelling "Encore! Encore!" when they threatened to stop. The boys agreed to one last song.

This time Alex let fly on the drums to open the piece, and TJ railed about her being here, then being gone, then being here again.

This song ended on one strong short note, and immediately all the guys abandoned their instruments. There would be no more cajoling for just one more. Kelsey was willing to bet that Nashville had their next stars on their hands, if someone would just sign them to a record label.

The guys surrounded the table, and threw a few 'Happy Birthday's her way before tearing into the food. The kids mostly served themselves, eating huge quantities of macaroni and cheese that was an unnatural shade of orange.

Kelsey didn't care. She wasn't policing anyone tonight, and she was certain she wore a permanent grin. The chicken tasted better than it had the last time she'd ordered it, maybe because of the thought behind it.

Alex was the first one up, even before the cake was cut. He excused himself saying he had a prior engagement, and he carefully packed away all his drums, which took long enough that TJ, JD and Craig had all eaten another helping and wolfed down cake in the time it took him.

TJ and Craig offered polite good-nights and one last 'Happy Birthday' before they slipped through the side door into the garage. Kelsey heard the garage door protest as they raised it, and that answered the question of how they had gotten into her back yard in the first place.

She frowned, she'd thought the door was locked.

"I borrowed your spare keys yesterday and hoped you wouldn't notice them missing." JD pulled them out of his pocket and held them up, dangling from one finger, until she took them back, slipping them into her own pocket.

"How did you know today was my birthday?"

"I checked out your driver's license when you weren't paying attention. I just wanted to get the date right." He looked contrite.

"I just can't believe I was such a sucker that you were doing all this when I wasn't paying attention." She pulled another piece of chicken from the bone with her fingertips. "You had Daniel in on it, too."

JD grinned, "Yup, and he did a good job." That elicited a high-five from Daniel who just laughed then helped himself to more cake. "He was supposed to get you to watch a movie with him, so we could set up without being heard."

"Mom almost fell asleep."

JD laughed, and Kelsey confessed, "It's true. I don't know how many times I've seen all or part of Peter Pan."

He didn't respond, and so she pushed the wording out. "Thank you for all this, when I said my birthday was coming up, I didn't intend for . . ." She swept her hand across the scene, even over to where only JD's guitar remained standing in its holder.

"I know you didn't. That's why it was fun." His eyes were sincere, and his smile was small, but it encompassed his whole face. "Presents."

Huh?

He jumped up and started picking up boxes from the pile that had been shoved to one end of the table. Each of the kids caught the cue and grabbed for them, pushing them in her face, with an 'open mine' or 'mine first'. Allie topped the others with "Mommy, it's nail polish, for our toes!"

Kelsey opened Daniel's first, which was a mini-muffin pan. To replace the one she'd burned. But, today she wasn't worrying, so she pushed aside the problem that he was paying attention. Andie's contained a tee shirt with silver filigree on it. "Wow, Andie, that's pretty. Thank you." That garnered a big hug and a smile.

Then JD sheepishly handed his presents over. The first came in a white box, and contained a gorgeous square-cut vase with a flare at the top. As she turned it from side to side, it set little pitter-pats going in her chest. While she reminded herself that JD was out of her league, she was grateful for the sign that she was coming out of the fog Andrew's death had left her in. "This is beautiful."

"You had a few along these lines on your mantle." He looked almost apologetic.

"I was never able to have glass in DC. So I started a little collection. Thank you."

The second present was a huge bouquet of short stemmed flowers, in a riot of reds and oranges, tied and ready to go into the vase, but far too many to fit in what he'd bought her.

"I tried to get enough so you could fill all your vases."

She thanked him again and again, as they cleaned up and put the leftover food into her fridge. It was dark already, so JD packed up his guitar and hauled Andie home, with her now usual sullen pout.

Kelsey tucked her kids into bed with a minimum of fuss because they were already worn out. Then she went into her living room where the Peter Pan menu was burning its way into the TV screen. She clicked the whole thing off, and admired her mantle, blooming in sunrise colors, then decided that thirty-two was looking light years better than thirty-one. She'd spent that birthday alone, in a city where she didn't know anyone, convinced that she had made the wrong decision, and crying her eyes out over Andrew.

Thirty-two had a surprise party and a live band that kicked some ass.

Yes, things were looking up.

CHAPTER 8

J D eyed the computer screen. The market was in his favor, and that made him happy. It hadn't been for a while, but these past two weeks it had turned around. He knew what it was to ride the tide—he'd been doing it all along. The pressure now was that he had a child that would lose everything if he failed. With everything else Andie had been through, she didn't need that.

He pushed a key and sold a huge quantity of penny-stock. The guys at the firm would laugh at him if they could see him now, if they knew how excited he was over two thousand dollars.

He looked down at the shirt he had simply pulled from the closet this morning. It said something about not drinking and driving, and insinuated getting sucked off in a car. JD cringed, shrugged the shirt off, and tossed it into the trash. He was going to have to go through his entire wardrobe and throw out at least half his shirts. If Andie ever started speaking to him, she would ask what they meant. He really wasn't up to lying or explaining.

For the first time he considered his current wardrobe. He

was wearing jeans and shirts and sneakers with holes, mostly as a grand F-you to his old way of life.

He needed to clean up. He was a father now, and he wanted the best for Anderson Winslow Hewlitt. She bore his last name, if not his genetics. She looked enough like him that he wouldn't spend his life fielding questions about whether she was his or not, and no one would tip her off. He and Andie could have that conversation maybe ten years down the road from now.

JD sucked in a deep breath. He was wearing thin with Andie. It didn't matter that she was a child and didn't realize what she was doing. The only time she spoke to him was to demand something from TV. And he couldn't afford it.

He wouldn't be affording them any time soon the way things were going. Supposedly, one of the execs from a big label had been in the crowd at last Thursday's show, but the guys hadn't heard anything. So there either wasn't anyone there, or whoever had been there had not been excited about them. Both options boded equally poorly.

A wardrobe upgrade and a job upgrade were in serious order. Hell, a whole life upgrade was called for here. He looked around the nearly empty condo. The PlayStation was about the only thing he had kept from his previous life. He wondered why he hadn't saved the leather couch or the nice end tables. He had simply thrown the baby out with the bathwater.

He noticed he had a serious tendency to do that. The wardrobe was just a symptom of quitting his job. He was even sloppier than the other guys in the band, and that was scary.

He took a moment to stop and think about what things would be like if he stopped reacting and started choosing. He was learning to think where Andie was concerned. He saw that Kelsey always seemed to stop and wonder what they needed, why they were doing whatever was pissing her off. Of course, she'd had a husband that turned out to be sick, and sometimes

69

violent. JD guessed you'd learn really quick to be thoughtful instead of reactionary in that case.

But if he thought it through, what would he choose? He scanned the room and decided he'd have a cushier sofa, something deep with soft pillows, in a dark color that wouldn't suffer if some of the guys spilled beer on it now and then. He'd hide the TV. He didn't want Andie to think that the TV was the main point of the room, which it certainly looked like now. He'd wear nicer looking clothes. Comfortable clothing existed that didn't have holes or logos.

He scratched his belly and saw his sale go through as the screen flashed—two thousand and some change. He calculated out half the change and decided to spend it. Kelsey had Andie until three or four, and it was only noon. Clicking the computer off, he grabbed a garbage bag from under the kitchen sink, then hit the closet and rifled through everything, looking at it with new eyes.

He couldn't even wear half of these things into the store to get new clothes. No one would serve him if he looked that ratty. He stuffed shirts down into the bag, and shoved his sentimentality in with them. He didn't need lewd reminders of white-water rafting trips or Mardi-Gras. He tied the bag and rolled it down the stairs, before stripping and climbing into the shower.

Not five minutes later he was towel dried, wearing khakis and a clean, plain, fitted tee, standing in the driveway. He winced as he turned the key in the car door. The car looked as much like an F-you to his old life as the clothes he'd just tossed. But he couldn't just toss the car. Even with the minor windfall he'd just gotten, he wasn't anywhere close to replacing it.

He climbed behind the wheel, grateful that the condo had covered parking that helped keep the car cool. He only ran the AC when he had to, mostly when Andie was in the car. It was dripping into the passenger foot well, and he was afraid it was going to give out any second. Quickly recalculating, he decided to spend a little less today, and leave some for the AC repair he was certain was coming.

Two hours later he was poorer in cash, but richer in shirts and pants. He was comfortable in his khakis and Doc Martens, he realized.

But not the car. It wasn't safe for Andie, he decided, as he glanced into the rearview mirror, where the new child seat looked anachronistic to the car around it. He just wasn't sure how he was going to fund this new car.

At three-thirty he walked over to pick up Andie. If it was just about him, or if it had been a daycare, he would have left her until the very last minute. They were both happier when they were apart. But he wasn't going to do that to Kelsey. She had told him you don't screw the babysitter, and while her meaning had been a little more literal, he figured it applied in this case too.

That was another thing that had to go: Kelsey taking care of them. It had been one thing when it had looked like Andie was going to come around. But she hadn't, at least not for him.

Both Bethany and another sitter that Kelsey had recommended, had watched Andie, and both had found her 'charming' and 'sweet'. JD wouldn't believe those words had been applied to his little hell-demon, except that he witnessed it with Kelsey all the time. It did keep him from feeling guilty that he was out three to four nights a week practicing or playing gigs.

He had racked up some serious trading debt with Kelsey as well. It seemed he was only paying his hours back about half as fast as he spent them. And he had no good excuse—Kelsey just didn't seem to need him.

He lifted her garage door, and then pulled it down, creaking, behind him, enveloping himself in the cool dark. With the spare key she had given to him after her birthday party last week, he let himself into the empty back yard.

Kelsey answered his knock with her headset on and a pained expression across her face.

"What's wrong?" He pushed his way into the cool and closed the door behind himself as she walked away pressing her palm into her ribcage.

"Don't worry, it's nothing." But she took a quick gulp of air.

He followed close on her heels, ignoring the kids because he could hear them playing together in the back bedroom. "It's not nothing and you're a bad liar. What gives?"

She shook her head then confessed. "It's hiccups."

He didn't buy that for a hot second. "Hiccups?"

"Yes, I've had them since two hours ago." And this time when she gulped he realized that it had been involuntary.

"So just sit really still for about five minutes."

She gave him a look that would have boiled cold water on sight.

"Mom! Andie won't let me have my dolly!" Allie appeared in the doorway, her face tear-streaked, perfect evidence for Kelsey's state.

"That is why I haven't been able to get rid of these."

"Yeah, I figured that out about two seconds after I uttered my stupidity."

That changed her expression to a grin instantly, and JD was proud of himself, until she hiccupped and winced again. Her hand flew back to her ribcage, her sweet hazel eyes widening.

"I could scare you." He volunteered.

She shook her head. "Can you let me lie down, uninterrupted, for about ten minutes?"

"You got it." He followed her into the living room, where she peeled off the headset before stretching out on the couch. He lowered himself quietly into the armchair that sat at a right angle.

Kelsey even had comfy furniture. It wasn't the leather he'd given up with his condo, but was nice enough despite the quilt thrown over it.

After a minute of contemplating the furnishings, he turned his attentions to the woman occupying the couch. Her long summer-tanned legs stretched from shorts to their perch on the armrest, looking casually graceful in white Keds. Her face was almost relaxed, except her lips held just the tiniest pout. And, oh god, don't let her open her eyes and catch him looking at her.

He glanced away, but his thoughts didn't change direction with his gaze. He bet, if he just leaned over and kissed her right now, that he'd startle her enough that those hiccups wouldn't ever come back.

He'd been having these thoughts for a while. At first, they had lingered undeveloped in the back of his head. Then he'd dreamed about her the night before her birthday, some erotic scene from a movie, only it was Kelsey crawling across the covers like a cat, wearing only some unidentifiable filmy white thing. In the dream it hadn't surprised him. It hadn't really surprised him when he woke up either.

He heard her deep intake of air, and her lips un-pursed, just a little.

He heard her voice. *You don't screw the baby-sitter.*

She'd been talking about Bethany, and she'd been right: Bethany was hot. But Bethany was twenty and acted twenty. Bethany needed a frat boy.

Of course, Kelsey had thought that of him, because he sure looked like his old frat-boy self. It had been a shock to find Kelsey's birthday on her driver's license. He'd startled when he read that her birth-year was before his. He'd done the math and figured out it was her thirty-second birthday. That put her just over three years older than him.

No wonder she'd been so shocked that he'd once worn suits and had a real job.

A vocal scuffle between all three kids caught his attention and pulled him from his thoughts. Hopping up, so that Kelsey wouldn't be disturbed by it, he broke up the mild melee and told Andie that it was time to start getting ready to go.

She protested, loudly, again making him grind his teeth. JD desperately wanted to not care, but if he didn't care, then Andie would be with a foster family.

He put up his usual battle, and finally got her shoes on her and the doll she had brought gathered up. As he stretched up, turning to go check on Kelsey, he almost ran into her. She had planted herself in the doorway, arms crossed over her chest.

"Are you feeling better?" She didn't really look it. JD hoped she hadn't gotten up, thinking he couldn't deal with his daughter. He could deal with Andie, just not well.

Kelsey absently replied, 'yes, thank you', but she didn't look at him. She stared at Andie. "Young lady, you owe your Daddy an apology."

"Why?" Andie sulked.

Oh, no. JD thought.

"Because, he's been nothing but nice to you, and you have been rude to him at every turn."

"So?" There was a defiance in her voice that he hadn't heard in a while. He had thought that maybe she was coming around, but perhaps she was simply seething quietly. "I don't need a Daddy."

Kelsey stepped into the room and squared herself off with his daughter. "Everyone needs a Daddy."

"No they don't!" Andie bordered on screaming. "Daniel and Allie don't. You are just fine with only a Mommy, that's the way it should be!"

JD almost stepped back, the look on Kelsey's face was vicious. She'd lost her husband just over a year ago, and he knew, even if Andie didn't, what a viper pit his daughter had jumped into. His response was almost to step in front of Andie and end this, but Kelsey must have seen some movement in him. While her gaze didn't stray from Andie, her hand came out in a subtle motion telling him to back down.

Her voice was soft, but deadly. "You have no idea how much Daniel and Allie would love to have a Daddy like JD."

"They can have him!" It was a full wail as she shoved past Kelsey and down the hall, they heard the front door rattle then slam as she let herself out.

"Jesus." JD let the breath out of his lungs as his body automatically followed Andie, the adrenaline controlling his movements when his brain didn't. His feet pounded down the front walk, then hit the sidewalk, skidding to a halt.

He frantically looked both ways, only to see the pink tail of her dress disappear behind the Henderson's hedge. He stayed put this time, only after two full, deep breaths did he realize that his teeth were so tight he was about to crack them.

A small hand appeared against his back, making him jump then sigh. "I wonder what Mrs. Henderson thinks of me."

"Only good things. I talked to her about Andie after that first day we met."

"Thank you."

He turned to face her, only to find that her eyes were swimming with unshed tears. "I'm so sorry, I thought I could-"

"Don't. It wasn't you. It's Andie. She hates me." He felt his hands reach for her, but stopped them. "She's great for Bethany. It's just me."

Kelsey shook her head. "It isn't you. I've watched her. She hates *men*. You said she kicked TJ, and at the party she wouldn't go near any of the guys. It's not you."

Even if he believed her, it didn't change anything. Andie wouldn't be happy with him. She simply refused.

He started down the sidewalk to fetch her from the Hendersons', but Kelsey put her hand flat against his chest. "Let me. I started it, and she'll be less trouble for me."

He agreed, still taking deep breaths. Already missing the feel of her hand against him, he watched as her long strides ate up the sidewalk. Turning, he went back inside to explain to Daniel and Allie where their mother had gone. At least they didn't hate him.

He watched out the front window until he saw Kelsey, hand in hand with a clearly petulant Andie, coming down the walk. What he wouldn't give to hear what they were saying, but they were beyond the glass and beyond him, both of them.

CHAPTER 9

Tuesday morning, he did something he hadn't done in what seemed like forever. He put his resume together. He procrastinated until he had done his usual investing, but an hour after that, it was done. He printed a hard copy and parked Andie in front of the TV, ashamed to realize he didn't feel any guilt about that at all. Then he tucked himself upstairs where it was quiet and began making phone calls.

Thirty minutes later, he'd emailed the resume to three different firms. It would be enough to get an interview. The past two and a half years might be an issue, though he figured he'd just say he'd been living off the same fifty thousand dollars that he'd come here with. In that time the fifty thousand had only dwindled by 1,676 dollars. Every last penny of principle that was gone was for Andie. He hadn't touched it once before she arrived.

Having done more than enough for one day, he packed Andie up and took her with him to band practice. She colored for the several hours they were there, and didn't make eye contact with any of them. He was in deeper trouble with her than he thought.

Wednesday, Andie was with Kelsey, and JD was glad that school would start in two weeks and that this wouldn't go on much longer. His heart sure didn't feel lighter, but he was doing the right thing. Andie would have a safe car, and the right education, and as many clothes as she could possibly wear.

When he shed his old life and high-tailed it to Nashville, he'd felt the weight lift, but right now he was just grateful that he had sitters that came to him, or lived next door, and that he didn't have to have Andie in his rat-trap car that often.

He let himself in through the garage again, and again found Kelsey with her headset on. She said a few words into the mouthpiece while she held up a finger to keep him quiet and quickly signed off.

"Hey, how was your day?"

It took just a moment to figure out that she was talking to him.

"Okay." He shoved his hands in his jeans pockets. "You know, if you need to work, you can call me and I'll take them."

She shook her head. "I'm used to working like this in the summer. I just close fewer loans. I did have some stuff come crashing down today, but the kids played great together."

Of course they did, Andie was a star-pupil for Kelsey. She peeled the headset and phone and put them in the cradle, declaring herself done for the day.

"You've done a lot for us-"

"Uh oh, where is this going?" She frowned at him, like he was about to take away her toys, and he stifled a little laugh, before he continued.

"And you're working pretty hard. I have Bethany lined-up for tomorrow night for practice, but Craig and TJ bowed out, so I'm free." He paused, not wanting it to sound like a date, which wasn't where he was going. He couldn't afford to, not with Kelsey watching Andie so much, not with her living next door. "I can't remember the last movie I saw, so I'm going to keep

Bethany and go out tomorrow night. If you want to join me, the whole evening's on me."

She eyed him like he was something she couldn't identify, and that worried him.

"So, what you're saying is, if I upgrade the babysitter to cover all three kids, I can have an evening with adult conversation and a free movie?"

"Nope." He shook his head. "The baby sitter upgrade is on me. And, if you promise not to whine, pout, or scream at me, I'll throw in dinner." *Uh oh, that started sounding like a date.*

Kelsey laughed. "I am so there."

JD couldn't stop the smile that spread across his face. "One rule: no talking about kids."

She stuck out her hand and they shook on it. She called the kids out of the back bedroom, then turned back to him. "So what are we going to see?"

"I don't even know what's out." God, that was sad, to not even know what movies were playing. He hadn't gotten to see a lot in the past three years of being dirt-poor, but he'd at least known what he was missing.

The kids traipsed into the room as she volunteered to pay for dinner.

"No." His chest sank. "I've got the whole thing. Please, don't worry about it." He didn't like the way the word 'please' had come out of his mouth, he was truly beseeching her to trust that he had the money. He almost laughed at himself for thinking she might mistake it for a date. There was no way Kelsey thought her younger, poorer neighbor was actually asking her out.

She explained to the kids that Bethany was coming tomorrow night, then asked if Bethany would be at her house or his condo. He stiffened at that, too. What was wrong with his place? Except that Kelsey's was perfectly set up for kids.

She walked away, talking as she went, "If they're here, then you can just carry Andie home, and we don't have to wake anyone up."

She made a good point, and he conceded before dragging Andie back home, against her will, as usual.

At five o'clock sharp the next night, he and Andie showed up on Kelsey's doorstep, and for a moment he felt as if he'd spent the whole last year showing up on Kelsey's doorstep. Bethany was already there, and so he offered Andie a quick hug good-bye, which she refused.

When Kelsey offered to drive, he felt the last straw hit. Suddenly, he didn't care if the AC leaked on her feet. He just pulled his keys out of his pocket and spoke up, "I've got it."

She actually smiled.

The evening was cool enough that he didn't have to worry about using the AC. Kelsey climbed in the passenger seat and stretched like a cat, "God, no one's driven me anywhere since . . . I don't know how long."

"When Andrew was alive?" He prompted.

"Andy was sick, he couldn't have a license, and I sure wouldn't get in a car with him. He was great, except that could change at any minute."

"Jesus."

Her only response was a nod.

"Your mother?"

A harsh sound, just shy of laughter, barked out of her, "My mother was an alcoholic."

"Wow," JD cranked the wheel into the turn, "I think your family was even more dysfunctional than mine is."

"We were hard to beat."

They still hadn't decided what movie to see by the time the bill came for dinner. Everything had been good until Kelsey looked at the slip with a worried expression. JD got mad. "Don't you dare touch that."

"Okay, I was just trying to help." She held her hands up. "I know what it's like-"

"Do you?" From where he sat, she had everything. Two perfect kids, a house, and spare money she had asked him again to invest for her.

Hazel eyes flared. "Yes, I do. And I did it in DC, where the house payment I couldn't make every month was several thousand dollars. I did it from when I dropped out of college until last year. I was the sole breadwinner for my family. Andy's medical bills wiped out anything spare real fast. So it was all on me. And there was no end in sight."

JD started to apologize, but Kelsey bulldozed right over him. "I had my mom and Andy and Daniel to take care of, and some days I think I had Allie just to make sure there was a greater number of sane people in the house. My mother up and died on me. Then the day after the last house payment was in, Andy dies. Things were finally looking up, and he goes and dies."

JD sat, chastised, while she was quiet for a moment, looking at her napkin in her hands. She was only right then noticing that she'd twisted it while she was talking. "Sometimes I think he planned it that way, that he did that on purpose to set me free."

"People don't time their deaths like that."

Her glassy eyes caught him square and held him tighter than any fist. "They do when they kill themselves."

His mouth fell open, but he shut it as soon as he realized he didn't have anything to say to that. It wasn't fast enough for her to not see it though.

The server appeared, and they didn't speak while he paid the bill. "Do you really believe he planned it like that?"

"Sometimes." She spoke again, softer this time, more subdued. "At least there's a good purpose for you living like this."

"There was a good purpose for you, too."

Her smile changed her face, "Yeah, but I was in a 'damned if you do, damned if you don't' situation. I didn't really choose it. It chose me."

JD shook his head, wanting only to negate the way she felt about it. "You were doing the right thing. You were taking care of the people you love."

That's what he would be doing, too.

The movie was uneventful; they opted for the last big summer blockbuster, and both decided they couldn't tell if it was good or bad. Kelsey laughed at him, and he realized that she had actually spent a good portion of the evening laughing. Aside from the really tense bill-paying moment at the restaurant, she'd been in a really good mood. It even seemed like she was a little lighter after she got that off her chest.

"I forgot to warn you," She started, "one of the symptoms of being a parent is that you get really picky about your movies."

"How so?"

"Well, you don't get to see very many, so when you do you really want them to count. If they don't, you can get really upset about it."

Something comfortable settled itself inside him and he told her about his week. "I hit this stock, I made over two grand, so don't worry about me and Andie."

Her head cocked to one side. "I don't really. I know I'm always offering to help out. But I do like doing it, and you two won't need us at all one of these days, and we'll all miss you."

He wanted to inject some words of his own into the conversation, but he only got out a disbelieving half-laugh before she was talking again. "I've been better since you two have been around. These last weeks, I've laughed more and seen the world around me more. Thank you."

"Well, you don't have to worry about us going anywhere any time soon." He told her about the Thursday night show, that TJ and Craig were meeting with someone tonight, but all he'd gotten was a text message that said, 'too hard-core'. It was just another 'no,' the reason didn't really matter.

At Kelsey's, he roused Andie just enough to gather her up and carry her back home, but just as he got to the front door she woke. Just alert enough to know she was being carried, she lashed out at him, landing a fist square on his jaw, as well as a solid kick to the ribs. To add insult to injury, she yelled at him, and ran to hide behind Kelsey.

Kelsey squatted down to Andie's level, "Baby, what's wrong?"

"I don't need a daddy. My Mommy said! I need my Mommy!" With that, she pitched herself into the armchair and let out a wail.

Kelsey looked at him like she was in shock, "JD, go get her birth certificate."

He stood there looking at the two crazy women in his life, and couldn't decide if he should just flee. But he shook his head and walked back to the condo. He rifled through the file drawers looking for the envelope that Texas CPS had sent him.

He was two inches from giving up, when the envelope appeared in front of him. Not for the first time, he wondered what Kelsey and Andie were talking about without him.

He locked his door behind him and hit the sidewalk.

In under two minutes he was back at Kelsey's. When he opened the door, he stopped cold. Kelsey sat square in the middle of the couch, her cheek pressed against Andie's head as his daughter cried. Wide hazel eyes looked up at him and Kelsey's hand snaked out reaching for something.

JD held out the birth certificate, but it wasn't the paper she took. Kelsey's fingers wrapped around his wrist and gently tugged him down next to her on the couch. There was only enough room to be flush up against the two crying females, and JD was at a total loss.

This time she took the birth certificate from his hand, and repositioned Andie, so that his daughter was still on her lap, but facing him now. "Andie, I want you to look at this. It's your birth certificate."

Andie ran one small fingertip across the embossed emblem in the corner, but didn't say anything.

Kelsey kept talking. "Everybody, when they're born, gets a birth certificate. And there are some rules about these papers. Do you know any of the rules?"

Andie shook her head. JD wanted to also—what the hell 'rules' was she talking about?

"Well, the first rule is that only the Mommy can fill out the birth certificate. So, for example, I filled out Allie's."

Andie nodded.

Kelsey kept going, her voice low and sweet. "It's the mommy who tells the hospital what to put on the birth certificate. She tells them the baby's name. Can you find your name?"

"Yes." Andie's voice was small, and she looked at the paper and, though she couldn't read, she did find her own name. "That says 'Andie'."

Kelsey smiled, "Actually, it says your whole name. Andie is your nickname. Like Allie, her whole first name is Allison. Do you know your whole name?"

"My whole name is Anderson Winslow Hewlitt."

"That's right, baby. That's exactly what it says, right there." Kelsey traced her finger along the page. "They put other things on here, too. Like where you were born," She pointed, then pointed again, "How much you weighed, that you're a girl." She smiled a little at Andie, and Andie just tucked herself back into Kelsey's arms.

This child didn't want him. He'd never been more certain of anything in his life.

"The mommy also puts her own name on the birth certificate." Kelsey pointed. "I bet you miss her."

Andie's voice was tiny. "A whole lot."

JD wondered again where all this was leading. He really felt he would be most useful if he handed them each a tissue and got the hell out.

"There's something else on your birth certificate, too." Kelsey tracked her finger to the other corner, to JD's name. "There's a line here for the father. Some mommies are married, and they put their husband's name in. Your mommy wasn't married was she?"

"No."

"Then she had a really important decision to make. She didn't like her own daddy, did she?"

Andie's voice was a whisper. "He was bad. He was mean to her."

Kelsey nodded. "I figured that. She didn't think you two needed a daddy, did she?"

"No, I don't."

"She was probably right."

JD's mouth almost dropped open. Just when he'd thought he knew where she was headed, Kelsey dropped that one.

"You two didn't need a daddy, you had your mommy. And you guys were just fine. But your mommy got sick didn't she?"

Andie nodded again, looking even sadder.

"Then it's a good thing your mommy was so smart."

Wide brown eyes looked up at Kelsey, waiting. JD waited, too.

"Your mom got to choose. She could leave the line for the daddy blank, or she could choose a really good daddy for her little girl. Just in case anything happened to her, she wanted to know that her little girl would be okay. And so she thought real hard, and she chose the best daddy she could think of, and she put his name down."

His chest constricted. Kelsey looked up, her hazel gaze a little foggy, and her smile fighting through the tears he had seen earlier. "Andie, can you read that name?"

Andie shook her head.

"JD, can you?"

He hadn't expected to participate in this, but maybe he should have. It didn't come out as clear as he would have liked, but he spoke it. "It says Johnathan Darcy Hewlitt."

"Who is that?"

He almost burst out laughing.

But Kelsey stepped in, as usual. She hugged Andie a little tighter. "He's right here. We call him JD, for Johnathan Darcy. It's his nickname like Andie is yours. JD is the daddy your mommy chose for you."

Andie looked up at him, her brown eyes scanning him for faults, like she was seeing him anew.

Kelsey continued, "Now you have to be really careful with him. There aren't many like him left. He's a really good daddy. That's why your mommy picked him. She even gave you the same last name as him, so you would know when you two found each other again. I'm really sorry about what happened to your mommy, I am, baby, but your mommy was so smart, she gave you the best present ever. She found the very best daddy, and she gave him to you."

Andie looked at him with a little frown, "Are you really my daddy?"

He nodded. "Yes."

"Okay."

That was it, no fanfare, just 'okay'. Somehow Kelsey had done it. Convinced Andie that he was a good guy. Even set things up for later when he would have to tell Andie she wasn't genetically his. And Kelsey hadn't lied, like so many people do to sugarcoat things to small children.

He held his hand out to her. "Are you tired, baby? Do you want to go sleep in your own bed?"

She nodded, her small hand sliding into his, and he realized, for the first time, what it really felt like to have a child hold your hand. The weight of it settled over him like a warm blanket.

Kelsey handed him the birth certificate, but Andie reached out for it. "Can I keep it?"

JD sighed. That was it. His thirty seconds of enjoying his daughter was over. "No, honey, this is a very special paper, and we only have one."

Her face sank, and she looked so sad it broke his heart, but she didn't whine or scream or fight. So for the first time, she truly won. JD realized he was in for a lifetime of losing battles to his daughter. "But I have an idea. Tomorrow we can go to the copy place and make you your own copy. Would you like that?"

Jesus, she looked at him like he had just volunteered ice cream for dinner, every night, for the rest of her life.

"You can sleep with it on your nightstand tonight." He started to turn to go, but she didn't give. Her little hand tugged on his, and he winced waiting for the kick, the scream, the tantrum.

"I don't have any shoes on." Her hands reached up for him. He wouldn't really have thought it possible, but he sunk a little deeper.

CHAPTER 10

Kelsey hadn't seen either JD or Andie all weekend. Daniel had asked after his friend, but all Kelsey could say was that Andie and JD needed some time to be just a daddy and his little girl. They would be back Monday morning.

Kelsey wondered if she was right. She wouldn't be all that shocked if the two of them just didn't show up tomorrow. But she would be disappointed.

She had gone this long without seeing them before, so it took a while to place what was wrong this time: JD no longer needed her. Andie no longer needed her. She wouldn't scream that Kelsey should be her mommy and JD wouldn't look at her like she could save him.

What was even more depressing was how lost she felt without that. All her life Andrew had needed her so much, and she couldn't 'fix' anything for him. But she had 'fixed' JD and Andie. She should be happy.

She almost laughed out loud and looked around, glad that the kids wouldn't see her getting so maudlin. Who knew if she had 'fixed' a damn thing for JD and Andie?

Maybe she'd sleep a little better tonight.

That was disturbing, too. She was far too tangled up in other people's lives. Despite her efforts, she didn't seem to be able to find any balance. She was either wound up in taking care of Andrew, or her grief, or Andie and JD. And Andie and JD were just people she had been nice to at Target.

It had certainly turned into more than that. She was watching JD's child on a regular basis. JD had thrown her the best birthday party she'd ever had. Andrew and her mother had never gone all out for her. They had been far too busy living in their world of 'everything's fine' to look up and see what anyone around them might need. And she had spent all her time making sure that world stayed fine for them.

Kelsey sat down at the table with her head in her hands. Good lord, she was an enabler! It stuck in her throat, and she swallowed hard to get it down. She'd told herself that the shrinks were full of it, but there it was. And in the end there had been no real solution, only the one Andrew had found for himself.

Kelsey took a gulp of air. Maybe she *had* enabled her mother's alcoholism. But if she had enabled Andy at all, she had enabled him to live—longer and happier.

She shoved the whole thing aside and went out into the backyard to play with her kids. Allie yelled at Daniel a few times, but he didn't yell back. Daniel still needed work in the getting-worked-up department. It was surely leftovers from Andrew. And even possibly genetics, also from Andrew.

If environment did play a part in Andrew's disease, then Kelsey had her job: make absolutely certain that Daniel's environment was safer, better, more open. Andrew had taken hold of Daniel's formative years, but she still had a few left to work with.

She had never confronted Andy about Daniel. Because Andrew had simply disappeared one day, then showed up years later with baby Daniel. Kelsey had always been afraid that if she tipped him the wrong way, he would just take Daniel and disappear again. For years it had woken her from sleep, ripping the covers away, and racing down the hall to be certain that her Daniel still lay sleeping in his crib.

Maybe that was why she'd had Allie. To have a child that Andrew's disease couldn't steal from her.

But Andrew had let them all go. Daniel was hers now, and hers alone to undo what had been done.

She called the kids inside and set them to brushing their teeth and putting on their jammies. Kelsey straightened the house while they were at it. After they were read to, and kissed, and tucked in, she settled in with a soda and a TV show. Her restless nights had left her tired and she passed out in the middle of the program.

"Kelsey?" JD's voice swam through the fog to her brain. Light pushed against her eyelids like hot fingers. Somewhere beyond her haze, JD spoke to her again. "Are you all right?"

"Mmmmmm."

To her left the bed sank and she rolled a little toward the weight, unable to stop herself. A warm hand lay against her cheek and, with the tiniest sigh, she leaned into it.

"Wake up, Kelse." This time the hand was less friendly and rattled her head until she blinked at him, letting the light in to sear her eyeballs.

"JD, go 'way." She pushed weakly at his hands, and tried to roll over.

But the hands stopped her again. Somewhere in her brain, she knew it was JD and that he was trying to wake her. Somewhere else in her brain was the firm belief that he was Satan incarnate, sent to earth to steal her precious sleep.

He rattled her again. "Kelse, I need to know that you're okay. You're scaring me here."

"Damnit!" Even while trying to fend him off, her brain reacted to the idea that she was scaring him. How many times had she stood over Andrew wondering if this would be the time that he wouldn't wake up? She couldn't do that to JD, even if he was waking her in the middle of the night. She threw back the sheet and slung her legs, less than gracefully, over the side of the bed and forced her eyes open. "I'm up. All right? What do you want, waking me up so damned early-"

The alarm clock glared ugly red numbers at her. 9:47. She rubbed her eyes with her fists and only after she had done it did she realize that she must look like a cartoon. And when had she crawled into bed?

"Okay." JD inhaled sharply, and she felt as well as saw him stand up and head out of the room. "As long as you're okay, I'm going to go now."

A second later she heard the door click behind him. Only a second after that did she realize that she was in a short t-shirt and underwear and nothing else.

Good move, Kelse, good move. She'd scared off her hot younger neighbor friend. *Oooops.*

It only took a minute to decide that her best course of action was to get dressed and act as though she flashed her undies to her neighbors every day. She grimaced, realizing the ones she was wearing said 'little devil'.

She threw on a pair of cotton knit pants and a new t-shirt, this time with a bra, and quickly brushed her teeth and splashed water on her face. The trip down the hall had seemed interminable, but at last she was face to face with JD, who was sitting on the couch while the kids watched their favorite cartoon.

She punctuated the whole thing with a wide yawn.

"The kids let me in when I got here. They said you wouldn't wake up."

"Oh, lord. Were they upset?" She flopped down on the couch beside him, ignoring her embarrassment.

"No, but I was." His hands searched for something, then found each other.

Well, maybe the embarrassment wasn't going to go away quite as fast as she had hoped. "I just hadn't been sleeping well, and I guess last night I caught up."

"Why weren't you sleeping?" His brown eyes filled with concern, only partially obscured by the hair that just kept growing longer.

She was *not* going to answer that one—not out loud anyway. So she shrugged.

Changing topics had usually worked well with Andy. Of course, Andrew had been emotionally impaired, and JD was nothing of the sort, but, hey, it was worth a shot. "How are things working out with Andie?"

He grinned. "Not perfect, but better."

"You weren't expecting perfect, were you? Because if you were-"

His hand came up, stopping her prattles and her worries. And instantly reminding her of the warm feel of it against her cheek, trying to wake her.

"No, I don't expect perfect. She speaks to me now, she just doesn't trust me or think I can do anything right. But it's a huge improvement. You should have been a lawyer."

She only nodded, blinking back the thoughts that she had once had serious designs on Law School. It was hard to hear now that she would have been good at it.

Again, he redirected her. "So how did you know to pull out her birth certificate? I'm still not sure I understand all of it."

She opened her mouth, then closed it, realizing that three

little pairs of ears were tuned to the TV, but who knew what they might hear. "Are you guys okay?"

They all nodded like good little TV zombies, and she stood and motioned for JD to follow her into the kitchen. Reaching into the fridge, she grabbed herself a can of coke, loving the icy feel and enjoying the pop and fizz as she opened it. Only after her first relieving sip did she remember to offer one to JD.

"No thanks." His eyebrows went up a few notches. "You're hitting that stuff pretty early today."

"I need the caffeine." She wasn't about to tell him she had a coke before ten a.m. just about every day. What was he, caffeine police? She propped herself against the counter, waiting for the fizz and sugar to support her from the inside. "I just remembered what you'd said about her mom possibly being sexually abused."

He nodded, the light going on.

Kelsey took another sip before she continued. "If there's one thing I learned from Andy, it's that we pass a lot of unexpected things on to our kids. I guess Stephanie passed on her wariness of men."

"That does fit pretty neatly with the way Andie's been acting." He shook his head. "She just doesn't quite trust me any further than she can throw me. But at least now she'll say so rather than screaming and kicking things."

Kelsey smiled. "We can work a trade."

JD groaned. "Not another trade. I can't ever pay you back for all your trades. I owe you so many babysitting hours that I should just adopt your kids." His eyes rolled.

"This won't be like that. Besides, I don't need to be paid back, but you could remember me when you're big and famous. I'd like to be remembered with a classic Ford Mustang. Teal, please. Leather interior. I can be patient."

He was laughing full out when he asked her about her latest trade scheme.

"I'll help you show Andie that you can be trusted. Kids learn by watching, and I'm female and therefore trustable. If I show that I trust you, she may come around. Like what do you most need her to do?"

"Take a bath."

Her mouth popped open. "Oh, I am so not demonstrating that one. Pick something else."

He nodded, "I figured as much. I really need her to let me brush her hair."

"She did it herself this morning, huh?" It was all gathered on one side with clumps sticking out.

His tone was droll. "You could tell, could you?"

She nodded. "That we can fix. I'll be sure and ask your opinion, and defer to you, obviously, several times a day."

He grinned, "I'm trying to find an argument with this. What's my role?"

Her shoulders lifted in a shrug. "We never knew what would set Andrew off, so we learned to tip-toe around and not raise our voices. Allie has come around, but Daniel got several more years of it. I need to show him that people can argue and they won't go off on a tear if they get startled or upset."

"So . . . we argue?"

She shrugged. "Clearly I hadn't really thought that one all the way out."

"I guess, if we concede and compromise at the end." His head tilted. "How off the handle are you going to get?"

"As off the handle as I feel like!" She mocked shoving him in the chest and trying to ignore the hard feel of it beneath her fingertips. "I have years of built-up resentments and tamped-down feelings."

But he couldn't keep a straight face. "Oh yeah, this is going to work out very well. Our kids are going to think we are insane."

"Well, we both have a good excuse. Meet me in the living

room." Back in her own bathroom she grabbed her shell brush and came back, holding it out to JD who was seated on the couch now. "Will you brush my hair for me?"

The children were too involved in the tv program; she didn't think any of them had heard her. But as Kelsey settled herself on the floor in front of JD, Andie glanced over her shoulder. She sent Kelsey a look of pure sympathy. "He's not very good at it."

One only had to look at Andie's own hair to wonder how bad JD could be. Kelsey yelped. "Ouch!"

"Sorry." He put the brush back at the crown of her head and started to stroke downward.

Kelsey flinched.

JD leaned over her, whispering in her ear. "You're supposed to be deferring to me. Show her that it's a good idea to let me brush her hair."

"I'm not actually sure that it is. She's right, you're bad at this."

Indignant, he sat up straight, even as Andie tossed the line over her shoulder. "I told you," she said without ever taking her eyes off the TV.

A growl of frustration found its way out of JD and he held the brush down in her line of sight. "Here, then, you do it."

He started to stand up, lifting one leg over her, but Kelsey grabbed at it, nearly pulling him back down.

Kelsey gave him a moment to get settled. "You've never brushed long hair before, have you?"

Leaning over her again, he glared. "Do I look like a stylist?"

"No." She grinned and held the brush back up, "Then you'll learn-"

"I don't really want to-"

"Shh! Watch." She held her palm against her head, and started at the bottom of a hank of hair, and using small strokes she worked out little tangles one at a time. "If you start at the top, you gather all the little tangles into a bigger knot that will never come out. Now you try."

He took the proffered brush from her, placed his palm against her head, and pulled the brush downward through a section of hair. She flinched, but just put her hands over his, indicating that he needed a little more pressure against her head, and smaller strokes at the bottom of the hair. After a moment, she was more aware of her hands over his than of her hair being brushed, so she let go.

He let out a small huff and worked on another piece of hair.

Within three minutes she had turned to pudding at his feet. She groaned.

"What?"

"No, don't stop. That feels good. I can't remember the last time anyone brushed my hair for me."

"That's taking it a little far, don't you think?" He whispered again. "I just need her to let me do it."

"Shhh! Brush!" She tipped her head back and waited. Within a minute she wasn't able to hold back any longer and she sighed.

"Oh my god. You really do like this." He stopped brushing.

"Shhh! Brush!"

He laughed. "Okay, but-"

"Shhh!" She leaned her head back again, exposing her throat.

He brushed it for her until the end of the kids' TV program. By then, she had become butter, tilting her head from side to side, to give him better access. She had become so boneless that she simply rested her cheek against his knee, enjoying the feel of soft old denim under her skin.

He skimmed his palm down her hair. "It gleams. You're done. My arms are tired."

She thought about protesting, but realized there was a better tactic. "You'll be back tomorrow to brush it again." She didn't really *ask*.

He changed tacks. "I'm going to take the kids today."

"What?" She perked up.

"You need the day off, you already overslept. I owe you a bazillion hours. I'll take them."

"Are you sure?" As soon as she said it, she wished she could swallow it back. While she had asked that question of everyone else in her life for years, it was insulting to an emotional adult.

"Yes, I'm sure." By the tone in his voice it had clearly been insulting to JD.

Damn.

"All right, then." Kelsey threw in a grin, hoping to cover for her gaffe, "Kids, you're spending the day with JD!"

Allie and Daniel hopped up and gave happy shouts. Andie simply didn't protest.

They worked together to get her kids dressed, and she walked them to the front door. "I don't really think the idea of letting you brush hair has soaked in." She spoke that line just to him, but the next one she put at overhearing decibels. "You'll be back tomorrow morning to brush it again, right? It gets lots of tangles at night." She smiled a false, but expectant grin.

"Dream on. Wednesday maybe. What am I, your hairbrush slave?"

"Yes!"

CHAPTER 11

Wednesday morning Kelsey set her can of coke out of sight before answering JD's knock. When she opened the door it revealed a dressed and smiling Andie, with a new shoulder length bob.

"You cut her-" She didn't get the word *hair* out of her mouth. "You cut *your hair*, too. Andie, I like that new cut. Did your daddy brush it this morning? Because he's going to brush mine, too."

"Nope!" And that was the end of Andie's conversation. She pushed past them and went off to search out Daniel and Allie.

Kelsey looked up to find JD glaring at her. "She's gone, you can just brush it yourself and tell her I did it."

Damn. "Please. We wouldn't want her to discover we were lying to her, that would destroy everything we've worked for."

That cracked his false glower. "You sound like a super-villain." He followed her inside, closing the door behind him. "Okay, but only for a few minutes. Get your brush."

"Whoo hoo." She practically ran out of the room, ignoring the voice at the back of her head asking her how sad was it that she was getting more gratification from cajoling her hot younger neighbor into brushing her hair than she had from any of the sex she'd had in recent years. She ignored the voice, handed the brush over to JD and curled up against his leg in front of him.

She realized, just after she had done it, that it was way too familiar a position for someone who wasn't her boyfriend at least.

She was going to examine that problem, but then he put his palm against her head and the brush into her hair, and she lost all train of thought.

She sat still like a rabbit, as though, if she didn't make any sudden moves, he would just keep going. It was the stupidest theory ever. He brushed her hair for about ten minutes, then handed the brush back to her.

He stood and stretched. "I have appointments today."

Not long after that, he was out the door. Kelsey was happy for him. 'Appointments' would be good. Maybe the band would get signed; that would turn things around. He seemed a little itchier every day about his financial situation. What was laugh-out-loud funny was that she was the financially stable one.

She had two months' worth of savings, and considered it the grandest coup. Half a year's salary in the bank? It probably wasn't going to happen for her in this lifetime.

This month was looking good. She could sock a little away, and maybe ask JD to take her on as an investing client. If he would take a commission, it could be good for both of them.

She made about six calls that morning before gathering the kids up to take them to McDonalds. She took them because there was an indoor playground, and that would be good exercise for them. And because it was her last day with all three of them.

The coming weekend was Labor Day weekend. On Tuesday, Daniel would start first grade and Andie kindergarten. Allie would most likely go home and cry all day. She so desperately wanted to go to school like the big kids. She just wouldn't be old enough until next year.

Also JD's birthday was Saturday. Kelsey had gotten him two passes to some whitewater rafting on the Tennessee River. She'd wanted to get four, for the whole band, but just couldn't afford it.

The kids lasted several hours, climbing, sliding, chasing each other and squealing with delight. They wanted her to watch what they did every moment, so she thumbed through a parenting magazine and looked up or cheered them on what must have been every twenty seconds or so.

After they were home again, she turned on the sprinklers for them. As she stood at the edge of the water's reach, she wasn't sure why she was so nostalgic about it already.

They were soaked and worn out by the time they asked to come inside at three o'clock. Kelsey plunked each of them into the tub and scrubbed them good, knowing that JD had been having a tough time getting Andie to oblige him. And no wonder, if Stephanie had been through what he thought. Truth be told, any five-year-old girl should refuse to let a strange man bathe her. Andie would come around as she came to trust JD.

An image popped into her head, as she remembered that bathing Andie was the first thing JD had mentioned he needed done—right after she'd volunteered to show Andie he was trustworthy. In Kelsey's head the tub was larger and deeper, one of those luxury models that was big enough for two, even if one of the two was a grown man. There were bubbles everywhere, and Kelsey imagined JD washing her hair.

Yup, Andie would get the picture. She'd probably grow up to be a flaming slut if she saw that one. But, hey, Kelsey would be in a seriously good mood.

The real problem was, it was crazy.

JD didn't return her feelings. He'd want a younger woman, one who didn't come with two children of her own. Kelsey told herself they weren't really 'feelings,' were they? Just unbidden images.

Kelsey stopped thinking about it and dried off and dressed each kid, then let them watch a few short shows on television. She sat on the couch with them flipping through the magazine she'd barely started earlier.

That was how JD found them when he tried the door. It gave, and in he came.

Kelsey had no issue with him just opening the door. But she didn't know *this* JD. Her jaw hit the floor.

She didn't move.

"Shut your mouth, Kelse."

His hair, the fresh cut she'd seen this morning, no longer hung into his face. It was combed up and back revealing all of his wonderful bone structure, and making him look handsome, or maybe dashing, and older. That may also have been due to the serious expression on his face that she couldn't quite read.

Added to all that was the suit—looked like Armani—in a beautiful silver grey. He was decked out from his new haircut to his shiny black wing-tips. He looked even better than she had imagined after he'd told her about being a stock analyst and wearing suits every day.

He looked nothing like her JD.

"Can we get a sitter for tonight?" He asked.

She shrugged, still bewildered by the sight at front of her.

His mouth quirked. "I'll call."

"Okay."

He looked her up and down. "You should wear something other than jeans."

What? Suddenly *she* wasn't up to *his* standards?

That was unfair, and she knew it. So she simply responded with, "Okay," again.

It was a full hour and fifteen minutes before Bethany arrived. Kelsey sat there in her cream colored dress and wondered where JD had gone. Was she even safe with this stranger?

Still she left the house with him. It seemed she was in for surprise after surprise. There at the curb sat a shiny new gold sedan. He ushered her into it.

"Is this yours?" She was incredulous. "Did you go out and buy the suit? The car?"

He had barely opened his mouth to speak when she caught on and railroaded him. "Did you get signed?!?"

Her chest swelled as she realized, and she knew her eyes showed how excited she was for him. And maybe also just how much she had come to care for him.

"No."

She deflated. "Oh, then what?"

"I'll tell you over dinner."

Kelsey tried so hard to hold her tongue and not pester him with questions. Luckily he started speaking and he told her a few things, if not the big picture.

"The car is a rental. I couldn't go out today in my old clunker. The suit is from the back of my closet. I kept a couple."

"Uh-huh."

JD wasn't smiling. He was far too serious to smile.

Kelsey was worried. What had he done?

He pulled into a restaurant in the nicest section of town. Two valets immediately appeared to help them out of the car. She could see into the parking lot, and this was about the cheapest car there.

JD walked in like he owned the place and spoke to the woman at the front. As she led to them to their booth Kelsey assessed the black dress the hostess was wearing and was certain it had cost more than her own.

Their booth was a semicircle and they each slid around to practically the middle. She found herself a little uncomfortable. This wasn't the man from her fantasy earlier.

This JD had all the qualities she would have said she wanted. He was self-assured, confident, clean-cut. He was uber-alpha-male.

He was also invulnerable and impenetrable.

She didn't like it one bit.

Their booth was very private, and she was glad, because if he didn't tell her what was going on, and soon, she was going to bust.

He ordered some drink she'd never heard of, and then upgraded the vodka in her bay breeze. Finally, the server left and she squared up to him, arms crossed, and demanded, "Speak."

"We're celebrating."

"What?" She didn't feel festive.

"I have my choice of two jobs." He grinned, but something wasn't right.

She didn't speak. The old Kelsey that didn't participate simply took over, and she waited.

"I had two interviews today, I had two offers. Both excellent money. One closer than the other. Less travel. Less money, but still plenty." He raised his glass as the server set it in front of him.

She raised hers, too, unsure what else to do. Her heart shrank. She clinked his glass, but to her ears even that sounded dull. "Doing what?"

"Making money. I'm good at it."

She nodded, and took way too big a drink of her bay breeze. Luckily he'd ordered her a very smooth vodka, but it still didn't go down easily.

He leaned over the table at her. "Say something. We're happy."

The server showed up again wanting their orders.

Both men looked to her, but she hadn't had a chance to study the menu, nor had she been able to listen when the server was spouting about the oh-so-delicious specials. "I haven't been able to think. You know what I like, you choose for me."

This JD didn't seem to think that was weird at all, and turned to the server ordering an appetizer and their meals. He also put in for a chocolate soufflé at the end.

Kelsey fought down a feeling that was far too close to one she'd felt before. The one she remembered from when she turned away from the oak tree in her DC back yard, and away from the body of her brother hanging from the sturdiest branch. The feeling of shock and disbelief.

JD turned his attention back to her, and it was like a physical thing. She could feel it. She'd felt his attention before, and it always made her focus on him. Now it made her shrink back.

"Say something, like 'congratulations'."

"Congratulations."

"Wow, your enthusiasm is overwhelming."

She shrugged, and fought for what little decorum she had. "I'm whelmed."

They sat in silence until the meal came. With each passing minute he tuned in a little more to her distress.

As he took the knife to his steak, Kelsey could see how upset he was becoming. And finally the dam burst and he spoke. "What, you don't like this? That you're not better than me anymore?"

She tried to break in on that one.

But he kept going, "I know you thought of me as some child, but I . . ." He just didn't finish.

Kelsey took the opportunity to counter with that one. "I *never* thought you were a . . ." *Oh, God, she* had *thought of him that way.*

He must have read it from her face. All he did was nod and look off.

She set down her fork, none too gently it turned out. "Okay, I admit it." She moved side to side until she got him looking at her again. "But I was wrong, dead wrong, and I figured that one out pretty damn fast. You have to admit that you do look a lot younger in torn jeans and old tee-shirts. But I'm not stupid. I realized really quick that you were an adult."

"Come on Kelsey. I saw your age on your driver's license."

She tried so hard not to wince.

"I know you see me as this younger kid. You have it all together; you took care of your mother and Andy for years, and I can't even take care of one five-year-old."

She shook her head. He hadn't been taught how to be a parent. He didn't get to start from the ground up. And the kid he'd been given fought him tooth and nail the entire way.

But she didn't get any of that out of her mouth.

"I was acting like a kid. I know it. I'm responsible for this child, but I don't even have a job. I can't go chasing some silly idea anymore."

She unclenched her teeth, searching, hoping for the right thing to say. "Tell me you *want* this job. That you're excited to start."

He didn't really smile. It was somewhere between a shrug and a head shake. "I'm excited to start earning money again."

"That's not the same."

"I know." He started eating his steak again. "But it's the right thing to do."

"Is it?"

"Yes." He muttered it around a bite of steak. She couldn't even taste her fish. Technically she could tell that it was flaky and tender. In her mouth it turned to cardboard.

Several bites later, she asked another question. "Have you told the guys?"

"No."

That started another round of silence, during which JD finished his steak and executed a perfect cross of his silverware atop the completely empty plate. From nowhere a server appeared and the plate disappeared.

Kelsey tried another tack. "Let me ask you something."

JD looked resigned. "Shoot."

"Don't you want Andie to follow her dreams?"

"Of course, I do. That's what this is about. So she can go to the right schools and have the right classes, and do whatever she wants." He pulled his napkin off his lap and slapped it on the table, looking angrier than she'd seen him all night.

"It doesn't matter what schools she goes to, or what education she has if she doesn't know how to go after what she wants. If she sees you dragging yourself to work every day, then that's how she's going to think life is supposed to be. Don't you want her to do what she loves? Don't you want her to chase after her dreams? Then you have to show her how. That's more valuable than any prep school time." She punctuated it with a huff.

He was still looking at the ceiling when he spoke. "You should have been a lawyer. Sometimes I really hate you."

"Because I'm right?" She was really hopeful. She tried not to be.

"You're not right, Kelse." He looked her square in the eyes, the JD that she knew, somewhere under the gracefully combed hair and perfectly cut suit. "You're all talk."

"What?"

"What are you teaching your kids? Did you want to write home loans for a living? Why did you do that?"

Her mouth hung open. This was supposed to be about him, not her.

"Close your mouth, Kelse."

God, he'd said that too many times.

She erupted. "I was at Brown, one year away from a pre-law degree. I tried to chase my dreams. But I *had* to quit! My family needed me."

"I have to, too. My family needs me now."

"It's not the same." Anger boiled in her that he thought any of it compared. "Andrew was suicidal. If I didn't stay home to take care of him, he would have *died*. There was Daniel, who was just a baby. I couldn't leave him with Andy. He wouldn't have been safe."

"My Andie needs me."

"Not like this!" Kelsey waved her hand at him indicating his hair and his suit and his grim expression. "She's clothed, she's healthy. If she had cancer and couldn't get treatment because of your situation, I'd be first in line behind you. But this isn't that."

"Listen to yourself!" His voice graveled. "You're right, but you're *wrong*. Andrew is dead. So stop living the life you had to when he was alive. Your kids are healthy, they're clothed. You've had time to grieve. Where are your dreams now? Why are you still writing loans?"

The fork she held in her hand clattered to the plate. The entire world shrunk to a space inside her head.

A few moments later, as it all soaked in, she emerged from her tiny shell to find JD watching her very intently. His eyes were warm and brown and full of concern. His voice was soft and comforting for the first time all evening. "You know I didn't expect all this from you. I thought you'd say 'If that's what you want.' and tell me you were happy for me."

She shrugged. "I'm not happy for you. But it's not my life. It's not my decision." She ate a few more bites of the cardboard fish before declaring herself done. "I told you I was working on flying off the handle a little more."

He laughed, and it was like something warm, that had been waiting inside, broke and ran, filling her.

He smiled a real smile that went across his whole face and filled his eyes. "We were supposed to be doing this in front of the kids."

She countered, "We're supposed to compromise."

He shook his head. "The band is breaking up anyway."

"Really!?"

"Well, we just can't stay together. We have nowhere to go. We lost our last studio, it was borrowed. I haven't sold a song, and neither has Craig, in over ten months."

She cocked her head to one side, thinking. "You're a garage band, right?"

A chuckle bubbled out of him. "I suppose."

"I have a garage."

"Kelsey." It was long and pleading, and had an underlying please-don't-go-there.

But she went there. "Andie will be in school next week. You can practice in the daytime when it won't annoy the neighbors."

JD shook his head. "Craig works days."

"He works at *Starbucks*. He can change his shift."

"We don't fit in. That's part of why we're having so much trouble."

"Exactly." She wanted to strangle him. "That's why you guys are so great. You have your own sound. And it's going to carry you so far, once you get over that threshold."

"It's been two and a half years."

She badgered him, just like she had all night. She *would* have made a good lawyer. "Do you want it?"

"Of course I do."

"Then why are you taking the one course of action that guarantees you won't make it?"

"I hate you, Kelsey."

"That's okay, the feeling's mutual right now. I hadn't planned on having this turned back around on me."

"All right. I'll cut you a deal. We use your garage, we keep going, and you apply to law school."

"I can't."

"Fine then. I'm taking the job."

"Let me finish." She ground her teeth, thinking even as she

did it that it was such a JD thing to do. "I'd have to take two more years of undergrad just to get to where I could test to go to law school. It's too much time. I'd be away from my kids too much. I might go when they are older."

"Cop out." He leaned back, and the server arrived with a mound of chocolate soufflé, surrounded by classy little dollops of whipped cream and a raspberry sauce strewn about.

"Hear me out." She held up her hand, and ignored the chocolate that would have called to her like a siren song at any other time. "I may go to law school when the kids are older." By his facial expression, he was still disgusted with her. "I always waffled between law school and ditching it all to become a photographer. I'll put my money where my mouth is. But I'm investing in photography equipment."

He nodded. "Then your garage should become a photography studio, not a band studio."

"It will. As soon as you guys move out. Which I have faith will be faster than I could get a photography set-up in there anyway."

He leaned forward. "If I don't take this job, I can't afford this dinner."

She laughed out loud, startling another diner near her. "I'll get it."

He shook his head. "You can't afford dinner here either."

She blinked, and remembered she hadn't seen any prices on the menu. "Dutch?"

He nodded. "Credit card."

Kelsey held one of the spoons out to him. "Then we had better enjoy this for all it's worth."

He agreed and they dug in. Finally, she tasted the food. It was worthy of whatever price tag they put on it.

"So what is the name of this band that's moving into my garage? I never heard."

"Wilder."

"It suits you. So who'd you sell that last song to?"

He shrugged, "It just wound up as a back track. It's not a single."

"Sure, but who cut it?"

"Tim McGraw."

She almost choked. He was one of the biggest names in country music. "*The* Tim McGraw?"

He nodded, looking a little embarrassed.

She wanted to yell at him. But she kept her voice as low as possible. "And you were going to *quit!*?"

CHAPTER 12

JD put Andie on hold for a little while that morning, while he called the two companies he was deciding between and told each of them that he wouldn't be taking the job. Each offered him more money, and each time he winced, his fingers pressing against the bridge of his nose. Man, that hurt. He'd had to explain to both of them, that he wasn't taking another job over their offer, he'd simply thought about it and decided not to take *any* job. After that, they wished him well and quit throwing money at him.

He wanted to laugh at that. He hadn't really *thought about* it; he'd had it beaten into him. But when he turned and looked at Andie, playing quietly on the floor with her pink haired doll, she looked up at him expectantly. He grew six inches. He felt lighter.

He *felt* like he was doing the right thing now.

For a brief moment it occurred to him that Kelsey had just moved a little further out of reach. But he shoved it down deep somewhere and told himself it didn't matter how far beyond him she was. Out of reach was out of reach, and further was probably better. That way he wouldn't do something stupid like try.

Kelsey had her kids in day care today, and he needed to get back online and make some money. He hadn't even checked his stocks yesterday, what with the interviews and the arguing with Kelsey. She was a formidable opponent. She'd argued him into altering his life, but he'd argued her into doing the same.

If only he could clear his head of the image of her, all sleep tousled, long bare legs draped off the side of the bed, no bra, bright blue 'little devil' undies. What made it worse was that it was fact, not some random image he had fabricated into fantasy. This was genuine Kelsey. He'd fled the room like his ass was in flames.

He punched some keys haphazardly, his fingers working from memory rather than thought. His stocks appeared on the screen in front of him. He turned his search to finding a new low penny stock to put the principle from last week's windfall into.

Forcibly, he turned his attention away from long bare legs and caramel colored pig-tails and focused on what he knew. An hour later he had an order and a prayer in for one thousand shares.

The weather had cooled, so he took Andie out to lunch then to the park. He wasn't up to making lunch. He wasn't SuperDad, and he wouldn't be anytime soon. One thing at a time. He had to get her trusting him, so he could keep her bathed and groomed. He didn't want her kindergarten teacher calling CPS. In fact, he didn't want them called at all now. They'd failed miserably at being the lifeline they had touted themselves to be. Now, they would only bring trouble. He had help. He had Kelsey.

He had one more day of summer.

Tomorrow he'd take all of them to the pool. Maybe Andie would let him teach her a little about how to swim. She flailed miserably, but if she made a few minor adjustments she'd be great.

Andie climbed the jungle gym like a monkey and made instant friends. Then she was playing with another, smaller kid and his sand pail, just digging like clams next to the swings.

Single mothers came and sat next to him and tried to start conversations. Looking around, he realized he was the only dad here, except for one guy across the park who looked way too granola. No wonder they were all hitting on him.

What had happened to him in the last three months? A year ago, if you had told him that, just by bringing a kid to the playground, women would be hanging all over him, he'd have kidnapped the nearest cute preschooler and hit the sandbox. But now he didn't want anything to do with them. They seemed desperate, or lonely, or . . . he didn't even know. But there was something wrong with each one of them.

"So, is that your little girl? What is she, five?"

He nodded, and pushed up half a smile at the edges of his lips. It was time to go home.

"She's a cutie."

"Yes, she is. Andie!" He yelled the last part, and somehow didn't add, "*Save me!*" Instead he turned to the woman who had parked herself beside him. "It was nice to meet you, but I'm afraid it's time for us to head out."

A quick up and down revealed that the woman was an attractive blond, late twenties or early thirties, with a killer bod and gorgeous blue eyes, and absolutely no sex appeal. Now he understood why married couples had no sex. Being a parent just drained it out of you.

He made peanut butter sandwiches and opened a bag of carrot sticks for dinner. Andie dipped hers in ranch dressing, and after choking down two of them to show how good they were, he joined her and smothered his, too.

~

He had Kelsey drive them to the pool the next day. They were all safer in her mini-van anyway. He paid everyone's way in, and Andie even let him show her a few strokes. She agreed to go into swim lessons the next summer. He'd had her for nine weeks. Yet he was making plans for next year. While it felt right, it still wasn't second nature.

For three hours Kelsey distracted him with that two-piece suit she sometimes wore. Being attracted to her was a real bummer, but it would pass.

For right now he pushed it aside by sheer physical exertion. He held Andie while she paddled around, reminding her to cup her hands, and showing her how to blow bubbles. He threw Daniel and Allie, who had no fear of going under water. Then again, they were both very capable swimmers. Allie let out wild shrieks each time he tossed her, and begged him to send her just a little further each time. It didn't help that Kelsey laughed each time, and told them to enjoy it because she sure wasn't strong enough to throw them like that. And, damn, was it a good workout. He figured dads really had no good excuse to turn to flab. Lifting thirty to fifty pounds at a shot was a great way to stay in shape.

No women came up and hit on him either. Although, that was probably because they thought he belonged to Kelsey. He wasn't sure what to make of that.

Later, Kelsey said she thought the kids were worn out. JD was supremely grateful. He'd been worn out himself about half an hour ago, but hadn't wanted to be the one to cop out on the last day of swimming.

They grilled hot dogs and hamburgers on Kelsey's tiny Weber grill in her backyard to celebrate. As he polished off the last hotdog and crumpled his napkin on his paper plate, Kelsey told him to sit still, and ran inside.

Confused, he waited. She emerged a minute later holding a small box that looked like it had been wrapped in plate copper. The top had 'JD' etched into it.

She held it out to him. "Happy Birthday."

As he accepted it she began gushing, about how it wasn't a big party and she didn't have a band to sing for him, but she hoped he enjoyed it.

"Stop." He smiled at her, feeling the same warmth inside that he was sure showed on his face. He hadn't expected this. "Quit making excuses; this is great."

Turning the box over, he looked for a seam and found the copper folded over in the back. Slowly he peeled it away, to reveal a cardboard jewelry box. He eyed Kelsey suspiciously.

She smirked. "That's just the box. I did *not* get you pearls."

He popped it open to reveal a printed internet page. His mouth opened as he read. "You didn't."

"I hope you like it. You can go any day they're open." She paused. "Tomorrow, if you want. The kids and I decided to start a tradition last year, and we drive up into this spot in Kentucky and go hiking, then we come home and pitch a tent in the backyard and sleep out. We have about three, really high-tech tents if you want to take one and go all day, then you can come back the next morning."

He couldn't believe what he was holding: a vacation of sorts. He hadn't had a real vacation in almost four years. He'd spent every trip visiting his parents, or picking up TJ from Texas when he'd convinced his brother to come out and sing. "Wow. Thank you."

Before he could think about it, he stood up and hugged her. She felt smaller in his arms than how he saw her. Her arms wrapped around his waist and she pressed the side of her face against his chest.

She was soft and warm and she fit him. The muscles in his arms threatened to tighten, and hold her just a little bit closer, a little bit longer. His brain made him let go before that happened, before things got awkward. "Why do you have so many tents?"

She shook her head. "Only Andrew knew. He kept buying them. He'd just come home with the latest gear. We have seven fishing poles. He used each of them exactly once. Most of them only in the back yard, practicing. So I couldn't return them. He opened each of the tents and set them up and took them down. It was like he wanted to be a survivalist or something, like at some time he would need to know how to pitch a tent in under five minutes."

She looked away, wistful for a minute. "I think when he was up, he was planning a vacation for when his meds stabilized and he was allowed to go camping." She smiled a sad smile, and JD regretted asking her to bring up the old memories. One thing that was clear about Kelsey was that she had loved and accepted this sometimes violent, always unstable man. And that she still missed him with all her heart.

Maybe for his own benefit, he put voice to that. "You still miss him."

She nodded, and he could see tears pooling at the bottom of her eyes, although she fought to not let them drop. "I always will." Her voice was whisper soft, but then it gained strength as she found her way back to the topic of the many tents. "They packed up so small, I hauled them here, thinking I'd sell them in a yard sale, but I haven't had one. I don't know if I could sell that stuff. But you should take one, and a couple fishing poles and there's even a campfire cooking set."

It sounded like more than he could wish for, and he was sorely tempted. But he didn't know how to accept a dead man's dream.

Kelsey made him. "Andy wouldn't have wanted it to go to waste. And neither do I. It's part of why we decided to camp out for Labor Day. Please, borrow them."

He agreed, and he was already making plans to phone TJ when he got back in his house.

He was simply stunned. Anderson Winslow Hewlitt had dropped into his life and left him with nothing but bad choices. That it was through absolutely no fault of her own only made the whole thing that much worse. He finally felt the tunnel didn't go on forever, and there was light.

Kelsey let him sit, and she gathered the kids up, handing out old mayonnaise jars with holes punched in the lids. She suggested that they catch lightning bugs, and that she'd already seen two of them.

JD held up his cell phone asked, "Do you mind if I call TJ and see if he's free tomorrow?"

TJ wasn't, but an hour and ten lightning bugs later he called back and said he'd moved some things around and he'd make it. JD closed his phone and told Kelsey he'd take her up on the offer to take Andie hiking with them.

She told him what to pack for Andie, and he thanked her again before he left. Andie had one small hand tucked into his, and her other hand wrapped around her lightning bug jar, which she wanted to keep for a nightlight. JD inspected the holes to be sure the bugs couldn't crawl out, before saying it was okay, and that she'd have to set them free before they left in the morning.

CHAPTER 13

JD leaned back into the swamp chair that he had found among the things laid out for him and TJ that morning. TJ was reclined in its twin.

He'd fallen out of the raft once and his ribs had taken a beating on the rocks. He was the hero of the boat, because he'd only fallen out the one time. Even the guide had gone over twice. That was because the rafting company had thrown together three sets of two guys who didn't know each other from Adam, but within three minutes they had all declared themselves real men and decided they were going down the roughest branch of the river.

JD wondered how his brother felt, both of them had put in more physical labor than they had planned. Thank God they had pitched the tent that morning as the guide suggested.

He looked over to TJ and decided to talk before his little brother fell asleep where he sat. "Can I tell you something?"

"You're gay?"

Where the hell had that come from? "No!"

TJ chuckled. "You're screwing your neighbor? Hence the fine camping equipment."

"No." JD sighed. TJ wasn't going to let him get this out. "The fine camping equipment belonged to the much beloved dead husband."

"Why not?"

"Why not what?" He frowned.

"Just because she's still in love with the dead husband doesn't mean she can't have some fun."

JD rolled his eyes. He only wished there was enough light for TJ to see how exasperated he was. But it wasn't worth the effort to turn on the wicked halogen lamp, also included in this morning's find. "Yes, it does mean that. And two, you don't screw the babysitter."

"Bummer."

"TJ, seriously, I have to tell you something."

"So, out with it man, I am about to fall asleep here."

JD took a fortifying breath. There was no telling how TJ would react to this. "You know Mom and Dad are coming by in October. Well, I haven't told them about Andie yet."

TJ sighed. "Jesus."

"I'm telling them this week. They'll meet her when they get here. I really want them to be good grandparents. I need your help."

"God, JD, that's really asking a lot. You have a kid out of wedlock. You know how they frown on that. They're going to have to admit that you were having sex, and a damn lot of this is going to come back at me. You know I'm Satan's kid for following you out here."

JD let a huge sigh take him over. Whether it was from sheer exhaustion or the topic, he wasn't sure. "You can't tell them what I'm about to tell you."

"Of course. You know I don't spill."

JD knew his brother was eminently trustable, or he never would have opened his mouth, "The thing is, I didn't have a kid out of wedlock."

"I'd say there's some serious evidence to the contrary, bud."

"She isn't mine."

TJ sat up for that one. "I'm sorry?"

"Stephanie put my name on her birth certificate, so the state handed her off to me. I was too shocked to really think straight."

TJ nodded, "I remember."

"A week later when the paperwork showed up, I realized she was about ten, maybe eleven months younger than I had thought, and there was no way she could be mine."

"Why didn't you give her back?"

"There was no one to give her back to. Do you know what happens to pretty little girls in the foster system?"

"Oh . . . God."

"Exactly." Good, TJ seemed to be understanding.

"Why didn't you find a family to adopt her? There had to be some other way. You don't need a kid."

"Believe me, I thought through every option. There wasn't another way."

"Jesus, Stephanie must have hated you."

JD let that one pass. He preferred to believe Kelsey's version, but he wasn't sharing that with TJ.

TJ frowned, it was about the last thing JD could see in the almost non-existent light. "So why won't you tell Mom? It might redeem you."

"No way. I'm already going to need you to help steer her away from bad-mouthing Stephanie."

"Why? Stephanie was all the things Mom is likely to say."

"Yes, but she's also Andie's Mom, and Andie loves her, and she doesn't need to hear it. She's been through enough without her new Grandma looking down on her."

TJ's voice had turned to understanding. "Yeah, Mom will cut her just a little slack for being blood, but if she knew . . ."

He didn't have to say the rest. JD knew what their mother would do. She'd rant and rave about sending her back to the state. About how JD was irresponsible enough without taking on a random kid to look after. And she'd do all of it within earshot of his five-year-old daughter. No wonder her two grown sons only visited on holidays. She had raised them Catholic, but had been about the worst Christian JD had ever seen.

"TJ, I need you to help me protect Andie from her."

"You got it, big brother." TJ stood and stretched. "Now if your magic girlfriend could just whip us up a studio, we'd be in business."

"She's not my girlfriend."

TJ started to protest but JD had had enough. "And she's giving us her garage. We can set up, and lock everything up there. And we can make all the noise we want from nine a.m. to two p.m. weekdays and whenever I can find a sitter for Andie on weekends."

"Are you serious?"

JD nodded, standing to stretch, and maybe to be on even ground with his brother.

"And you aren't sleeping with her?"

JD shook his head.

"Maybe you should ask her. I think she's said 'yes' to everything else you wanted. Seriously, you should just ask."

Tuesday morning was the weirdest morning in his life. He hadn't been this keyed up when it had been his own first day at school. His heart beat faster, and he wondered what the other kids would be like. What the other parents would be like.

Andie was at the door with her thermal lunch bag in hand, telling him to hurry up. She had even let him brush her hair. Another point for Kelsey.

A knock at his door made him jump, but he knew it was

Kelsey with her kids. She smiled calmly when he pulled the door open. "Nervous?"

"Hell, yes."

"Daddy, we don't say 'hell'."

He looked back over his shoulder at this sweet little angel, who, just weeks ago, had been a hell-demon. "I'm sorry, honey, you're right."

Kelsey grinned at him again, she looked cool and collected in jeans and a white tee-shirt. She was ready for the first day of school, no doubt. He simply gathered up Andie and her backpack, which was on wheels. What was with the wheels? How many books was she going to have?

They started walking the three blocks to school. And, of course, after the first block Andie didn't want to carry the Tinkerbell backpack, and when she dragged it she did a really bad job. He wouldn't have known it was possible to do a bad job dragging a wheeled bag, but she sure did. Eventually he gave up and slung it over his shoulder. It bothered him until he saw a dad full-on wearing a pony backpack, then a second carrying a Barbie lunchbox.

When they reached the gates of the school, Kelsey, Allie and Daniel dropped them off at Andie's kindergarten class before traipsing off to find first grade. Only Allie seemed in tune with his trauma, but she had a huge hug for Andie, and only a simple wave for him.

Andie found her room number, and waited patiently while he hung out and met the teacher, a nice older woman who immediately set him at ease. The next classroom over was run by a sweet, young beauty, who looked to him like she'd be cake before ten a.m. She was already having difficulty fending off one near-leering dad. How was she going to handle the twenty kindergarteners who were filing into her room?

But then Andie's class was starting and he had to pay attention. He was sitting on a square of carpet and feeling like a kindergartener himself. The teacher lectured them on the importance of promptness and having homework handed in on time. *Homework? In kindergarten?* He filed that away under 'ask Kelsey'. After a quick tour, the parents were all promptly dismissed.

A few parents had introduced themselves and their kids, but he'd been so focused he didn't think he'd retained any names. JD walked home alone, the streets were empty of all but a few random people.

The three blocks disappeared in no time, now that he didn't have small children cutting the pace. He worried about Andie in her kindergarten class. Then he worried that he worried about her when she had seemed just peachy.

The house seemed quieter when he let himself back in. Even though twice a week she had gone to stay with Kelsey, today it just seemed emptier. Still, he parked himself at the computer and went to work. He sold one stock for a nice profit, not quite as good as the last one, but enough to keep them afloat. He decided to park some of it in savings, just in case.

At noon he headed back out the door to pick Andie up, his nerves cranking up, wondering how she'd fared her first day. As he turned the corner on to the main street, Kelsey swung by in her van. She honked and he nearly jumped out of his skin. The passenger window peeled down and she leaned over. "Will you wait for me? I'll be just a minute."

With a nod, he turned and followed to her house. He jogged to get to the garage before her, lifting the door so she could park. He made a mental note that an automatic garage door opener would be a good Christmas gift. Then he reached in to help with the bags.

He didn't speak until she said she was ready to go, only they'd piled all the groceries on the kitchen table and not put anything in the fridge. When he pointed that out, she just laughed. "First day of school getting to you?"

"What?"

"Look in the bags, silly."

He hadn't been called 'silly' in ages. He saw computer memory and cables in one bag. Another bag held plastic encased lenses and camera equipment.

He started picking out pieces and examining them. She had reams of heavy-weight, high gloss photo paper, as well as what looked like hand pressed stock. There was a brown jug of chemical and an accompanying wide, soft-bristled brush. There were lenses and cases, and . . .

She laughed at him again. "Come on, we don't want to be late. It's the first day of school."

Kelsey grabbed his hand and pulled him out the front door.

His hand was still in hers half a block later when his working jaw finally produced some sound. "You did it."

"Yeah, to the tune of about a thousand dollars."

"Really?"

She nodded, a little grimly. 'Yeah, I'd better be good at this."

"Oh my god." He felt like a slacker. The guys hadn't even moved into the garage yet. He tried to stay focused on Kelsey and her project. "Have you done anything that I've seen?"

She nodded, "All the pictures of the kids in the house. Except the ones I'm in, and I even did a few of those."

He blinked. He had thought the photos were done by a pro. He'd thought maybe Andrew had had a talent for it. He squeezed her hand. "You're going to do just fine."

"Thank you." She tugged, urging him to go a little faster. "We want to be waiting at the gate when they come out."

Three minutes later they were at the gate, and two minutes after that kids started pouring out the front door. The kindergarten and first grade came out a side door for the little kids.

JD let out the breath he didn't know he'd been holding.

Andie didn't look any the worse for wear. Not even a little

confused at the sea of five-year-olds swarming around her. Daniel found Andie before she spotted them, and brought her over. Neither child said 'hello' or how their day was. They simply asked if they could have pizza. Apparently there was an after school sale, at a buck per slice, the whole first week.

He almost swore right there at the entrance to the kindergarten, with both Andie's stern older teacher, and the younger, somehow still fresh-as-a-flower teacher looking at him. He bit his tongue. He had no cash on him.

Kelsey smile and produced a five she'd tucked in her back pocket. "The first week there's always pizza."

As though that just explained everything.

TJ plugged in another extension cord, and JD prayed it would be the last. They'd used Kelsey's garage to power themselves at her birthday, but they hadn't done a full set-up. He prayed they wouldn't blow a fuse and shut down her whole house.

The kids were off at school and daycare. Craig had gotten his Starbucks shifts moved, and they were starting their first practice in permanent digs since he and TJ had ditched the old studio where they'd lived.

Craig plugged in, strummed a cord, and tuned up. "So, JD, tell me, how'd you swing this? You fucking her?"

"No!" God, he was so tired of getting asked that.

"Don't bite my head off." Craig actually looked offended. "I just wanted to know if our digs are tied to your dick."

TJ laughed, and jumped in, keeping him from replying with the exasperation that was building. "No, and he won't either. You don't screw the babysitter. He's been good, he's keeping it in his pants."

JD shook his head. "She's also my next door neighbor, I am not touching that with a ten-foot pole."

Alex actually snickered from behind his drum set.

Of course, TJ jumped on that. "She's not my babysitter. Can I touch her with my ten-foot pole?"

"Can we all please keep our hands and other body parts off the hot neighbor?"

There was a chorus of *'damn's* as JD glared at all of them. "She gave up her garage for us. She also talked me out of taking the corporate job I was offered and into sticking this out with you dipshits. So maybe you should just show a little respect . . ."

The voices all came on top of each other, "You were going to quit?" from TJ.

"She did save our butts." from Alex.

"Did he just ask us to 'show some respect'?" from Craig.

Oh yeah, he'd turned down money and stability for this. He hit a hard chord, "Just play."

CHAPTER 14

K elsey felt she had settled into the rhythm of work after the first week of having the kids in school. What she wasn't prepared for was the itch. She'd never felt it before, this desire to just quit. It was harder to start loans in motion and harder to do the necessary follow-up.

She wanted to be outside with her camera. She'd spent tons of money and she was getting a handle on how to use the equipment. In addition to shopping, she'd emptied the linen closet the first day of school. The second day she'd ripped out the shelving, while Allie rotted her brain on TV all day. Her daughter had seen almost the entire collection of Baby Einstein. She was going to be brilliant but with severe emotional problems.

Kelsey caved and sent her to daycare the next day. It was way better than being at home with a mother who was busy installing a counter into the old linen closet, and still wondering where to put the linens that had been in it.

She liked that the band practicing created a soundtrack to her day during school hours. She couldn't quite hear the words but there were tunes and voices coming from the garage all the time. She remembered how much she had liked them when they played for her, but, until they'd started up in her garage, she'd forgotten just why.

Thursday she forced herself to work only on her loans. And she worked her ass off, knowing that if she didn't her boss was going to call and wonder why she wasn't getting anything done, and that there wouldn't be any food on the table come October.

Friday she went out in the yard with her camera, and photographed ants until she convinced herself it was all right to go into her own garage and listen to the band in there. Sneaking in the side door, she tried not to disturb any of them. It was no use, they all noticed right away, but none of them missed a beat.

Feeling awkward, she waited until the song ended then motioned to the camera in her hand. "Can I practice on you guys?"

They looked at her with something akin to revulsion in their eyes. For a moment she wondered what the hell she'd done wrong.

It was Craig who spoke up, "We're supposed to be practicing." He leaned away from the camera as though it might bite.

It dawned. They thought she wanted them to model for her. "No! Keep practicing. I'll just take photos while you do, if that's okay?" She held her hands up, "feel free to say 'no', it's all right if you do."

Alex looked at each of the others. "While we practice? Sure, why not?" That was all the thought he paid to it and started playing again. Kelsey grabbed her camera, clicking off shots.

The camera was new to her, and she'd been getting a grasp on what it could and couldn't do. It was high time to try it on some actual people.

She caught sweat in midair, flying from Alex. She caught his sticks in a single frame, when they'd been a blur to her eyes.

Craig using his whole body to hit a final chord. Later JD and TJ sharing a mic.

She groaned when she used up the photo card. The damn thing held three hundred photos. So she had three hundred to sort through on her computer. She could spend hours just wading through them. She might never come out of the office.

But that was what this whole photographer thing was about, not just messing around like when she'd toyed with the idea. So she thanked the guys and fixed herself a ham and cheese sandwich and loaded the photos into her new huge memory bank.

She chewed as she waited for the pictures to start appearing. Then she stopped chewing. It took a good twenty minutes to pick and choose from nearly identical takes, just keeping the best ones.

The ham sandwich sat, forgotten, while she skimmed through what she had taken. This camera really beat the old one all to hell. She'd wiped out nearly half her savings on this stuff, and today she felt it was really worth it.

She was feeding page after page of high gloss stock into her printer. Five by sevens weren't big enough, she was making eight by tens. She'd turned out at least five of each of the guys and another fifteen of two or more of them together.

Kelsey hit the print button again, as her stomach growled. The ham sandwich still sat to the side of the computer, which was really a bad thing. She was going to ban herself from having any food near her equipment, just as soon as she finished this sandwich. Her eyes wandered to the clock that lived in the lower corner of her computer screen.

2:37

Holy shit! No wonder she was hungry. She sat down somewhere around noon, if she remembered right. Pulling the last print off the tray, she gathered what she had done and headed out to the garage.

Only as she pulled open the door did she stop to question her decision. Until they all turned to look at her, she hadn't considered the possibility that they might not want her bothering them again.

"I- uh, I- . . . I'm sorry." She stammered. Kelsey couldn't remember the last time she'd stammered. "I didn't mean to bother you again. I just wanted to thank you for letting me take pictures earlier."

They all nodded at her. JD at least produced a smile.

"I'll just leave these." She motioned to the stack of photos in her hand. But there wasn't a flat surface anywhere that wasn't covered. There were notepads, cords wound up and tied, sheet music, cases, and things she couldn't identify.

Alex stood up to take the pages from her. "Thank you." He gave a polite smile and started to set them on top of another pile. "Shit. Guys, come here."

She started to back out the door, wondering what he'd seen, and sorry that she'd clearly interrupted. A hand grabbed the side of her shirt, then let go to take hold of her hand and pull her back in. TJ had a firm grip on her and wasn't going to let go.

"I'm sorry I interrupted."

He shook his head. "We were about done anyway."

Craig's voice broke over the murmurs from the corner. "Damn, these are great."

"I told you she was good."

Kelsey perked at the note of pride she heard in JD's voice, but it was TJ's eyes searching her own for something. She just wasn't sure what.

JD's voice came through clear on the phone. "I was going to get Bethany, but Andie asked me to call you first. She hasn't been there in a while."

A while was five days. Then again, she'd been here so much this summer that Andie probably did feel the loss. Kelsey knew she did, and so did her kids. They'd asked after Andie on more than one occasion, but Kelsey had put them off, thinking JD and his daughter needed time to be together. And she needed the time to shake her growing attraction to JD.

"Of course I can take her."

"Thank you." There was an audible sigh of relief. "I was afraid you would already have plans."

She almost barked out a laugh. Plans? Plans required a life, friends. "No, I didn't have plans that night."

As though she might have had some on another night.

"I may be late."

"That's okay." Late would be fine.

"Listen," His voice turned low, like he was saying something confidential. Or maybe that was just her mind at work. "The guys really liked the shots you took of us the other day."

"Thank you."

"You're really good."

She smiled and couldn't help herself even though she knew he couldn't see it. She would have just told him to come over, but her kids were already in bed, and probably Andie was, too.

"TJ's threatening to have the one of the two of us singing blown up and framed and sent to my mother."

"Oh, I can do that." She could easily get it enlarged. She'd registered at a print shop as a pro, and would get the resale price. "I'll get it framed—"

"No! It's a joke. I'm- I-" That was it. He let the conversation flounder.

"What? I thought that one was pretty good. It—"

"It's not the shot, Kelse. My mother thinks I'm a moron for giving up a good life to come out here and . . ."

"Chase your dream?"

He laughed. Even though it was low, she heard it through the line. "Something like that."

"She doesn't really, does she? She realizes how good you guys are, right?" Surely he was exaggerating.

"My mother has every faith in us. She's quite convinced that we'll never be able to support ourselves. I'm being a foolish child by doing this." His voice was just shy of flat. The only thing she could distinguish in it was a touch of wistfulness.

"That can't be right."

"Get over it, Kelse." He tightened his voice. "My mother got me my first guitar and insisted on getting me lessons. She says now that she regrets that with all her heart."

Kelsey felt her chest squeeze as she realized he was serious. "How?"

"And to make matters worse, I got TJ involved. There wasn't much I could do that would have hurt her more. I stole her baby."

"Jesus, JD." That was the worst thing she thought she'd ever heard.

"The last thing she wants is a portrait reminding her of what she considers the worst mistake ever. And speaking of the worst mistake ever, there's something else I've been meaning to ask your help about."

"Okay?"

Only after a moment did she hear him sigh. "I can't tell you now, but sometime. Maybe on the walk home from school tomorrow."

"All right, then. I'll talk to you tomorrow."

He said good-night, then hung up, and for a moment she simply sat with the phone clutched tightly.

She couldn't remember the last time she'd had a phone call like that. It had felt . . . intimate.

Kelsey sighed. If nothing else, JD opened her eyes. She'd been living a very solitary existence.

Now she had a real friend. One who called her at night and asked favors of her. No one did that, not before now. Her mother and Andrew had simply fallen apart, maybe because they knew she'd pick up the pieces for them. Kelsey had friends in college, but never let herself get close. Maybe because she always felt like any moment she could get called back.

But now Wilder had a job on Tuesday night. And JD needed a babysitter.

She looked around the living room with new eyes.

For the first time the house felt permanent. She couldn't get called back. She was her own master, and she was going to cultivate all the friendships in front of her: JD, Andie, even Craig, TJ and Alex, some moms from church and school.

She traipsed upstairs to put herself to bed, and fell asleep wondering what JD needed, and how to tell him what she'd figured out.

CHAPTER 15

The next morning dawned a clear gray. Kelsey dressed her kids for mid-weather: that horrible phase where you didn't know if the day would turn cold or blazing hot.

The kids were halfway through their bowls of cereal when JD and Andie showed up on the front doorstep. Kelsey swung the door wide without even looking; it could only be them. There was no one else who showed up at 7:40 in the morning.

As they headed out, they all looked up at the sky. "Should I drive?" Kelsey knew JD couldn't offer, his car wouldn't hold all of them.

He shook his head. "It feels like the first real day of fall. It won't rain before we get back."

With that prediction haunting the back of her mind, they started out. They all walked the extra block to drop Allie off at daycare. She fussed, but was grateful that JD and Andie were there for extra hugs. Normally, Kelsey dropped Allie off second, but she wanted to find out what JD needed.

The little troupe turned toward the elementary school then, and went the last two blocks to the school. As soon as Andie and

Daniel were through the gate, they had forgotten about the parents watching to be sure they made it inside.

Kelsey turned to go, then realized that JD hadn't. "Come on, bud, she's safe."

He looked chagrinned. "Do they just keep getting bigger? Don't answer that. They do. I know that."

A laugh came out of her, and she was grateful for the feeling. Little by little, her load was getting lighter. "They do just keep getting bigger. And you do stop periodically and say, 'oh my god, when did she grow?' Just one day their clothes don't fit anymore and you can't lift them."

"Is that why people want more kids?"

"Maybe." She cocked her head at him as they wandered back down the path. Parents walked in front and behind them, and a few stragglers hurried late kids toward the school doors. "Do you? Want more kids?"

He laughed, so hard she could almost see tears in his eyes, and shook his head. "I've barely got a handle on the one I have." He sighed. "That's what I wanted to talk to you about."

"Shoot."

His hands went into his pockets, which she'd learned by now meant he had something to say that he'd thought about, but wasn't sure of. "My Mom and Dad come out to visit every October, on their way to Italy. They go on pilgrimage every year, so that's when they come by. They refuse to spend Thanksgiving or Christmas in the country."

"You and Andie are welcome to spend the holidays with us." It was casually thrown out there. But the quick catch in her chest said more. Friends, she reminded herself. For the holidays. Something she had never had before.

"Thank you, but that wasn't what I was after."

"Oh." Something lost, even though she'd never had it. She steadied herself. "What was it then?"

"I finally told them about Andie yesterday. The yelling may have blown out your phone lines."

"That bad? They aren't excited about having a granddaughter?" She took in a breath. Who were these people? Her own family had blocked her in every way from her own dreams and life, but they had done it by circumstance. No one had ever told her she couldn't or shouldn't be a lawyer or a photographer. Her mother and father had given her money for college, or whatever she chose to pursue. "Or is it that they don't consider her their granddaughter?"

His hands pushed deeper into his pockets. "That's part of it. They're very Catholic. So having a child out of wedlock is a huge sin. On top of everything else I've done."

"So . . ." She spent a second getting her thoughts together. "Don't they see what a good thing you've done for her? It's a big deal JD, raising a child that isn't your legal responsibility."

"It's not that big."

That was typical JD, and she said so. "It *is* that big. Most people would have sent her back. They would have made up some excuse about why they really couldn't do it, or wouldn't be the best place for her, and they would have sent her back to the state of Texas. You kept her."

"I thought about sending her back."

"Yeah, well, you're human. Please don't tell me what you did was a sin. I can't tell you how many nights I dreamed of putting Andy in an institution and setting myself free. I feel enough guilt about those thoughts, don't you go adding to it."

He switched gears and surprised her. "They don't know she isn't my biological child."

"You didn't tell them? Are you picking fights? Or are you saving it for later?"

"No. That's going to be Andie's decision to tell them someday. As for right now, it's really important that they not find out that she isn't genetically related."

"Do explain." She paused, and waited until he filled the empty air. They were in front of her house now and she simply went up the front walk and in through the front door, knowing he would follow.

"Andie is in their bad graces for being born. I'm in for having a child out of wedlock. My mother has never understood the damage her tongue can do when she doesn't pay attention to what she's saying. If she knows about Andie, she'll yell at me to send her back, and she'll tell Andie, in some way, that she's inferior."

"Ouch." Kelsey reached into the fridge for a coke, and without thinking, grabbed a second one for JD.

He raised his eyebrows at her, but she kept her face steady. Sure it was only 8:15, but she'd been up for an hour and a half. He didn't say anything about it, just popped it open within seconds of her own sharp fizz and took a drink.

"My mother is so convinced that she's right about everything, there is every possibility she'd feel it was her duty to notify the state of their error. She might dig up Andie's biological father and convince him he belongs with his child."

There was something in his face, and she debated saying it, so she half-assed it, and regretted it as soon as it was out of her mouth. "That would be bad for Andie."

JD didn't half-ass it. "It would be awful for me." He took another slug of his coke. "I still think life would be easier without her. But this is what it is. Easier isn't better. I worry about her even when she's at school. But she hugged me the other night. Just out of the blue. Did it again this morning." He shrugged, "She came and crawled into bed with me when she woke up today. I don't know why she put her faith in me, but I can't break that."

Kelsey held her can up to him, and made a dull metal thud when she clinked the two together. "Congratulations, you're a Daddy."

He laughed a little, then swallowed the rest of the drink, before crushing the can in his fist, and tossing it sideways into the trash. It was such a guy thing to do.

Just to be silly, Kelsey tried the same. It took too long to finish the soda. Her 'crush' was more of a mild dent, and her shot went awry.

JD laughed at her, then said he had to get out to the garage. She held back telling him what she'd come up with about the band. There was a better way to tell them.

She called and left a message with Bethany, asking if she could sit that night. Then called Maggie to see if she would want to go out?

Kelsey waited for the cars to arrive.

Alex passed by her front window first, and she would have missed him if she hadn't turned around right then. She dropped the laundry she was folding and went after him; she was pretty sure she'd scared the bejezus out of him. But she convinced him that she absolutely must take his portrait right now.

The light was perfect she said. That wasn't a lie. Wasn't five minutes of his time a great exchange instead of rent? She placed him in front of the too-white fence that stood around the yard, and snapped him from head-on, from the left, the right, down low and up high with her standing on the picnic table.

He held only his drum sticks, both clutched in his left hand, and tried to look comfortable. But he didn't quite pull it off. He looked put out. And he looked a little wary.

Kelsey thanked him and set him free, snapping off one last shot as he walked away. Then she got Craig and TJ aside as they pulled up against the curb. TJ was naturally in a good mood. The day she saw him sour she would be afraid the earth was cracking in half. So she used Craig first. He was suspicious of her no matter what she did. From the look on his face, she couldn't derive much better torment than making him pose for portraits.

He propped his bass on his foot and balanced it there with a bored look that suited him perfectly. So far they had each been wearing jeans and a dark shirt. Craig's had a logo on it, but Kelsey was confident that she could erase it.

TJ was less of a bother than the other two. She messed with him a little bit, fussed with his hair like a mother hen, straightened his shirt. Posed him and re-posed him. All for the purpose of getting him a little put out. Seven minutes later, when he couldn't hide it anymore, she started snapping photos.

JD was last. He was too easy going, too willing to pay her back whatever she asked, feeling too indebted. She had to seriously perturb him.

"I really want to get your silly side." She walked up to him, camera hefted in one hand, and brushed his hair out of his eyes. It was so hard to stay in the moment as photographer, when touching him felt so right. She set the camera down, and played with his hair for another minute, telling herself it was for the shoot.

The damn fool was all too happy to oblige.

She sighed, not knowing how to get what she needed out of him.

Craig did it for her.

"Hey, pretty boy! Get your butt in here, we've got to run the set."

JD hopped. "I've got to go. We'll get this later."

"No!" She thought fast. "I need it now. I have to show them to someone this evening. Please?" She put what she hoped was the right dash of desperation into her voice.

"I-" He paused. "They're waiting on me."

"I know." She held her hand out, like that would stop him if he wanted to go. "Please, just a few more minutes."

At last, he gave her a wary look. He wanted to be practicing, didn't understand her. It all showed in his face. He looked her in the eye, even though his head and his body were leaning toward the garage, where he wanted to be. His hands were itching to play something, and she could see it in the way he held the guitar.

She snapped rapid photos from different angles. It was perfect.

"All right." She sighed. "I guess you can go now."

Before she could break face, she turned and walked inside. All the while in her brain a little voice was going *Yes! Yes! Yes!* When she was sure he wasn't looking, she turned and rapidly squeezed off one last shot of him walking away.

Kelsey called clients while she downloaded pictures and ate a granola bar. Tomorrow she would ban food at the computer.

She filled in info online and promised herself that she would pull full credit reports on each client after the kids were home. The granola bar was polished off, and her memory was loaded.

Kelsey lined up all the low shots, then all the left shots, and so on. She chose what she would use, then spent the rest of the morning editing. She removed the picture from Craig's shirt, killed spare shadows, a lone bleach spot on Alex's jeans.

A sharp knock at the back door jolted her. She was just starting to relax when she heard the knob turn. Quickly, she hopped up and bolted for the office door. Only JD would just come in that way, and she was just getting the door shut behind her as he walked up.

"So, did you get what you need?"

"Yeah." She tried to sound less than stellar about it. She didn't want him to know, just yet.

"Can I see?"

"Please, no." *Distraction!* She couldn't think of anything, so she threw out what was true. "I've been staring at those for so long, I'll go cross-eyed. I'll show you tomorrow."

Just then her stomach let out the strangest noise.

JD's jaw dropped. "Was that you?"

"Yes." She grimaced. On the upside he wasn't asking about the pictures anymore.

"Do you want to grab lunch?" He looked at her sideways.

"Yes!" Finally, her hand unclenched from the office doorknob—as though JD might try to wrestle his way in to see the photos. As if she could stop him if he tried. "All I have in the house is a little bit of lunch stuff for kids. I haven't been grocery shopping in . . . too long."

That was because of the camera. She was spending all her free time with it.

He took her hand and pulled her away, out the back door and through the still vibrating instruments in the garage. "We'll have to come back this evening and pack."

She nodded.

"Who are you showing the photos to tonight? I thought you were going to watch Andie?"

She flushed red. "I'm sorry, I should have asked you." *Oh, this was bad.* "I just assumed you wouldn't mind, I got this appointment and I booked Bethany."

"That's okay. Maybe we'll all go somewhere after school tomorrow. I know Andie wants to spend some time with you."

Kelsey cringed.

"Hey!" He stopped on the sidewalk, turning square to her. "You said you weren't going to do that again."

"Do what?"

"Flinch."

"Oh," Her breath let out. He'd scared her. "I wasn't flinching, I was feeling guilty. You told me Andie wanted to spend some time with us, and I just assumed she wanted the kids."

"She wanted all of you, but she'll be fine." JD led her up the back steps to the condo, "I can make spaghetti, broccoli, macaroni and cheese . . ." He looked a little more chagrined as he listed each item.

Kelsey wanted to laugh so badly, but she tried to hold it in. "I wasn't expecting flaked salmon salad."

"Good, because that isn't coming."

He wound up making eggs and sausage, and complimenting her on the prospective client she was meeting tonight.

Guilt wormed its way a little deeper. He was cooking for her and congratulating her on a fabrication.

As they sat down to eat, he brought up his mother again, "They'll be here the week before Halloween. You and TJ are the only ones who know. Please don't tell." Eggs disappeared from his plate at an alarming rate.

"It's not mine to tell." Kelsey shook her head. She didn't reveal everything about Andrew. "She's your daughter, it's your decision. I'll tell you if I think you're making the wrong one, but I'll abide by it."

"You would tell me?"

"Yes." She nodded. The old Kelsey wouldn't. But the new Kelsey, the one that was taking pictures and living in the world around her, would.

"You think this is right?"

She thought for a moment. "*Right* is a big word."

His plate was nearly clean, one last triangle of toast was left, and he ate that even as he looked at her funny.

"I don't know if there is 'right' or 'wrong' in this. I think your decision is the best one for Andie. I don't know if it's the best one for you."

JD nodded. "I'm good with that."

She couldn't finish all that he'd piled on her plate, and she pushed the remainder at him. "I have to get back to work."

"Me, too." He stood and saw her to the back door. "Why don't I just pick the kids up at school? That way you'll get an extra half hour of work in."

Something inside her softened. Kelsey stood in the back

doorway, "You know, I don't think I've said how impressed I am by what you've done."

He snapped a little straighter. "What do you mean?"

"All of it. It's impressive, giving up your job and moving across the country to try your hand in a field like this. Then Andie got slammed at you, and you just rose to the challenge again. Most men wouldn't have done either."

His head tilted, his hair falling over one eye. Apparently he hadn't had it cut that short. He made a striking portrait standing, and Kelsey wished she had her camera. She could see the strength, what the rest of the world couldn't see at the surface of him. There was compassion in his eyes, and a straightness to his spine, that said he did the things he believed in, and that he would be the one to stand up when he felt someone needed to.

She said a quick thank you, and turned down the steps. She wondered what was showing in her own eyes as she had looked at him.

CHAPTER 16

JD and the rest of Wilder made their way out onto the stage. He was always hoping for a crowd that was ready to go, but the bar was at a low hum, not a wild thrum. At least they knew how to handle this. They'd done it enough.

He picked up the guitar he'd set in the stand on stage earlier. The stage was cramped, but again, they'd worked that way before. With a smooth, innate motion, he flipped the guitar strap over his head and made a few minor adjustments until it no longer felt like the guitar was something he was holding, but simply an extension of his arms. While he looked out over the crowd trying to pick out anyone who might be an agent, his right hand reached down, fingertips absently walking through notes.

For a moment he thought about Kelsey, and hoped that she was doing well with her client tonight. She'd need her garage long before the band got anywhere. Then Alex tapped the beat for the first song of the set, and he started it with a gusto that JD wasn't sure he could match tonight.

He didn't count the rhythm, it just came to him. His hands knew when and what to start without his brain, and he was transported to that place where he was just playing. There was adrenaline, because this wasn't Kelsey's garage, but a real bar with real people watching. And you just never knew who. He cranked up his efforts.

They did a ballad next, the one he had sold to Tim McGraw. TJ didn't announce that JD had written it, nor did he say it was a cover. He just started singing, and one by one the instruments joined in to back him up. They had added a longer instrumental to give TJ a vocal break. They launched immediately into a third song, and Alex wailed on his drums. His kit took up most of the small stage and JD swore he was getting a wind off Alex's sticks.

The crowd changed. Faces were looking at them now, instead of at each other. The floor, which had walking room when they'd started, was now packed. JD scanned up and down the long bar in the back, only three people were facing the bartender. That was good, as long as one of them wasn't an agent.

After the sixth song they stopped for a break. The crowd had clapped and cat-called, and that was good, too. For three minutes they talked out what they needed to, adjusted what required it, and let TJ be quiet for the few moments in his life when it happened. JD rolled his head around on his neck. He held himself with every muscle taut while playing; most people didn't realize what a workout it could be. When they were ready again, he turned back to the audience and played a chord. Instantly the crowd reconvened.

Why wasn't there a damned agent here? Or someone, anyone, who worked with a record label? Wilder could command this crowd. With one chord the floor had filled up again, just waiting for them to play. It was the end of nights like these that he felt they could make it.

He tried his best to wipe the surliness off his face and just enjoy playing. Finally, he reminded himself that an agent or manager might be out there, and he'd better look salable.

Four songs later, he saw her.

She was laughing with the woman next to her, and had on more make-up than he had expected, but her face was turned toward the stage. Kelsey finished what she was saying and looked up at him, meeting his eyes, even while he continued to play. His fingers jerked just for a second, but he saved the riff, and didn't think anyone would notice. When his hands didn't need his brain again he looked up at her. She smiled.

JD tried to deny the shift that occurred in him. But he wasn't truly able to.

Kelsey was here. She had come to see them.

She raised her margarita glass in salute, and he couldn't stop the return smile that hit his face.

He played the rest of the set, keeping one eye to her. At one point her table emptied, and he lost her for a full song. He was just convinced that she'd gone home, when he spotted her closer to the front.

He didn't know what to do with the relief he felt. So he turned away from where she sat now, almost directly under him.

JD wasn't one to be timid about women. He asked them out, he made his play, he lived with the results. But this whole mess with Kelsey was going too far. There were a million and one reasons to squash it before he sank any deeper.

For one, she was older. She'd want someone stable and able to give her the life she deserved.

Two, she was his friend, and the pull inside him would fuck that up.

Three, she was his baby sitter, and in her own words, *you don't screw the babysitter.*

Four, she lived next door to him and walked the same route to school. When she found out about his feelings, they would both have to go way out of their way to avoid each other.

Five, there was Andie . . .

He kept counting as far as he could.

It was a damn long list.

He tried his best to focus on the music. He wasn't going to blow his chance with whoever was in the audience over a woman he couldn't have.

Finally, the set ended.

The crowd called for an encore and, flattered, the guys played another song. And another before the bar manager shut them down. He had to clear the place out by midnight on weeknights. Lights were going up in fifteen minutes.

Turning back to the table that was almost smack up against the stage, he found Kelsey right where he'd last seen her. Her empty margarita glass twirled lazily in her fingers, but she didn't seem any the worse for wear.

He wanted to jump down off the stage and kiss her.

He wanted to not want that. So he tamped it down.

"I see your girlfriend showed up." TJ almost startled him out of his skin.

"She's not my girlfriend."

"Your face on her boob says otherwise."

"What?" He looked. She was wearing a clingy little black tee-shirt, just like the one her friend had on. She had stolen the Wilder logo that Alex had put on his bass drum last year, and she had assembled the photos she had taken this morning into what looked like it had been a group shot. She and her friend were wearing the first ever t-shirts for Wilder. His head was on her left breast. "TJ your head is there, too."

"I know. That's cool."

JD couldn't stop the words before they came out. TJ was his brother, and would read him like a book. "What's cool? The shirt or your head on her breast?"

"You aren't going to ask me to 'show some respect' again, are you?" TJ walked off to talk to Alex and Craig.

JD moved out from under his guitar strap and set the

instrument in its cradle. In two short steps he was at the edge of the stage and bent down, hands pressed to his knees. "I can't believe you did that."

She pulled the bottom out, to show off the whole design, and looked apprehensive, "Do you like it?"

He didn't get to answer.

"That is so cool." Alex was right behind him.

Craig was too, "That's what that shit this morning was about."

She nodded, and JD turned to see all of them staring at her breasts. Her friend showed off the matching shirt and drew some of the attention away. Kelsey shrugged. "You didn't look edgy enough until I pestered you."

Craig conceded, "Good point. They do look really great. You have more?"

JD looked at Kelsey, who had no idea what a coup she'd scored. Craig didn't concede to any one person, ever. Not that JD had known anyway. He'd take a vote-down, but to come back and tell Kelsey that her pestering that morning had been a good thing, that was unheard of.

"I can make more." She stepped back.

"I want one." Alex called from where he was disassembling his drum kit.

Craig and TJ chimed in, and somehow JD didn't get anything said.

Kelsey took note, then changed the subject. "I want you guys to meet my friend Maggie." She gestured to the redhead with her. "Maggie, this is Wilder: TJ, Craig, Alex, and JD."

Maggie held her hand up, and offered a firm shake to each of them. JD didn't like touching anyone at the end of a set. He always felt grubby, but Maggie's pristine hand couldn't be ignored. She smiled up at him, and her fingers lingered a little long. There was no mistaking what that smile was about, but he kept his own neutral. There were a million reasons not to get involved with anyone right now.

He turned back to getting their gear in order and heard Maggie talking to Kelsey. "We have to go. I have to get back to my sitter."

But he didn't hear Kelsey respond. Just then the lights went up, and the manager cleared out the last of the lingering guests. JD continued winding cords and strapping them together, until he heard the manager speaking to Kelsey and Maggie.

"I'm going to have to ask you ladies to leave. We are no longer open to the public."

"She's with us." JD didn't know where that came from, but he tried to back it up with his demeanor, now that it had been said.

Kelsey gave a reluctant shrug. "Maggie's my ride."

"I'll give you a ride." *Home.* He should have said 'ride home'. He refused to turn and look at TJ, there was no telling what his brother would have to say about that Freudian slip.

"Are you sure?"

He shrugged. "You have to wait for us, but it's not like it's out of the way."

"Thank you."

He went back to the job of clearing their stuff from the stage, while Kelsey said good-night to her friend. The redhead let the manager show her out the front door, and JD did more clean-up before he turned back to Kelsey.

She didn't have time for him, though. She was chatting with Alex, about the shirts. "It's great. I need the advertising and so do you. Trust me, unless you all flat out refuse, I'm going to use these for my business, too."

She would convince them all that she wasn't doing them any favors. JD had begun to believe that she wasn't really capable of holding back if someone needed her.

He glanced up and saw that she had Craig's attention, too. "I

149

have pictures of you all walking away. I want to put them on the back."

Craig looked wary, but Kelsey fixed that, too. "You should all come over tomorrow and see what I have. Then we'll modify the shirts. If you bring me a shirt, we can make you each your own."

That won her a spot in all their hearts.

Even TJ looked up from his very careful cord wrapping. "Can I bring a tank top?"

"Sure. I don't see why not." Then she launched into something JD hadn't expected. "See, the way I figure it, you guys are doing something wrong."

"Thanks." It was Craig, but it wasn't harsh.

JD abandoned his work for a moment; this he wanted to hear.

"No, really." She held her hands, palm out, toward them. "Maggie, she goes out all the time. I don't think she's seen a movie in five years, but she seen tons of local bands. She's never heard of you. Why not?"

"Because we suck?" Alex volunteered.

Kelsey laughed, and JD realized she had every one of them eating out of the palm of her hand.

"That is clearly not the case." Her hands waved around, looking for a purpose. "I'm guessing you guys have been too busy playing and not spending enough time doing advertising. I need the portraits for my business, and these are perfect. So I just made the shirts. You might consider giving them out, or selling them at your next job."

"Who's gonna pay for our shirt? You just said no one's heard of us."

The manager walked up to them, "You guys quit jabbering and clear out. I want to go home."

They all turned back to work. Apparently so did Kelsey. While they loaded equipment into their cars, making trips out into the alley and back, he heard Kelsey ask the manager what the till looked like for the night. And how did that compare to other Tuesdays?

They all walked out to the alley as the manager turned the bolts behind them, but the guys clearly weren't through questioning Kelsey. She was answering each question with a clear point.

"Listen, why don't we just reconvene at my place?" He put his hand on the driver's side door handle, ready to go.

"I'm starving." TJ was probably feeling their new cash, however small it was, burning a hole in their collective pocket.

"Me, too."

JD was unofficially the keeper of the money. The most reluctant to spend it, he had been the natural choice. But for some reason when Kelsey's voice added in that she, too, could use something to eat, he suggested they order a pizza.

She slid into the passenger side, and he cranked the engine, grateful that it didn't embarrass him.

Once they were on the street, he turned to Kelsey. "The shirts are amazing. I can't believe you did that for us."

She shook her head, but he didn't let her deny it.

"So, how did things go with your client tonight?"

Her laughter ricocheted around the small car, hitting him several times. He still couldn't believe she'd just shown up.

"I lied. No client."

"You did that just for us?"

She looked sideways at him, as though he were nuts. "No. It's for me, too."

His hand wanted to reach across to hers. And it pained him to realize that if she were anyone else, he would. Instead, he simply clutched the shift so his hand couldn't move. "You didn't really need any Fabio pictures."

It wasn't a question, but it opened the topic. Kelsey responded. "No, I was just trying to get you to look at me with something other than kindness. I needed something with some attitude. It was hard getting you to give it."

He'd felt so bad, trying to get away from her, but he'd been stuck between a rock and a hard place, and she'd caught exactly that in the photo.

Alex and TJ both tailed them to Kelsey's house, and she ran inside to set Bethany free after saying they should just meet at her place. The guys shrugged, and continued carting the equipment back into the garage. They didn't set it up, but they had to get it under lock and key. JD shuddered to think what might happen to the band if any of their stuff got stolen. They really couldn't afford to replace it. Leaving it in a car was a sure way to get it ripped off.

As Alex, TJ and Craig followed him in the back door, JD held his finger to his lips. The kids would be sleeping, and he didn't want to deal with an awake Andie. He didn't let any of them utter a word until they met up with Kelsey in the kitchen. She was thumbing through a phone book and muttering.

"I haven't been this hungry since . . . was someone smoking weed in that bar?"

Craig looked at her sideways, "You would even know what it is?"

She almost snorted in return. "I went to college. I'd know it if I smelled it. I wasn't always a mom."

They spent far too long ordering the pizza, then Kelsey let them raid the fridge for drinks, and she started back in while they were guzzling sodas like there was no tomorrow. JD for one was going to spend his morning walking Andie to school like a zombie and then climbing back into bed.

"So I was trying to figure out why Maggie hasn't heard of you. Then I realized that there's nothing in print. No shirts, no posters. You need a manager."

"And you're going to be it?" TJ looked her up and down.

"No way. I don't have that kind of talent or those

connections. But I will do what I can until you get one." She shrugged. "I really thought I'd be more of a 'groupie' if you don't mind."

Craig shrugged. "Sure. Why not?"

JD wanted to slap him upside the head. *Why not? Because you never agree to anything this easily.* When he wanted something from Craig it was like pulling teeth. For a moment he paused as an odd thought hit. Was Craig into Kelsey?

Kelsey was speaking again, and all three of the others were listening with rapt attention. JD decided he'd better focus, too.

"I asked what the take was at the bar tonight, and what it was on other nights. You guys helped them pull in more money than they do without a band, and more than some of the other groups."

"Okay?" Alex was taking mental notes and you could tell from his expression.

"You all should be playing Friday and Saturday nights. But you probably won't until you can prove that you're good for business. So we need to advertise the next job you have."

Craig nodded, understanding, but shrugging. "We don't have a next job yet."

Kelsey smiled that smile, and JD knew what was coming. "You're back at McMinn's next Wednesday if you want it. One of you has to call Jeff and confirm by tomorrow, or he's looking for someone else."

"Are you serious?" TJ lifted Kelsey into a fierce hug and twirled her around her own kitchen. Her squeal of glee was punctuated by the doorbell, which JD ran to get before the pizza man rang it again and woke up the kids. His brain stayed a little too focused on the kitchen, and he tried shaking it off. He wasn't successful until he reminded himself that TJ wasn't going to liplock with Kelsey right there in front of Craig and Alex.

He paid for the pizza out of his own pocket, saving the band money for later, then walked the boxes back into the kitchen. TJ finally set Kelsey down in favor of food, and JD fought one last time to remove her from his brain. *Jeff?* She knew McMinn's manager on a first name basis after one night? And *TJ?*

No. He wasn't going to get her out of his system easily.

All of them, including Kelsey, tucked into the pizza. The guys were on their second and third pieces each, as Kelsey daintily finished her first and started talking again. "There's tons of places around town to put up posters. I have an account at the printers. I can get real posters. If you want them."

They all agreed that they did, and Kelsey started explaining their options. The vote was unanimous for more of the cheaper black-and-whites.

"That's what I figured you'd say." She motioned to her shirt, "I thought we might use this shot for the poster."

"What about something else?" Craig asked.

"Well, right now we need to keep the name and photo simple and repetitive, make it recognizable around town. So the posters and even the t-shirts ought to all be the same."

TJ was leaning his face into his hand, his elbow propped on the kitchen table. "Where did you learn all this?"

"My roommate was a marketing major in college." Kelsey smiled and picked up one of the last pieces of pizza. She took a bite, and when she finished it, she broke the silence. "The question is: do you want to go with this, or is there anything you want to change?"

They all admired her chest for a while, then she stopped them. "If we can go quietly, we can look at what I have on the computer, or if you want something really different, we can shoot more tomorrow."

"I like what we have."

"This is good."

"Tomorrow's for sleep."

JD didn't weigh in. Just followed the others down the hall he was already familiar with. She opened the door to reveal a pristine office and she sat down at the computer. Kelsey began opening photos. Individuals of each of them, some headshots, some each of them walking away.

She pulled a print on some filmy paper off the printer, and gingerly held it out to them. It was each of them walking away, composited to look like they had just been standing there together, and had all scattered. "I was planning to put this on the back of the shirts, but I didn't get done in time for tonight . . . It's an iron-on."

Kelsey put it back in the printer tray. "Okay, here's what I can do."

For the next hour she flipped them through photos, until they agreed on one. They altered the logo in a way she suggested, to make it look a little more hardcore and a little more country.

With a few keystrokes she changed Alex's drum logo to match. They all nodded. Finally, they laid out the poster, upright, name on top, then photo, followed by block letter info underneath.

"When you advertise, McMinn's will make more money, and you'll get invited back, and you can demand more pay, and maybe even move to Friday or Saturday nights. You'll also get your name and faces out there. The more people that recognize you, the more other bars will want to hire you . . . It's win-win-win."

"It's two thirty a.m." Craig scratched the back of his neck. "I need to get some sleep."

TJ said good-night and followed his roommate out the door. Alex lasted two seconds after they did, and JD was left standing there with Kelsey, both of them suddenly dog tired.

"I don't want to carry Andie home."

"Then don't." Kelsey couldn't hide a yawn. "Just show up tomorrow morning around seven with a change of clothes, and her school stuff. Maybe you can walk them in while I hit the printers." Her hands flew to her face. "Oh, god, that's less than five hours away."

"Okay."

It was all he could muster, but he went and checked the bolts on the front door before letting himself out the back.

CHAPTER 17

Kelsey met him at the front door the next morning, looking far too chipper for seven a.m. "I hate you." He growled out.

"Good morning to you, too." She gave a false fifties-housewife smile and motioned hostess-style for him to enter. She then waltzed back over to the table where three pajama-clad kids were eating cereal and grabbed her can of coke.

"Jesus, Kelse. It's seven a.m. and you're already hitting the sauce."

She held out a second can to him. "I'm awake and perky. Do you want one?" She sounded like she was straight out of Leave-it-to-Beaver. She threatened to throw the can to him.

He growled again, and stalked over to yank the coke away from her. He might as well drink it. She was alert enough to do impressions and he was barely upright.

When he found his voice, he went over to Andie, who had previously looked like she didn't care that he was there. But now she launched herself into his arms. "Daddy!"

"Morning, baby." She almost toppled him, but he held on, the weight of this child sweet in his arms. He stood and grabbed Andie's hand. "Let's go get you dressed, baby."

As usual, Kelsey saw him as he wondered where to do that and prevented him from even asking. "Use my room."

He led his daughter down the hallway to a room he had never really seen before. Every time he'd been in here it had been dark or Kelsey had commanded his attention in her 'little devil' underwear and naked legs. He didn't want to pay attention now. So he tried to focus on getting Andie ready for school.

Was Andrew such trouble that Kelsey had learned to anticipate questions and bring whatever was needed to avoid violent storms? She didn't seem to act like it had been that bad. His picture, a whole family picture, was beside the bed on the small table. Andrew was blond-haired and blue-eyed. No one would guess that the almost too-good-looking man in the photo was mentally ill or violent. They certainly looked to be the perfect family.

"This room is pretty."

Andie's voice pulled him away from mulling over the photo. The room *was* pretty. It was soft without being frilly, feminine without feeling girly. The dusty red comforter across the big bed was still rumpled from use. It looked inviting against the creamy yellow walls. Large pieces of dark furniture and a patterned chair in the same reds and yellows filled out the rest of the room.

He laid Andie's jammies over the arm of the chair without thinking and tied her shoes. He pulled out her brush, and Andie eyed him warily. JD sighed. He didn't have time for this, but he also knew that if he took a step backward, then he would have to make up for it later. Usually in spades. He turned away. "Fine, I'll see if Kelsey wants her hair brushed."

He went into the living room and sat at the edge of the

couch with his knees apart. In just a minute, Kelsey ushered Allie and Daniel out into the living room, dressed and shining.

He held up the brush. "Do you want your hair brushed?"

"Yes." She smiled widely, and before he knew what to do, she had plunked herself onto the floor between his legs.

He did what she'd taught him: started at the bottom and worked his way up. He held his hand against her head if there was a tangle. He also did what she probably didn't realize she'd taught him: stroke with long clean lines from the crown of her head to the tip of the long hair. He did it in every direction, placing the brush just above her ear and pulling back until he ran out of hair, and from underneath, pulling up.

Kelsey responded the way he figured she would: she made low humms in the back of her throat. She turned her head side to side, giving him better access, and placed her cheek against his knee, resting it there.

He kept going, knowing that the whole thing had turned vaguely sexual, and still not quite willing to stop. When she curled a little tighter against him, brushing her breast against his calf, his jeans tightened a bit, and he decided he had to call the dogs off. "Okay, that's it. You're done."

She didn't move.

He nudged her, "Kelse, I know you love this but you have to get up. The kids have to get to school."

It was Daniel who pointed out the problem. "She's asleep."

"What?"

Daniel looked askance at the both of them. "This is what happens when you stay up past your bedtime." He shot a questioning look at JD before walking away. It was just enough to make JD wonder if the kid knew what kind of thoughts sometimes went through JD's head about his mother.

He nudged her a little harder this time. "Kelsey. Wake up. We have to get the kids to school." He didn't stop rattling her until she moved of her own will.

She sucked in a breath. "Wh- what?"

"You fell asleep."

His explanation fell by the wayside, as she stood up and stretched her arms over her head, leaning from side to side and exposing little slices of smooth skin where her shirt gapped above her jeans. He noticed all of it. And wished he hadn't.

"Okay, kids, JD is walking you to school today." She gathered thermal lunch bags and light jackets.

"Nope." JD countered. "We're all walking today."

"Why?" She looked up at him, mussed, and blinking, and beautiful.

"Because you just fell asleep on your living room floor. You are not driving to the printers by yourself. You walk with us."

Daniel looked up at her, big-eyed and stern. "No complaining, Mom. You're the one who wanted to stay up late."

JD had to laugh. It sounded so like Kelsey.

She blinked again and disappeared into her room, then reappeared with a thin sweater drawn over her shirt and stuffing her feet into slim sneakers. She ducked into the kitchen for a minute, and when she emerged she was accompanied by the pop and fizz of a fresh can of soda.

JD shook his head at her even as he held the door open. She was the last one out, and his hand was at the small of her back before he was even aware of what he was doing. He pulled it away, locking the door behind him. "You've got a bad habit there, Kelse."

She turned and glared over her shoulder, even as the kids went down the sidewalk single file, looking like an old Norman Rockwell painting. "Bite me. I'm a single mom, with small children. I get my coke." She cradled the drink to her, despite the hint of chill lingering in the air.

After that, the walk was pretty uneventful. They took Daniel and Andie to the gate at the school, then cut a few blocks over to drop Allie off at day-care, with Kelsey cringing as they left the property. "I've been running up a bigger bill here than I planned."

JD nodded. "Everything is cheaper without kids."

She nodded, but stayed silent.

JD turned around, walking backward down the sidewalk. "Isn't this the part where you extol the virtues of parenthood to me? Remind me of what I have? How money doesn't compare to love?"

Kelsey smiled sweetly at him. "Nope. If you don't know that by now, there's nothing I can say to change it. It's okay to gripe about money and how much they cost, I won't doubt your love for your child."

JD nodded, but inside he smiled.

It was only two blocks to Kelsey's house. She darted in to grab the things for the printer, but then seemed surprised that he was going with her.

"Kelse, you fell asleep once already this morning. What if you fell asleep at the wheel?"

Her eyebrows went up.

JD continued. "Who would take your kids?" Her mouth pursed, then opened, but he didn't let her speak. "*I* would. Do you really want me to be a single Dad with *three* kids? I don't think anyone does."

She laughed at him, as she often did. "You'd be fine. You'd find some beautiful young wife to help you out and all would be well."

They climbed into his car and headed just five or six blocks down to the print shop. The guy at the front counter greeted Kelsey by name. Several copies of the photo as well as a disk copy were handed over with an explanation.

"Ready by five." The man assured them.

She smiled at him. "So we eat an early dinner and take the kids out postering."

Without saying anything else, they climbed back into the car, and he dropped her at the curb to her front walk. He was afraid she would barely make it to the bed.

~

They did exactly as Kelsey had suggested, eating dinner before all driving over to pick up the posters. All five of them headed in, and JD tried not to show what it meant to finally see his band on a real poster.

The thick stack of glossy paper was heavier than it looked. Kelsey paid for the posters on her account to avoid the mark-up, and he made a mental note to put a check in her hand before the night was over.

Then they hit the town looking for blank walls and old posters they could cover. When they found a good one, Kelsey pulled to the curb and popped the trunk while JD helped all the kids get out.

A homeless man stepped up to him and asked for money. First putting the kids behind him, JD pulled the last three singles out of his wallet. He couldn't refuse anyone in need of help, even though it wasn't much. He'd been pretty broke himself sometimes. The man was gracious and walked away.

Kelsey pulled out eight of the posters and she held up the top row while JD rammed the staples in. The kids held up the bottom row, poorly, until he knelt down and lent a hand, showing Andie and Daniel how to line up the edges. There was almost no hope for Allie, who was holding up a single poster that had folded over on her.

"Where's Allie?" Kelsey feigned. "JD, have you seen Allie?"

Allie giggled.

Daniel put his fingers to his lips, and motioned for Andie to play along. "I haven't seen her in a while, Mom."

Andie shrugged.

Allie giggled again.

She still had a tiny baby voice, and she called out from under the poster, "I'm in here. I'm stuck."

He pressed his own lips together. "I hear her but I can't see her."

"I'm under the poster!" She yelled it at the top of her little lungs.

He lifted the edge and found her with her hands still holding the poster to the wall, just as he had instructed. He hammered the staples in and hollered. "Okay, everybody! Back in the car!"

The kids ran screaming, and jumped in. He and Kelsey buckled each of the kids in a pretend rush and drove off to find the next blank wall.

They plastered up lines of posters, covered doorways on shops for rent, and wrapped telephone poles. They wore themselves out and called it a night with four hundred posters left to go.

At the front of Kelsey's house, they all wearily climbed out and dragged themselves across the grass. The kids hadn't complained at all. They had been given jobs, and worked hard only knowing that it was for JD. Each kid had 'helped' to the best of their ability, which sometimes wasn't much, but didn't matter.

"Well, that was fun." Kelsey smiled, even though she was clearly exhausted. "The kids will sleep well tonight."

He nodded and said good-night, holding Andie's hand as they walked around the corner to their condo.

He had a big day tomorrow. He and Craig had four hundred posters to get up. It would certainly go faster, but he doubted it would be anywhere near as much fun.

The following Wednesday McMinn's was turning away customers.

CHAPTER 18

October had come in on little cats' feet. Wilder was doing better and better. Craig had to cut back his shifts at Starbucks. The band was playing three and sometimes four nights a week, with a Friday or Saturday night booked most weekends. They even had a standing gig at McMinn's on Wednesdays.

Kelsey had enlisted Maggie and they had sold over two hundred t-shirts with the Wilder logo and her photo on them. One day JD saw a total stranger walking down the street wearing their shirt.

Each week, they were going out and putting half sheets with up-to-date info over the old info on the posters. Craig told her she was brilliant when she said she'd designed them that way on purpose. Kelsey was a single mom, and single moms knew how to do things without any unnecessary work. Time was precious.

She'd racked up a ton of babysitting hours with JD, but she wasn't all that anxious to get them paid back. He did watch her kids a few times when she met photography clients. She'd even shot a wedding.

The band had taken her out for a nice steak dinner to

thank her for helping them turn things around. Kelsey agreed to accept the steak but not the credit. All the posters in the world wouldn't mean a damn thing if the band wasn't any good. She had simply helped them tell the crowd where they'd be.

Andie had learned her days of the week and colors, and Daniel had taken to writing and drawing stories. It seemed like she stapled a stack of paper for him to 'make a book' every day. Allie was counting the days until next fall when she, too, would get to go to school.

JD and Andie were coming over for dinner. It was happening more often these past two months. Maybe once a week they were all together. Tonight it was pizza, and JD and Andie were bringing it. Kelsey hollered out to her kids. "Okay, TV off, we have to make the salad."

She heard two sets of small feet heading into the kitchen. She chopped and handed off lettuce, tomatoes, carrots, cucumbers and raisins for the kids to toss. Then she had them carefully set the table.

They had just slid the chairs back into place and set up the third booster seat for Andie, when the front door clicked. None of them bothered with knocking anymore. Not JD or Andie, not the band, not even Alex, who was the most soft-spoken of the whole group.

"Hey, we're here." JD hollered out.

Allie and Daniel went screaming out to find them, and Kelsey started pouring drinks. She realized as she did it, that she didn't even ask what he wanted, or what his child should have, anymore.

He appeared in the doorway to the kitchen, the smell of hot pizza wafting from the table behind him. He didn't say hello. His hands were jammed deep in his pockets, and she knew what was coming. "It's tomorrow."

Kelsey nodded. His mother and father were coming, and he

dreaded it like someone was going to remove a limb. "You look pretty upset."

"When you meet her you'll be upset, too."

Kelsey now wanted to meet this woman just to see if she was as bad as JD said. TJ agreed with him, so there was probably merit. But her own mother had drunk herself into oblivion, and her brother had fits and threw things. She understood that his mother didn't approve of him or TJ, but how bad could her *behavior* be?

She motioned them all to the table, and she and JD made the kids finish a small pile of salad each before they could have pizza. He didn't speak much, just nodded at Andie's talk about meeting her grandparents.

So Kelsey changed the subject. "What was the most interesting thing at school today, Andie?"

"Todd put thirty paper towels down the toilet, so when I had to pee, I had to walk over to the other classroom." She took a bite of pizza, and chewed thoughtfully.

Leave it to a kindergartener.

She tried the adult next, and they ran down the list of the upcoming week's Wilder events. "It's good," she smiled. The guys had four shows this week, one at their biggest venue yet.

JD smiled as wide as she had ever seen. "I know. I'm solvent."

"Really?"

He nodded and downed almost another whole slice of pizza at the same time. "It's been so long since I was *ahead*. I want to do something for Andie, she's been so good through all this. I just have to get through this thing with my mother first."

Kelsey didn't say anything.

"I'm afraid my mother's going to undo all that Andie and I have built." Andie and Kelsey's kids had asked to be excused, so JD spoke more freely knowing that the kids wouldn't hear. "You're going to be there for dinner tomorrow night, right?"

"Yes, me and the kids." She chewed for a moment. "Where is

there? Your table isn't big enough, the five of us barely fit around it."

"I got a new table. With a leaf-thingy in the middle."

"Cool. Are you cooking?" She tried to hold her face straight while he panicked.

"Only a little, you said you'd bring-"

She caved quickly. "I was kidding. Of course, I'm bringing chicken and dessert."

"That was mean."

"I know," she grinned before she polished off the last of her pizza, "and it was fun."

They joined the kids in the living room for the rest of the movie, and Kelsey flipped through a magazine. JD did the same.

"This," he held up a page, "this is absolutely correct." It was *10 Things He Wishes You Would Do In Bed*. "It's good to see you women are staying educated."

"Uh!" She rolled up her own Cosmo and threatened to whack him with it. "You should just be grateful! I don't see *7 Ways to Remember Her Birthday* or *How to Buy Jewelry* in your magazines, it's all just T and A."

"Like this isn't!" He frantically turned pages until he arrived at *This Month's Man Without His Shirt*. "Look!"

"That's one picture! One! And he's wearing jeans!"

"They're unzipped!" JD held up the photo for her to see.

It was a blond surfer guy with green eyes, ripped abs, and great arms. He wasn't her type; as in, he wasn't JD. Kelsey didn't say that. "He's hot, that's okay. Please, the girls in men's magazines are in their underwear, if anything."

JD conceded, and went back to flipping pages. Kelsey looked up when she saw the credits roll. "All right guys-"

The phrase died on her lips, the kids were all asleep, piled up like little logs. She turned to tell JD, but he, too, was out cold.

Extracting herself from the couch, Kelsey tiptoed out of the room and grabbed her old Nikon 70mm. Slowly, she turned the dimmer switch up, then down again, trying to get the light just right, then she began snapping off photos.

She didn't know how long she'd been at it, but she stopped herself when she realized that she had an overabundance of pictures of JD. Unlike the digital photos, where she could just erase them, there would be negatives, evidence of what she'd done.

She shouldered the camera, telling herself she should wake him up, but she just stared. His face was so interesting. *As a subject*, she told herself. His straight nose looked noble in some way, and dark lashes fanned out against his cut cheekbones. His lips were full, and she could imagine the way his eyes sometimes closed when he sang. Pulling her gaze away, she saw where his shirt had come untucked, and she couldn't hide a smirk. He could easily give October's *Man Without His Shirt* a run for his money.

She forced herself to put the camera away, then carefully carried each of her kids to bed, thinking she should bring the camera and get some photos of JD and his family tomorrow. She would send them to his mother later. Just to be nice.

Without much extra thought, she lifted Andie and settled her into the opposite end of Allie's bed from where Allie was curled into a tight ball. The two girls had shared the bed this way more times than Kelsey could count now. Neither would be upset or surprised if she woke up in the middle of the night.

Her arms felt light afterwards. JD usually carried the bigger kids, and he did it with such ease. He opened stuck windows. He lifted heavy things for her. Kelsey kept telling herself that it was for Andie. That Andie needed to see Kelsey asking JD for help, and trusting him and his opinion. But she did trust him. It was wonderful having a man around—to have someone find her on a ladder changing a light bulb and feel strong hands grasp the ladder and hold her steady. Or simply shoo her down, and do the job.

When she entered the living room JD was blinking rapidly, still reclined against the arm of the couch. She grabbed his hand and tugged. "Come on, big guy. I can't carry you to bed."

"Hmmmmmm."

She wasn't sure what that tone had meant, but he'd been thinking about something.

On unsteady feet, he let her pull him down the hall to the office. She had a futon in there, and she left him in the doorway for a moment to set it up. When she turned back she saw that he'd shucked his shirt.

Oh, god.

She tamped that down. She'd seen him in a bathing suit numerous times. This was different though, and her thoughts took off on a wild rampage, while JD seemed to have fallen asleep standing up. It appeared he knew where he was though, because he'd crawled across the bed and sprawled on his stomach.

Kelsey drew the covers over him. For her, not him. His jeans hugged his ass, and his bare back was giving her thoughts that she was too long without a man. She refused to back-calculate.

She made it to her own room, where she crawled under her own covers. She couldn't think this way about JD. She was finally participating in the world. JD and Andie had become her family. It was like when Andrew was mid-swing. When he wasn't manic, and wasn't depressed, he was amazing. He was helpful and fun and smart. JD was all of that, and his mood didn't change unpredictably. Her kids very much needed a male figure in full control of himself.

She *could not* screw that up.

Having a crush on her younger friend was about the worst thing she could do.

CHAPTER 19

K elsey sniffed the air, the chicken smelled fabulous. She had spent an hour slicing oranges and added raspberries on top of the seasoned chicken. She wished she had some fancy dish to serve it in, but she didn't. She'd never bought anything glass or china while Andrew was alive. She examined the danger potential of every object if it were to be broken or thrown. Now, she had to spend her money on camera equipment and kid stuff that was far more important than serving dishes.

She still wished she had one. Any little thing that would help soothe JD's Texas housewife mother would be a blessing. Kelsey half expected the woman to show up in white gloves.

She half expected the woman to comment on the fact that Kelsey had seen her son in his skivvies this morning. Apparently, he'd shucked the jeans, too, sometime during the night. And she hadn't closed the door all the way. So her walk down the hall to the kids' rooms yielded a fine look at JD's backside and the non-returnable knowledge that he wore boxer-briefs. And wore them well.

She reminded herself that JD was in his twenties. He'd be dating women a good decade younger than her. She reminded herself that if she didn't check on the chicken she'd burn it, and how was she to explain that one at the dinner table with his parents? *Why, yes, I was thinking about your son. He does have a great ass.*

No, that would not go over well.

She pulled the chicken out and turned off the oven. She loved the steamy heat of the kitchen on cold evenings when the weather was at that stage where it couldn't quite decide what season it was.

She hollered out for the kids. "Are you ready?"

They both appeared in the doorway, carefully dressed to meet the family. "It's almost time to go."

Kelsey spent a few moments getting herself ready, then she lined the kids up and entrusted Daniel with the apple pie she'd made this morning. Grabbing pot holders, she picked up the chicken and marched out the door. Allie was already around the corner and Daniel was following her, apple pie carefully balanced in front of him.

With measured steps, especially given that she was doing all this in heels, she made her way over to JD's. She wondered what they were walking into. JD and Andie had spent most of the afternoon with his folks, having rushed off after the soccer game to change and pick up TJ.

Kelsey saw Allie had reached the back door, knocking her little heart out and yelling, "We're here."

JD opened the door, smiling first at Allie then looking around for the rest of them. She could tell when he spotted her, still out on the sidewalk. He said something over his shoulder and came down the walk to her, thanking her profusely while lifting the heavy dish of chicken like it was a sheet of music.

He led her up the back step into the kitchen, where more food awaited. He leaned in, placing his mouth near her ear, and Kelsey couldn't stifle the shiver. It wasn't his lips she got, but his voice. "She keeps telling Andie that she doesn't look like me.

And she's made more than one remark about children born out of wedlock being a sin."

Kelsey cringed, thoughts of his lips all but forgotten.

He shook his head, "My only consolation is that Andie doesn't understand what 'out of wedlock' means."

TJ gave her a brotherly hug and Kelsey was surprised to see him in pressed pants and a button down shirt. He had even combed his hair out of his face. JD, who had dressed a bit nicer than usual for his parents, hadn't.

They all sat down for dinner, and TJ was unfailingly polite. He made every effort to turn the conversation away from Andie and her arrival. He talked about what she'd been doing in kindergarten, and smiled at her. For this he earned his mother's gratitude for helping out his brother in this 'untenable' situation.

JD was definitely getting the short end of the stick. Mrs. Hewlitt referred to her sons as Johnathan and Thomas, and Kelsey as 'Mrs. Conklin'. Kelsey didn't bother to correct that she had never been married. She didn't think it would reflect well on JD. When she gave it a little thought, it could look pretty bad —two kids, different fathers. Different mothers, too.

Mrs. Hewlitt also made comments about the condo. 'It was nice, for not being a house.' 'It would be more suitable to his purposes, if he just fixed it up.' And she straight out asked what he was doing to remedy the situation of Andie not having a mother.

Kelsey watched JD snap when his mother asked if he had called 'that sweet Lisa he had been in love with in Texas.' She also offered a sugar-coated but pointed look at Kelsey when she referenced *that sweet Lisa.*

"Mother, Lisa wasn't sweet. She was doing cocaine off my counter-tops."

Mrs. Hewlitt's hand went to her chest. "I'll believe no such thing. She was a sweetheart."

Mr. Hewlitt raised his eyebrows, but went no further. He looked like an older version of his two sons. They would age nicely, but neither of them was like him. He was a non-issue in the shadow of his overpowering wife.

"For the record, I was never in love with her." JD grumbled.

Mr. Hewlitt did the one smart thing Kelsey had seen him do all evening: he changed the subject. "Our travel group is actually going to make it to Bethlehem, this time. It's going to be quite a pilgrimage."

After that, each of the adults took turns re-directing Mrs. Hewlitt when she started in on one of her sons. By the time the meal was finished, Kelsey had had enough.

JD won. Andrew may have thrown things, and yelled, and said things that cut right to the core, but in the end he apologized. Mrs. Hewlitt meant it.

When everyone got up afterwards to go into the living room Kelsey volunteered to clear, just for some peace. But she was outmaneuvered, and Mrs. Hewlitt cornered her while she was scrubbing her baking dish.

"It's so nice of you to help JD with Anderson."

"Andie's a sweet girl, and we love having her." She braced herself. She could feel it coming, she just couldn't see from where.

"Johnathan mentioned that you were older than him. You must be . . . what, thirty-eight? Nine?"

She spoke through locked teeth. "I'm thirty-two."

"I just don't understand. I'm not sure what a woman your age would want from a man she can't possibly have a relationship with."

Maybe I just want to screw your son's brains out.

But she didn't say it. It wasn't true anyway, that wasn't what she got from this relationship. "JD needed help getting adjusted to having a daughter, and my children needed a strong male role model. It just worked out."

"Your husband?"

Kelsey didn't correct her. She'd felt her own claws pop out and she needed to keep them behind her back if she couldn't keep them sheathed. "He was ill throughout their whole childhood."

"Hmmm."

Damn that woman. Even the 'hmmm' was disapproving.

"Mom!" JD's voice rang sharp from the doorway, "Stop pestering Kelsey, we want you in the living room."

His mother smiled as sweet as honey, and turned her back, dismissing him by action as well as words. "I'm needed in here, Kelsey and I are just catching up."

JD faced Kelsey behind his mother's back, looking panic-stricken and helpless. Kelsey smiled at him. "We're fine." She wanted to add, *I can hold my own.*

When he was gone, his mother started in again. "I'm not trying to be judgmental."

That was a crock of shit if Kelsey had ever heard one.

"But you aren't really helping my son."

"Oh?" This she had to hear.

"The more you help, the longer he can go on pretending that he's doing fine. He's not. He needs a real job and a wife. He needs to fail, so he'll finally come around. I know it's hard to watch someone hit rock bottom, but it's the only way to help."

Kelsey closed her mouth.

Then she found her voice, "I understand what you mean about watching someone hit rock bottom. It is very hard to do. My mother had troubles, and I realized that the more I helped the more I prevented her from getting real help."

"I'm so glad you understand-"

Sweetly, Kelsey cut her off, "Having been through that, I can solidly say that your son is in no such situation. JD has held that band together, and it's starting to pay off. They're earning money." Two could play at this, "It takes a long time to get a venture like that off the ground, but your sons are very talented."

She so desperately wanted to throw Andie in this woman's face. That her son had taken on someone else's child and turned things around, simply because he was needed. Instead, she bit her tongue. "And don't worry about me getting in the way of him finding a wife. Musicians are sexy as hell, and the women are lining up for him. I'm just his neighbor." She finished drying the dish and set it on the counter.

She smiled, saccharine to the core, and turned to lean against the counter. Her hands were on either side of her, in a way that the doctors had always said invited attack. She was just thinking, *Bring it on, bitch,* when she looked up and saw JD and TJ standing at the entrance to the kitchen. Their eyes were wide as saucers, and they stood dumbfounded.

Perhaps she had laid it on a little thick.

His mother was quiet. From what Kelsey could see while she dried one of the dishes absently, Mrs. Hewlitt was planning her next attack.

Even though she'd clearly gone too far, Kelsey was glad the old battle-axe needed time for a rebuttal to that. She just didn't want to still be standing here when it came. *Shit.* She'd brought on World War Three, when she was supposed to be buffering things. She was a trained buffer from the moment it became obvious that her little brother was beyond the scope of normal. Why couldn't she have held out one more night?

TJ found his voice first. "Mom, Andie's been waiting patiently to show you her drawings. Come on." Unlike JD's earlier attempt, he brooked no possible disagreement, taking her hand and pulling her away.

The woman gave one last smile to Kelsey as she followed her son out the arch. It looked sweet, but underneath it was anything but.

JD walked into the kitchen, and opened his mouth but no sound came.

Oh, shit. She'd screwed everything up.

His mouth worked, but still no sound.

Her chest squeezed. He had every right to hate her, to never speak to her again. She kept her voice hushed, but it rushed like water over rocks. "JD, I'm so sorry, she just made me so mad that I -"

He closed the distance between them, the arm around her back clasping her tightly to him, in direct contrast to the other that was bracing his hand over her mouth to shut her up.

"Don't be sorry. That was amazing. I've never seen anyone shut my mother down."

He removed his hand from her mouth and smiled.

For a moment he stood there, holding her flush against him.

She thought he might kiss her, and she hadn't yet made up her mind about how she felt about that, when he did.

On her forehead.

CHAPTER 20

K elsey stayed in most of the next week, closing one home loan and starting another. The check from the one she'd closed would be big, but wouldn't show up for another week. Money was getting tight. So no nights out with Wilder for a bit.

She booked a family at the elementary school for portraits. She'd placed an ad in the school's monthly circular, and she'd been getting inquiries.

Maggie was set to attend the Saturday show at the Troubadour, but the real coup was that Maggie was going to go with her friend Brenda. And Brenda was an agent with one of the smaller local labels.

Kelsey could feel her own heart beat faster just thinking about it. But she didn't tell the guys. JD said they played every night like there was an agent in the audience, because you just never knew.

She tried not to think about JD kissing her on the forehead. Or what it might mean.

She dragged Allie shopping with her, while Daniel and Andie were at school. The very fact that she had thought that

Daniel *and Andie* were at school today told her how attached she had become to JD and his daughter.

Somewhere after filling her cart, she found herself standing in front of the music department. She didn't think she'd bought a CD since college. But she was in the country music section before she knew what she was doing there. Admission came as she scanned for Tim McGraw. Grabbing his latest release, she read the publication date. It was this year. She put it into the cart, ignoring Allie's pleas to hold on to it.

She placated her daughter by buying her a My Little Pony miniature that was hanging in the check-out line, something she never did. Allie was happy brushing the pony's hair and showing off the absurd sparkles on the rump. Kelsey didn't understand the allure of small, ridiculously colored, plastic horses, but Allie sure did.

When they got out to the car, Kelsey rummaged through the bags. When she found the CD, she tore apart the cellophane and jabbed the theft-proof stickers with her key until they gave. Popping the disc in her CD player filled the car with Tim McGraw's unique sound.

"Mommy, who is this?"

"It's Tim McGraw, honey." But she didn't say any more. She yanked out the booklet that came with it, and scanned mercilessly until she found what she was after.

John Hewlitt. The fifth song.

It had to be. So she punched the skip button until it was on the right track. A guitar picked notes off, until the voice joined. It was Tim McGraw singing, not JD. And in Tim's voice it sounded like he'd lost his lover.

But the words weren't that specific. They spoke of "when I was your golden boy" and how you sometimes had to leave, and better yourself, even when those who loved you couldn't understand. Even if they wouldn't love you anymore.

In Tim's voice she heard the regret and longing, and right there in the parking lot at Wal-Mart, she broke down and cried.

~

"Kelsey!"

She heard her name through the dream. JD was calling to her but she couldn't see him.

"Kelsey!" It was getting louder.

"Wake up!" And more specific.

She fought through the haze to the hand tapping hers, to the none-too-gentle jostles to her shoulders.

"Wake up!"

She sat bolt upright, terrified. "What's wrong? The kids?"

"Nothing's wrong!"

Her alarm clock said 2:42. The pitch black around her said that was 2:42 *a.m.*

JD was beside her bed, holding her hand, tugging her up. "I have news."

He pulled her down the hallway, while her eyes blinked and her brain turned over. In the kitchen he flipped the light on to blind her.

"Ah!" She raised her arms and shielded her eyes from the bright-burn.

"Here."

She heard the fridge door open, and the pop and fizz of a fresh can of coke. He pressed the cold metal into her hand, and obligingly she took a drink. "So, I'm guessing Brenda signed you."

"What?"

She immediately regretted it. He deflated like a popped balloon.

"Yes, she offered. You knew? . . . Of course, you knew."

Somewhere in the bright she saw his hands wave then settle on his hips as he wandered the kitchen. "You've been our angel all along. I don't know whether to hug you or hate you."

She could feel the caffeine hit her system. He was right, she did have a habit. But like all good addicts she ignored it. "The hugging I'm on board with, the hating, not so much."

He snorted.

"Why would you hate me for this? I thought it was what you wanted, I'm sorry if-"

"Shut up." He grabbed her and twirled her around, open coke can and all.

For a moment her breath caught on the thought that he would kiss her.

When he finally set her back down, he explained. "I was going to hate you for not telling us. But I'll let you defend yourself first."

She took another slug of the coke. "You said you play every night like there's an agent out there. I didn't know if she'd make it, or even what kind of music she worked with. I guess I didn't want you getting your hopes up if it was nothing."

"What are you, my mother?"

She was fully awake now, and that burned. "Ouch."

"Yeah, you deserve it. You should have told us."

Leaning against the counter, she crossed her arms and conceded. "You're right. I won't do it again. Forgive me?"

He smiled. "Always."

It turned out Brenda was anxious to sign them. Kelsey had never seen the guys so keyed up.

JD walked the whole way to drop off Daniel and Andie with his feet about ten inches off the ground. Kelsey felt the need to grab him periodically and tug him back down to earth.

When they returned to her house, Craig, Alex and TJ were all sitting around the table waiting. Kelsey wasn't surprised. She'd given them all keys, and she actually felt safer than she ever had, knowing that anyone casing the house saw four sturdy men coming and going all hours of the day.

One by one they stood up and hugged her, and thanked her.

"I didn't do it. Maggie knew Brenda. She liked you guys, she said she was bringing Brenda."

They disagreed.

She wound up cooking pancakes. Allie was the only calming influence on them. You knew things were keyed-up when Allie was the calm one.

Her daughter had grown so used to having them around that she thought nothing of asking Craig for his last sausage patty. What was more surprising was that he simply handed it over. "Here you go, squirt."

"I'm not a squirt."

"Yes, you are." He stuffed the sausage in her mouth, making her giggle.

God, the world had simply turned upside down.

After they left, she and Allie played card games and watched far too many children's shows waiting for the phone to ring.

The call didn't come. Four grown men burst through her door at 2:33 p.m. acting like schoolboys. Even Alex was effusive. Only JD stood calmly by, his eyes wide open and bright.

It took a good ten minutes to get the whole story. Brenda had explained the contract, and they all agreed they were probably seven kinds of fool, but signed on the spot. By noon, one of the other partners at the agency had them booked to play that weekend's nearby Cornbread Festival, and they had to have a single ready to sell by then.

"Holy shit!" That was her own voice. She didn't apologize, even when Allie began yelling "holy shit holy shit holy shit."

Craig told her she was right.

The guys even agreed to stay home with Allie while JD and Kelsey walked over to get Daniel and Andie, if they could raid the fridge. There was something in JD's eyes that made her give them free reign.

It took JD a full block to start talking.

"She wants to put us on tour. To cut the album over the next month, then put us on the road. Opening for whoever she can find."

"That's amazing. That's great. But . . ."

"I can't leave Andie for that kind of time."

She smiled. "I've got her. You go. I guess we weren't thinking ahead, but anyone who signs you is going to want you to tour." She shrugged. "So . . ."

"I can't ask you to do that."

She laughed. "I don't recall being asked. I volunteered."

"I can't leave Andie for that long. It might be a month at a time." His hands were in his hair, and she was afraid he was about to bald himself.

"So I said I couldn't tour like that, and I bowed out. I told them to sign without me."

"JD!" Her heart clenched. He'd already given up everything for Andie. Everything but this, and now-

She saw it, "The guys didn't let you. They won't tour without you."

"How did you know?" He stopped dead on the sidewalk, almost causing another late dad to run smack into him.

"Because they're not stupid. You said yourself that you guys sounded good, but when you got TJ in you finally found your synergy."

"But that was TJ."

"*You're* not stupid either JD. You wouldn't tour without Alex or Craig. Why on earth would you think they'd go without you?"

He nodded. "Brenda said she understood about kids. That she'd work something out. Even if we couldn't tour."

Kelsey turned to look at him. "You'll tour. I'll keep Andie."

He started to protest but she cut him off with a shake of her head. They were at the gate.

JD changed the topic. "You don't seem that excited about this." He lowered his head until his gaze was level with hers. As though he might look into her head. "What's going on in there?"

"I'm *very* happy for you. I'm just not as *surprised* as you. It was always just a matter of when. You really are that good."

His shoulders sagged and his head tilted. "You had faith in us all along. Thank you."

He enfolded her into a huge hug, right there at the gate of the school. His arms were a strong band around her shoulders, and she could smell the leather of his bomber jacket as she pressed her face into it. Her arms slipped around him as she reveled in how solid he was.

That was how Daniel and Andie found them.

Kelsey broke the news. "Guess what?"

Two bright faces looked up expectantly. "Wilder is playing at the Cornbread Festival this weekend, and we can all wear our t-shirts. Then they're going on tour."

JD explained to Andie that he was really sad to be leaving all of them, and would she be okay with Kelsey? Andie screeched like a howler monkey at the thought of all those slumber parties.

JD's mouth quirked. "Good to know I'll be missed."

Socking him in the arm playfully, Kelsey felt her own early start to missing him. "You'll call every day."

"Yes, I will."

They were almost to the front door, when JD grabbed her hand and held her back. She watched as the kids were greeted with a little too much enthusiasm by the rest of Wilder, then turned to see what JD was going to say. "I want you all to come to the festival, but I'll get Bethany to go, too, so you don't have your hands too full and so you can stay and see us."

"Sounds like a good plan."

CHAPTER 21

Saturday night came with food and lights and an array of bands. All four guys showed up in their usual jeans and black tees, but this time with cowboy boots. The kids stuffed their faces with cornbread and spent a good part of the afternoon running around the petting zoo and waiting for pony rides.

JD disappeared with the band an hour earlier, and it was about time for them to come on stage. Kelsey was holding Allie on her shoulder, and she suspected her daughter was already asleep.

"Bethany, is Allie out?"

"Like a light. And Andie here's getting fussy. Should I take them home?"

Kelsey nodded. She'd wanted them all to see JD. But anyone who made serious plans past a child's bedtime was a fool, and she knew it. "Yup, take them."

Reaching out, Bethany took a limp Allie from her. She had Daniel and Andie each give Kelsey a kiss before the three of them formed a hand-chain and went off in their matching Wilder shirts.

Suddenly Kelsey was all alone in a huge crowd. She knew the guys who would be going on stage in a few minutes, but that was it. She found a tent pole to lean against, at that moment very tired. She figured JD was running on pure adrenaline by this point. Like the good Dad he was, he was at the soccer game bright and early this morning. He'd spent the afternoon here with the guys, doing sound checks and rehearsal. When he wasn't doing that, he had led the kids through the petting zoo and stayed with them for a late dinner. And, of course, the whole week had been crazy for all of them. They had cut the single Brenda had chosen: the makeup sex song. Of course, Brenda re-titled it, and rightly so, in Kelsey's mind.

The band that was finishing up was very twangy and spangly and heavy on the fiddle and steel guitar. A good-looking middle-aged man asked her to dance, and she surprised herself by saying 'yes'. It was, after all, a two-step, and she knew what to expect.

He was a passable dancer and a passable partner, and Kelsey was flattered to be asked, but grateful when the song ended and the band thanked everyone for coming out.

Kelsey stepped away, then stilled the second she saw the guys come out into the lights. This was the first time she'd ever seen them on a real stage. This was the real deal, with spotlights and rigging and the whole nine yards. She was in awe.

That's how Brenda found her halfway into the first song.

Brenda's grin was pure pride. "The boys told me you were the pretty brunette with pigtails. But I remember you now."

Kelsey almost chafed at the mention of 'boys', but then realized that Brenda had every right to refer to them as 'boys'. "The shirt probably gives me away."

"Not so much." Brenda shook her head, and pointed out a small handful of black tees with Wilder on them.

"Wow."

"I hear it's your work on that shirt."

Kelsey just nodded as Brenda told her they wanted to use it on the front of the single cover and on more posters and t-shirts, and she was going to get paid for it.

The two women watched the entire set, Kelsey mostly with her mouth open. She didn't know if it was because her photos got picked up along with the band, or because the guys were just so good. They got the crowd rocking and yelling and dancing, and buying singles and t-shirts. Whatever Brenda had done was working.

TJ stopped the set for a moment to breathlessly introduce his 'brothers' onstage, and then they played the last song. It was one she hadn't heard before about love right under your nose. She didn't notice until the lights went out that Brenda had disappeared, but that made sense, hers was a small time record label, looking to get bigger. Brenda was everything: agent, manager, producer.

The stage stayed black for a while, and she simply remained where she was. Her legs were tired and her head was tired. The next band didn't cut it.

Just as she was straightening up, she saw JD walk down a flight of steps all but hidden around the side of the stage. He'd changed into a green t-shirt, and she couldn't see his face. Even as he walked down the steps he pulled the cowboy hat a little lower.

Cowboy hat? She didn't think she'd ever seen any of them in a cowboy hat. She was on the verge of laughing until he was right beside her.

"Nice hat."

He looked sideways at where she still leaned against the pole. "Our big debut, and all you can say is 'nice hat'?"

"Yup." She rolled her head to the side to see him under the brim. "You guys were awesome. The crowd loved you. Brenda seems to think you're the next big thing. But the hat—the hat is a shock."

He didn't ask, just took her hand and pulled her out onto the dance floor. "I saw Bethany leaving with the kids just before the set."

Kelsey knew her regret came through in her voice. "Yeah, Allie was already asleep."

"I figured that, since Bethany was carrying her like a sack of potatoes."

He led her once all the way around the floor before she commented. "I'm boggled. First the cowboy hat, then the two-step." Her eyebrows had to be so high as to have left her head entirely. He was much better than Ken had been, too. But maybe that wasn't so much a surprise. JD felt like a perfect fit at everything he did.

"Now, baby, where am I from?"

"Texas." She grinned.

"Any other questions?"

She laughed until he shut her up by spinning her in about three different directions.

CHAPTER 22

J D was astonished at how much fun Halloween was with a
child. He'd pestered Andie no end, making sure her angel
wings were perfect. He'd bought her pristine little white
shoes that Andie begged Kelsey to glue huge bows onto. And
he'd nearly broken down and cried after Andie said she'd
chosen to be an angel to be like her Mommy.

They hopped down the back steps at about 4 p.m. to head
over to Kelsey's. JD was surprised that the sidewalk didn't look
worn where one or the other of them had walked it a thousand
times.

"It's not even dark yet!" Andie was clearly concerned by this
fact, and he wondered if she thought people were going to turn
away a beautiful five-year-old in full costume just because it
was a tad too bright.

"We're going to eat something first. But it will probably still
be fairly light when we go. It's a school night." He hadn't felt so
strongly since his own school days that there ought to be
mandatory movement of the holiday to a weekend.

They rang the bell, which they never did anymore, and

grinned at each other when they heard Allie and Daniel come running.

The door was thrown open by a small Peter Pan, waving a foam sword. Allie/Tinkerbell clapped, jumping up and down in place, and JD was almost glad he'd missed Andie at that age. Although it was entirely possible that Allie was just nuts and not all kids were jumping beans at that stage.

Kelsey called them all back. "You're letting the heat out." She walked over to the table placing a pile of steaming fettucine alfredo in the middle of a spread that already included salad, a bowl of peas, and a pile of garlic bread.

JD blinked, he thought maybe they *ought* to vent the door and let some of the heat out. Kelsey could keep the food steaming just by standing near it. She was in a pink I-Dream-of-Jeannie outfit that showed off a killer figure and an expanse of smooth waist. How was this a woman who'd had two kids? It tumbled out of his mouth before he could take it back.

She flushed a sweet shade of pink, and shook her head. "Only one. Andy brought me Daniel." She ruffled the little boy's hair.

Okay, how was this a woman who had had a child? But this time he kept it in his mouth. "You look great." Then he faltered. "I didn't know I was supposed to come in costume, too."

She waved them all over to the table, "You weren't. Just this afternoon Maggie invited me out to a party tonight, and we wrangled Bethany into babysitting by bribing her with double pay." Her nose crinkled and he wondered if she was casting a spell. "I didn't invite you, because I thought you'd want to spend the evening with Andie."

She was right, of course. Wilder was leaving the next morning to head out on tour. Brenda had poured huge money into having an old tour bus revamped to get them out there.

Some band had gotten too big for their britches and bailed on opening a tour of new artists. Brenda decided it was divine intervention that she was sitting on not one but two new acts, the other a female vocalist with a voice like God's own hurricane. Since neither of them could tour full time together they'd share the tour.

JD agreed about the divine intervention part. He'd also heard Hailey Watkins sing and he agreed with the hurricane analogy. And he did want to spend the evening with Andie. He just also had a driving urge to follow Kelsey to the party and fend off . . . everyone?

The kids wolfed down their dinners without a fuss. Five minutes later they were out in light that was only slightly dimmer than full sun, and hitting the neighbors up for candy. He and Kelsey hung back at the sidewalk, letting the kids go ring doorbells and yell 'trick or treat'.

After the second time a man had looked up from the kids to see Kelsey standing there in full Jeannie gear and asked her if she needed some candy, too, Kelsey's arms crept around her waist. The kids were already hopping and skipping their way to the next house, so he leaned in close and whispered in her ear. "Why did you wear it, if you're uncomfortable in it?"

Her head turned when she spoke to him and he nearly missed what she was saying, he'd caught the scent of her shampoo and some wild soap or perfume, and his body reacted without much decision from his brain.

"—the only thing left in my size. It's Halloween and the stores are cleaned out."

He nodded. He had no stake on her, and he knew it. Every time he'd thought he might have caught some interest from her, something else came along and made him think he was wrong. Like now, here she was walking down the street in a sheer top and gauze harem pants that he could see her legs through. There was some trick of the fabric that no matter how hard you looked you couldn't see her ass. And he was trying. He was certain everyone else was going to try, too.

She had to see she had the perfect opportunity to let him know if she was interested.

And she didn't.

He took a deep breath. She deserved to be happy. Tonight was as great a time as any for her to meet someone. He grabbed her wrists as they snaked across her bare belly again, and pulled them to her side. "Put your arms down, Kelse. If you've got it, flaunt it."

The tour bus seemed so cool when it pulled up on the busy street in front of the condo. The driver was making the inaugural pick-up. Brenda warned them that this wasn't going to happen again, from now on they'd have to get their own butts to the bus on time. His had been the last stop, and TJ, Alex and Craig were all gathered at the front window waving to him. Then they all spilled out onto the sidewalk to admire the side of the bus.

The Wilder logo was under the front windows, and on the back half of the bus was that same photo Kelsey had doctored of the four of them. She and Allie had come out to see him off and he carried Allie around showing it all off.

When he got back around to the sidewalk, Kelsey was hugging each of the guys in turn, and JD got himself in last, twirling her around and enjoying the feel of her in his arms far more than he ought to.

He promised to call every day, and then the guys were all on the bus, whooping it up and opening beers. Then they hit the road for real. They played Memphis that night, at a small amphitheater that filled as they played. Amped up, they'd happily boarded the bus before the rest of the acts were done and headed off for Jefferson City, Missouri. They played some county fair then played Kansas City with the rest of the tour that night.

They learned real fast how to sleep on the bus. The thing actually had bedrooms for each of them—though 'bedroom' was stretching it. There were four three-and-a-half-by-eight-foot cubbies. The upside was that they came with soundproof walls and sliding doors. The room kept out most noise. If only it was also motion-proof.

The beds folded up into the wall. When it was down, it was comfortable enough, once you got past the fact that it was suspended by metal wires bracing from the outer corners to the wall. After the first night, when it didn't drop him despite all the bouncing, JD got to trusting it.

On top of everything, adding to the surreal quality of the whole trip, Kelsey was no longer their only groupie. Hot chicks were swarming the stage and hanging out afterwards waiting for them. JD figured that most of them were after anyone who walked by. In his head, he heard Kelsey's voice telling his mother that 'musicians are sexy as hell.'

He'd always thought it was the money and the fame that made them attractive, but Kelsey must be right. Wilder sure wasn't famous, and he didn't see anywhere near as much money here as he had as a stock analyst. When they came off stage they were tired and sweaty, yet there were the girls.

And the guys indulged. Craig went through condoms faster than water bottles—and managed that even within the ground rules that only serious attachments got onto the tour bus. Serious, like "your wife" serious. Craig had asked for that rule, seeing early on that 'women were nucking futs' as he put it.

JD had never entertained the thought that he'd be 'swamped' in women. Then, in Vegas, they got panties thrown on stage, and it was all JD could do to not stop the music and ask what the hell was going on. They sold their single by the fistful, so apparently *someone* was actually listening to the music. But he felt he'd stepped into the twilight zone, and he desperately wanted to go home.

That feeling got even worse, when the beat behind him stopped for a moment, and he turned to find Alex unwrapping something red and lacy from one drum stick. Alex then motioned to the girl who had thrown the panties to wait on the side of the stage. She happily obliged and jumped up and down like Allie for the remainder of the set.

When they finished, to whoops and cat-calls, Alex ran off and gathered the girl into a lip-lock the likes of which JD didn't think he'd ever seen. Alex and the pretty brunette then disappeared.

In fact, JD was the only one on the bus when the call came later that night. Alex said he would fly in to Phoenix in the morning to meet up with them. JD scrubbed his hand over his face, and called Kelsey.

"Wow, it's late." Her voice was an anchor in what was becoming a crazy storm.

"I'm sorry, I didn't mean to wake you."

"You didn't. I was up."

She was wondering what was going on with him, he could hear it in her voice. He'd already called earlier today and talked to the kids after school until he'd lost the signal.

"We just played a casino. It was crazy."

"Where are you?"

She knew he was in Vegas, and he knew she wanted the specifics. "I'm standing in the parking lot behind Harrah's. I can't get back on the bus; I can't deal with that. We've been given another," he looked at his watch, "two hours to go drinking and gambling. And whoring."

"So why are you standing in the heat in the parking lot?"

"It's not that hot."

She waited him out and he gave in. "I'm a Dad. I make peanut butter and jelly sandwiches in the morning. I pack juice boxes in my daughter's lunch. I walk to kindergarten twice a day. The other guys, they're used to this. Craig and Alex are out there partying. I just can't handle this touring anymore. . ."

"You have to do it." Her tone of her voice was soothing, but the steel he heard under it was not.

"I don't want to let the guys down, but I don't really know that I can."

"Because this is what you wanted. You love being out on stage. It shows in your eyes, and in the way you hold yourself. You may not like this part of it, but you do like some of it. Enjoy that part. Besides, if you stop now what are you going to do? Be a stock analyst again?"

He cringed.

"This is the gateway to what you really want to do." She lowered her voice as deep as she could. "This, too, shall pass." She laughed. "So you ought to enjoy it while you have it."

"Thank you." He breathed out.

"So get your butt out there and drink and gamble, while you can. We're fine here. We miss you, but we're doing all right."

He smiled. "I'm so proud of you, too." She'd said earlier that she had booked two new clients for family portraits, which she was making her mark by doing around town, rather than in a studio. He'd felt guilty about that. She didn't have a studio because Wilder had her garage. But Kelsey was one of those people who made lemonade.

There was a silence over the line, and while it didn't seem to bother either of them, JD signed off and went off to do what she had told him. Tucking his cell phone into his pocket, he walked in through the grand double doors to Harrah's.

After wandering around the outer loop, following the wildly patterned carpet trail, for about half the casino, he spotted the blackjack tables. He hadn't done this in forever. He spent another ten minutes finding the cheapest table that he could, thinking back to when he'd been here for meetings, and testosterone demanded that he play hundred dollar minimums.

He pulled out a couple of twenties. Seven hands later he'd doubled his money, and downed three of the drinks that just kept coming, when a tart blonde thing in something spandex sat down beside him.

Her hand touched his arm in a way that was almost possessive, and she smiled an invitation, "You're from that band that played tonight, aren't you?"

CHAPTER 23

H e sat with his head in his hands, elbows perched on spread knees while the whole place jostled and bounced with every little dent in the road, and JD felt his stomach turn over. He'd barely made the bus.

If TJ hadn't called when he did, missing the bus would have been the least of what was making him sick. He'd like to attribute it to the rum and cokes; he wasn't sure how many he'd had. All he knew was that there was about a hundred dollars in Harrah's chips in his pocket and Harrah's was getting smaller in the distance with each passing second.

TJ's call had found him in the tart blonde thing's room, about to do something he hadn't thought through at all.

His stomach rolled again.

TJ was sitting on the floor, cross-legged in front of him. "It sounded like I interrupted something."

"You almost did."

Craig came out of the plumbed closet that was referred to as a 'bathroom' only because of the lack of more appropriate terminology. "Dude." He shook his head at JD as though he'd caught his band mate stealing.

"What!?" JD lifted his head too fast, but the liquor was going to swirl in his stomach regardless of what he did. "You guys have slept with every unattached female from here to Memphis."

Craig scratched his head and lit up a wicked grin, "They weren't all unattached."

TJ laughed at that, and JD felt the world spin as the bus hit a pothole, or maybe another car.

Still he ranted. "God! Alex didn't even make the bus. He followed some chick who threw her lace thong on stage. Who are you to judge me? You both have fucked your way across America."

TJ's voice was calm. He didn't respond with the emotion that JD had laid out there. "And you haven't."

The entire world came to a stop around him. His brain quit functioning, and his cells stilled.

Somewhere in the fog he heard TJ and Craig's conversation, Craig asking, "Is he finally going to admit—"

"Give him a minute, sometimes he's a little slow."

"Slow!? He should be institutionalized if he's really this slow."

"Just about some things."

JD couldn't participate, he was too busy watching all his carefully constructed denial crumble around him. He took the beating. "Oh, shit."

"There you have it!" TJ stood up, removing himself from JD's direct line of sight. But JD didn't raise his head, it was enough to watch Craig and TJ's feet as they linked arms and square-danced in front of him.

That only lasted a few turns, before Craig got down in front of his face. "You'll feel better when you say it."

JD didn't agree. His mouth didn't work yet. He was still trying to keep breathing, and wondering how he could have lied to himself all this time.

TJ joined in. "Come on, say it."

His chest didn't expand all the way, but the lack of oxygen was almost welcome. He tried to work his mouth. Nothing came.

TJ resumed his perch on the floor. "You gotta say it."

He finally found his voice. "I'm in love with her."

Craig let up a war whoop, startling the driver, who luckily only swerved a little. "There now, don't you feel better?"

"No, I really don't." JD shook his head. "You guys knew?"

"Yup." Craig smiled again, "Everyone else always figures it out first."

His heart knotted in his chest, dread spreading to all corners of him as a horrible thought took hold. "Does Kelsey know?"

"I don't think so." TJ patted his shoulder.

That was all he could process in one night. Placing his palms against his knees he pushed himself upright, "I'm going to bed."

"Sweet dreams!" Craig called to his retreating back, and JD heard them talking about him again as he shimmied his way down the narrow 'hall' to his room.

"Will he be easier to live with now?"

TJ answered. "Probably not."

JD ignored them and slid his 'door' open. Carefully he unfolded the bed, and climbed onto it before sliding the door closed. He had a sneaking suspicion that the bus had housed a female band before them. He was just too big to fit most of it.

His thoughts swarmed and things emerged from the jumble. He hadn't realized it until now, but he'd never truly been in love before. What a shame that this one was going to get wasted.

He thought of her in his kitchen, telling his mother in the sweetest voice where to stick it. For a moment he wondered what she would have done if he'd kissed her then, like he'd wanted to. He'd almost gone in for the real thing, and had chickened out, instead kissing her forehead.

He thought of sitting at the dining room table, and eating

dinner, talking with the kids about their day at school, but this time knowing that she loved him back. That after the kids were in bed, they'd go off to *their* room. That she'd let him make love to her. That she'd want him to.

He squelched the thought.

He heard strains of the Dixie Chicks coming from the front common area. Apparently the rooms weren't really soundproof. "Taking the Long Way" drifted back to him, and spoke to him on too many levels.

He fought for sleep and found it. But he woke twice in a hot sweat only to find that his hands were not tangled in her hair and her mouth and naked body were not pressed against his.

The third time he woke it was because the bus stopped. A loud roar, like a train bearing down on him, rattled the whole thing, and JD thought that might be a fitting end for him.

He pushed the sliding black-out shade from the window just a touch, but it was still enough for the glare to blind him. Daylight. His night was over.

He found jeans and haphazardly stepped into them. Figuring he looked about like he felt, he thought maybe the others would know to stay away.

There were voices in the main room. Foolishly, he walked toward them.

TJ and Craig were eating frosted flakes around the table they'd folded down. The bus shook again and JD realized they were at the airport. Then the driver opened the doors and Alex walked on followed by the girl from Vegas.

TJ didn't acknowledge her. "Hey, Alex, what's JD's problem?"

Alex frowned, "What? That he's in love with Kelsey?"

"See?" TJ looked at him even as he shoved in another bite of frosted flakes.

"Thank you." JD was pissed that his unrequited love life was bigger news than the fact that Alex had brought the girl from Vegas onto the tour bus.

Craig, at least, had the decency to point that out. "We agreed, 'wives only'."

Alex grinned like a maniac. "I know. It's all taken care of." He held up his left hand, still interlocked with the girl's. Both were sporting thick gold bands, hers with a sizeable diamond square in the center. "I want you all to meet Bridget."

"Holy shit!"

JD wasn't sure who said it. But the world had just gone to hell.

They went back to Nashville by way of Arkansas. Bridget became a fixture on the bus, and Alex was clearly besotted. JD didn't want to like her but it was hard not to. She said she'd never done anything like that before, and she'd lived in Vegas all her life. Even TJ asked, "Does that mean she's never thrown her panties on stage before or that she's never gone and married a musician on the spur of the moment before?"

No one had an answer.

JD called the house at 6 p.m. The guys were on his case like white on rice, and if they had their way, he'd dial and say, "Good evening, good to hear your voice. Were you aware that I'm in love with you?"

Luckily, the driver was off smoking, and right now JD was grateful for the man's bad habits. Ben always had his ears open. He probably knew about Kelsey before last night, too.

He sucked in a breath each time he heard a click on the line. But it was just the cell phone crossing the distance. The message came on in Allie and Daniel's voices, and at least that made him smile. He listened to the whole thing, but didn't leave a message. He went back to his speed dial and held down the next number, it went to her cell phone.

That, in and of itself, was telling. Even TJ occupied only one speed dial button.

She answered on the third ring. "JD!"

"Hi." He froze, his tongue stuck to the roof of his mouth. His brain had no idea what to say to her. But Kelsey picked up the thread.

"Ignore the background noise, remember Saturday's soccer game got rained out? Well, the make-up game is tonight. Our kids are kicking butt."

A cheer went up in the background, and he smiled.

She spoke to someone next to her, and then her voice gained clarity, "Where are you?"

"Little Rock. On the bus, in a gravel parking lot behind an arena."

"A whole arena? That's great."

"Yeah, we're booked as fill-in's tonight."

"Where are you tomorrow?"

"I don't begin to know. I miss you so much."

"We miss you, too." Her tone was wistful, but he'd wanted *I miss you, too.*

Another cheer swelled in the background, this time Kelsey joined in, before apologizing profusely for screaming in his ear.

"It's okay. It's just good to hear your voice." He stretched his jaw, figuring that he'd be deaf by thirty-five between that yell and the amps every night.

"I'd put the kids on, but Allie won't sit still and Andie and Daniel are out playing."

"That's okay, just give them each a kiss for me, please. Goodnight." *And one for you, too.* Again, he didn't say it.

Holding the phone down in front of himself he clicked the call off. He'd made it through round one. How many more rounds he had to go, he didn't know.

He walked across the gravel and in through the back door of the theater. Hands were everywhere, running wires, setting up drums, adjusting lights. In just a few hours the lights would be turned down and people would be finding seats and buying beer. The lights wouldn't even go dark before Wilder came out. And no one knew who the opening act was.

Except Kelsey. And she was in Nashville.

He woke up in time to beat everyone else to the front of the bus. He was dog tired, but he had reason to be awake. He was watching the flatlands of west Tennessee start to buckle and roll. On the east side of the state, the land would give rise to the Smokies, but he wouldn't go that far.

Nashville was only about an hour away. A scene from a movie came to mind of a young couple standing on a Nashville roof top and yelling at the top of their lungs, "Look out music city, 'cause I'm here now and I ain't never goin' back!"

He'd wanted to do that when he arrived. But he'd been so wired from the drive from Texas. And he wanted to find a place to live. He had put it off, thinking there'd be another day. But he still hadn't yelled from the rooftop, and here he was, pulling into town, on his tour bus, with his face plastered three feet high on the side.

He'd been looking at that picture every time he'd stepped off the bus these past few days. In it his hair had fallen in his face. His head was turned, and he looked back at the camera cautiously. He'd wanted to find a tiny reflection of the camera and Kelsey there, but he couldn't. He wondered if that was what she saw when she saw him—the old shirts, and the young rebel expression.

They passed the road sign saying 'Nashville 30mi', and he hauled himself off the 'couch' and went down the hall rattling doors. "Time to get up and pack, we're almost there."

Craig liked to grumble, but he was a talented songwriter and a brilliant man. And he would never let it be said that he wasn't sharp enough to be the first one in line for the shower. One by one, they came out front as they got closer to home.

Familiar restaurants rolled by. People on the street ignored them, except for a little girl in a stroller who waved at the bus. Ben took them through the streets in the same order he had before. That meant TJ and Craig were the first ones off.

TJ gave him a hug. "Welcome to the big time, brother."

JD hugged him back, thinking that the little kid he had tormented was grown. "Thanks TJ."

"Thanks go both ways, big brother." He and Craig each hopped the last step down to the ground in front of the apartment complex. Some girl walking out saw the tour bus and soft cased guitars slung across their backs and gave them the full eye up and down, followed by an impressed smile.

Get used to it, little brother, he thought.

Alex and Bridget were next.

She hugged JD tightly and Alex slung both their bags over his shoulder as he descended the stairs. He saluted with his drumsticks and a smile. JD wondered how Alex was going to explain his new bride.

Last one on, he dialed Kelsey.

She squealed and didn't bother with 'hello'. "Where are you!?"

"Two blocks away."

"I'll be right there!" The line went silent.

JD slipped into his jacket and wearily dragged his guitar to where it fit casually across his back. Holding onto the bars behind Ben, he waited on his feet.

He saw her standing on the corner, waving as the bus neared. Of course, she couldn't miss it if she tried. The trim was painted the same brown-to-orange and vivid midnight she had picked out.

Even before they got near the curb, JD had his duffel in

hand. He looked for the kids, but since it was ten in the morning, he wasn't surprised not to see them. For a moment he was glad to save the jumping and excitement for later, glad that it was just Kelsey now, as weariness settled even further into his bones.

As the bus ever so slowly pulled to a stop, Ben flipped a switch and the doors opened, letting in a gust of cold air and the huge smile on her face.

JD didn't know how he got to the ground, but his feet were planted and the duffel was dropped and Kelsey was in his arms before he consciously thought about it.

As she slipped her arms under his jacket, he rested his cheek against her head, oblivious to the cold, aware only of her in his arms, holding him as tightly as he held her. He breathed in, letting the smells of her soak in, and the feel of her alter everything within him.

It was the first time that he'd touched her since he'd known. He wanted to stay here on this curb, like this, for however long he could. But she stepped back, letting the wind in between them. She grabbed his hand and reached down to get the duffel bag for him.

He was laughing even before she attempted to stand upright with the bag in her hand. She gave another good tug and only got the front end of it up. "Lord, what's in there?"

"Everything." He brushed her fingers away from the handle, without letting go of the hand she held, and hefted the bag. He liked that he could lift it when she couldn't, even if it was a little caveman of him.

The wind came at them as she led him back to her place, but he didn't care as long as their fingers were intertwined. She tugged him along, and he went more than willingly, willing to simply enjoy the feel of her skin for as long as she gave it.

Her voice carried on the wind, back to where he trailed her. "You look . . . tired . . . ?"

So much more. But he couldn't say it.

Turning around, she faced him, seemingly unconcerned that he refused to let her hand go. "What do you need? Food? Water? Sleep?"

"D, all of the above."

"All right." She laughed at him, "What do you want? We can get a steak, or Mexican, we can go to-"

"No!" He cut her off, planted his feet and refused to go another inch. "No restaurants, *no* fast food, and no wheels. What I wouldn't give for a peanut butter and jelly sandwich."

She tugged at him. "I have that. I also have some leftover lasagna in the freezer. It doesn't go quite as fast without you around. Would you like that?"

It sounded like heaven, and he didn't respond with anything other than a sigh.

She finally unclasped her fingers from his to open the front door, and ushered him inside in front of her. As he passed by, she lifted the guitar from his back and carefully propped it inside the front door. He let his duffel thud to the floor just beyond the front entryway, happy in the knowledge that he understood her well enough to know it wouldn't matter.

She ushered him to the table, and offered him tea, which he took. "I'm sorry I don't have a beer or anything." She wrinkled her nose.

"Please." He downed half the iced tea in one gulp, "We had a beer or two after every show. That, combined with the really bad eating habits we had, was enough to make me quit. Tea is perfect." He liked her fussing over him. She may not feel the way he did, but she cared, and he'd take what he could get.

"The lasagna won't be ready for another hour. I have to thaw it, then heat it up." Her head tilted to the side. "You want to go lie down, and I'll get you when it's ready?"

Nodding, he stood up and stretched, tall iced tea glass in hand. She took it from him and put it in the sink before following him down the hall. He turned toward the office, where every light was on, and photos adorned the walls.

His eyes trailed from one to another. She must have hung photos from the jobs she'd done while he was gone. He didn't recognize all the faces, but he recognized her hand in all of them. Another photo was open on the computer screen and in the process of having some digital altering done. There was a box around a shadow, but he didn't know what it was for. He realized he had interrupted her work-

"Not in here," Her voice came from right behind him and he turned to look at her. She pointed down the hall to her room. "I have to work. Take my room."

"Are you sure?"

"Yup."

He was shocked how disappointed he was when she turned to go to the other half of the house, presumably to start the lasagna she had promised.

Alone, he wandered through the partially open door, into the sunny room with the red comforter and thought he'd never seen anything so inviting in his life. Every last drop of energy in him died and refused to reignite.

He toed off his shoes, and peeled his shirt, leaving it in a puddle on the stuffed chair. It looked a bit out of place there, too masculine and messy for the French country print of the upholstery.

He peeled back the covers that were still mussed from this morning. As neat as she was otherwise, the woman couldn't seem to make a bed. He crawled in.

His last thought was silent behind his moan. Oh God, the whole bed smelled like her.

CHAPTER 24

She *did* have to work. But that didn't mean she'd had to give him her bed, did it?

Kelsey clicked the mouse and made up for the failings of the sun. Minus her print costs, the new work would leave her with a decent chunk of change.

Not like when she'd closed that house in DC, but enough. Half went into her regular account and the other half went into savings. Things were still tight, but she was getting along okay.

The timer dinged at her, nearly startling her out of her seat. Time to pull the lasagna out of the oven. Happily ignoring what else the timer signified, she breathed in the smells of the kitchen and pulled open the oven door.

She set the dish on the stove top to let it cool, and the cheese on top gave off the slightest of sizzles as it gave up a couple hundred degrees of heat. Lasagna always took a while to cool.

It was now unavoidable. Kelsey turned toward her bedroom, reminding herself that it was all okay. She'd seen the man in his boxer briefs, so this couldn't be that bad. Or could it?

How was she going to react to seeing him in her bed?

With the shades pulled, it meant she could only make out the edges of him under her covers. Well, halfway under, and whether or not he was clothed was anybody's guess. The part she could see certainly wasn't.

She told herself she wasn't admiring him, just letting her eyes adjust. He was lean and muscular, and looked stable and wild all at the same time, even with his eyes closed and his mouth just a little open. She fought the urge to grab her camera, and decided she couldn't put it off any longer.

Sitting on the side of the bed, she reached out one tentative hand to touch his skin and shook him. "JD, the lasagna's ready. Time to wake up."

"Hmmmm?" He rolled over onto his back, and for just a moment, when his eyes first opened she wasn't sure what she saw in them. But it didn't matter. Who knew where he was when he first woke up?

She pulled her hand back, and tried to ignore the bared chest he'd exposed to her. "Are you still hungry?"

"Mmmmm hmmmm."

He blinked a few more times and closed his eyes as he used his arms to push himself almost to sitting. She watched with a bizarre fascination as the covers fell back and revealed . . . jeans.

That was probably a good thing. Who knows what would have happened if she had jumped him? Not for the first time, she wished he'd been born five to ten years earlier. But wishes didn't change things, and she was a master at accepting what she had, and making the most of it. She would simply do the same now.

Pushing off the bed, Kelsey walked out of the room, calling back over her shoulder, "Meet me in the dining room when you're ready. I'll be the one with the steaming plate of pasta."

"Mmmmmm."

Shaking her head as though that might stop the images

burning into her long term memory, she went about being domestic. She'd been everybody's mother since Andy was three-ish and first diagnosed. Her own mother didn't handle it well, and so Kelsey simply took over.

Grabbing two plates and two glasses and two forks, she helped herself to a square of the lasagna. She hadn't planned to eat this early, but she was hungry now that she smelled it. Pouring herself ice water, she sat down and waited.

She was just wondering if he'd fallen back asleep when he walked out, still shirtless, blinking those amazing eyes. Thankfully, he reached into his duffel bag and pulled out a clean shirt before heading any closer to the table. She didn't think she'd eat all that well if he insisted on sitting down to lunch that way.

He tugged it over his head as he went by, and a flash of skin at his waist was close enough for her to reach out and trace her fingers along. But she didn't. Kelsey blew on the bite she had carefully cut, and waited for him.

When he sat down across from her he looked up. "Thank you."

"For what?"

"Feeding me. Letting me sleep. Not jumping down my throat wanting all the details."

She shrugged. That's what friends were for. But she didn't say it. Instead she raised her glass to him. "Here's to Wilder's first ever tour."

He clinked his glass against hers, even though his expression was tentative. "Many happy returns." He let out a sigh. "I can't wait to get back to normal."

"Yeah, aren't you guys going to start cutting your album tomorrow?"

He rubbed his hands over his face. "I know, be careful what you wish for."

"So tell me about it."

He lifted a forkful of pasta to his mouth and started in, "There were groupies. Everywhere. And, I love women as much as the next man, but as a species . . ." He shook his head, "I don't want to offend you, but women in general are nucking futs."

She laughed at him. "But men are better?"

"Oh, God, no. Case in point, Alex."

She raised her brows, and chewed a bite of lasagna.

"Remember I said he stayed in Vegas with that girl? Well, I didn't tell you the whole thing, I wanted to tell you in person, because it's crazy."

Kelsey waited for a Fatal Attraction story, but wasn't prepared for what she heard.

"He showed up at the Phoenix Airport the next morning married to her. Her name is Bridget and he just told his parents about her something like an hour ago."

"Did she come back with you?"

"Yes." He was still shaking his head over that one, apparently thinking much the same as she did about Alex. "She's really very likable."

"But he just met her at the concert and then ran off and married her that night?"

"Yeah." He stood to help himself to another serving of lasagna, the first had disappeared a few sentences earlier.

When he returned, she shrugged, "Well, you know what they say—still waters run deep."

JD laughed like she'd just told the best joke in the world, and Kelsey had to blink a few times. Finally, he got it together enough to speak. "She's hot. And she threw her red lace thong right onto one of his drumsticks. I think that's about as shallow as water can run."

Kelsey conceded her point, and silently admitted how happy she was to have him back.

The kids climbed him like a jungle gym when they came to the gate and saw JD there. Daniel made sure he was staying for dinner, and JD looked at her for answers.

"Of course, you're invited."

"I don't want to impose."

Andie laughed, "It's not a problem, they love having us!"

Kelsey had to laugh, too. How many times had she told JD exactly that?

They all trooped the two blocks to Allie's daycare, where she gave a shrill yell and launched herself into his arms. JD made it worth her while by scooping her up in a bear hug that almost crushed her.

Kelsey was pretty certain that her kids didn't understand that JD wasn't theirs.

It was Sunday morning when Kelsey was getting ready for church that she realized that it had been four days since JD returned home, and this was the first outing she would take her kids on by herself.

She was glad to have only Daniel and Allie with her. She needed the peace of the service, and the moments by herself while the kids were in their Sunday school classes.

The sermon drifted in one ear and out the other. It wasn't all that interesting, and she knew it would have a point—they always did—but she didn't feel like waiting around for it. Instead her thoughts turned to wishes. Keen ideas of JD sleeping in her bed the first day he'd been back. He'd only been there an hour, but she swore she could still smell him. That tormented her on a nightly basis.

She shook herself out of it in time to hear the moral. It was about how God tests us, in sometimes unusual ways. *Amen to that*, Kelsey thought.

She stayed and talked to the other parishioners, many of

whom had noticed she was missing last week. She'd have to ask JD if it was okay to bring his daughter to church with them when she had her.

They went and fed the ducks at the pond, which they did most weeks. The ducks seemed to recognize them, although Kelsey struggled with feeling a little incomplete. Andie had been here with them last week, not to church, but to the duck pond. For a brief moment she catalogued how different her life would be right now without JD and Andie in it. The sheer number of things that were affected was scary. There were so many things she would miss if JD were to stop speaking to her, or feel uncomfortable.

That alone was impetus to keep her feelings to herself. If JD made any moves, she'd gladly return them, but that was a big *if*. And she didn't see it coming on the horizon.

Monday morning the front door opened at 7:30 and Kelsey was alarmed that it felt like the sun shone just a little brighter with JD and Andie in the room. She was way too attached, and she had no way to extricate herself. She knew she would have to ride it out.

After they'd dropped the kids off, JD took her out for breakfast before going in to the recording studio for the day. Brenda called her and asked her to do the photos for the album cover. The guys had met with her usual photographer, and Brenda didn't like anything he'd given her. Kelsey was pleased to hear the woman say it didn't compare to what she'd captured. Of course, the caveat was that she knew these guys by heart, so it wouldn't translate into any other work. *But hey, you don't look gift horses in the mouth.*

The guys would be home until the day after Thanksgiving, and Kelsey had two free mornings of their time to shoot everything she needed. She had a JD moment right in front of him, "There's not enough time to really plan this out! I just-"

"I understand exactly how you feel." He gave her a sad smile across the dinner table that night. "But we'll give you our best. Hell, Craig even trusts you, and that's rare."

"Daddy, don't say 'hell'." Andie speared another broccoli and shoved the whole thing into her mouth. Kelsey debated whether or not to correct a child who was eating her vegetables.

"You're right, baby." And JD just let the slip go by. "So I wanted to have Thanksgiving at my place."

"You're going to make a turkey?" Kelsey speared her own broccoli and twirled it on her fork. She hoped she looked like she was eating it, but her kids weren't that stupid.

"Is that disdain I hear?" JD shot her a look of half-hearted offense.

"Just surprise."

"So you'll help me?"

That made her bust out laughing. It was good to know they were invited. She was getting so accustomed to her life not just being about her and her kids. That had to be a good thing, right? "Of course. Who are you inviting?"

"Not you guys."

"What?!" Daniel had apparently been paying attention. "We don't get to come?"

JD smiled at him. "Yes, you do. You don't get an official invite, because you don't need one." His gaze shifted from Daniel to looking at her. "You're family."

That satisfied Daniel, who went back to pestering Allie and Andie.

Kelsey couldn't help what she felt inside. "Thank you." She beamed, she knew it.

"It's true." He shrugged it away, but he could afford to. Kelsey, on the other hand, had no other family than those at her dinner table.

JD didn't let her get too introspective. "I'm inviting TJ and Craig, and Alex and Bridget, although I don't think they'll come.

I suspect they're having Thanksgiving with his family. That should be plenty."

"Sounds like." She hoped Alex and Bridget would come, she hadn't even met the girl yet, and Thanksgiving was only a week away. "Are we doing traditional? Potluck? What?"

"Potluck is scary with TJ and Craig, maybe we could make them bring rolls or something."

She smiled, "Can they make the little yams with the marshmallows?"

Shaking his head, JD speared a slice of ham, "No way, if TJ makes it, all three kids will be diabetic before the end of the night. If I make Turkey and Ham and Pies, can you bring veggies?"

"Of course, do you need me over there to help watch the turkey?"

JD's plate cleared during the conversation. As was usual with him, it was as though a wind had simply swept it away, but he'd eaten the whole thing. Thanksgiving with three, if not all four, guys was going to mean a lot of food.

JD stood at the counter helping himself to another serving, just like family. "When does the turkey go in?"

"Depends on when you want to eat and how big the turkey is."

The look he gave her said he had no idea about either, so she ball-parked if for him. "Between seven and ten."

"A.M.?"

She nodded, "A.M. I'll be there."

"Thank you."

"That means the kids will be running around your house all day."

He just shrugged, "That's what Thanksgiving is." He sat back down with another heaping plate, and it was all Kelsey could do to keep her eyes in her head. Would she ever get used to the amount of food the man consumed? His voice distracted her, "What's stupid is that's exactly what my mother wants: a house full of grandkids on holidays. She could come and have that, but she's so stuck on having it be just so, that she's missing the whole thing."

CHAPTER 25

Unfortunately, the days Brenda gave Kelsey to get the photos were back to back. The first morning was a total waste. It was a waste of film, time, and effort. JD was the only one who tried, and as good-looking as he was, he was a terrible model.

She couldn't capture the way his smile lit him up because he was working so damn hard at it. Craig was stiff, and TJ and Alex were like puppies. She was sorely tempted to roll up a newspaper and whack them with it.

After lunch at a nearby burger joint, she tried getting a neat shot at the river. Of course, it turned out Alex was afraid of bridges—not heights, just bridges. She'd never heard of anything so nuts.

Next, she suggested a hike. Anything to get them moving naturally.

"Hiking?" That was Alex.

"Are you afraid of hiking?" She hadn't meant to be so harsh.

"Fine!" They went, bewildered, while Kelsey followed, camera in hand.

Eventually, the guys wandered back to a small clearing, and

she showed herself, telling them to set up and play. They did, doing an oddly updated version of the old 'King of the Road'. She wandered around taking photos from all angles. There was hope for those photos. It sure couldn't be worse than this morning.

She made JD drive her while Craig, TJ, and Alex followed in Craig's car. With a wild flourish that nearly made JD wreck, she got him to pull into the first of two open spots on the side of the street. Craig barely managed to tuck in haphazardly behind them, before getting out and asking, "What the fuck was that?"

"Abbey Road." She pointed to the cross walk down the street.

"It's been done." He pointed out.

"Because it's good." She shot back. After five tries, while they'd been bickering and complaining about the chill, she'd enlisted a swarm of high-school girls who'd just gotten dropped off at a nearby bus stop. They were in knee socks, white shirts, and navy blue skirts. She couldn't have planned it better.

"Walk again!" She yelled down the block, her camera aimed to take the photo.

About forty shrieking teenagers went chasing down the street after the guys, who broke form, looked scared as shit, and ran. Kelsey almost laughed too hard to get the shots, but she got all of them. Until Craig spotted her laughing and pointed her out to the guys, who then turned and charged her.

She warred between fleeing and getting the shot. But, deciding bravery was a necessity, she planted her feet and snapped off what she could before they stormed her, JD swooping her up and slinging her over his shoulder. The girls came up right behind them.

"You did a great job, ladies!" Then she looked down at the guys from her perch above JD's shoulder. He held on tight to her, his arms wrapped around her legs. "Would you gentlemen care to give these nice young ladies some autographs?"

She was drowned out by questions from the girls. "What's

the name of your band?" "Where did you go on tour?" "What's the name of your next single?"

She snapped shots from up high until JD realized he couldn't balance her and sign autographs. It was almost a full thirty minutes before the girls had gotten all the autographs they wanted. They were all excited about maybe appearing in the album photos. When the last one left, the guys turned on her, but it was JD who spoke. "There's going to be payback."

She stepped back. "Payback? I just made you a ton of new fans!"

"Payback." It was just a statement, but he moved too fast for her to get out of the way, and he'd slung her over his shoulder again, camera and all.

From hanging upside down she complained. "You know the only thing I can get a photo of from up here is your ass."

"Feel free." He called over his shoulder. "Guys, I think we'll see you tomorrow." And she saw the sidewalk rotate and slip past as he walked off with her.

She tried hollering out, "Tomorrow, nine o'clock!"

"Yeah, yeah." They hollered back at her. She was pretty sure TJ waved. She was too far away to yell before she finally gave up, and sank down.

When he set her on her feet without warning, all the blood rushed the wrong way and she swayed just a moment until she felt the car behind her and JD's hands through her jacket. With a deep breath, the world righted itself, except for the part where JD was practically in her face. "What was that Kelsey? School girls?"

She shrugged, "I'm sure some of them were almost legal." She didn't know where that had come from, and she tried to ignore that she had mistakenly steered the conversation that way.

He was looking right at her, into her, "I don't want a school girl, Kelse."

Her breathing stopped, all of her braced. He looked like he might kiss her. So she panicked. Without thought, she started jabbering. "The pictures are great though!" She pulled the camera up in between them, pushing buttons until she had the slide show on the screen.

They were great photos, but she wasn't sure what she'd just done.

～

The second day, they worked all day. For lunch, she gathered them in a booth in an old-time restaurant with a mini-jukebox at the table, then asked them how they got started together.

Pulling up a chair, she snapped more photos to add to the heaping pile she already had. She ignored her own food as it grew colder, fascinated by the story, and the view she had of it.

JD pointed across the table. "Craig and Alex were in another band. What were you guys called?"

"Roadrage." Alex had the grace to look a little sheepish.

Putting in her own two cents, Kelsey stayed behind the camera. "What happened to that band?"

"Band fight." Craig supplied around a bite of burger. "There were songs about murdering people, and . . ."

JD picked up the thread of the story again. "I was here, songwriting, and looking for a band. I was actually walking down the street with my guitar in my hand, as though someone might stop me and ask me to play." He shook his head. "I'd been here a year, and played the Bluebird, thinking I'd made it. Then I played again, and again, and got a card from a distributor, looking for new writers. Mostly I got my music 'on file' and not very often picked up."

"We literally ran into each other." Alex laughed. "Craig and I were storming out of the studio. We packed everything we could and bolted."

"Smack into JD." Craig grinned, "This sweet little country boy from Texas."

JD barely stopped his eyes from rolling, "They were so punk, Craig had a bleached Mohawk."

"Turned out we all lived in the same building with a bunch of other starving wannabe musicians." Alex shook his head. "JD was the only talented one. So we decided we'd just practice together until we each found a better match."

JD threw a French fry and turned to Kelsey, "After a while it was too much work to make fun of each other, and we just kind of melded. About six months after that, TJ said he wanted to come out. I told them TJ had a better voice and better front-man personality than me, and since we still were figuring we might go our separate ways, they didn't care."

"I'm the glue that holds this little ragtag band together, ma'am." TJ smiled at her, and Kelsey couldn't help but laugh.

Craig shrugged, wadding up the paper wrappers littering the table in front of him. Without effort or thought he chucked them over two, thankfully empty, tables making clean shots into the trashcan. Kelsey caught that, too and Craig added, "It worked, it just fused. I haven't heard anything else out there like us. I like that. You just know when something clicks."

Apparently they all did. Just then, by some unspoken agreement, they all got up and began clearing the table. JD set her forgotten food aside for her to bring in the car, and in a few minutes she was nibbling the less-than-stellar burger in his passenger seat.

They made a roundabout tour of town, stopping in a few key places Kelsey had already scouted, and a few she hadn't. Finally, the light was starting to dim, and they all sat on the courthouse steps, exhausted and trying to look casual and a bit rebellious. TJ was the only one who pulled it off with any measure of skill.

They squirmed one way, then another, trying to appear comfortable and relaxed. They looked anything but. Finally, she gave up and called off the dogs. All the guys moaned in relief, and like the true band they were, they all collapsed across the steps, exhausted.

With a grin, she caught what would be the last photos of the shoot, walking in closer until she was standing directly over them. "Come on guys, look sexy."

TJ raised one brow in a too-good mockery of a soap actor. Craig just shook his head and grinned. "Darlin' I always look sexy, can't help it."

She and JD laughed.

Alex's cell phone chose that moment to ring, and he answered it, still lying on his back and looking up at the sky. "Hey, baby."

It was clearly Bridget. If she hadn't heard the words Kelsey would have known anyway by the sharp pierce of envy she felt. Alex's whole body changed. His voice softened, every part of him was aware only of who was on the other end of the conversation. His eyes lit up.

Kelsey pulled her gaze away. Alex was younger than her, and there he was, all in love. It didn't seem fair. After Andrew, she knew everything there was about life not being fair. Case in point, the remarkably sexy man helping her gather her stuff. He was just a nice guy, and didn't need her clinging to him.

Five minutes down the road, JD's hand found her shoulder. "Something wrong?"

Everything. "Nothing."

He clearly didn't buy it, but let it slide, and in a few minutes they had pulled into the parking spot under his condo. Without thinking she went around back to the trunk and gathered up the camera equipment she had. Then she grabbed a small case. "What's this? Violin?"

A wicked grin spread across his face, effectively erasing her lingering melancholy about Alex and Bridget. "Baby, I'm from Texas. It's not a violin—"

She grinned, too, and joined him for the last three words. "—it's a fiddle."

"Will you play for us?"

He nodded, grabbing the guitar as well. "I usually sing Andie to sleep when it's just us."

She was walking away, grateful that her face didn't show. She was suddenly jealous of Andie. All this time he'd been singing to his daughter and Kelsey hadn't managed to hear him.

While she heated up leftovers and ate her dinner, conversation stirred around her, and she sat in a bubble of her own little sadness. It wasn't really self-pity, it was just . . . lowness. And it was familiar. She'd felt this when Andy was diagnosed, even though she'd been too young to categorize it. Then again when he'd disappeared at 17. She'd lived in it for so long after Andy had died. But here it was again, and so she kept her mouth together through most of the meal, nodding here or there, and not participating much.

The kids left in a flurry of activity and she got up to clear the table. But JD was around to her side, stopping her, his hand gentle on her arm. "Kelse, what's wrong?"

She tried to say 'nothing', but it was too much of a lie.

He leaned down, looking in her eyes, clearly worried. "Baby, you look like you're about to cry."

She was appalled to find that he was right. Even as she shook her head, fat drops welled in her eyes, and spilled over. She didn't know where this had come from. This life she had now was so much better than the one she'd lived just a year ago. But now she *felt*, and she felt so keenly. What had been missing didn't matter before, but now it did.

His arms slipped around her, steady and sure, and only a fraction away from what she really wanted. Leaning in the doorframe, he pulled her between his braced legs and folded her against his chest. "Can you tell me?"

She shook her head 'no,' feeling his soft t-shirt against her cheek.

"Is it me?"

Yes. "No." Her voice was tinny and hollow.

For a few moments he just held her there as she cried. Not great heaving sobs; she didn't have the energy for that. She hadn't lost anything. She just wasn't going to get what she wanted. And for the first time in her life she didn't think she could just chalk it up to fate.

His hand stroked her hair and his cheek rested against the top of her head. It was almost perfect, but almost wasn't close enough.

"Are you thinking about Andrew?"

She nodded to that one, copping out. It was true, just not *the* truth.

After that he didn't say anything, just held her until she had it together enough to pull away. Then he looked at her, his hands smoothing her hair. "Feel better?"

She nodded, wiping at her face. "I don't know where that came from."

The front of his shirt was wet from her face, and she pointed at it. "I'm sorry."

"It'll dry." He shrugged, and set about clearing the table. They worked in a companionable silence, with him bringing the dishes from the table and her putting food away or rinsing dishes and loading them in the washer. It was so domestic, she almost cried again.

When they had the table cleared and everything put away, he grabbed his guitar. "It's getting close to bedtime. Andie won't get up in the morning if I don't get her into bed by eight." He paused, "But you probably know that as well as I do."

"Yeah." A smile graced her lips.

"So, let's go have a sing-a-long. Would that cheer you up?"

"Absolutely." Trailing him down the hall, she hollered to the kids, "Clean up! JD's going to sing for us!"

JD hollered, too. "Everybody's going to sing!"

The door to Daniel's room opened and Kelsey sighed. It looked like a tornado had struck, and she warred with herself about making them clean it up before JD played. She finally decided just to make them pick up what was necessary to have enough room to get to Daniel's bed. "Let's all go into the living room then."

The three kids ran down the hallway, a parade of soft bare feet and chattering voices. "My Daddy plays real good! Wait 'til you hear him."

Glancing back at him, Kelsey saw the flush on his face, she couldn't hide the grin. It was good to know he could blush. "I'll bet he does."

JD gathered them in a circle on the floor and pulled out his acoustic guitar, setting it across his lap. He gave it a strum, his gaze somewhere not in the world around him, and he began playing with the keys, slightly altering the sound. Kelsey didn't hear a problem, but he kept at it until he was satisfied. JD didn't notice Andie shushing the other two, explaining what he was doing. But Kelsey had seen.

With a blink he entered reality again. "Okay, what are we singing?"

No one volunteered.

"Alright, then. I suffered through a darn lot of Dixie Chicks on the road, and now they're in my head."

He hit a few chords before she recognized the piece. Kelsey never considered anyone but the Dixie Chicks singing their songs. In a measure she'd changed her mind. "Taking the Long Way" was all new with only a guitar and JD's clear baritone.

When he hit the bridge, he looked up at Kelsey, "I know you know this one. You own the CD."

Her nerves skittered. Her voice was passable at best, but she opened her mouth and gave it what she could. He smiled as he sang with her, the look changing everything on his face and encouraging her to go a little louder.

Her heart fluttered in her chest, and the sweetest sound was his voice across her own. But it was over too soon, and JD was asking what else they wanted to hear.

Andie jumped up and clapped, "Do the kisses song."

"The kisses song?" He smiled as he said it. While Kelsey was clueless, JD obviously knew what Andie was asking for.

The guitar filled the room again and he started in, this time JD's clear voice was accompanied by Andie's sweet small one.

Kelsey saw her own kids enjoying the song, and watching JD with a focus she hadn't seen in them before. But even while she was watching she was listening. The rich sounds would linger long after JD left.

JD and Andie put their faces close for the chorus.

His eyes turned to hers as he sang about wanting a full house and a rock and roll band.

Daniel requested "Should've Been a Cowboy" next, and JD had them all singing. Kelsey didn't think she'd let go like this in forever. This was her family. And they were all smiling.

They did three more songs, with at least one voice joining his each time, before Allie requested 'The Itsy Bitsy Spider'. Kelsey waited for 'no', but it didn't happen. JD simply nodded and lifted the guitar out of his lap and reached back for the violin.

Again, he mentally disappeared for a minute to tune the instrument, but when he looked up, he cued Allie to start singing. With a few bewildered blinks, she softly began. Inside of two notes, JD had pegged her key and was accompanying her. Allie sang it three times through, her eyes getting wider with each round.

Kelsey wanted to stop time. Her kids were happy, truly happy. She now had the same size family as she'd had previously, but she was willing to admit that this one was better. *Oh, God, Andrew forgive me.* The weight that had been lifted from her when Andrew died became even lighter when JD stepped up to really share the load.

He didn't vacuum her living room, or do her laundry, but she had a sounding board that she trusted. She had someone to tell her that they saw she was doing her best.

In the next minute, JD declared it to be past bedtime, and Braham's Lullaby floated out from the bow as the last song of the evening.

CHAPTER 26

JD's arm reached out to catch the cup as Allie set it, tottering, on the edge of the table. The lightning reflexes were only part of how he'd changed over the past four and half months. "Allie," He handed her the milk, "Put it up the right way this time and pay attention."

Chastised, the small girl took the cup from his hands and, much more carefully this time, placed the milk on the table before using her fingertips to scoot it back. JD's own fingers reached out and found Allie's hair to ruffle. She smiled at him then ran off to play with her brother and Andie.

The kitchen smelled fabulous, thanks to the pseudo-traditional turkey and ham he and Kelsey were baking. They'd argued that morning about how to prep the meat. Eventually, Kelsey had given in, letting him and Daniel stuff whole cloves of garlic 'up the turkey's butt', as Daniel had put it.

Kelsey stood, hip propped against the counter, steaming asparagus on the stove, and baking yams with marshmallows and refusing his help. She had on a sweet, striped apron that read 'never trust a skinny chef'. Clearly intended for someone larger, it took on an evil tone wrapped around Kelsey's slim shape. He smiled from his vantage point at the table. He could see the kids playing in the living room from where he sat, and he could watch Kelse, checking things and stirring things, and making his house smell better. Look better, too.

She came over to him and pulled a cucumber stick off the plate in the center of the table. She'd intended it to keep the kids from getting too hungry or cranky before the meal was served, but they'd both been nibbling at it, too. It was just another Kelsey flourish.

Her skirt swished around her knees as she sat next to him and crossed one ankle over the other. It didn't help him that she was wearing what looked to him like red, heeled, dancing shoes, with a thin strap holding each to her ankle. Her sweater sleeves were pushed up, and a few wisps of her hair had mutinied in the heat, escaping the twist at the back of her head.

He leaned forward, putting his elbows on the table, as she picked up another cucumber stick. "You look amazing."

She blushed sweetly, but just kept nibbling.

"Seriously," he continued, "you look too nice."

She ignored him.

"Kelse, my brother will likely be coming in jeans. Craig just got a new tattoo, and he's wanting to show it off. If Donna Reed meets them at the door, they'll flee." He flung out what he hoped was the deciding factor. "Then we'll have no bread."

She still looked at him with a frown. "I don't look like Donna Reed at all."

"Okay," He pointed to the apron, "I'll concede to Donna Reed meets A-Touch-of-Evil, which is definitely better, but . . ." with his hand he gestured up and down her outfit.

"It's Thanksgiving. You dress up!"

"Says who?"

She was silent for a moment. "They do."

"Who are 'they'?" Here he was picking another argument, and not really sure why he'd done it.

"The great and infamous 'they'. 'They' say a lot of things." She smiled and chomped the end of the cucumber in punctuation.

"They have no jurisdiction here." He stood up, towering over her, "You need to loosen up, let your hair down . . . literally."

Before she could stop him, his hands came up and pulled out the clip holding it all in place.

Her hands fluttered as she reached up too late to do anything about it. Only after a minute did she utter, "Hey!"

He handed her the hair clip with a flourish worthy of a butler, but the look on her face wasn't decipherable. "What was that for?"

"Only what I said." But what he thought was that she looked sexier with her hair in waves from having just been undone. And for a moment it was too intimate, seeing her like that. Parts of him tightened, and deep down something loosened. He spoke to cover what was swirling inside him. "Don't want you scaring away the guests."

"Thanks." It was wry, and she got up to attach the hair clip to her purse so she wouldn't lose it. Then she ran her fingers through her hair to undo the tumbled look, which greatly disappointed JD until the doorbell rang. He'd hear no end of it if Craig and TJ walked in and found Kelsey looking tumbled.

As it was, when he answered the door, TJ hung back on the porch and asked him if he'd solved his 'problem' yet.

"No." JD worked at squelching that thought right away. He couldn't live with TJ riding herd on him. "The real problem is that it's unsolvable. So stop asking."

"Oh, brother," TJ offered up a pat on the shoulder that made JD afraid his younger brother was going to try to sell him snake oil, "Nothing is unsolvable."

"You're right," He whispered harshly. "I'll just chain her in the basement and keep her as my sex slave."

TJ mused that one for a minute, until JD literally knocked him upside the head. "Clean your brain out."

JD didn't wait for a response, just turned and went back into the bright kitchen to see Craig handing Kelsey a bakery bag of rolls, and Kelsey graciously taking them from him as though he had threshed the wheat and milled the flour himself.

Craig wasn't one for basking in praise, spoken or unspoken, and he turned it around, gesturing to Kelsey, "What's with the Mrs. Cleaver get-up?"

Before he could say anything, she turned to JD, who had paused in the doorway. "I hate you." And she brushed past him out the door.

Not knowing what else to do, he turned to Craig, "What the hell did you say to her?"

He shrugged, "We brought rolls? It really seemed directed at you."

When JD looked out beyond the back steps, she had already disappeared. She hadn't seemed all *that* mad. He hoped she'd be back in a few minutes.

Fifteen minutes later, he was getting worried. "Craig, I think you really offended her."

"That was at you. What did *you* say?"

His head hung down of its own accord. "That she looked like Donna Reed."

TJ turned to Craig, the jury deliberating, "Well, that's a crime."

It wasn't a crime. She'd looked beautiful, just overdressed. He shouldn't have said anything. He leaned back against the counter, looking at the food, bubbling without Kelsey there to play chef. He checked his watch, if she wasn't back in five minutes he'd call her. He'd grovel. Maybe he should just go over and fetch her back.

He planned out what he should say.

Four minutes later he had most of his speech prepared, and he was putting on the finishing touches while he waited for the seconds to tick off. She had thirteen to go when the back door swung open, letting in a blast of chill air and Kelsey in a long coat.

She had darkened her eyeliner and her lipstick, her hair was fuller and curling around her face. She peeled the coat and dropped it across the back of a chair, but it wasn't the coat that had their attention.

She was in a very short skirt, with black fishnet stockings hugging mile-long legs all the way down into some wicked black leather heels. Her shirt was long-sleeved, but laced all the way up the front with a black leather thong. She'd tightened the laces until they looked like they'd give way at any moment.

"Happy now?" She stared them all down, then went over to the stove to check the asparagus. She found it lacking and put it back over the heat. She checked the oven, and JD doubted she was aware she'd let them see that her legs went all the way up.

His hand reached out and covered TJ's eyes. His own tongue had difficulty staying in his mouth.

She stood back upright and fixed each of them with a hard stare. "Well?"

TJ was having difficulty not laughing, and she gave him a dirty look until he explained. "Oh, I'm not laughing at *you*, you look stellar. I'm laughing at him." He pointed to JD. "I don't think you could have come up with a more fitting revenge."

Kelsey looked like she was about to question what his brother had just said, when she was sidetracked by Craig. He had the balls to walk a full circle around her, checking out the goods, and JD felt his blood pressure rise with each look Craig gave her.

"Kelsey," Craig's voice was smooth. "I didn't know you had it in you. You look like you belong sprawled across the hood of a very expensive sports car."

JD waited for her to blow.

But she smiled, a sweet smile that was out of place with the rest of the get-up. "Since I was going for full-on 'slut,' I'll take that as a compliment."

"It was meant as one." Craig grinned back and left the room to commandeer the video games from the kids.

Allie came racing into the room just then, her arm extended, holding her dolly out for her mother to see. She pulled up short. "Mommy, you changed."

Kelsey nodded, "And I did it to suit the whim of a man. I hope you don't ever make the same mistake."

"Okay." Allie looked at her weird, then turned away, the dolly forgotten.

JD simply put his head into his hands and tried to remember how to breathe.

TJ laughed a low whisper into his ear. "Oh, you are so fucked."

JD thought his brother was most likely right. He toyed with the idea of pulling her aside somewhere and telling her, *either screw my brains out or stop tormenting me.* But he didn't think that would go over very well.

Half an hour later she declared it time to set the table, and made them get out the table cloth she had brought. Even though she no longer looked like Donna Reed she wanted everything set to look as though Mrs. Reed had been there.

They all ate dinner with the kids alternately picking at things and wolfing them down. JD ate quite a bit considering his eyes never saw his food. He was working so hard at not looking down Kelsey's shirt. Craig didn't bother trying to hide it, and that earned him a few dirty looks from JD. Surprisingly, Kelsey didn't seem to mind, and that started a deep seed of fear growing. Craig wouldn't. He just wouldn't.

After they finished with the main course food, TJ hauled out chocolate ice cream for the kids.

Andie and Daniel over-indulged in the ice cream, excusing themselves to go moan in the living room. Only Allie stayed to shovel away a full two pieces of pumpkin pie. And Kelsey rested her chin on her cradled fingers. She looked pleasantly tired, which ate at his heart. He was sending Andie home with her, because the guys were all due at the studio parking lot at four a.m. to catch the bus.

"Well, that was good." Kelsey's red lips curved into a sated smile, and for a moment he could imagine that it wasn't due to the food.

The guys were all leaned back in their chairs, happily stuffed. Craig moaned. "That was great. It was way better than anything we're going to eat in the next eight days."

"Mommy, may I be excused?"

Kelsey smiled at her daughter and the clean plate in front of her. "First wipe your face, pumpkin."

TJ helped out, and Allie raced off to the living room, somehow not stumbling like a drunken sailor from all the sugar she'd consumed.

Kelsey planted her palms on the table and pushed herself up to standing, again most likely unaware that the move pushed her cleavage even higher to strain at the laces of her shirt. She began clearing the dishes, leaning across the table in a housewifely gesture that was innocent in itself, but yet again gave glimpses right down the front of that amazing, god-awful shirt.

JD couldn't stand up. Craig, of course, did, popping right out of his seat to offer to help clear. For this he was bestowed with the sweetest of smiles. TJ laughed again in JD's ear before he left to go keep an eye on the kids.

Yes, it was all going to hell in the pretty little hand basket Kelsey had hauled her stuff over in.

Craig helped to load the dishwasher, and for the briefest moment JD remembered the scene with his mother, and Kelsey's words that *musicians are sexy as hell*. Was Craig?

With a grunt and a shove, he pushed himself away from the

table and wandered into the living room to nurse his ire. TJ was blasting aliens from a version of the old Atari Space Invaders game, but when he finished he looked up at JD, sprawled in the corner of the couch. "Don't worry, he's not into her in any way other than to torment you."

Only the kids showed any sign of life, and later they bounced upstairs as the guys turned on the recorded football game from earlier. Craig and TJ eventually drifted off to their apartment, leaving him alone with Kelsey. TJ had insinuated that it was JD's job to say something to her tonight. But what that might be, he didn't know.

She stayed in the middle of the couch, neither coming closer nor scooting away. Lying there, she looked sweet and mussed, and dressed for sex, and he couldn't remember when he'd wanted her more.

JD had fantasized about her. Looking at her now, he wondered who hadn't. But it had been from a distance, and now, she was right beside him. What if he leaned over and just fitted his mouth to hers? He could blame it on the outfit, but it came from somewhere so much deeper inside than that.

Later, when the game finished, he used the last of his strength to haul himself up off the sofa and offer her a hand. She accepted and threw her weight against him, finding her footing on those long heels and longer legs. "We need to round up the kids." With a great breath in she yelled up the stairs, "Kids, it'll be time to go in twenty minutes."

A couple of "Okay, Mom"s came from the landing, as Kelsey turned to him, "Sorry, I couldn't gather the strength to walk over there."

"That's all right." He yawned and stretched and attempted to reclaim some of his energy.

Ten minutes later she had the leftover food packed and ready to go. The only things that waited until morning were his guitars.

"Okay kids!" The three of them tromped down the stairs in a line, marveling at the dark beyond the windows, finally believing Kelsey that it was bedtime. It was incongruous seeing those words come out of her pouty mouth. She looked nothing like the mother of this brood.

When she was ready to leave, she couldn't carry everything. Food containers were stacked on the counter, Andie's bag waited by the door, her own things—dishes, the table cloth and napkins—were in the basket with the pale green bow.

She couldn't leave it, it needed to be washed, she'd forget where she'd left it. She protested in a far more practical manner than her outfit suggested.

JD grabbed Andie's bag, slinging it over his shoulder, and grabbed the stack of food containers. "Let's go."

"Thank you." She slipped silently into her own long coat, grabbing the basket and another bag, and ushering the kids out the door. With only a few mild fumbles, he managed to get the door locked behind him, and they traipsed down the dark sidewalk through pools of yellow light, following the rhythmic click of Kelsey's heels.

She let them in the front door, turning on lights as she went from room to room, and sending the kids off to get ready for bed. JD lingered, helping orchestrate the brushing of teeth, and getting all three kids into big 'Wilder' t-shirts. Kelsey kissed them all, then went out to the kitchen to find room in her fridge for everything she had brought, finally finding space for each container and putting two pans into her own sink to soak.

She leaned against her hands, facing the window over the sink, and he wasn't sure if she saw him as clearly in the reflection as he saw her.

Her voice came to him on a soft sigh, much like the ones he'd imagined. "You should stay."

Stay.

It set up a ricochet in his chest, and he took a step toward her, his breath catching inside him before she finished.

"The office bed is open. I am *not* working tonight."

She turned to face him, seemingly not having noticed his blunder. "You don't look like you'll make it back. Like I'd find you curled up on the sidewalk in the morning. I'll get you an alarm clock."

He nodded, following her down the hall to the office and turning back the sheets that she'd left on for him. Shrugging out of his shirt and jeans, he crawled under the covers.

Maybe ten minutes later she came down the hall, padding on bare feet, and making his eyes really open for the first time since dinner had settled. Ready for bed, she was in an oversize shirt that hid all of her but for her well-toned arms and legs. Her hair was brushed down from the vamp look of earlier that evening. Her face was scrubbed of all make-up, and JD was grateful for the privilege that he was allowed to see her like this.

She handed him an alarm clock and wished him good-night before turning and walking down to her own room in the glow of the hall light.

CHAPTER 27

"Hey there, stranger." Her voice was soft in his ear, and he leaned back against the built-in sofa on the bus. TJ and Craig were out, milking what they could out of the few hours they had before the bus pulled out. Alex, who was now a lovesick fool, had gone into his own room, presumably to call Bridget as he did every night. JD held his cell phone, making his own nightly call, and didn't miss the comparison.

If he closed his eyes he could imagine she was right beside him, and not bouncing a signal off of satellites and mountain tops between them. "I miss you."

"We miss you, too."

He said it every time, waiting for when she would respond that she, herself, missed him. But it wasn't tonight. "Why are we whispering?"

"Andie's in bed with me." He heard a soft rustle in the background that could only be the slide of the butter yellow sheets he knew she had on the bed.

"How's she been?" The conversations were often inane, but almost more comforting that way.

"She's been a hellion."

"What?" His eyes opened and he leaned forward. "Is she back sliding?"

"No." A soft laugh came through the line and filtered down into his chest, releasing the knot of tension that had formed. "She's a child, she has bad days. She threw a temper tantrum and we had to leave the grocery store."

"Oh, Kelse, I'm so sorry. I don't want to make extra work for you." He couldn't do this at the expense of Kelsey. He couldn't do anything at the expense of Kelsey.

"It's not a big deal. She came and crawled into bed with me a while ago and apologized for her behavior."

"She did!?"

"Yeah. Your little girl's growing up."

And he wasn't there to see it. He sighed. "You are the reason I've been able to do this, knowing that Andie is with someone she loves. Thank you."

"Stop thanking me. It's good for Daniel to see her throw a tantrum every once in a while, and to see that no one blows up at her, and that we all love her anyway."

JD cringed, not for the first time wondering how such an intelligent woman could have married a man with Andrew's problems. Maybe he hadn't had them then. Maybe he'd hid them. One day JD would ask.

Just then, the bus door opened and Craig came up the stairs with an open beer in his hand, "Hey, Cowboy, talking to your girlfriend?"

JD opened his mouth to protest, even as TJ followed Craig up the stairs, looking a little too sotted to make his own remark. But Kelsey beat them both to it. "Tell the guys I say 'Hi'. I'm going to go before I wake up Andie."

"'Night."

"Night." She hung up while the words *I love you* tumbled off the edge of his brain. He didn't say them. He hadn't said them before, and he wouldn't now.

He managed to call earlier the next night and talk to each of the kids. Then he kept Kelsey on the phone for another hour while the bus rumbled underneath him. When he hung up, he told himself he was going to give Kelsey whatever she needed—time, money, space to grow her photography business. It was only what she'd given him. He played with a little extra care for the rest of the tour, now that it wasn't about him.

They were home for seven days in the middle of the month. He spent all of them at Kelsey's. They decided it was easier than moving Andie back and forth, and he simply got out of her office early in the mornings. He was at the studio during the day, but he worked the schedule, with the help of the others, so that he could be available to walk to get Andie and Daniel after school. He took Allie several days so Kelsey could do what she needed, finally feeling like he was starting to pay her back.

They settled into an easy rhythm right away, with both of them rising early and getting ready, before getting the kids up and out the door. Kelsey's nose would be red every morning by the time they got back to her place, but she would still go straight to the fridge and pop open a can of coke. "I thought I smelled snow this morning."

He shrugged, "It hasn't done more than a light dusting the whole time I've been here. But we need to get going, I don't want to have shopping left to do while I'm on tour."

"Let me get my list."

He waited. As a man, he, of course, had no such list. At least he had some money. They had all been getting regular paychecks from the label for a month or so, and that was his Christmas fund. He was still playing his stocks online, although he hadn't been able to devote as much time to it as he would have liked. But he also wasn't at home spending money a lot of the time.

She appeared at the door to the hallway, her jacket back on, her hair pulled up in a fuzzy, ear-covering headband. In her gloved fingers, she clutched her precious list. "You've never done this before."

He frowned. "I've Christmas shopped before."

"Not for your own child."

"Of course not. I've never had my own child before. But I've shopped for kids before." He led her out the front door, waiting while she operated the lock with the smooth movements of a woman used to the cold.

She trailed him to his car, skipping along like Allie. "I'll try to keep you out of trouble."

He almost laughed at her. The way she was bouncing it would likely be Kelsey who needed to be kept out of trouble. "I don't think that's a problem, I don't even like Christmas shopping."

They shivered until the heat kicked in, and he gave her the low-down on his poor Christmas beliefs all the way to the mall.

Kelsey gave him a half-smile. "All the more reason for you to get into this."

JD agreed. He wanted Andie to know he had chosen her gifts with care, and that they would be things she wanted. She was already likely to get something terrible from her grandmother.

They pulled up in front of the mall, which the parking lot showed to be way too full for his tastes. But it was only going to get worse, so he didn't protest, just climbed out into the frigid air and went around to get Kelsey's door.

Three hours later they left. He had done more shopping than he had ever done in a mall in all his years combined. He cursed Kelsey for being right. He'd gotten caught up, and Kelsey had matched him purchase for purchase.

It didn't escape JD's notice that they had each bought for all three kids, indiscriminately. They would be celebrating Christmas together, with both Craig and TJ coming over, since Craig had no affection for his own family, and TJ didn't care to join their parents in Switzerland.

That meant that Kelsey had to buy fabric, as she insisted on making a matching set of stockings for all seven of them. If he wasn't so enthralled by her, he would have left her there. The fabric store was insane—it made the mall look like a ghost town. And this crowd was all old ladies, ooh-ing and ahhh-ing over each other's hideous choices of sparkly and patterned fabrics to sew their own Christmas clothes.

Kelsey wound her way through bolts of cloth and scary women, and JD attempted to follow. When he was asked to make a decision about which fabric he liked better for the top of the stockings, he refused. He made a different decision instead.

If he was going to get taken to the mall and dragged through the fabric store at Christmastime, he ought to be getting laid by the woman doing the dragging. He didn't want anyone else anyway, and he'd certainly had his pick of willing women recently.

Everything else was in place, they were living in the same house right now. Just for a few days, but that was plenty of time. They'd celebrate Christmas together. The kids were so entangled, with him being gone all the time, they probably already thought they were brother and sisters. His joining Kelsey in her bed would be only one small additional step.

Okay, it wouldn't be small at all.

If it were that small, it would have already happened. But he was getting tired of getting pestered by the guys. He was tired of watching her walk away in those jeans that hugged her ass. And he was tired of sleeping in a different bed, and keeping his thoughts in his head.

He reached out and took the fabric out of her hands, "It's perfect." He ignored her surprised expression, and laced his fingers through hers, dragging her out of the back corner. As much as he wanted to, he wasn't about to kiss her here, or pull her down amidst the red and green velvets in a crowded fabric store. "Let's go check out."

She tugged the other way, "We have to get it cut first. The cutting line is over there."

"We have to wait in line before we can wait in the other line?"

She nodded, and he held on tight to her hand. He finally released her when he opened the car door for her and her purchases. But she didn't seem to think anything of it. They drove back to Kelsey's place in relative silence except for the grumbling of her stomach, and they made grilled sandwiches to eat on the walk over to get the kids. They picked up Allie first, and between the food and the children she didn't have a hand to hold.

He felt like he was in junior high all over again. Except his fantasies about what he would do when he did get the girl had been decidedly tamer back then. The kids overwhelmed the afternoons and made dinner into an all evening event. There wasn't much opportunity for him to steal a kiss when he could get her take on it, rather than have commentary by the kids. And that evening, when they were watching TV after the kids had gone to bed, he chickened out.

It was just him and her. No buffer. He sat there, next to her on the couch, unable to follow the program because of his wandering brain. If she didn't want him, then how would he pass it off? If he acted casual, like he was just trying to get laid, that would upset their friendship as much as telling her he was crazy in love with her, if she didn't return his feelings.

What a mess. His fingers plowed through his hair and he stood, "I'm going to bed. See you in the morning."

He wandered down the hall, back to his old friend the futon. He washed his face and brushed his teeth, wishing he could simply brush out his brain and be done with it. But he couldn't, so he peeled his shirt over his head, and tossed it in the laundry, and purposefully added some arrogance to his thoughts. *She should get used to seeing me half naked. She should get used to seeing me all naked.*

With that he managed to talk himself into a straight-backed stride down the length of the hall, except she was watching the TV, not him. A little of the air left him. He'd have to try again tomorrow.

The next morning, he let Kelsey sleep in while he gathered the kids around to do laundry. Telling them it was a game and the winner got two scoops of ice cream, he managed to create a bevy of excited, if not overly helpful, workers. They sorted colors and darks and lights and argued a bit.

At eleven, she wandered out in her big t-shirt and a yawn, and asked what time it was. Her eyes bugged and she hugged him, thanking him—with only her t-shirt and his jeans between them. But she didn't seem to notice. She was simply too happy about sleeping in.

Then again, the woman wasn't stupid. She was walking around her house, with a red-blooded American male within scenting distance, wearing only a large shirt, and assumedly some panties. She *had* to know what she was doing to him.

He chickened out again that day.

He even went to church with the kids and her the next morning. Andie wanted to go, which he figured made it a far better church than any he had ever been to. Older people patted the kids on the head, and the kids seemed to like it. Andie spotted someone she knew, and ran off to talk. Feeling utterly out of place, JD slipped his own fingers through Kelsey's again. Again, she didn't seem to notice.

Maybe she thought he was gay.

He'd been trying to think up every way that she could possibly think it was all right to walk around the house in that night shirt, every way she might imagine that she wasn't turning him on. His mind wandered and, pulled by her hand, he simply trailed along, a leaf on the surface of a stream. When chimes sounded, the stream changed direction and pulled him into the church itself, an old wooden structure with stained glass and worn but loved pews.

The kids sent Kelsey, then him, down the row before piling in, taking the last spots on the aisle. Two hymns in, he found out why. There was a children's benediction, and his daughter, the hellion he hadn't been able to take to Target six months ago, was sitting pristinely and listening intently. Stephanie must have raised her well to start with. Certainly Kelsey had helped. He liked to believe he'd had a hand in it too, but he wasn't certain.

Several people approached after the service and asked Kelsey if he was her husband. Each time he waited to hear what she would say. Each time he held tightly to her hand, defying her to introduce him as 'just a friend'. Each time she responded with, "Oh, we're not married." But she didn't elaborate. To their credit, no one got up in arms about her bringing a man and his child to the church when she wasn't married to him. Of course, there was no reason for anyone to get up in arms. It wasn't like they were sleeping together. *Yet.*

Afterward, they stopped at the store and all piled out. The kids seemed to really enjoy each getting fifty cents and going to the bakery, where apparently they were recognized, and each picking out a few day-old rolls or such to feed the ducks. The baker helped them decide, then all piled back into the car. Each child clutching a bakery bag as they headed off to the duck pond.

Even the damned ducks recognized the kids.

As glad as he was to see Andie happy and on schedule, he felt heavy that his small daughter had a whole life he was unaware of. His only consolation was that he'd left Kelsey in charge of that life, and she was apparently doing a better job than he ever had.

They changed into play clothes after they got home and he

played t-ball in the front yard. JD decided they should play at the duck pond next time, but he didn't say it. He wouldn't be here the next time. He'd be on the road again—starting at seven-thirty tomorrow morning.

That evening he chickened out again.

JD hauled himself out of bed at five a.m. His chest ached, and his head hurt. His brain protested by shutting down. The urge to crawl back under the hot covers was strong, but he fought it. He wanted to help get the kids ready for school, both to see them before he left, and to help ease the load on Kelsey, one last small time before he hit the road.

Straining against the need for more sleep, he pushed himself into the shower. Still, he got himself shaved and dressed and out the door. He walked to his condo, the cold air biting at him and waking him far better than he ever could have himself. Quickly, he re-packed the things he had taken to Kelsey's. He grabbed spare cables, extra picks, and blank pages of sheet music. He set his three guitars by the back door, not daring to leave them in the car even while he was getting the kids ready for school. Then he headed back.

He unlocked the front door to find the lights on and sleepy children brushing their teeth. Kelsey was making shuffling noises behind her bedroom door, presumably getting dressed. With little thought, he set about getting out cereal. He made sandwiches and bagged baby carrots. The kids emerged as he was lining up lunch bags with backpacks.

He talked to them while they ate, helped get them into their clothes, and generally enjoyed being around them and Kelsey for these few last minutes. Breakfast was special because it wasn't going to happen again soon.

He had to leave just before they did. So he grabbed each of

the kids, giving them a big hug, an 'I'll miss you,' and a kiss. Without stopping to let his brain think it through and ruin it, he did the same to Kelsey.

It was just a touching of lips, no passion, no soft sighs or seeking tongues. But in that moment he lost his innocence. He now *knew* how his knees would threaten to give way. He *knew* that his fingers would clench at her of their own accord. He *knew* the feeling of the oxygen pooling in the bottom of his lungs, and what it felt like to breathe her in. That one tiny touch would rob him of breath for days to come.

He set her down before it could look like anything other than what he had shared with the kids. But it had already become so much more. "I'll see you in eight days."

He looked at each of them, hoping his bland smile shaded the racing of his heart, and that the roaring in his head didn't mask anything they were saying. He walked out the front door.

Later, he didn't remember fetching the guitars or the drive to the studio parking lot. But he was there and the guitars were in the backseat. He climbed onto the bus knowing that his promise to himself to catch up on sleep was now worth next to nothing. The others loaded on after him, each slinking into his room and closing the door firmly.

JD threw his bag into the corner, and pulled out the acoustic guitar along with a pencil and a pile of blank pages. A melody had been rattling in his head for several days, but he hadn't thought anything of it. Now it was congealing, and he could hear the specific notes of the guitar and the bass intertwined. And he had words.

He finished playing it through for the third time as TJ emerged from his room. "That's good. You just write that?"

"Yeah, pretty much." JD scribbled one last thing.

"I'm too tired to make a comment on the power-ballad quality or the fact that you obviously wrote it for Kelsey."

"Good, then don't."

TJ yawned, the movement of his jaw finally forcing his eyes all the way open. "Tonight's too early, but we should be able to try it out by Wednesday's show. Where the hell are we going to be Wednesday?"

They practiced the piece on the bus that day, and played late at a concert of new and unknown artists. JD was pretty certain that Wilder fell into the second category more than the first. He wore himself out on stage, working for Kelsey's photography studio.

JD didn't even remember where he was when he fell asleep that night. And he didn't know where he was when his cell phone rang far too early the next morning.

Without thinking he hit the 'accept' button and was immediately rewarded with a scream. His heart raced. "Kelse?"

"Listen!" He heard noise getting louder in the background. But the volume kept cranking and he realized she was playing their single.

"Huh?"

"It's on the *radio!*"

"Oh!"

Stunned, he stood up, the backs of his knees hitting the edge of the bed in the confined space and making him plop back down on the mattress. The support wires allowed for a little bounce, but, as always, it held.

This was it. They'd been playing forever to get on the radio.

He pushed back the door to his cubicle, and went down the hall rattling the accordion doors of his band mates. He heard several "huh"s and a loud "go away".

He laughed. "Say good morning to Kelsey!"

TJ popped his head out, "Damn, from the look on your face, she gave you a BJ from all the way in Nashville."

JD ignored his baby brother, even the crass remark didn't get past his smile. He heard Kelsey laugh on the other end of the line and say, "Better!"

"We're on the radio back home, guys." Into the phone he said, "Crank it up, Kelse!"

She obliged, likely holding the phone right in front of a speaker and turning the volume to a deafening level.

By the time the song finished, all four of them were standing there, in the small bus hallway. The DJ's voice came on in a honey smooth drawl, and she announced the title and their name, saying she'd heard their next single already and thought Nashville would be hearing a lot more from Wilder.

The guys' screaming probably deafened Kelsey as much as the radio had.

But her laughter was what replaced the tinny sound of the radio as she turned the volume down. "Okay, I've got to get off the side of the freeway now."

"Oh, my God, Kelse. Go, get somewhere safe. Thank you." He smiled and started to say something else, but TJ's voice overrode him.

"I love you, Kelsey!"

Craig joined in, "I love you, too, Kelsey!"

Alex whooped before adding his own, "I love you, too, but don't tell my wife!"

JD turned away from the expectant faces and spoke directly into the phone, "I love you, Kelsey."

"I love you guys." Again, not what he'd wanted. But he'd take it.

The bus rumbled into the studio parking lot the night before Christmas Eve. JD worked desperately to squash the nerves he was feeling. What would Kelsey say about that kiss?

She probably wouldn't say anything, they had talked on the phone every day, and nothing had come up. Maybe she was waiting to attack him in person. If she attacked him with her lips he'd be thrilled.

Weary and loaded to the gills, each of the guys practically rolled down the steps of the bus, gear getting lugged into cars. They said beaten good-byes and drove off in slightly different directions.

JD drove himself home and dragged himself into Kelsey's arms. The kids would just have to wait while he got what he needed. She hugged him back like he was a soldier returning from a war. He only wished the soldier wasn't her brother.

For Christmas Santa went insane. Small toys dripped out of stockings, and piles of presents were stacked around the house. JD stole Kelsey's stocking before they went to sleep and filled it before creeping back into his own bed.

The kids woke them at six, running screaming into his and Kelsey's rooms that Santa had come. JD couldn't think of a better alarm clock than that. They tore into presents and squealed at things as silly as socks with frogs on them. JD's heart stopped at a sixteen by twenty black-and-white framed photo of his and Andie's faces nose to nose. Kelsey smiled a secret smile and wouldn't reveal when she'd taken it.

In turn, he insisted on fastening the locket he'd gotten her around her neck. He heard her small gasp when she saw it. Though he'd imagined several things she might say, what she actually did was better than what he had thought up.

"How much did you spend on this? It's beautiful." She fingered the work on the front and opened the tiny clasp.

He bordered on lying when he answered, "Not too much."

Within moments, she had him and the children gathered around for a photo, which she then printed in miniature. She let him fumble again with the clasp at her neck. Her nearness and the way his hands kept brushing the skin at the base of her throat turned him on far more than it should have. It wasn't right, he knew, to be in lust like that, standing there in front of the children, on the holiest of days. He pulled out the tiny photo that came with the locket, and cut around the one she'd printed then went through the fabulous torture again after inserting the new photo in between the gold sides. Only then did Kelsey let them resume opening their presents.

Later Craig, TJ, Alex and Bridget came over.

Kelsey had begged a wedding photo out of Bridget earlier, and gave them a tasteful black and white that was hand tinted and framed. TJ got a Wilder Poster. But Kelsey had re-worked it so that TJ was the sexy front man. It looked like something a teenage girl would hang on her wall, and TJ thought it was the coolest thing he had ever seen. Craig got a pair of super faded jeans with a Celtic/tribal black tattoo down one leg. He liked them until he looked more closely and saw the band's name worked into the design. "Holy shit. Thank you, Kelsey. Can I wear them onstage?"

"Sure!" She was flattered by the praise, and her smile hid the tiniest flush in her cheeks. JD slipped just a little further in love with her. And felt just a little further away, his own framed photo seemed to pale a little in comparison. Simply because she had put that effort forth for everyone.

Only much later that evening, when she was stuffing scraps of wrapping paper into a trash bag, she confessed to him. "It was easier getting stuff for the guys. To me, they are the band. You're not. I mean you are, but you're more. I just hope I did okay."

That alone was more than enough. "You did great."

They fell asleep on the couch on New Year's Eve. At eleven. A half-drunk bottle of champagne between them. JD had hoped for other effects of the alcohol, but had no such luck.

Six days later, when the band was rolling out again, JD offered a repeat performance. He grabbed each of the kids for a hug and a kiss. This time Kelsey lined up, an elfish grin on her face as she waited her turn. "Mom, you're next!" Daniel warned her.

"It's Kelsey's turn?" JD looked at the little boy, thanking him for helping out, even if he didn't know it.

"You can't forget Mommy!" Bless little Allie, too.

He mocked a heavy sigh. "All right."

Kelsey was giggling when he wrapped his arms around her ribs. Lifting her straight off her feet, he held her close, her laugh catching in her throat. When he saw her eyes, he didn't wait for comprehension. He just kissed her.

Not the simple peck of last time.

He lingered, kissing her softly while he let her body slide down his, slowly putting her back to her own feet. Then once more, the pressure of their lips together soft and sweet, before he broke it off.

His brain rode herd on his breathing, fighting to keep it under control, "I'll be back in seven days."

Turning, he walked out the front door, but he'd thought in that last look at her that her eyes had been wide and bright.

CHAPTER 28

For a moment, Kelsey simply stood there, just inside her front door, her fingertips touching her lips. The touch seemed to clarify that just maybe she hadn't imagined the whole thing.

"Mommy got the best kiss." Allie was grinning.

Kelsey blinked. There were still small children gathered around her, depending on her. "I did. Didn't I?"

But the kids didn't answer. They scattered to get ready for church.

Kelsey breathed deeply and shook her head. Whether the kiss meant anything or not, she had to get to church, and that meant getting dressed, and being sane.

But she didn't think sanity was going to be happening anytime too soon.

Once the kids' story at the front of the church was finished, and they wandered off to their respective classrooms, her mind took off like a race car. That had been a real kiss. Was it because he could? Was it because he wanted to? Was it because he had a kid and figured a single mom, the one next door even, was the easiest target? The questions rattled in her brain throughout the sermon, and by the time the last hymn was sung, Kelsey was no closer to God or to an answer. But she had about thirty theories floating through her head.

Like a robot, she took the kids to the store and smiled at the baker. Andie almost got pecked hand-feeding a greedy duck because Kelsey wasn't paying enough attention. She changed them into thick clothes when she got home, and sent them all into the back yard, praying they would be fine, and that God would hear her prayers even though she hadn't been very attentive today in church.

Her brain turned to its new task. She dug out the itinerary that JD had left for her. An hour and a half later she had searched every airline for flights to every destination on their tour. She could make St. Paul on Wednesday night. She called Bethany, knowing only deep disappointment when she got the sitter's voicemail.

She was chasing that kiss.

It was the best thing she had felt in years, maybe ever. And she had to follow it. The money was worth knowing if there was anything more behind it, if it was a momentary whim or just an appeal to scratch two itches.

She clearly couldn't answer the question on her own. If Bethany could keep the kids overnight, then she could find out.

She had served lunches and played a game of almost-badminton when Bethany called. Kelsey took a deep breath hoping that the sitter could cover her. She answered the phone, pressing it tightly to her ear. "Hello."

"Hey Kelsey, what did you need?"

She almost laughed out loud. What she *needed* was to know if there was any emotion behind the kiss her best friend had given her, and if she could get it again, with tongue please. But she asked Bethany about watching the kids.

Bethany, of course, couldn't commit. She had to check her calendar. Kelsey was afraid her 'cheap' last minute plane ticket would go away. But she hung up, agreeing to wait out Bethany's schedule, if not to do it patiently. So she watched the kids play and tried to find some Zen.

The steel bands constricting her chest were pretty anti-Zen. She was uptight, the way she'd always felt while Andy was spending one of his storms. She just had to wait, and could do nothing about it. Desperately, she tried to convince herself that if it didn't come together, then it wasn't meant to be. But that was painful to accept. She knew if JD told her that it wasn't meant to be, she could accept it. If he told her in words or if she got there and he was with his girlfriend, then she'd know.

If she sat here all week, she wasn't sure she could do anything when he got back. It was different having guts when you'd spent money you didn't have, when you chased a tour bus across several states. But if he just walked in the door, would she have the guts to ask him what he meant?

She played with the kids, set them in front of a movie. Tried to work and couldn't get a single thing done. She checked her email, but reading it was strain enough. JD had seriously messed with her head.

She'd thought he'd sent her into a tailspin last time. She told herself it was just a peck and it was no more than any of the kids had gotten. He'd thrown both of those arguments out the window this morning.

At seven, her cell phone played her a Wilder tune that she'd downloaded as the sitter's ringtone. *Please have good news.*

"Hello, Bethany?"

"I have good news." The girl's voice was cheerful, and Kelsey smiled.

In fifteen minutes, she had a ticket for Wednesday afternoon. She would arrive in St. Paul just in time to get to the venue and get in. They weren't opening for anybody big, and she prayed she could find someone selling a ticket out front. She booked herself a hotel room there for the night, and she'd fly back the next morning.

For a moment she just sat there, thinking. The plane ticket, the hotel room, the scalped concert ticket, the babysitter, the rental car—she was running up a hefty tab. But when she closed her eyes, and let her sense memory take her back to when he'd kissed her, she knew it was worth it. She might just get her heart broken, with a very expensive blow. But she might come out all the better. Her smile was huge for the rest of the evening.

The kids asked her about it. She told them she was going on a short trip, and no, they couldn't go. But she didn't tell them where or why.

The kids played games, and watched a few educationally appropriate shows. Kelsey tried to read a book. She downgraded to a fashion magazine and still couldn't stay focused. Her brain was running circles and thinking in swirls. Every thought began with *if* and she couldn't control the speed of her breathing. The song bursting forth from her pocket only made her jump sky high.

It took half a second to realize that Wilder was not, in fact, having a concert in her jeans, but that her cell was ringing. She looked at it: JD. That made her breathing more erratic. But she forced herself to calm down, or at least to do her best imitation of it, and she answered. "Hey."

"Hey, it's getting near bedtime so I just thought I'd check in."

Her mouth pulled up at the corners, and there was nothing she could do about it. Just the sound of his voice made her smile. Her brain ignored the fact that he seemed to be calling about the kids and not to profess undying love. The call wasn't over yet. "We hit church and the duck pond as usual. The kids played in the backyard and got red noses."

He laughed. "Can you put them on?"

"Sure."

Then one by one the kids passed around the phone, telling

JD the same thing, only with halting English and digressions about the spider they saw or the dog they felt they needed to get. Allie began every sentence with 'because.' She often started the same sentence five times, the exact same way, but JD's responses were positive and patient.

Kelsey felt her heart swell.

Allie said good-bye into the phone, and Kelsey took it from her, only to find that her daughter had turned it off.

JD didn't call back.

Oh, well. Maybe the kiss was nothing. But the way her fevered brain was working she would have to make the trip to know for certain. When he called the next afternoon on the walk back from school she didn't tell him either.

Tuesday she had to practically bite her tongue not to say anything. Snow came that night, but it was only a light dusting. She had Bethany come over and bestowed on her the keys and instructions, although mostly Bethany already knew where everything was.

The kids all squealed with glee at the thought of having Bethany over. Kelsey was pretty certain that Bethany didn't follow her instructions to the letter. But, then, as a child neither had her favorite sitters. A late bedtime here or there never killed anyone.

She had purposely waited until after JD called to have Bethany over, she couldn't let one of the kids spoil the surprise by blurting out that she was going to go visit him. And thankfully they hadn't on Sunday; after that, they'd seemed to forget about it. Kelsey disentangled Allie from Bethany's leg, and broached the subject of Bethany driving the minivan.

"Sure." Bethany shrugged and smiled. It took people a while to realize that the girl was really quite intelligent. She was simply fairly agreeable. "I don't know how I'd get all those car-seats into my coupe."

"Exactly. Plus, if it snows, I'll feel safer having the kids in the heavier car."

"That makes sense. And you can take my car to the airport. No sense taking a shuttle or anything." Bethany smiled again, and played a quick game of Go-Fish before she went home.

That evening, Kelsey felt her adrenaline kicking in, and she wasn't sure if she could stand another twenty-four hours of this. She could feel her heart beating inside her ribcage, and far too often her brain had to take over total control of her breathing. But she felt like she had to do this. She was scared and excited and nervous, and had no idea what she'd find.

At least she'd be there Wednesday night. And she was glad that, if things didn't turn out well, she'd be able to slink home and lick her wounds for a few days before she had to face him again.

She barely slept, tossing and turning, and eventually figured she ought to make her waking time useful. So she got up and started to pack. She was determined to get everything into two carry-on bags. Her purse would go into the second along with her usual flight entertainment: music, a book, a magazine, gum . . . she needed a list.

Around five a.m. she slid into the other side of the bed. The side nearest the door was covered with possible outfits for tomorrow. She had to be comfortable on the plane and in the concert, because there wouldn't be time to change. And she had to look single and sexy, without looking slutty. She'd heard the guys around the table on several occasions, waiting until after the kids left, talking about this groupie or that one that had thrown herself at him.

Apparently there was a whole sub-culture of women who went after unknown bands, wanting to get there first. Kelsey guessed they were going for numbers. If you fucked enough starter-band guys, some of them would make it big and you could claim you'd nailed them when.

That gave her pause, and ruined her chances for falling asleep quickly. She didn't want JD if he didn't want her, or even if he just didn't want her exclusively. She would have to remind herself of that repeatedly during the trip. She wasn't sure when she fell asleep, but the alarm woke her at six forty-five.

Blinking and suddenly wide awake, Kelsey knew what she was facing today. She got the kids all ready, reminding them several times that Bethany would pick them up and that they were to do what Bethany told them and to mind their manners. She had to tell Allie three times that she'd be back tomorrow afternoon. Even Daniel got exasperated with his little sister. "She said, *tomorrow afternoon.*"

That was a good sign. It was another indicator that Daniel was slowly starting to turn into a kid. He had probably been even more traumatized by both Andy's life and his death than anyone had realized. Kids who lashed out made their feelings clear to everyone. Kids who were quiet were easier to believe when they said they were okay.

Kelsey walked them to school, all three kids jumping and squealing about the two inches of white fluff that had fallen during the previous night. Daniel wanted to know why school was open.

She rubbed his head through her gloves and his knit Tennessee Titans hat, "Baby, it's probably going to melt before noon. So you enjoy it now, okay?"

"All right." He grumbled. The grumbling was good, too.

She gave both the big kids extra tight hugs, and watched them get into the building before she tugged Allie's hand, leading her toward daycare. Allie hopped along, singing some little song that Kelsey didn't register right away. After a minute she realized her daughter was working her elfin voice through *Go To Bed Mad.*

"Lovely."

"Thank you!" Allie beamed, completely missing the dry tones in her mother's voice.

She was great until Kelsey tried to leave her at daycare, then Allie pitched a fit. Normally she was pretty good about drop-off, but it would figure that today was a bad day, because she was leaving. Then again, that was probably why Allie *had* chosen today to have a fit. Kelsey gave her a second, and then third big hug and kiss, then told her daughter that she loved her and she'd be back tomorrow. She talked up Bethany, knowing that Allie would be excited about that. Then she walked out of the daycare with renewed respect for Andie, who watched her father leave for a week or longer with great manners.

That, of course, slid into a thought of JD. Kelsey missed him. And that slid into a thought of JD leaving, and that last leaving had been the best.

She set out what she was going to wear—the great jeans she had bought a while ago, a sweater that was sheer enough to be clingy and sexy, and fuzzy enough to be warm. It also had a great tendency to slip off her shoulder. Then she finally decided on some heels. Her feet might hurt, but she didn't think she'd notice, so why the hell not?

With her bags waiting by the door and two hours to go, she crawled under the covers and attempted to sleep.

After several forced deep breaths she was at the Cornbread Festival with Wilder on stage. Then the band disappeared. Kelsey searched for them in the crowd, only to wind up face to face with JD.

The world melted away beyond them and his hands were in her hair, holding her so he could kiss her. As though she might try to get away. His mouth was hot and seeking, and she kissed him back, unconcerned that the rest of the world was gone. His lips molded to hers, putting pressure on her to open to him, and she did willingly. She felt his tongue invade her mouth the way he was invading her other senses, as he backed her against a brick wall of a nearby building, holding her there with his own body.

Reaching out, Kelsey grabbed him and pulled him closer, as though they might climb inside each other, fighting for dominance in the war their tongues were waging. He pressed against her, allowing her to feel how aroused he was, and she pressed back in a sign of acceptance. His hands left her hair, even as the kiss continued, and wandered briefly over her shoulders, tracing her ribs, and coming up under her breasts. He took the weight of her in his hands, her shirt having long since disappeared, and his thumbs grazed her.

Kelsey gasped for breath and sat bolt upright, staring in disbelief at the darkened room around her. In the next second her alarm beeped at her startling her again.

God, why couldn't she have stayed asleep just a little longer? She'd been making love to JD at the Cornbread Festival.

Still, she hopped out of bed, noticing how warm she felt, and wondering if the covers had been too hot or if she had. She dressed and fussed, and finally pulled on her jacket, checked her tickets and headed out the door.

She drove to Bethany's and traded cars, thanking the girl again. Then headed out to the airport. For a brief moment she wondered what in the hell she was doing.

When she remembered that he'd kissed her, really kissed her, Sunday morning before he left, she knew why she was here, and she got her feet walking toward the airport. The air was warmer and drier inside, and she breathed a sigh of relief, before relegating herself to waiting in various lines.

The plane was midsized and unidentifiable from any other. Finding her seat, she got as comfortable as she could, given that she was stuck on endless loop fantasies about her next door neighbor. She tried to sleep, but then decided against it; she always felt gummy when she woke up on a plane.

After several hours and several cans of coke, her ears started to pop, signifying that they had begun their descent. Although that didn't last long—the pilot quickly informed them that they had entered a holding pattern as the weather was causing problems.

She'd come all this way—she couldn't miss the show now, not for this. She tried to find some Zen, but only found her own stupidity. Of course there were weather problems, she was hovering over Minnesota in the dead of winter. What had she been thinking?

In that moment, she felt that last kiss slip through her fingers. As though, if she couldn't get to JD here, there'd be no second chance.

Instead, she tried to have patience. She excused herself to the ladies' room and did her make-up, at least they were making nice smooth circles around the arena in St. Paul. And then she buckled herself back in and waited again.

Finally, they touched down with more than the usual bumps but Kelsey didn't care. She had her gear over her shoulder and was in the aisle early enough for the flight attendants to give her dirty looks. The car rental took forever as usual, and she finally drove off in a compact that wasn't at all what she reserved.

Right after she got her seat adjusted in the tiny car, her cell phone rang. The faceplate displayed only two letters: JD. She turned on the radio and answered. "Hey!" And tried, desperately, to sound normal.

"Are you all right?"

"Oh, yeah." She kept it short. She said she was in the car—which was true. And implied that she was around the corner from the house—which wasn't. She told him she'd call back in a few minutes with the kids—which was a blatant lie. And promptly hung up on him.

She hightailed it to the theater about an hour away, freezing her ass off until she figured out where the heater button was, and thinking that her destiny was to not make it in time. But she didn't give up, even after two wrong turns and a parking spot that guaranteed her heels would get ruined in the sludge that blanketed the lot. Kelsey no longer cared.

She pulled her cash and ID from her purse, stuffed it in her pockets, and headed toward the lights.

With the weather what it was, and the fact that the show should have already started, there were more people selling tickets than buying, and she got one on the cheap. Which was cool, because it was the only thing on this trip that had been cheap. She even managed to snag a pit ticket, which would be fun while Wilder was out playing, but the main group was one that she wasn't overly fond of. Maybe she could find the guys after their set and hang out with them. JD said they usually had a few hours before the bus took off. That was *if* they hadn't already played and disappeared.

She hit the ticket line, and when it scanned, she slipped into the next line to get wanded for metal objects. The security was worse than the airport, and she wondered if she could get cancer from all the scanning.

She wasn't stopped again, and managed to beeline past the long lines for beer and liquor, hoping that she hadn't entirely missed the guys. The place was only starting to fill, and there was an announcement on the Trinitron that the whole show had been delayed an hour, because the main band was on a flight that was delayed. Kelsey almost laughed out loud. She knew what they were caught in, and she didn't think an hour was going to cut it.

She found an empty seat in the first row, thinking she'd move when the owner showed. But after ten minutes she was bored, and didn't even have anything to do with her hands. She'd left the cell phone in the car, so she couldn't call and say she was here. And she didn't think she had what it took to talk her way backstage. There was a bleached-blonde with deep-dark roots and almost no clothes trying that very thing with one of the security guys. She was not succeeding. Kelsey wasn't up for that.

She wandered out to the ladies' room, then into one of the long lines, where she could get a glass of white wine. It turned out to be a small plastic cup, and while it was in fact white wine, it was hardly what she'd choose. She returned to the seat that wasn't hers and nursed the wine, almost falling asleep about half an hour into the cup.

Just as she polished off the wine, she heard music in the theater. Within a minute, a local radio DJ walked out onto the stage to welcome everyone and thank them for waiting.

In that short time, the pit became about five times as full as it had been earlier. The radio announcer called a few seat numbers at random until he had a winner, and he gave out a T-shirt for the station and tickets to the next concert they were hosting. Then he got down to it.

"All right, ladies and gentlemen, our first act is backstage warming up. And if you've been listening to your radios, then you already know and love these first guys. We've been getting such wonderful responses to their first single we just had to have them here tonight."

Kelsey smiled. She felt a personal note of pride at the warm welcome the guys received, even though the announcer was slick as oil and paid to say whatever made the crowd happy.

"All the way from Nashville, Tennessee. Give it up for Wilder!" He disappeared as the lights all went out. The crowd went nuts, and the pit roared to life.

Kelsey felt she was being swept up in the tide. She heard the opening chords of *Here and Gone, Again*. As the lights drifted up during the first few notes, they were directed mostly on the stage, even though there was still some light floating over the audience, as an acknowledgement to the fact that the whole crowd hadn't shown yet.

At the end of the song, TJ spoke to the people he could

barely see. He did the usual thank-the-city for coming out. He asked if they were ready for another one, and the guys burst into *Go to Bed Mad*. The pit had started with the usual standing, then maybe swaying, with the slower *Here and Gone, Again*, but now they started really dancing. It was clear from the mouths moving that a decent number of them were familiar with the song.

Kelsey couldn't keep her jaw shut. She scanned the crowd, dancing along with them despite feeling a little lost. When she looked up again, JD frowned at her, just a bit. It took her a moment to realize he thought she looked like herself, he just didn't believe that it was her. He leaned over to TJ to sing the main line, then casually wandered back to her side of the stage, and looked again.

But the song ended, and TJ announced another, leaving her no time to really communicate with JD while he was up there. Oh well, she sighed and sang along. She knew this one by heart. No one else in the audience did. She felt just a little superior for it.

Again JD wandered to her side of the stage, scanning the audience, which was clearly hard to do by the expression on his face. Only then did she think of what it was like to be up there. The lights were in his face, and the guys might never know she'd been here tonight if she didn't find a way backstage. So she pressed her way toward the front, and she smiled up at JD as he passed by.

His expression as he hit the last chord was fleeting, but clearly dumbfounded. He got it together, giving no acknowledgement to her other than the look of surprise that had crossed his features. As he turned, she saw that he mouthed something to TJ who was sweet-talking the audience again.

Kelsey decided to pay attention.

"This one is new, and . . ." Whatever JD had mouthed stopped him from what he was about to say. Smooth as silk, he changed tacks. "Well, we need to know what y'all think of it, so afterwards I'll ask and you ladies out there let me know." He grinned something wicked, and laughed at his brother while JD and Craig both changed guitars.

Kelsey was positively riveted to the spot. She hadn't had a band in her garage for too long. They had a new song, and she hadn't heard it. In a few moments the guitars joined each other for what was obviously soft and low. The drums were all but non-existent in the background, and TJ started with eyes closed and mic-stand clutched like a lover. He sang about what *I am*. A man, a friend, a shoulder to cry on . . . Then the *I am* again, but this time, scared, alone, in need . . .

After a while she realized that the song had no true chorus, just a repeating but subtly changing melody, with intricate but soft guitar work. And it had TJ, who milked the love song for every last drop. Damn, but the man could give Sinatra a run for his money. By the end he had every female in the crowd in love with him, and anyone who straggled was brought to heel with the last line, sung almost entirely without back-up, and played for everything it was worth. "In the end, all I am . . . is yours."

Oh, yeah, as she looked around she wouldn't have been surprised to see crying women throwing themselves at the stage. No wonder they had all those groupies. Any woman would screw the man who sang her that one. Especially TJ. He needed to sing a song about beating his wife just to get back down to where the human males were.

While his brother and Craig changed guitars back to the Fenders both men preferred, he asked the ladies what they thought. Kelsey nearly went deaf at the screams, and she shook her head. When she looked up JD was laughing at her. It only lasted a moment, before he looked away. He was on stage, he couldn't just hop down and have a conversation with her.

They went through several other songs before TJ announced that it was the last one of the night. This one Kelsey knew Craig had written, and ended on one strong note, both vocally and instrumentally. Then the lights went down. For a moment she was in the dark, and aside from the shuffling and the sounds and smells around her, she was just alone.

It was over. Wilder was gone. All of twenty seconds later, the lights came back on, almost full bore, but the curtain was down, and any sign of the guys had disappeared. The radio announcer came back out, thanking the crowd, asking what they thought. Again there was the usual screaming, but Kelsey wasn't caught up in it. She figured that the guys had seen her. But maybe they didn't know how to get her. Maybe they thought she'd make her way back stage. She figured they might be calling her cell phone right now, but she'd left it in her car.

There was nothing holding her here, and she had cell numbers for each of the guys. Surely, she could get a hold of one of them and see if there was any chance to . . . hang out? grab dinner? at least to say hello face to face. The announcer's voice caught her from behind as she was halfway up the stairs, "They'll be signing autographs in the lobby, and selling copies of their album in just a few minutes."

Kelsey smiled. With a new spring in her step, she bounded up the carpeted stairs, hoping to be one of the first on scene for the autographs.

She was. She was also among the sanest. There were screaming girls that radio-station employees were herding to a set of doors with a curtain and a table set out with Wilder CDs and eight-and-half-by-eleven reprints of the guys. Kelsey smiled at the display, fingering the album. She hadn't seen the final thing—the total package with the disc and all the photos with the fold out. One of the people behind the table in a Wilder t-shirt asked if she was planning to buy it. Kelsey was tempted except she probably didn't have to. "Oh," Her hand flew to her throat at she realized he thought she was probably attempting to steal it. "I designed this, I was just looking at it."

"Uh-huh." His look said it all. Like fifteen girls every night claimed they had designed the album as a cheap ploy to get in with the guys. Kelsey was offended. As a cheap ploy, that had to be somewhat original, right? But she heard a voice she knew, and looked up.

"She did design it. Let her back."

Craig smiled at her, and enfolded her in a fierce hug. "Kelsey, what the hell are you doing here?"

By the time he finished the question, the rest of the guys had come out the door, and the security guys had ushered her in behind the curtains rather than let one of their wards out. "I came to hear you in concert!"

She grinned, but it didn't last long, before she was enfolded in another hug from behind.

CHAPTER 29

"Kelsey!" TJ whirled her around and grinned. "This is awesome. I can't believe you came all this way."

She glowed. She knew it. Never had she expected the guys would be this excited to see her. She really had figured that she'd be something of a nuisance, but she so desperately wanted to see JD that she hadn't cared.

Alex hugged her, and girls in the crowd were starting to glare at her, JD just managed a wave, and a confused grin, before management pulled them all to the table to sign autographs. JD looked up, "Can you wait for us?"

"Oh yeah." But after a few minutes it was clear they weren't going anywhere for a while, and she excused herself to run to the car for her purse. When she got back in she was freezing, and had to fight her way back to the edge of the curtain. One girl recognized her and offered her fifty bucks to introduce her to the guys as an old friend. Kelsey refused, then double refused, when the girl said she just had to meet *that* JD. Kelsey figured fire might have burned in her eyes for a moment, because the chick finally backed off.

Kelsey slipped through the curtain, after Alex reminded

them that she was with the band, which nearly made her laugh out loud. She loved that she was *with the band*.

She pointed to the stacks and asked, "Can I have one?"

Alex picked up the nearest one and said "Sure."

When the clerk glared at him, he glared back, "She took all the photos, including that one on your shirt, and we lived in her garage for months. Give her the damn album with a smile."

Kelsey blinked. So did the clerk, who uttered a soft "Okay." Thanking him, Kelsey promptly tore off the cellophane and security stickers.

She was still examining the contents when the guys were herded back through the doors and turned to take her with them.

They walked like they knew the place, even though her itinerary said they were only here for today. They wound their way down a long dull cinderblock hall that went deeper underground and eventually opened into a large room. There were people milling about, mostly with headphones on, and saying things into the microphones while tapping buttons on walkies attached to their waists. Tables draped in white paper were loaded with food and as they went by each of the guys grabbed something and encouraged her to do the same. But she was too keyed up to be hungry.

Eventually, they hit a series of dressing rooms. They all stopped, turning to her. "So you came all this way to see us?"

"Yeah." She smiled. "I hadn't seen you all on a real stage before."

"Are you here for a while?" Alex leaned against the wall, waiting.

"Just overnight, I have a room."

"We can go out." TJ smiled. "I want food. Serious, sit down food."

Kelsey felt the smile get a little more stuck on her face. Somehow, on stage, they really had become a little larger than life. And she knew she was intruding on whatever they usually did, "I don't want to get in the way."

But they didn't let her finish. "No, this is great." "You're not in the way."

So she agreed.

But then TJ turned to Alex. "Listen man, I didn't want to say anything before the show, but Bridget called the bus and she was in a serious snit. You have to go work that out before you go anywhere. I am not fielding another one of those calls."

Kelsey started, it was the first she'd heard of any marital anything other than pure bliss. JD leaned over, "Bridget upset is someone you don't want to be too close to."

Okay. Kelsey just accepted that with a little nod. Alex groaned as he went into his dressing room, muttering something about "It was good to see you."

Craig and TJ went back to get more food, and she was left in the hall with JD, who was looking at her like he still wasn't quite sure she was there. Finally, he shook his head, "Come on."

He led her to the fourth door and walked inside. "I stink. I have to shower."

As proclamations went, it wasn't quite what she'd been hoping for. But he closed the door behind her and grabbed her a bottle of water from an ice bucket on the mirrored counter and motioned for her to get comfortable in a chair, before he disappeared into the tiny bathroom carved out of a corner of the room.

She heard the water start, and promptly stood up to survey the room. There were a few magazines lying around, but the room was fairly obviously for generic use. A bowl of candy and granola bars and fruit sat quietly to one side of the long counter. Aside from the cowboy hat and leather bag with clothes falling out of it, nothing in the room spoke of JD.

Just then, the water turned off, and Kelsey resisted the urge to startle, like she was snooping or something. A minute later the bathroom door opened, and out walked JD, white towel tucked low around his hips, and his hands rubbing another one across his head. His broad chest and lean legs were on display for her whether that's what he intended or not. Kelsey took a second to adjust her gaze from full-on stare. From under the towel, he looked up at her. "I can't believe you're here."

She almost gulped. This was more of what she had hoped for, but it didn't really tell her anything. "Yeah, me either. It was a bit of a whim."

"Where are the kids?"

"With Bethany, at home." She looked at her watch, "Probably still up watching TV."

He laughed then motioned her to get out of the room. "I've got to change."

She gave one brief thought to telling him she'd prefer to stay, but figured it wasn't quite the time. So she headed out into the hall, and decided to entertain herself with the foldouts from the album, when Craig and TJ came back by. "Hey, Kelsey."

She looked up at Craig, still in his stage clothes and still wearing a look that said he'd worked hard up there. "Hey."

"Listen, we've got to shower, and there were these two girls before the show. We're going to meet them out at the bar across the street, then we'll call and catch up to you and JD."

"Sure." She went back to reading as she tried not to lean against the rough cinderblock. They walked through another door just as the one behind her popped open. JD emerged, clean, combed and smelling wonderful. He wore jeans that molded to him and his leather bomber jacket over a black t-shirt. Her eyes took it all in, but she tried not to let it show.

"I'll just be one more second." He smiled.

Of course, while she was working up what to say, he was heading in and out doors. He opened the door across the hallway. She hadn't been looking, at least she thought she hadn't, but some girl greeted him at the door wearing nothing but black lace underwear and a matching bra. JD said something to the girl and closed the door behind them.

Alone in the hallway, Kelsey's heart sank.

There it was—what she'd flown so far to find—the answer. Just not the one she'd wanted. She considered just walking back up the long ramp and heading home, but right then the door clicked open, and JD spoke again to the girl who was draping her arms around him even as he peeled them away, "Just sit tight a little while, you might get lucky."

He pulled the door shut and turned to face her, but Kelsey protested, her hands coming up between them as though she could ward off the squeezing in her heart just by holding him at a distance. "Don't let me keep you from something."

He laughed, "You're not. Trust me, she'll keep."

"Okay." She sighed the word, not able to fight it even as he took her hand and laced his fingers through hers. She should really reclaim those fingers, she thought. There was a definite war here, between the warmth of her hand in his and the coldness generated by seeing a half-naked woman waiting for him.

"Let's go get Craig and TJ."

"They said they would call and catch up to us."

He nodded, his fingers squeezing hers a little tighter. "Okay, then. I'm going to grab my things and throw them on the bus. We can call a cab."

"I have a rental car." She said it even as he went back into the first dressing room and grabbed the cowboy hat, settling it low on his head, and slinging the bag over his shoulder. He never let go of her hand. If only there hadn't been that girl in her underwear, there wouldn't have been anything to temper her giddiness.

"Is it okay if I just bring my bag and you drive?"

She nodded. Kelsey would have considered making a bold play for him at the car or invited him to her hotel. Not that either was an option now, because she had promised herself that him being interested in her didn't matter at all if he wasn't interested exclusively in her.

They approached a set of double doors, and Kelsey could feel the temperature drop several degrees.

"Where's your jacket?"

She startled out of her thoughts. "Huh? Oh, in the car."

"Here." He didn't say anything else, didn't ask if she wanted it, just shrugged out of the bomber and wrapped it around her. It engulfed her, both in size and warmth. The deep smell of him made it feel like she was wearing her boyfriend's letter jacket.

Kelsey scanned the parking lot trying to get oriented. The lot was crowded with far more cars than when she had arrived, and she wasn't sure which way she was facing. After a minute she found a direction, and they slugged off through the dark mush.

Once they were safely inside the car, she cranked the engine to let it warm and started to slip out of his jacket. He turned, "What are you doing?"

"I've got my jacket in here."

He laughed, "Yeah, and it's practically a block of ice." He motioned to his jacket. "Keep it, the car will warm up."

"Thanks." She slid it back up around her shoulders and asked where they were going. Just then his cell phone rang. She waited while he answered it, and started to feel the tension ease out of her when the heater finally started producing something warm.

JD pocketed the phone. "That was Craig. They aren't going to make it. Apparently there are a couple of willing females involved." His eyebrows went up.

Kelsey put the car in gear, figuring they'd at least get out of the parking lot. "So what do you want to eat?"

"I don't even know what's open, but I like TJ's original idea of a good sit-down meal. We've been eating crap this whole trip. We should have cooked more at Christmas."

She pulled into traffic, and they drove for twenty minutes, with JD looking at her phone GPS for clues. Four streets later they saw a diner and decided they were tired of looking. Still in his jacket, Kelsey followed him in, his fingers somehow once again laced through hers. They slid into a vinyl booth and ordered burgers and milkshakes from a woman who seemed happy as a clam to live in the cold Minnesota winter and wait tables late at night.

Kelsey looked up to see JD eye her sideways. "I still can't believe you came."

"Clearly I had to, you guys haven't been in my garage for a while, and you've been working up some new stuff." She thanked the waitress for her milkshake, and had a brief moment wondering why she'd ordered something so cold when the weather was like this. She felt like a teenager in a soda shop. "I really like that new love song you guys did. You wrote it, didn't you?"

"You can tell?"

She shrugged, "It just sounded a lot more like your hand than Craig's. It was definitely something a little different, and it had great . . ." She motioned her hand around, not sure what the words were to describe the way the lyrics had wound round on themselves. "And TJ sold it for all it was worth. Your brother has enough charm for ten men."

"We can't all be perfect."

Kelsey was a bit shocked he'd taken it that way. "Are you serious? All that charm is wonderful on stage, but face to face you never know if he's giving you a real answer."

"I don't know that he is. That's a good way of putting it."

Their burgers arrived and Kelsey bit in, her stomach rumbling and urging her to go for another bite.

JD swallowed the huge bite he'd eaten. "I wish we could go sightseeing while we were here. But we're always too busy to see any of the places we travel through."

"We can do some sightseeing from the car if you want."

He smiled a sad smile. "I'd love to but I have to be on the bus in another hour and a half. We pull out at eleven thirty sharp."

"Well, we'll get a little in, and then I'll drop you off, and head back to my hotel." She dipped one hefty steak fry into a mound of ketchup she'd poured and enjoyed the smell before she ate it. The waitress came by as Kelsey had her mouth full, but JD ordered them both waters. Something else loosened in her chest just then. She'd been thirsty and about to order it herself.

They ate for a few more minutes, then the waters arrived, and JD swallowed his like he'd been dry for a year. "Have you checked into your room yet?"

She shook her head.

"You should stay with us on the bus tonight."

Before she could respond, he started up again. "I'm wide awake, and it's a total bummer that we have to leave from here so soon. We can drop your rental car off and catch a cab from the airport. You can trade your ticket for a flight out of Chicago." Suddenly he stopped talking and just sat there, waiting for a reaction from her.

It was all she could do to finish chewing her bite of burger. She needed a sip of water. As she opened her mouth, he spoke. "That's okay, it was just a thought. It'd be fun to have you on the bus."

"It would be fun."

So he just watched her, waiting for her to make a decision. But there was no real decision to make. She hadn't come all this way to toss and turn in some cold hotel bed. She'd save the price of the room—that was a bonus. "Sure, why not?"

His grin lit up his whole face and made the world change color to something brighter, something deeper. Kelsey hid behind her burger so he wouldn't see what she was thinking. She couldn't remember the last time anyone had been so happy to have her. Sucking in a breath, she forced herself to take a bite and act calm. But it was too difficult to do when you just realized that you were in love with the man across the vinyl booth from you. Never mind that it probably wasn't returned. She had come for an adventure and she was going to get one, it seemed.

She finished what she could of her burger in silence, and the waitress asked if they wanted dessert. Kelsey did, if for no other purpose than to have something to do, something to occupy her mind and keep her from being so obvious. But JD insisted they had to go if they were going to get the car to the airport and get back to the bus in time. Kelsey excused herself to the ladies' room.

She checked her face in the mirror and tried to see if she looked different. She was thirty-two years old and she'd never really been in love before. She hadn't let herself. Andy had been the love of her life. She'd adored and hated her baby brother equally. Now, as she looked for changes, she wondered again if maybe he hadn't set them both free.

She gave her face a bit of a wash, as though the water might rinse away the color that threatened her cheeks. Then she wound her way back out to the table, where somehow JD had already paid the check and procured a big white paper bag.

He stood and reached for her hand with his free one, the other holding up the bag. "I got us four slices of apple pie, and she insisted that we try it with cheddar cheese."

Kelsey's tongue turned at the thought of cheddar cheese on the apple pie, but she was far more interested in the fact that JD had taken her hand every opportunity he'd had tonight. She'd eat cheese on her pie with a smile on her face for more of this.

JD pulled his jacket around her shoulders, again walking in the freezing air in only his shirtsleeves. But he didn't seem to mind, even going around the car and opening her door for her.

He popped open the GPS while she waited for the heater to kick in, then navigated their way back to the airport. They dropped the car in the rental return lot and pulled their bags out of the back seat. JD took hers from her, slinging it over his own shoulder. Kelsey wasn't overly surprised; his mother was a pain in the ass but she'd raised two men who knew how to treat a lady. He didn't even let her hail the cab, although she was only holding her purse and the white bag of pie slices.

Tucking her into the backseat of the cab, he told the driver where they were headed, adding that he needed to stop at a convenience store. Kelsey eyed him, but he dragged her into the 7-11 with him, where he bought three cold cans of coke and a half gallon of vanilla ice cream. The cab sat outside, racking up the fare while they waited in line. JD paid for all of it, then paid the driver, too when he pulled up right beside the bus.

He popped out of the back, letting the cold air in as he stood.

Kelsey could see out the driver's window that TJ had come down the bus steps, his arms wrapped around him against the night. "I see you made it back. We were starting to get worried about you. How was Kelsey?"

CHAPTER 30

"You can ask her yourself." She saw JD grin at his brother, then reach a hand inside the cab and help her slide across the backseat. He pulled her out of the car and closed the door.

"Kelsey!" TJ smiled at her, then at his brother, his expression changing, but Kelsey couldn't decipher what it meant. He gave her a hug then led her up the bus steps. "Welcome to our humble abode."

She laughed.

When JD climbed the steps behind her, the driver pulled the doors closed and stepped on the gas. The motion didn't bother any of the guys, still TJ had to grab her arm to steady her. Craig and Alex came out and greeted her as well, but fairly quickly the others all disappeared into their rooms. Kelsey suspected that their speed may have been due to females waiting behind closed accordion doors. Wasn't that why they hadn't made it earlier?

JD was missing for a moment, but he quickly appeared out of his own room having shed the bags inside. He flipped down a table top, and motioned for her to slide onto the couch that sat directly behind it. Taking the pie bag from her he pulled out pieces and asked if she wanted hers with cheese. Kelsey refused, then made faces at him while he nuked a slice of cheddar right over his.

"It's a southern thing. Just tell me you'll try a bite."

She shook her head, "I don't know."

She sat and watched while he pulled out a coke for her, and scooped ice cream, serving the desert on dinnerware that was nicer than what she had at home.

He slid in next to her and proceeded to try to get her to eat a bite of the cheese covered pie. His slice was gone in moments, and hers followed soon after. He asked about the kids. So she told him stories, promised him that Andie's behavior had been fine, and soothed him that it was all right for her to have his daughter this long. He promised her this touring thing was going to slow way down here really soon, and Kelsey told him she was looking forward to that.

Later, they decided the pie hadn't been big enough and they nuked the last two pieces. Again he put cheese on his and insisted that she try a bite. Only this time he came after her with the fork full of pie and cheese.

"No!"

He waved it around like you might to a small child who didn't want to eat his strained peas. "Come on, Kelsey, it's good. Try a bite."

She shook her head, her mouth clamped together.

"You'll like it. I promise."

She shook her head again, stifling laughter, until he manually tried to get her to open her mouth. First with his finger on her chin, which almost worked. But when his fingertips traced her lips, they parted in surprise at the ripple that spread through her. He fitted the fork into her open mouth and she bit down in surprise.

He had only fed her a bite of pie, but his eyes held hers in a way that seemed to have nothing to do with pastry. Only as she sucked in a breath did she realize that the pie was in her mouth and it actually was good.

She said so. "Ohhhh my God."

"Here, have another." He held up the fork again, giving her another bite. And another, until he'd fed her the remainder of the pie.

"That was so good." The words just tumbled out of her mouth.

But another voice interrupted. "Can you two go to bed? It's two thirty." Alex stood in his open doorway, scratching his head and blinking sleepy eyes.

"Oh, I'm so sorry. We'll be quiet." Kelsey felt so bad. She'd woken him up in the middle of the night on a moving motel.

"Sorry, Alex." JD scooped up the plates and put them into the sink. He carefully folded the table back up and secured it in place, before grabbing his jacket in one hand and her fingers in the other. He led her down the short hall, just across from Alex's doorway and into his open one.

Kelsey's eyes almost bugged out of her head. The room was so small, and there was nowhere to sleep. She almost said so, when JD unfolded a bed at her waist height, much like the table top had. He added a few pillows while she still stood in the open doorway. "You sleep on that?"

"Every night. It's fairly comfortable."

She eyed the thin strings supporting it at each end. "It won't hold both of us, I'm surprised it holds you."

"I can clear out underneath, and you sleep on it."

"No! It would drop me on you and kill you in the middle of the night." That thing looked scary. The mattress looked plenty fluffy and it was somewhere just wider than a twin, but those little strings were too weak. She said so.

"They're wire, Kelse. They'll hold, I promise." He scooted over and she backed out the door to make room. Turning, he sat himself on the high bed and bounced, promising again, "It'll hold."

"You maybe."

He grabbed her and pulled her between his spread legs, closing the door behind her. Wrapping his arms around her waist he leaned back, lifting her off her feet. He gave a few test bounces while she tried not to squeal. "See, it holds both of us."

"Okay! Set me down." She whispered it, not wanting to wake Alex again.

He let her slide down him until her feet hit the ground, but he didn't let go. The friction sparked something and his grin faded to a hot look in the dim light through the window. She couldn't breathe. Couldn't think with him looking at her like that.

Just as fast as he had grabbed her, he released her.

A sharp stab of disappointment hit her square in the chest, until she felt his hands. His fingers traced her jaw, and she held perfectly still, breathing slowly, not wanting it to ever end. Her eyes drifted closed as he followed the lines of her face to her lips, and there was nothing she could do to stop her head from turning and pressing to his fingertips.

She didn't see him coming but she felt him, his breath was sweet from the pie, and she could smell whatever aftershave he'd used. It took forever for his mouth to find hers, but when it did she felt enchanted—suddenly awake from a long sleep.

There was nothing tentative about this kiss. His mouth molded to hers, changing pressure, nibbling along her lower lip. His hands held her steady, and he explored her.

Her own hands crept up his arms, loving the feel of him, solid beneath his clothes, strength sliding off him in waves. Her arms slipped down, locking around his waist. The simple act of lacing her fingers and holding him there brought him just a fraction closer. JD didn't need any other signals.

He changed the kiss. His tongue traced her lower lip and

slipped into her mouth when she sighed, bringing with it a flood of heat. For a moment she just enjoyed being tasted. He was pure sex in the middle of a lonely life. So she leaned into him, with her body, with her mouth, with her tongue, giving back what he was giving her.

She didn't know how long they clung like that, just tasting, but his fingers found her hair, and tilted her head back, gaining access to her throat, and kissing her there over and around the locket that he'd given her, while his hands traveled down her back and slipped under the edge of her sweater. He wrapped one arm around her while his mouth slipped down into the wide open neck the sweater revealed. His other hand slid up under the front, finding her bra, and creating a deep need to lean into his touch.

A sigh reached her throat, and he stopped. It took only a second, and no second thought, to look at him. His eyes found hers, giving no indication why he'd ended what was wonderful. While he watched her face, she felt his fingers tickle at her waist, grabbing the hem of the sweater, and it was a moment before she realized he was silently asking permission to take it off. Languidly, she raised her arms, saying yes, and the soft fuzz slipped up her torso and past her lips which gasped as she felt his mouth on her breast.

His teeth grazed what the sweater had revealed even before it was over her head. His hands roamed her body, and her bra simply went missing, leaving her bare for his fingers to explore. His tongue touched the tip of her nipple, sending her nearly over the edge, and she realized that she wasn't close enough. One leg slipped up over his, and when he realized what she was doing, he grasped her hips and held her steady. His fingers gripped through denim, while she shifted and climbed him, until she straddled his waist and he held her flush against serious evidence of his desire.

He kissed her mouth again, while she pulled the long sleeved shirt up his chest, waiting until he pulled his arms down, maintaining the kiss until the last moment when she tugged the shirt over his head, him breathing like he was tortured to not be in full contact. She dropped it, not caring where it was so long as it was gone.

His mouth found hers and their hands worked at the same purpose, maintaining as much naked skin contact as possible. His chest was hot and solid pressed to her breasts, and she rubbed up against him feeling wanton and wanted. One of his hands splayed warm over her bare back, the other grabbing her hip and locking her to him while his body moved in a way that left no uncertainty about what he wanted to do.

She moved against him, a sensuous 'yes.' He toed off his shoes, that movement alone creating friction in the right places and making her crazier. She reached back to peel the heels from her feet, making her chest jut forward. And he took full advantage. All she could do was feel, and he was lifting her, rubbing against her, and setting her down on the soft mattress. His mouth left hers, making a slick path behind her ear, down her throat and over the tip of one breast. Her fingers found his chest and touched ridges of muscle that made her stomach clench and flat nipples that made his. The textures of him ranged from smooth to rough, but every inch of him burned with fever.

He left her, and again she felt a momentary panic. But her jeans were moving, down her hips, and off the end of the bed, until she was lying there in only her necklace and a white lace thong. He traced the edges reverently then kissed her navel, making his way back up until he was lying beside her and pulling her knee up and over his hip. He watched her face while his hand slid down her belly and under the edge of the lace. Her eyes glazed when he found her, his fingers testing, slipping and rubbing.

Her hips moved in response to his touches, wanting more,

and feeling too much. She bucked against his hand as one rough finger slid inside her and the groan was from his throat, not hers. Her own hands searched the front of him frantically, flying until they reached the edge of his jeans and popped the buttons open, shoving down the band of his underwear until he fell free, thick and heavy, into her hand. He pushed against her fingers, and she focused just long enough to see his own vision go hazy. She wrapped her hand tight around him and enjoyed the feel of him in her control.

His breathing labored like her own, and his whole body moved in response to her touches. His eyes slipped closed and she leaned in to kiss him, fusing their mouths together in a common want. But abruptly he pushed away, pushed her hands off of him, and stood. She would have felt scared, but she was still hot and still wanting, and suffering from the lack of him. With careful movements he shed the last of his clothes, and stood naked before her, then reached out and removed the lace that was her last hiding place.

For a moment, he simply looked at her, his eyes roaming what lay before him, want shining bright in his gaze. She felt the bed shift as he came back beside her, and his body heat reached her before his fevered skin did. His mouth had no trouble finding hers again, and for a minute he kissed her like that was all he was allowed to do. But his kisses made her heady, and she rolled against him, challenging him to do the same. He answered.

For a few seconds he fumbled, the rip of foil and the feeling of his movements let her know he'd put on a condom. She saw him move over her, finding a place for himself between legs that easily parted for him.

His fingers trailed reverently along her skin as though she was satin, not human, and they found her ready. Her hands inched up the bands of pure muscle along his arms, and her body drew toward his, magnet to iron. Finally, she felt his thick head at her entrance, and she pushed against him, desperately wanting.

Slowly and by degrees he tortured her, rocking into her inch by inch, when she so hopelessly needed all of him. When, at last, he was fully inside her, his mouth found hers again, sealing them together in every way possible. He moved just a fraction deeper and set off a reaction she was helpless to stop. Her orgasm took her, undulating her hips against him while inside her muscles clenched around him, released and clenched, in an endless series.

When at last she came around she was nearly limp in his arms, his body still locked inside hers. His eyes were bright in the near black, and he watched her as he moved again. Her mouth was open and she could taste the scent of him, smell how they were joined, and breathe in his thundering heartbeat. They touched, skin to skin, and his body moved in her the way it had promised when they were still partially clothed.

He set a slow rhythm that changed lyrically as he drove himself deeper into her heart. She fought to meet him measure for measure. He made love to her for ages, taking her where there was no world beyond the touch of his body, then building the pleasure even beyond his own steel control. She watched as he snapped and became animal lust, taking her in a way that she fought to give back to him. Only, as he pushed over his own precipice, he took her with him. She felt his release as his body struggled to create something lasting beyond this moment, and hers stroked him, making both their climaxes stronger.

They lay tangled together in sheets and sweat, laboring for oxygen, and desperate for each other. Later, Kelsey felt her breathing regain a pace akin to normal, although how she'd ever be normal again was beyond the haze she was in. JD pushed himself away, against her fingers that clawed at him wanting to keep him there as long as possible. But maybe it was good that one of them was thinking about the condom.

He stood in the tiny space at the end of the room, facing away from her, and Kelsey languished in the night air, feeling it cool her wet skin. There was still barely enough light to see, and Kelsey breathed in one big lungful, knowing that he had pushed away only to return more fiercely several times before.

But he didn't come back. His breathing labored again and he walked the tiny confine as though pacing a larger room. He was clearly at a loss, and Kelsey rolled to her side, getting worried but not scared. Not until her hand slipped under the pillow and found the large pile of condoms he kept stashed there. Looking up, she saw his hands go into his hair, and cold fingers went into her heart. She waited, knowing she hadn't been the first one here, and wouldn't be the last.

His words only confirmed her thoughts. "I shouldn't have . . . It wasn't supposed to go like this."

He may have been at a loss, but she wasn't. Tears welled, unbidden and unstoppable, in her eyes, and she rolled away attempting to hide them. But he was JD, her best friend, and she'd never really been able to hide anything like this from him. Where would she hide now anyway, when she didn't even have a shred of clothing on?

His voice came to her again, "I should have been clear first. Kelse?"

She didn't answer him. Couldn't.

The cold in her heart had seeped out to everywhere.

"Kelse, I'm sorry, don't cry. Baby, please."

She'd been on the verge of growling out that he shouldn't call her 'Kelse' when he'd switched to 'baby', which was worse.

"Did I hurt you?"

He'd climbed up behind her on the bed, and his hands were in her hair. She pushed them away even as she shook her head 'no'. *You didn't hurt me, I did.*

His hands left, but she could feel him, restless, on the mattress even though she couldn't see him. She curled herself along the edge, trying not to touch, and fighting for control of those tears.

The only thing that he even attempted to reach her with was his voice. "Do you miss Andrew?"

She blinked, wondering what in the hell he was asking, when she realized that she hadn't said enough about her brother and he'd mistaken the man for her husband. Now was not the time to correct him, and she answered with true words, if not the truth. "Yes, I do."

"I'm sorry. I didn't know. I shouldn't have done it."

She tightened every muscle, hoping that he would get the idea. She didn't want to talk, didn't want to hear his apologies.

It worked, because he lowered himself along the mattress behind her, careful not to touch or even invade her space any more than necessary. She didn't know how long she lay there before his breathing evened out. She didn't think her own ever would.

Quietly, she stood up, and slipped back into her clothing.

CHAPTER 31

JD woke tangled in sheets that smelled like sex, like *her*. Visions and feelings assailed him as his eyes blinked slowly open. Kelsey kissing him back with all she was worth. Kelsey opening for him. The feel of her naked against him was a sense memory he knew he'd never shake. The smell of her on the sheets around him proved it wasn't just another of his very vivid dreams.

He had made love to Kelsey.

Then he remembered the rest.

He had made Kelsey cry. He'd fucked it up, literally, and needed to fix it now before the problems solidified in the daylight.

She wasn't in the bed with him, and he figured she had simply slipped away, to the bathroom, or maybe even out to the common area. Wanting to rectify things, he pulled on jeans, and with a second thought a t-shirt. She might not want to be reminded of his bare body and although it hurt to think so, he would be considerate of that.

He could lose her as a lover. Hell, he already had, and he

would have to live with that. No options. But he couldn't lose her as a friend.

He pulled the sheets up close enough to being straight, and folded the bed into its niche in the wall. He startled when silver things dropped out at the hinge. Even as he was bending to pick them up, he realized they were the condoms he had grabbed, and there were something like fifteen of them there. He'd just grabbed a huge handful, praying that he might get to use one. He had. And only one.

JD stuffed them into his bag, and pulled back the folding door. She wasn't in the common room. Only TJ was. And his brother was buried so deep in his coffee that he didn't even acknowledge that JD had come up.

There was water running in the bathroom, so he leaned against the wall and waited for her. Wondering what he would say, and not even knowing how she would look. If she would face him like any other morning, or if she would be bleary eyed and hide herself back in the bathroom.

At last, the lock turned and JD straightened, but it was Alex that emerged from the tiny cell.

JD assaulted him. "Was Kelsey in there?"

Alex shot him a look saying he'd flipped his lid, but JD didn't care. "No."

He ran the five steps to the common area, this time catching TJ's attention. "Where's Kelsey?"

"With you."

He shook his head. His breathing raced; a panic like he had never known set in. He wondered if she had somehow slipped past him and was in his room again. He looked. No Kelsey. He stuck his head through Alex's open door, then assaulted Craig, knowing that Kelsey liked him and may have crawled in after leaving him. Craig didn't even get upset, and JD assumed that his terror showed on his face.

She wasn't there. All four of them converged in the common

area toward the front. His voice strained, giving away his feelings, but he didn't care. "We're on a moving bus. Where could she have gone?"

Alex looked at him askance. "I thought she was with you. She was a two-thirty last night."

That made TJ and Craig raise their eyebrows, but Alex kept talking. "I thought I heard some noises that would indicate things were going well."

"You did." JD laid it out there. It didn't matter what his friends knew. Nothing mattered except finding Kelsey. "We did, but I made her cry."

TJ stood up, putting his hands on JD's shoulders, but he couldn't stand being touched, even by his younger brother, and he shrugged the hands off. TJ spoke anyway, "Listen, JD, the bus wasn't in constant motion. Maybe she got off. Where are her things?"

JD barely heard the end of the question. He slammed toward the very front, crossing the line he wasn't supposed to while the bus was in motion, and he got the driver's attention, "Ben, did the woman who came on last night get off?"

Ben nodded. "Yup. About four-thirty."

"But she didn't get back on?" Horrifying thoughts assaulted him. Had Ben left her there? Was she stranded?

"Said something about fetching a car and getting her flight."

JD felt his heart slow. He wasn't sure he believed Ben. Surely Kelsey wouldn't have . . .

But he ran back and checked his room. Sure enough, both her bags were gone. Kelsey had left, voluntarily, in the middle of the night. She had gotten off at an unknown gas station somewhere along the freeway.

JD sank into the corner of his room, sitting on the floor, feeling the rumble of the bus beneath him. A while later TJ joined him, having asked a few more questions of Ben. "She got off about halfway between St. Paul and Chicago and told him she would get one of the local rental car companies to drive out to her. She said she was heading back to St. Paul."

JD didn't respond, but his brain did. She had decided to wait at a gas station, for a stranger, rather than stay on the bus with him. It was easier to drive hours out of her way, than stay and let the bus drop her off at O'Hare Airport.

All he could think was that he had made mistake after mistake.

Every scenario he'd played in his brain before yesterday involved him telling her how he felt *before* any sex happened. He'd held his beating heart out to her last night, but hadn't said so.

"What happened?" TJ's voice was like his posture, beside JD on the floor, simply offering support.

JD knew he didn't have to answer, but he had no control of the words pouring out of him. "Everything was great, but after, when I realized I hadn't told her . . . I didn't get a chance to. She started crying."

"Jesus, JD." But TJ's voice was full of sympathy.

"She misses her husband still. I guess she wasn't ready. Then she disappeared." His breath came in gulps as he realized the ramifications of Kelsey not speaking to him.

TJ's arm slung around his shoulder. "I just have a hard time believing she didn't feel the same way about you. It seemed it was always written all over her face. She'll come around."

"No." JD didn't believe that. Kelsey had always been decisive. She stuck to her guns, she wouldn't have run if she'd intended to turn around.

"Sometimes women are just slow to see what's in front of their faces. People say it's men, but that's not always true."

JD prayed his brother was right, but he didn't believe the plea would be answered. He prayed that Kelsey was all right.

TJ fished through the leather bag in the corner, pulling out his brother's cell phone. JD stared at it as it was slapped into his hand.

"Call her. Find out if she's okay."

JD nodded, hitting speed-dial. It went straight to voicemail, sending his heart pounding again. What if she wasn't okay? What if she was beside the road, or something had happened at that gas station?

TJ watched, and tried again. "Would the babysitter know where she is?"

JD nodded and punched through his contact list until he had Bethany. He waited while the phone rang, his hands close to full-on shaking. He didn't know if Kelsey would ever speak to him again, but worse, he didn't know where she was, didn't know if she was safe.

"Hello?"

"Bethany! It's JD."

"Oh hey, how are—"

He cut her off, he didn't have time for pleasantries, "Do you know where Kelsey is?"

He heard the frown in her voice, but she answered. "She called a few hours ago, said her flight was a little late and asked if I could pick up the kids at school. Is that okay? Are you coming back?"

His breath expelled, and his shoulders sighed. Kelsey was okay. Her phone wasn't answering because she was in the air. "No, it's okay. Thank you, Bethany."

He simply hung up, unwilling to listen any further, unable to carry on a conversation.

"She's all right." TJ could tell just from watching JD's posture.

"She's on a later flight."

"Okay." TJ's hand rested on JD's shoulder while he stood. Silently, he left.

In a moment, JD was alone in the corner of his room, his

head resting in his hands. He didn't see how things had gone so wrong, when they had felt so right. Maybe they had only felt that way to him. In his head, it hadn't been sex, it had been something he'd never experienced before. Afterward had been something he'd never experienced before either. He'd had no idea how to handle it, and clearly he'd handled it wrong.

Those same thoughts cycled through his brain. Never really changing, just seeping deeper and deeper into him, down into some level of acceptance of what had happened.

At one point, TJ had brought him food. JD had wanted to tell his brother where to put it. He was spoiling for a chance to yell his frustrations at someone. But he discovered he hadn't the energy.

Later, the bus rumble changed underneath him, although JD barely noticed it until it bounced him around too much. Just then he felt the bus stop, and the small lurch as the brake was set.

Again TJ came to sit beside him. For a moment he just sat, offering his presence. But he was TJ and it wasn't long before he offered his voice, too. "She should be home now, right? With the kids?"

JD looked at his watch, somehow it had become four in the afternoon, and from the view out the window, he was very much in Chicago. He nodded.

TJ simply picked up the cell phone that JD had left lying beside him on the floor. It hadn't rung. She wasn't calling him. "You always call her when we get in."

JD didn't answer, so TJ punched buttons until he found Kelsey's number. JD didn't pay attention until his brother handed him the phone, "It's ringing."

He panicked, his thoughts and heart racing, but TJ saw that and talked him down. "You always call her when we get in, you can't change that now. You have to go on tonight. And you clearly need to hear her voice."

What if she hangs up?

He didn't get to worry further than that, because her voice answered, sweet and unsure. "Hello?"

TJ left the room, and JD closed his eyes, using all his energy for the conversation. "Hey, Kelse, it's me, JD." He didn't know why he'd said that.

"I know."

"I just wanted to see if you got in okay."

Something in her tone softened. "Yeah, I'm here, and so are the kids—"

She sounded like she was about to hand him off, so he butted in. "You gave me a hell of a scare. I just had to be sure you were all right."

"I'm sorry. I didn't mean to. I just had to . . ." She didn't finish.

"I know. I just needed to hear your voice." He sighed, too tired to think of anything else to say. "Can you put Andie on?"

"Of course."

A few moments and a few shuffling noises later he heard his daughter, bright and cheerful, "Hi, Daddy!"

It was exactly what he needed.

Somehow he made it onstage that evening. The guys asked nothing of him, except that he hit his notes. He spent Friday in a haze, trying to figure out what to do to fix the rift between himself and Kelsey, but he came up with no solutions.

When the bus stopped, they had only half an hour to unload. But TJ showed up in his room again, and handed him the cell phone. "Call her."

JD shook his head. "I called her yesterday. She's okay."

"You call her every day. And things are not okay. I can see that in your face." He held the phone out, waiting for JD to take it from his hand. But JD didn't. TJ continued, "I would imagine her face looks much the same. She needs to hear from you. Call her."

Still JD simply looked out the window at the unfamiliar skyline that had come to a standstill. He didn't even know where they were, and he didn't care.

What he did know was that TJ was almost right. Kelsey probably didn't need to hear from him, but he needed to hear her voice. Needed to put every patch in place before he had to face her. So he took the phone.

TJ looked at him, "Good boy."

At any other time, it would have been insulting, but right now it just passed by. TJ stood in the doorway just long enough to see that JD dialed Kelsey's number, then shut the pocket door, and left him with his thoughts and the ringing of the phone.

It rang long enough that he wasn't sure she would pick up. The dreary sky outside beyond the bus let loose, hitting the window with a smack of rain, and keeping him from hearing any noises from the phone.

Her soft voice startled him. "Hey, JD."

"Hi." It bothered him how he warmed because she had simply picked up and deigned to speak to him. For a moment he couldn't think of anything else to say, but he realized if he didn't speak, things would only get worse. "I wanted to see how you were doing."

"Do you want to speak to the kids?"

"No." His voice sounded weary to his own ears, "I want to talk to you. Tell me what's going on."

She could have interpreted that any way she wanted. "I got a check from the label."

"And?"

"It's huge." There was a pause. "I thought I would take the kids on a small vacation later."

"You deserve one. Maybe you leave the kids with me and you

go with a friend." He smiled, until he realized that he might wind up babysitting while she went on an overnight with a date. His stomach turned at the very thought, but he worked hard to hold steady.

There was a pause. He had caused it, they had never had pauses before, but after a few seconds ticked by unused, she filled it in. "Brenda called me. They wanted to know what I would do with photos of their girl band. For t-shirts, a poster."

He gave her what she'd given him. "Of course she did. You're an amazing photographer. You'll get it."

"Thank you." She didn't pause, but her voice was soft, as though she couldn't quite commit herself to the volume required to be excited. "I have to research the band. So, if you could watch the kids a few nights, I could go see them perform."

"I'll be back on Sunday at six a.m. Any time after that will be fine."

He heard a trace of a smile. "You don't have to watch them the day you get in. Maybe later."

"Whatever you want." He meant that about more than just the babysitting, but didn't know how to say that. He would give her anything, except unlimited space from him. He just needed her too much.

When he hung up, he hadn't spoken to the kids at all. He wished he'd had time, but repairing things with Kelsey was far more important.

That night he went on stage remembering what he played for: Kelsey's studio.

He asked her Saturday evening when he called if she had started clearing the garage for her portrait shop yet.

She hadn't.

She asked if Alex and Bridget had patched things up. As far as he knew, Alex had fixed them that very evening. If only he could do as well.

This time he asked if he could let himself in and sleep on the futon, so he'd be there when Andie woke up.

She hesitated.

After all the times that she had led him in there and sent him to bed, all the days he had just stayed there when the layover between tours was too short, she hesitated.

He was about to promise that he'd stay in the back room, that he wouldn't come climb into bed with her, when she said, "Sure, that would be okay."

"Thank you."

It grated. He'd never had to ask her before. Never felt the urge to thank her profusely just for letting him stay. Of course, he had never before pushed himself on her and made her cry.

They hung up and he went about getting into the theater and getting his bag into his dressing room. All the while, he was thinking that he knew he hadn't forced himself on her. She'd been willing, at the time. But maybe if he'd talked to her first, instead of just kissing her and totally losing his head, they both would have realized how she felt and not made such a colossal mistake.

Of course, if they had talked, and he had told her how he felt, she might have pulled away just as much. Maybe it was better the way it had gone down. He had a chance to redeem himself.

The only problem was that he knew what it felt like to be inside her—to have her kiss him back and move with him. But he wouldn't have that again, and the knowledge only hurt him. So he shoved it to the far reaches of his brain.

He went out on stage and tried to smile. He played for the people in the audience, trying to convert new fans. They would support him in the coming months, if the band could rack up the numbers. He did a fine job of faking it, until they got to *I am*. The song was now a knife twisting deep in his chest.

He realized that he had written that song too close to the heart. He hadn't played with anything to make the song work better. He'd simply told it exactly as it was. The problem now was that he recognized that he was all those things in the song. Except for one, *hopeful*.

TJ sang the last line in the spot light. The instruments were quiet; the way it was intended to be. It was a damn good thing, too. Because, by that last line, his jaw was clenched tight, and it was all he could do not to smash his guitar in frustration. But country fans weren't used to musicians smashing instruments on stage.

So he pulled it together and made it through.

They hit the road for the last time, and he packed everything before falling into a deep sleep of exhaustion. Dreams came in senses, not stories. And when he jolted into reality with the stopping of the bus, he could still smell her on his sheets.

He blinked awake, dressed and brushed his teeth before getting off the bus. This made him the last one off. Only TJ addressed the Kelsey issue, with a hug and a 'go get'em,' before leaving him to drive home himself.

Problem was 'home' was his condo, and 'home' was Kelsey's house, too. His car arrived at the curb without knowing how he'd gotten there. The sun had peeked out from behind clouds while he had driven.

Still he pulled out his instruments and hauled his tired and fearful feet to the front door. Using his key, he let himself inside. The kids rushed at him, already awake and up, screaming and clamoring for hugs and kisses.

He grabbed each of them in turn, giving a bear hug, and asking how they were. But there were only the three kids, and it didn't take that long.

Kelsey had stood at the fringes of the frenzy, in her oversize t-shirt, but this time she had pulled on sleep pants, and JD felt the loss right there with the idea that she had already altered things because of Wednesday. She would glance at him, meet his eyes, and offer a forced smile before looking away.

Still, he did it. He stood up and looked her square in the face, and held his arms out to her.

She hesitated until he felt the sting of rejection.

Then her feet started to move. She came to him, and the hug she gave him was stiff and awkward, but it was all he was allowed to hope for.

She started to pull away, and he wasn't going to hold her too tight, to keep her there. Instead he waylaid her by leaning over and speaking into her ear. "I'm sorry."

He felt her head shake 'no' from where she had leaned against him. This time she whispered. "Don't be. It was my fault."

"No. It was mine."

CHAPTER 32

JD ran home to get nicer clothes before they all went to church. Andie walked with Allie and Daniel, the three of them chattering endlessly. Kelsey was clearly in control of the little group. And he wasn't included.

It was the same thing they'd done plenty of times before. Only this time he didn't hold her hand. She didn't even scoot closer to him after the kids had left for the story, she remained a full seat away on the hard pew. She didn't relax during the sermon, her eyes didn't wander, and she stayed a little too focused.

On the surface everything was fine, they functioned together. The details made a world of difference, and a world of hurt. His mind had wandered during the sermon. He almost felt her moving against his fingers, thought about what she looked like lying there naked, and how her eyes went hot with want when he'd shed the last of his clothes.

Church was about the last place he should have been thinking of that. Her skirt was meant to be proper—it wasn't improper, certainly no one looked at her funny for wearing it to church—but it skimmed her curves so that he could see the dip of her waist and the flare of her hips. The sweater covered her from chin to fingertips, but it was white and soft and fuzzy and begged to be touched.

However, her posture made it clear in no uncertain terms that her clothes were lying. She was not to be touched. Most certainly not by him. Kelsey sat stiff and formal and the few smiles she offered him were much of the same.

Afterward, he trailed them to the bakery and the duck pond, talking to the kids, helping them talk to the baker. He kept the aggressive ducks away, and after the mini-van arrived home he thanked Kelsey profusely, took his daughter, and ran.

He only made it as far as his condo, but it was far enough. He was out of Kelsey's sphere, and he began to breathe. It was just a simple matter of taking in oxygen, but he hadn't been able to do it properly since he walked in her front door that morning. He still wasn't doing what he used to. He wasn't sure he'd ever really breathe again. At least now he was able to move the air in and out of his lungs and sustain his functions.

Andie was the only thing that relaxed him. She chattered about school and crayons, about Daniel and Allie and how they had eaten green eggs and ham again. For once he was grateful that his daughter could talk from one subject to another, never needing a pause. They watched a little bit of TV that Andie had chosen, but she was constantly pausing the program to add her own two cents. He taught her how to play Parcheesi, and they went two rounds before he shuffled her off to bed.

He read her a story and tucked her in for the first time in a week. He had one more week of touring at the end of the month, then they would play locally a bit more and spend time working on their next move. Of course, the great irony was that he had plenty of time to spend with Kelsey here in a few weeks.

JD pulled the covers under Andie's chin and kissed her on her forehead.

"Daddy, why are you sad?"

He highly suspected she was stalling, trying to keep him there and talking, but he also felt he couldn't brush this one off, not if he wanted to encourage her to talk to him in later years. Kelsey had told him that kids don't hear what we say, but they see what we do. "I lost something wonderful."

"Can you find it again?" Her head cocked.

"No, baby, it's gone." He patted her hand where it curled around the sheet. "That's why I'm sad."

Andie smiled. "We can find you a new one."

"No, there was only one."

"Oh." She frowned a bit at him, "I'm sorry, Daddy."

"Me, too." He kissed her soft forehead, and turned out the light.

Now with nothing to do, he looked for a way to fight the echo of the words he'd said. Kelsey was irreplaceable.

JD started to ring the doorbell Monday morning. But it was seven thirty, she *had* to be expecting them. He didn't remember ringing the doorbell before and he'd be damned if he'd give that up, too.

He pushed the door open, startling Kelsey as she picked up an empty bowl of cereal from in front of Allie and disappeared into the kitchen.

He forced the conversation, hollering out, "Good Morning."

"We'll be ready in just a minute." But she didn't come back out. Didn't look him in the eye. Just shuffled her kids around and pulled heavy jackets on each of them.

Kelsey looked tired, like she wasn't sleeping very well, and JD figured she was just as upset as he was. Only, while she was upset about what *had* happened, he was upset about what hadn't. Again, there was nothing to do for it, nothing except pray that things came around, that they could work out something between them and get it back to good.

They dropped all the kids off, including Allie, who was a chattering puffball of leopard print. She grabbed his hand that last block and told him that they'd gotten her adorable coat just the previous week, while he'd been gone, and wasn't she beautiful? He told her she was, and purposefully bit his tongue to refrain from saying 'just like your mother'. That would only make things worse. He wondered if Kelsey had dropped Allie off last to have less time alone with him.

He shoved his hands deep in his pockets, to keep them warm, and to stall the itch to hold her hand in his. That wasn't going to happen again. He'd tried for more and failed. To keep his mind from wandering back to places he couldn't go again, he spoke, "What are you up to today?"

"I'm meeting the new band. Talking about anything specific that they want. Then we'll schedule a shoot."

He nodded, "It sounds like they want to use you again, and they should. What you did for us was phenomenal."

"Thanks." But her response was dry and lacked any depth. "That was easier, I know you guys. I know how to get what I needed out of you."

He shrugged. "I'll bet you can do it again."

She didn't respond and they walked the rest of the way in silence, parting company at the corner with only the most cursory of exchanges. JD climbed the back stairs to his condo while his heart shattered into pieces again. He truly could have sat in the corner and cried all day, but he wouldn't let himself. There were things to do, things he owed her.

So she found him that afternoon in her garage.

She drove past in the mini-van and must have squealed to a stop, because she almost immediately ran around back to see him. She pulled up cold at the sight, making him wonder what the hell he'd done wrong now. It looked damn good to him.

"What is this?" Her tone was downright frosty.

He didn't know how to respond. He'd expected excitement, at least a smile. "Your studio."

She looked the garage up and down. All the remnants of the band had been removed: he'd swept, installed a railing to the ceiling connected around three sides of the garage, and long cloth backdrops hung from rods so they would slide in whichever direction she wanted. He'd bought the variety of colors and textures the supplier recommended. Two umbrella shaped lights with diffusers slid up and down mounted poles to provide light from any angle she wanted. But she didn't look happy about it.

He couldn't bear the expression on her face, and he backpedaled. "Look, if you don't like the ones I chose, you can return them and get what you want."

"You should return all of it and get your money back."

He was stunned. "I thought you wanted a studio in here."

"I do."

She didn't elaborate.

So he pushed, "Then what's the issue?"

"I know what this stuff costs. There are several thousand dollars here."

"Yes, and . . ." He waited, but not long.

It was like someone had lit her on fire. She would have been magnificent to watch, if it hadn't all been aimed at him. "I don't want your money. You don't owe me anything. I made a horrible mistake, but *I* made it." She pressed her fingers to her heart. "You throwing money at it makes it worse."

It hit like bricks. She felt like a whore, like he was paying her for the other night. And it was his turn to go up in a flash. He'd never been so insulted, and by someone who was supposed to know him better than anyone else. His voice slid out like ice, "This was my plan for my first paycheck from way back when we were signed. It was a god-damned present. A thank-you for everything you did. If you want to trash it or burn it or return it, that's your prerogative. But if you want to throw it back in my face, that's too bad. Because my face won't be here to throw it at. It's a damned *gift*."

The wrench he didn't realize he'd still been holding slipped from his fingers, hitting the cement floor with a clang to rattle the windows.

He didn't look at her.

Didn't care if she was stunned, or mad, or what.

JD simply walked away.

CHAPTER 33

JD drove to pick up Andie that afternoon, and wondered why the hell he'd been walking in the cold all this time.

He knew, of course. He'd been walking because Kelsey walked. And because he got to walk with her. Rather than drive right back home and have Kelsey know he'd been flat-out avoiding her, he drove Andie to Chuck E. Cheese's for an early dinner of things that weren't very healthy. But they were healthier than whatever he might make for supper in his little black rage.

His cell phone rang and he answered it even as he plucked off the long chain of tickets he'd won at skeeball and handed them to his daughter, who jumped up and down. "Hello?"

He realized his mistake right away. He hadn't checked the caller ID. If it was Kelsey, he was pretty sure he'd hang right up.

"Hey," It was TJ's voice, and relief rushed through him. "I was just calling to see if you two had managed to patch things up."

Yeah, that was a big laugh. JD told Andie to go play or trade in her tickets. With an eye on her, he wandered back to their booth, "No. Not at all. I didn't think it was possible, but now it's worse."

"Shit." The way his brother said it, the word had three syllables. JD thought it was still a few syllables shy of where it would really express the situation. "What happened?"

"I put up a portrait studio in her garage."

"Yes, I see. You are clearly a very bad person." Then his tone changed from sarcasm. "How the fuck does that make things worse?"

"She decided I was paying her for the sex the other night. She said that being with me was *her* mistake, and my throwing money at her only made it worse."

A woman looked at him with a curled lip and furrowed brows—like he was a monster.

JD was about to tell her where to stuff it, when he realized he'd spoken at a fairly normal volume in the middle of kiddie land about whether or not he'd treated his neighbor like a whore.

"Oh, hell JD." He could practically see his brother pacing the tiny apartment kitchen. "I have to say I expected you to yell at me for interrupting the two of you having hot monkey sex."

"Yeah, that's not going to happen."

"I still say it will." TJ had some sort of belief in this shit. He'd always had it. He'd believed that he would marry his high school girlfriend. Never mind that everyone else could see that one was over before it had started. Or that JD was pretty certain his brother had cheated on the girl. TJ just wasn't the most reputable source for predictions of everlasting love.

"Well, it won't. I'm done."

"JD, you two just need to talk abou—"

JD hung up on his brother.

JD drove Andie to school the following morning, and picked her up the same way. He saw Kelsey walking with her kids, but he didn't wave or anything. He'd been icy and numb for about forty-eight hours. He figured that was good, he was in for a world of hurt when the cold wore off, and there wouldn't be much he could do about it. At least this way he could function.

He fixed macaroni and cheese with applesauce for dinner and served it on paper plates with plastic spoons so he wouldn't have to wash anything. He figured Andie would get her daily allowance of polyvinyl. Then he looked at the calendar and marked a big black X exactly one week out.

On that day he would have to start cooking healthy meals and stop sleepwalking around. But he had until then to refuse to feel anything. He figured he was entitled.

As part of his entitlement he sat on the couch and watched stupid TV, flipping channels each time there was a commercial, and giving Andie cursory help with her tracing-letters homework.

About an hour later a knock came at his back door. JD dragged himself to his feet, mentally shuffling through the possibilities. Alex with Bridget problems, Craig with TJ problems, or TJ come to talk about Kelsey problems. If it was TJ he'd just close the door again.

But it was Kelsey, and she looked scared. "Help me."

Blood flooded him, the panic was instantaneous, she needed him. He grabbed her arms and looked her in the eyes. "What is it?"

"I fucked up." She was on the verge of tears, and he wondered who was in the hospital. "I'm sorry. I've messed everything up between us."

He felt the tension seep out—not all the way, but most of it. He didn't speak.

"I shouldn't have slept with you. I gave you the wrong idea. And I'm so sorry."

He waited.

"I know you better than that. I know you wouldn't try to pay me. I was just so upset." Fat tears had welled in her eyes and now spilled over onto her cheeks. He wanted to brush them away, but checked the urge. He simply stood there in the open doorway, letting the heat out and the cold in. And waiting.

"I can't handle not talking to you, JD. I can't stand this."

Neither could he really, but she kept going, not letting him talk.

"I lost Andrew because I had no other choice. But I have a choice here, and I'll do everything in my power to keep you. I love you."

His breath sucked in, and he stepped toward her. When she said that, he couldn't have stopped himself from taking her into his embrace if he'd been told the entire world depended on it.

Her voice came to him, this time from the front of his sweater where she'd tucked her face. "I can't lose you. You're my best friend."

Again with the letdown. He didn't know how many times he could survive getting dropped from a high place.

Kelsey's arms were wrapped around his waist where she'd snuggled herself into the hug she'd wrangled with that 'I love you.' He had been a fool, not anticipating the 'like a brother' that came after.

She tipped her head back, to look up at him, but when he finally looked at her face her eyes were squeezed shut. She spoke in frightened tones. "Say something."

He sighed and hugged her. He did it because she was pressed into his arms, and because he knew he had no chance in hell of successfully pushing her away. He resigned. "We'll work it out."

Her sigh was audible, but she didn't open her eyes. "Thank you. I can't stand us not talking."

Neither could he, but he didn't say so.

This time she looked. "Tell me you and Andie will be over tomorrow morning to walk to school."

"We'll be there." He told himself he was seven kinds of fool.

"I have to go. I left Daniel in charge." She wiped at her face as she turned to head down the steps.

JD just watched her go, and saw her turn around at the bottom. Her hand rested on the railing, and she looked up at him with big, soft eyes. "And thank you for the studio. Once I realized I was being an idiot, I realized that I love it."

"You're welcome."

Her smile was genuine and wide, if painted with the remnants of tears. Then she wandered off into the night.

Brenda Lyle sipped at the glass of merlot Kelsey had served. JD leaned back in his seat nursing his own glass of beer, glad that he hadn't said yes to the wine. He could smell the foul stuff in the women's glasses from where he sat.

Kelsey had invited Brenda and her son over for dinner, and him and Andie, too. The kids were off playing in the back, and Brenda was explaining the label she'd co-founded while Kelsey cleared the table. He'd offered to help, but like she always had lately, she'd refused. And in those jeans he couldn't say he really minded watching her walk away each time she came back for a different set of dinnerware.

Brenda spoke again, pulling his attention away from Kelsey's gorgeous ass. Which was probably a good thing.

"We all worked for different big labels, and we realized that no one there was in charge of their own life. Not even the artists. We were all a slave to the label." She shrugged and took another sip of the merlot. "So we mortgaged our houses, and John Abbott put in his inheritance and we started HeartBeats."

JD nodded. "That's why you were willing to take us even though I couldn't hit the road all the time."

Brenda nodded. "I wanted to see my kid grow up. It was one of those there-just-had-to-be-a-better-way situations. Speaking of: you guys are on hiatus from touring for a while now. I know you need some time with your little girl. Hailey Watkins stepped up and filled this next week's roster for you guys."

JD smiled and relaxed a little. It would mean that he could help Kelsey out for a while. That would be a nice change. Maybe they'd be around each other enough to sort things out and ease off the rough edges. Right now they were in an uneasy truce.

Brenda spoke again. "Kelsey, I want to talk to you about the Straight Up contract tomorrow."

JD warmed inside. His girl had gotten the go ahead to do the photos for the up and coming girl-band.

Brenda turned her attention back to JD, and he almost laughed. The woman had quit a job she was a slave to, but the job was clearly her passion. She couldn't *not* talk business at the dinner table. But since she was delivering only good news so far he let her. "Wilder may be off tour, but you guys are going to be interviewing on the local radio stations, and a few around the area. We're going to get you to two places a week, hopefully at drive time, if that's okay."

"Like where?"

"Memphis, Atlanta, Louisville, Charlotte." She grinned. "Houston, Dallas and Austin if we can swing it."

His heart fell. "I won't really be home then, will I?"

Brenda made a stern face. "Don't look at me like that. You'll puddle-jump out early and be back in town by noon."

Kelsey piped up. "I'll take Andie to school. I'm right here."

She'd been a little overly helpful since her apology. He'd have to find a way to curb that. He just wanted Kelsey back again.

Brenda talked about the other players at HeartBeats. "John's going to have your album in Target and Wal-Mart before the month is out. Lisa's going to get all the interviews lined up. And Bart wants to get you back into the studio to record *I am*."

She discussed a few options for it since they missed getting it on the album. Brenda couldn't decide if they should release it right away or hold it for the next album. "It's evolutionary to your other work really."

"I know." Kelsey agreed, "It's my personal favorite."

JD couldn't help the wry twist that curled the corner of his lip, or the thought that freight trained through his brain. There was a perverse joy he found in the irony. Of course she loved it, it was hers.

After the wine had time to clear from her head, Brenda gathered her little boy and took him home. JD started to gather Andie, too, but the kids had made a monumental mess. Kelsey was scrubbing dishes and loading the washer, so he directed all three kids in clean-up.

When Andie picked up an elf, and he realized that her pants were too short, too small. He told her so.

"Nuh-uh!" The protest startled him.

"Andie, they don't fit."

Daniel looked up at him with a sage expression. "They fit fine. She's wearing them like Mom does."

JD looked at Daniel wondering what in the hell the kid was talking about. "Your Mom does not wear high-waters."

Daniel obviously didn't know what that meant, but he countered anyway. "They're too tight."

JD thought about the way they hugged her curves, and how his hands itched to grab her. Those jeans made other parts of him itch, too. "You're right, they are too tight."

He bent over, laughing to himself, to pick up another pastel colored pony and saw the heeled boots standing in the doorway. His eyes followed them up long thin legs, to where they created a small gap before her sweater, showing off a sweet piece of skin that he could no longer touch. The sweater clung to curves that were also hands-off. But her face was devastated, her mouth hung open, and she stood stock still.

"Kelse?"

"No, it's okay." She turned and fled down the hall while he blinked.

For a moment he stood there unable to think of anything to say. He could explain that the jeans were too tight because they turned him on. But she sure as hell didn't want to be reminded of 'that night', which was all that telling her about his thoughts would do.

He looked around Daniel's room for something sharp enough to cut a few good veins. So he could bleed to death before he choked on his own feet.

CHAPTER 34

K elsey sang softly to herself as she did the dishes. The
guys were in the back, playing video games with the
kids. Bridget was egging them on. She'd gotten to know Bridget
better in the time that the guys had been home now. She had to
agree with JD—Alex had done well for himself. The girl was
really very likable.

She filled one of the pots with soapy water and sang through
a squeal from the back room. Her brain wandered to JD. She
wanted a family and a husband. JD would want a good time.
He'd had fatherhood shoved down his throat, he wouldn't want
more responsibility now. She wasn't kidding herself thinking
that was why things fell apart. It was just that they wouldn't
have worked out in the end, even if everything had been
different.

The voice startled her, so she almost dropped the dish she
was rinsing.

It was TJ singing the next line.

Her hand went to her heart. "You scared the crap out of me."
As soon as she said it she felt ten years older. That was
something old people said.

"Sorry." Even his laugh and his apology were musical and charming.

"Can I help?" As he asked it, he picked up a serving dish off the table, not waiting for an answer. "I talked to my mother today. She asked if JD was still seeing that hussy."

"Oh." Kelsey scrubbed at the dish a little harder. She hadn't known he was seeing anyone. "What hussy is that?"

TJ laughed again. "You! I told her that JD was, in fact, still seeing the tramp."

"Thanks a lot."

He brought another pile of plates in from the table. "Hey, if she'd had anything good to say about you, I wouldn't still be speaking to you."

Kelsey laughed herself. Although she wished his mother would like her, she wondered what good it would do anyway. It felt really good to talk to someone without the underlying tension she'd been living with for almost a month. "I thought you were her better son now."

"Please. JD was always number-one-son in more ways than just birth." He shrugged and collected silverware like what he was saying didn't bother him in the slightest. "By the time he ran off here, and she turned it on me, I was old enough to know better. I never bought in the way he did."

He grinned, and she couldn't see it, but Kelsey bet there was a world of hurt under there. "You know, Andrew threw things and raged, but at least I knew he loved me."

"How did you get Daniel? JD said he was Andrew's from a previous marriage. Why didn't he go back to his birth mother? If you don't mind me asking."

"No, I don't mind." Kelsey shrugged. "About a month before Andy died, he assigned me guardianship of Daniel. He showed me Daniel's birth certificate, and the 'mother' line was actually blank."

"Andrew never told you?" TJ took the heavy dish from her

gloved hands and loaded it into the machine like a pro. "Wasn't he married to her?"

"Oh, I have no idea about that one. He disappeared for three years. I didn't know where he was or if he was alive. But he showed up one day, sitting in the living room in my mother's rocking chair, with this baby in his arms."

TJ stopped what he was doing and stared at her. "You seriously let your husband disappear for three years, and show up with another woman's baby that you raised?!? Kelsey, do you hate yourself?"

"He wasn't my husband." She laughed. Oh, god, she had to straighten them all out. "He was my baby brother. I forgave him everything."

"He was your brother?"

She nodded, tears welling up just from thinking about Andrew. "He was my pride and joy when he was born. And my mother had something in common with yours—she didn't want anything to look less than perfect. So when we realized that Andy wasn't normal she didn't get him help right away. She figured he was so young she could just discipline him out of it. She didn't want to deal with it so I took care of him."

"What was it that was actually wrong?"

She shook her head, the tears falling. "I still don't know. He was diagnosed as bipolar with poor impulse control, but he had elements of both paranoia and schizophrenia."

"Jesus."

She shrugged, her heart squeezing at the pain she knew Andrew had lived with. "The doctors loved him, he was a fascinating case. But sometimes he hated himself so much. And sometimes I think he planned the whole thing. I had just made the last house payment, and he knew I was so happy to be free of it. And him signing Daniel over to me—I didn't question it. I was always so afraid that Andrew would disappear and take Daniel with him that I didn't ask him why. I didn't dig. And then he killed himself." A fresh round of tears fell, and things she hadn't known she'd hidden became clear. She bit her lip and pulled off the dish gloves before apologizing to TJ, "I'm sorry, I don't know what this is."

"It's okay, that's what it is." He held his arms to her, simply because she was a person in need. She walked into them cleanly, no baggage, no walls, and cried there.

After a moment he stepped abruptly away. She'd probably gotten to be too much for him. He wasn't his brother. But no one was, or ever would be. And she didn't get to have his brother. So it was a bad situation all around in her estimate. TJ polished that off with, "I have to go." And he fled the kitchen, calling for JD.

Kelsey sniffled a few more times and then turned back to the dishes. It was as good an excuse as any to take a little time and get herself together. She scrubbed the dish TJ had brought in.

It had been her grandmother's—one of the few family heirlooms she hadn't sold off to pay for Andrew's treatment. So she loved it.

That was where TJ found her when he returned about fifteen minutes later. "You doing okay?"

She nodded, and figured changing the subject was the best way to not burst into tears again in front of an unwilling man. "What did you run off for?"

He shook his head, like he was getting rid of a bad memory. "I was after JD, but it seems he isn't talking to me."

She washed another two forks, then handed them to TJ who had taken up a dishtowel and was graciously drying the silver, piece by piece. "Really? What did you do?"

"What makes you so certain it's my fault? You're as bad as he is." He put down the towel and walked out of the kitchen.

~

JD was home most of the time. Kelsey walked Andie to school on the days the guys had radio interviews, and she walked along with her portable radio when they interviewed at a local station. He sounded great, intelligent and likeable, although there were a few listeners who called in saying they couldn't distinguish the brothers' voices on the air. Kelsey didn't have that problem.

JD's was the one that sounded cold.

He'd built some distance in between them again. Although she couldn't really peg when it had started, she knew it was there. And she couldn't really be sure it was just between them. He seemed pissed at everyone lately. Hence the cold voice on the radio.

She had closed a loan that morning. She'd done it simply because she'd started it two months ago. It had taken forever, due to the couple changing their minds, then calling back and starting all over again.

She wondered if it would be the last one ever and thought that it probably would. She'd banked some money for the studio, and JD had spared her spending that, so she had a small bundle of savings. She had shot a few portraits in there over the past week and the clients had been really happy with them.

Tomorrow she would look at buying advertising space.

Today she would pop open a bottle of champagne and celebrate.

She pulled open the fridge and searched the back for the split that she'd stashed there. She closed the fridge without grabbing the bottle. Her heart sank. JD should be here, celebrating the last of the loans. He was the one who talked her into this. But he was barely speaking to her now. He handled the transactions between them, shuffling his child and her children back and forth. But that didn't change her feelings for him at all.

Okay, that was a lie. Now she hated him almost as much as she loved him.

She forgot about celebrating the last loan, and slunk off to the back to work on touching up the photos.

She was still neck deep in shading and lighting when the voice came from behind her. "Are you ready?"

He didn't call her 'Kelse'. He just showed up, and barely spoke.

He did much of the same on the walk to school to pick up the kids. He mentioned that he would be in Atlanta the following Tuesday and could she take Andie to school with them in the morning?

She considered telling him she had to check her calendar.

At least he was human to Andie. His daughter jumped and skipped, and chattered non-stop about her day. Only Daniel seemed sensitive to the tension between the adults. Just when she thought she'd gotten Daniel back on track, she knocked him off again. And the things that knocked them both off the track had all been related to JD.

She considered just cutting him off. Tell him she was glad for the time they'd been friends but—

"We're going to California!" Andie skipped, her breath coming out in little puffs.

"When?" That was news to Kelsey, but maybe Andie would tell the story if her Dad wouldn't.

"For Spring Break! We're going on an airplane."

"Wow." Daniel's eyes got big. Kelsey didn't think he'd ever been on a plane that he was old enough to remember. "That sounds like fun."

Kelsey questioned Andie herself. "Where in California are you going?"

"Bear!"

She hadn't heard of any place called 'Bear', but JD filled in the blanks without any emphasis or excitement. "Big Bear Lake. Our parents took me and TJ there several times when we were kids. I always wanted to take my own kids there. And I can finally afford it, so we're going."

Kelsey just nodded. "Is TJ going, too?"

"No." His voice so flat she would have thought it was recorded if she hadn't seen his mouth move.

Andie twittered on about fishing and boating and living in a cabin. Kelsey and JD both kept their mouths shut, until Andie asked Daniel what they were doing for Spring Break.

Daniel shrugged. "I don't know. We didn't do anything last year."

Kelsey felt a spurt of guilt. It wasn't that they hadn't done anything for *Spring Break* last year. It was that they hadn't done *anything* last year. She'd only wanted to get her feet under her. Daniel asked her if she had made plans for them. "We'll do something."

She ruffled his hair, feeling like a bad mother, because it hadn't really occurred to her to go somewhere or *do* something for Spring Break.

Andie piped up. "You should come with us!"

"Oh! No!" Kelsey felt the burning need to stop that one before it got started. Just the thought of vacationing with JD drained her.

"That's a great idea!" Daniel started jumping around, too.

"Yeah," Andie sang, "We have plenty of room, right, Dad?"

JD didn't even answer.

That was it. Kelsey reached out and took Andie's hand. "Listen Andie. The person who pays for the vacation is the person who gets to invite other people. So—" It was a good lesson, she just didn't get to finish it.

Andie turned to JD, "You have to invite them, Daddy."

JD stopped on the sidewalk, his hands in his jacket pockets. "It's not a bad idea."

Kelsey was sure her mouth hung open. So she did the only thing she could think of to keep from being upset that he wouldn't even say 'shut your mouth, Kelse' like he used to. "You kids run up ahead and let me and JD talk about this one."

She turned to him, "What are you thinking? You've barely spoken to me in the last week. You want to go on vacation together?"

He shrugged. "I've missed you."

"Well, all you had to do was open your damn mouth!" She whispered it, and prayed that the kids wouldn't hear, and that they were far enough from the gates of the school that there weren't other people's kids behind them to complain to their parents.

"Come on, Kelse. There's an elephant in the room. Maybe a week under the same roof will help get rid of it."

"You're serious!" She couldn't believe him. He barely spoke to her for weeks, then wanted to share a vacation? She wormed out of it. "I'm sure I couldn't find flights at a reasonable rate anyway."

"I've got it covered." His face still didn't show any emotion.

Kelsey simply didn't answer him. By her counts the man had gone mental.

A full block later he spoke again. "Is it because TJ isn't coming?"

"TJ?" God, the man baffled her. "What does this have to do with him?"

He only repeated the question. "Is it because TJ isn't coming?"

She sighed. "Let me be more clear: this has nothing to do with TJ. It has to do with the fact that this is the biggest conversation we've had in a week."

His hands were still jammed in his pockets. "Is this how you want it?"

She was exhausted from being so tense when she was around him, and she was still tense a good portion of the time she wasn't around him, too. "Of course it's not how I want it. I miss us being friends. I just don't know how to go back."

"Then come with us."

"Fine." She gave in. It wasn't going to be a vacation at all. Not for her. He'd be looming over her, and she'd be wanting things she couldn't have, and—

She looked up and the damn man was smiling. A real smile.

"What the hell are you grinning about?"

He shrugged.

CHAPTER 35

They spent the next week getting ready. JD flew in and out of Atlanta in a heartbeat, just as Brenda had promised. They dug out Andy's old fishing poles for themselves and bought some small ones for the kids. Kelsey had no idea you could get Superman or Scooby Doo or even Barbie on a fishing pole. But they had one of each as proof.

They also got little inflatable air mattress sleeping bags for the kids. JD wasn't able to get a larger cabin at such late notice, so that meant the kids would be sleeping on the floor—a fact they were all quite happy about. They went back out later in the week to get her kids suitcase sets like the one Andie had. It came with wheels and an airplane carryon, and that seemed like a good idea for a cross country flight.

JD asked her several times what he should pack for Andie, and was mortified at the amount she suggested. But he made her smile—really smile—for the first time in a while when she asked him, "You've never traveled with a kid before, have you?"

They stood in line at the airport check-in waiting to go through security. Luggage was piled around them. He shook his head. "I traveled plenty *as* a kid."

"Not the same." She held her hands up. "I didn't *make* you do anything. But if a kid's going to wet the bed or vomit, they'll do it on vacation where things are unfamiliar."

He blinked. "Thanks, this is sounding like a lot of fun."

"I didn't plan it, you did."

After that they fell silent. Even the kids kept their mouths closed in awe of everything swirling around them. Kelsey saw other families go by, harried mothers holding small hands, Dads who were lost, other families doing fine in the middle of their mountains of luggage. But the problem was they weren't *other* families.

She could dream about it every night until the moon exploded, but it wasn't going to happen. JD didn't want to settle down, and he was in the best position to never have to. These days he had plenty of money and plenty of groupies. She couldn't—wouldn't—compete.

They made it onto the plane without any mishaps. The kids insisted on sitting together in the middle three seats. Leaving Kelsey and JD in two together. JD didn't look like he'd ever be comfortable. Still, he got settled, and the kids sat down with their carry-on bags and each unpacked a book or a hand-held game and got lost in that.

After they reached altitude, even she got bored enough to fall asleep against the window. Almost immediately JD shook her awake, her head resting against his shoulder.

It was barely noon in Vegas when they landed. Two hours later, they were in a rented mini-van and heading out of town. It rained on them on the drive up to Big Bear Lake, and she pointed out the sheets of water she could see falling through the mountains to the kids. But all three were already passed out cold.

JD drove, eating up mountain road at a steady pace. He wasn't inclined to stop or admire the scenery. She'd looked back over her shoulder into Vegas once as they'd left town, but the smog was more than she could stand to look at. She was finally glad she'd never been.

The town of Big Bear was quaint with little gingerbread houses, and rows of motels and cabin clusters along the roadside. There was really only one main drag and the lake ran the whole length. JD handed her an email confirmation with the info for their cabin and a map that was printed on a legal-sized piece of paper.

She directed them to a single cabin along a side street. When they woke the kids, all three snapped-to like they'd never been asleep. They all wanted to run screaming into the pool.

Once JD assured her that it was heated and supposed to already be turned on and warm for them, she helped the kids change into their suits. JD brought in suitcase after suitcase, and sorted them between the rooms. He gave Kelsey and her kids the larger one and Andie took notice, begging to sleep in the same room with Daniel and Allie.

Kelsey looked up at him, dripping in baggage, "I don't mind."

"No." His voice was harsh, and he continued with his luggage sorting. "You have all three kids all the time. They'll never sleep if they're all together. I . . ." He trailed off, shaking his head.

Seeing that Andie desperately wanted to join her kids, Kelsey protested that he had paid for the whole thing, he should get to enjoy it.

After a few minutes he asked her very politely to shut-up, were they going to argue about everything?

She obliged, then made the kids wait while she climbed into her own suit. She'd packed her old one piece, after that comment about her jeans being too tight. She slipped into it, glad that it was black, even if it did have insets of sheer mesh.

The kids went screaming out the back door and she followed them with an armload of towels. Daniel cannon-balled in, slipping back into his kid persona, for which she was grateful. Allie and Andie gingerly took the steps down but squealed in delight that it was warm and Kelsey should join them.

She considered it, but the hot tub looked way too inviting to spend any time in the pool. She was more than happy to find that it, too, was already heated. Because the hot tub was in the far corner of the yard, she had a good view of JD walking out in his suit. Damn, but that man made the water around her boil hotter just by walking by. She was so screwed. He looked at her and she was sure it showed on her face. Luckily, he went right past and dove into the deep end of the pool.

After they played for an hour, Kelsey scrubbed the chlorine off of them, and got everyone ready for an early dinner. When they got back in after eating they were all exhausted, and the kids promptly passed out. Kelsey and JD both begged off and went to bed not half an hour later.

The next day JD took them out to ride the Alpine slides. Daniel was the only kid tall enough to go down by himself, and JD was the only one who'd ever ridden before. So after a quick explanation and a chairlift ride to the top of the mountain, Kelsey tucked Allie in front of her and tried not to hold the brake too tight. Her daughter yelled, "Faster!" the whole way.

JD was waiting at the bottom with Daniel and Andie, laughing like a loon when they arrived. "I could hear her all the way down here."

He only laughed harder when Allie asked very politely if she could please ride with him next time, Mommy was just too slow.

Kelsey put her hands on her hips. "It was my first time down. Fine, little traitor, go with him."

Andie was more than happy to ride with her, and for that Kelsey was grateful. She had decided to wear her sundress and she needed a kid sitting in front of her to keep from being indecent. They rode the chairlift behind JD and Daniel and Allie. Andie didn't talk much on the way up, which was a good thing. Kelsey's mind had wandered.

Even though she had a clear view of his ass in jeans, that wasn't what she was thinking about. It was that, even though she couldn't hear anything, she could see that he was perfectly at ease with her kids. And just at ease with her having his kid. He talked to Allie, and nodded in response to her. JD easily talked Daniel through jumping off the lift and put his hands on Allie's waist, lifting her out of harm's way, but setting her feet down quickly enough that the little girl would feel like she'd done it herself.

Kelsey's heart squeezed. How could she not be in love with this man? She wasn't going to get over it. That was just a big, fat, hairy lie that she'd been telling herself.

JD was standing waiting for them, and lifted his daughter out of the seat, as though she was no heavier than an infant. He set Andie down, and turned back to Kelsey, "What's wrong?"

She shook her head. "Nothing."

He gave a tight nod, knowing that she wasn't going to tell him, and stalked off. She thought about it the whole way down the slide, only partially paying attention to braking as she went into the turns. He wanted her to talk to him. But she just couldn't make herself say the words that would destroy everything.

Things eased up during lunch. Maybe JD had realized there were some things she wouldn't tell him and he was learning to be okay with that. They actually laughed and got along while they ate, and the kids all had good behavior, so Kelsey got them bouncy balls out of the red-topped toy dispensers down the street.

She was looking in the window at cowboy boots and hats,

and it wasn't but a minute before Andie joined her. The little girl looked up. "I never had any cowboy boots."

"Yeah? Neither have Daniel and Allie. I guess it seems kind of wrong to live in Nashville and not have a pair of cowboy boots." She decided to buy Daniel and Allie some after they got back home. JD, however, had decided to buy some now.

They all trailed into the store, Kelsey taking back the bouncy balls while they were shopping. But without the balls to occupy their hands the kids all wanted to try on boots. She let them while JD helped Andie into a pair that was brown and pink with silver buckles on the side. Andie was in heaven.

Allie had chosen a red pair, and Daniel had gone after something that looked like he needed a Harley. But with the prices what they were, Kelsey just tucked the colors and styles and sizes away in her brain for birthdays. JD started trying on pairs for himself. Like he needed another pair.

That was when Daniel brought her the purple and green snakeskin boots and insisted that they were exactly what she should have. Just to be silly, Kelsey agreed and tried them on.

Eventually, the kids brought her a pair that she liked. Kelsey tried them on and admired them. Aside from the price tag they were perfect. But since the kids would have to wait until their birthdays, it would hardly be fair to buy herself a pair now.

"Those look great."

JD had come up behind her in the full length mirror.

"Yeah?" She turned a little bit. "I don't think I'd wear them with this sundress, though."

"Why not? It looks sexy."

Her head snapped up. She couldn't believe he'd said that.

He instantly apologized. "I'm sorry. I suppose I gave away the right to say things like that."

Her heart pounded. "I guess."

"You tell me."

She still didn't know what to do. It wasn't good to have him telling her things like that. She'd fall into his arms so easily—so casually—but god if it wasn't wonderful to hear. "I don't know."

He looked away, standing in his second-skin jeans, boots in hand, and white socks on his feet. "Tell me when you decide."

She nodded, but he didn't see her. Kelsey unzipped the boots she had on and started calling for her kids.

"Here, I'll put them back." He held out his hands for the pair she'd just stepped out of. "I'm going to get these," he gestured to the masculine and utilitarian looking black pair hanging from his other hand, "And Andie's. Do you mind corralling the kids while I check out?"

She nodded, even as she removed the stuffed animal from Andie's hands. "There's an ice cream shop across the street, want to meet us there?"

They ate ice cream, went swimming again, and ordered pizza in for dinner when it started to rain. JD took them out Bowling that night.

The rain kept coming, making them run to the car, and get more than a little wet in the process. By the time they got back to the cabin, it had quit, and there wasn't a cloud in sight. The kids protested being put to bed even though it was past ten. But as soon as they quieted down, they went right under.

Taking a book with her, Kelsey turned on the lamp and curled up on the couch. She was two pages into the chapter she'd started when JD walked by in his bathing suit with a towel over his shoulder. "Come with me?"

She shook her head. "It's too cold to swim."

"Hot tub." He smiled.

The thought of being alone with JD, in the dark, in the hot tub, at night, with only the woods behind them . . . "The kids are in here."

"We'll only be in the back yard."

Her heart pattered in her chest. But there was the problem. "I can't."

Understanding, he nodded. "Come out if you change your mind."

She looked back down at her book but she didn't see the words. They swam in front of her face, and even so she turned the page to look like she was reading, faking it until she heard the back door shut. Only then did she put the book down and let her breath suck in. Had that been a nearly blatant invitation to sex in the hot tub?

She wasn't certain, but her brain sure went there. She tried to shut it down, but couldn't. Then she figured that maybe she shouldn't. So she let herself imagine that she went outside in her bikini. That he kissed her and stroked her in all the right ways. That part of it she was sure of, he'd done it before. Her breathing sped up just thinking about it. But then she got to the part after it was over and he said something like, "thanks" or "God, I'm tired now, see you in the morning." That was the part that kept her inside.

CHAPTER 36

I t rained again the following morning, and they made their way out for brunch. In what seemed the pattern up here, it cleared up quickly, and they took the late morning boat tour for an hour and a half, which was about an hour too long for the kids.

After a vote for fishing, they made a quick stop for bait then pulled out fold-up chairs and set up shop at the edge of a stocked pond. Despite horrible technique, Allie caught the first fish only half an hour in. The kids had no idea what to do. JD coached from the sidelines but Kelsey was pretty certain none of the kids was really listening to him.

Eventually they got it into a bucket where JD pulled the hook out with a few fingers tucked under the gills and a quick flip of his wrist. He tried to hand the still wriggling fish off to Allie to hold it up for a photo. Allie squealed and refused, but posed with JD holding the fish for her.

Kelsey caught the next one, but when Daniel caught another right on her heels, she wound up pulling her fish up by herself. All hands were helping the six-year-old. She managed to haul the silver devil up into the air, then clumsily swung him back where she could grab at his body. The whole time she was certain the line would snap and the fish would go flopping into the dirt. But instead she got a good grip around his middle and managed to drop him into the bucket.

Overcome by an attack of the willies, she wiped her slimy fingers on her jeans, while she made faces.

"Kelsey! What are you doing?" JD was beside her in a flash handing her a towel. "You're ruining your jeans!"

"Oh come on, these are the bad jeans."

"They're great jeans. They look really good on you."

She tilted her head sideways and decided to call him on it. "Come on, JD, I heard you. They're fishing jeans now."

"I—" He made a face and turned away, then he turned back. "Just tell me it'll wash out."

She breathed deeply, and wiped her hands off on them again, her palms still felt wet and slimy. "They'll wash off."

JD walked away to help the kids.

Later, once the fish were iced and put away, Kelsey got the kids ready for dinner. "Okay, everyone, shoes."

"How about these?" JD hauled out a few stuffed bags from the stop the previous afternoon.

Andie jumped up and down, "I can wear my boots?"

Kelsey sent her own kids back into the room to grab their sneakers, but JD caught them as they went by and handed each child a box. Eyes went wide as Allie and Daniel opened the boxes to reveal the boots each had tried on the day before. They immediately plopped on their butts in front of him to get help pulling them on.

Kelsey was almost mad. Her heart hurt. He had to quit being so great. "JD, you didn't have to."

"I know. I wanted to." He pushed little feet down into the boots and had all three kids showing them off in a moment. He turned back to Kelsey. "Now these aren't the same sizes they tried on. The sales lady sent me back and suggested I get a full size larger than what fit, so they'd last longer."

Allie, at least, remembered to thank JD and launched herself at him. Kelsey thanked him, too, before heading back to fetch her own sandals. His arm snaked around her waist as she passed by. "I didn't forget you."

He pulled out a huge box and opened it to reveal the butter-soft, stitched pair she'd tried on the day before. Her mouth hung open. "JD, these were expensive."

He pressed his lips together. "You're welcome."

"Thank you. Oh, my god, thank you."

That at least made him smile. "You need help getting into them?"

She laughed, thinking that having him handling her legs and zipping her boots would only cause more problems. "I think I'm okay."

When they were all ready, they traipsed the three feet out the front door to the car. Kelsey thought they looked touristy with all of them in their new boots. That was okay, they *were* tourists, and the kids were happy.

Dinner was fabulous, and far more expensive than Kelsey would have chosen. When JD had gotten up to take Daniel to the bathroom, a nice woman came over and told Kelsey how lucky she was. That all three of her children were so well behaved. Then the woman added on what a handsome husband she had, too.

That startled her, and she said 'thank you' without explaining that it wasn't true. That they weren't all three her kids, and he wasn't her husband.

"You okay?" He asked over his steak.

The man was always sensitive to her moods, and it was really starting to piss her off. "I'm fine."

They hauled full, sleepy kids home after that, forced them to brush their teeth, and together went through the two rooms kissing foreheads and telling them to sleep well.

Again JD emerged twenty minutes later, asking if she wanted to join him in the hot tub.

Again, she refused.

For dinner the next day, JD presented their catch, perfectly cooked. Each of the kids took one bite and made a face.

"Catching them is fun," Andie spoke up, refusing to take another bite. "Eating them is yucky."

JD ate piece after piece, the little bites disappearing into his mouth. Knowing how much he usually ate, Kelsey figured he was burning more calories than he consumed eating the tiny flakes he got.

"Look guys, it's good." She took her own forkful of flaky trout and put it in her mouth. She was helpless to stop the grimace she made.

"What?" JD was looking at her as if she were Judas.

"It's fishy."

"Of course it's fishy. It's fish!" He ate another big bite to show them how good it was.

"No." She didn't take another bite. "Tuna steak doesn't taste like this. I've had Mahi Mahi and swordfish. They don't taste like fish-smell."

He sighed, and set his fork down. "Those are deep sea fish. We're on a man-made lake."

He looked at each kid one by one. Allie scrunched her nose. Daniel didn't do anything, but he wasn't touching that fish. Andie shook her head.

JD conceded defeat. "Who wants to go get burgers?"

Kelsey was fairly certain she was the first one up. She raced the kids to the car, stopping just long enough to throw the salad, uncovered, into the fridge. She hollered to Daniel to get the bread. Being Daniel, he carefully set it on the counter before bolting out the door. Kelsey didn't care that they were all dressed for a backyard barbecue. She was in her cut-off jeans shorts with her new boots, and was grateful that her button-down shirt was reasonably presentable.

By the time JD climbed in the car, the rest of them were buckled in and waiting with smiles on. Kelsey sought to console him. "It wasn't how they were cooked. It was the fish."

"Uh-huh." He started the engine. "Someone had to stay and double bag those fish, so that bears don't wander into the backyard while we're out."

Kelsey kept her mouth shut during the ride, and they all let JD pick the place. Kelsey almost groaned, the burger was so good.

The kids wanted to swim after dinner, but Kelsey saw clouds gathering and decided maybe they could put the radio on and play a game. That way they could get inside quickly if need be.

But the rain didn't come, and they shuffled the kids off to bed a little while later. JD went into the kitchen to put his beloved fish down the garbage disposal piece by piece, so Kelsey made her way out to sit on the picnic bench and enjoy their next to last evening at the cabin.

The sky was deep velvet, filled to bursting with little stars shining. Clouds skidded across the moon too fast to drop water. The air was just warm enough that she didn't go inside to change into pants. So she sat on the table, enjoying the air and the music and the peace. She relaxed, and took a moment to be grateful that she had come. JD was right, there was an elephant in the room. At least now they were speaking again. Now things were getting better. She sat a few more minutes just soaking in the feeling of solitude.

Until JD came out and perched himself beside her. For a long time, he didn't say anything. When he did open his mouth, it wasn't anything she'd expected.

"I saw you with TJ a while ago."

"Huh?" She had no idea what he was talking about. Unless he meant in the kitchen, but that had been nothing—

"I would just recommend that you not fall in love with my brother. I don't think he wants what you want." JD didn't look at her. His posture looked relaxed at first glance, but she knew him better than that.

"Trust me. I'm not going to fall in love with your brother." *How could I? When I'm already in love with you?* But she didn't give it voice. Instead, not liking where that might lead, she changed the subject. "Listen, please don't think that I don't appreciate it, but you don't have to do all this. The studio, the vacation, the boots—we don't need those things. You don't owe me anything."

He still didn't look at her. "On the contrary, I think I owe you everything."

She wanted to press him, but didn't think it would work. So Kelsey reverted back to her old method of silence.

She didn't have to wait long.

"I'd had Andie for three weeks when I met you. I couldn't do a thing with her. Then you came along, and started making things work."

"That's because I was a female—"

But he wasn't done, and didn't seem to care that she was speaking. "I'd been in Nashville for two and a half years. Maybe I am talented, but I was as talented then as I am now. Only after you came along did I begin to make a living at it. I think I actually owe all of it to you."

Kelsey waited, wanted to be sure that he was finished. "You've paid me back. I have a photography studio in my garage. I have clients and the equipment I need. You gave me the kick in the ass to do it. And the whole time I was taking the risk, I knew you had my back. That means the world to me. No one really ever had my back before. Thanks."

They sat there, looking at the sky, staying quiet, until the music stopped and the sultry female voice on the radio announced that it was nine-thirty on Thursday night and that meant it was two-step time.

JD grinned and hopped off the table top, holding out a hand to her.

Kelsey accepted as he pulled her to him, waiting for the voice to stop and the music to start. The first song was fairly fast, and he spun her breathless around the grass. The second wasn't quite as lively, but still up-tempo, and Kelsey was grateful for the commercial break. She slipped in through the sliding glass door and grabbed a bottle of water out of the fridge. She was drinking it outside wondering where JD had gone when he emerged. He slid the door shut on quiet runners. "They're all asleep." He smiled.

Then he pulled the water from her hand and drank half of it.

"Uh!" She protested, and he gave it back, grin still on his face while she drank more.

He took the bottle from her hand again and, setting it on the table, pulled her back out into the open grass and into a solid hold, where he proceeded to spin her around again. She was breathing heavily when the voice said, "Okay, a slow one for you lovers out there." She didn't make a decision, just followed as she was pulled tighter into his embrace, and danced around the yard.

She didn't fight it. She couldn't. His arms around her created a safe cocoon she'd never had with anyone else. The feel of his chest where her cheek rested against it matched the smell of him through the thin fabric of his t-shirt. He kept perfect rhythm to the slow song. Though she couldn't hear the words, she didn't need to. She just needed to stay here, like this, oblivious to everything else.

She just needed him. It must have shown on her face when the music ended and she looked up at him. Because she didn't say anything, and neither did he. JD simply closed the distance between them and kissed her.

She kissed him back, her arms tightening around his waist, her weight leaning into him just a little more. His tongue found hers and his hands found their way up her back, holding her where he had better access. He changed the kiss, making it deeper still, as though she could take everything that he had to give from that contact. For just a moment, he broke the kiss to suck in air.

Kelsey drew in her own breath. And with air came thought.

Quickly she moved her hands around, and pushed against his chest, keeping him at bay if not the feelings. She knew how this would end, and she wouldn't survive it again. She was still barely surviving the last time. "I can't do this."

CHAPTER 37

"Then don't kiss me back." She heard JD pushed the words out through clenched teeth, but they were audible even as he turned away.

"I'm sorry." Her shoulders slumped, and suddenly it was too cold without JD holding her. "You're right, I shouldn't have. But I can't be your road whore again."

He whirled on her, his face a mask of uncertainty. "My road whore?"

"You know, one of those girls who—"

"I *know* what a road whore is!" He roared it so loud she thought he'd wake the entire town. "What the hell did I do to make you think you were a road whore?"

She didn't know where to start. She'd have to tell him that she'd fallen in love with him, so he'd know that she knew she had concocted everything she felt. Her jaw worked, but no sound came out.

He made sound. "Was it the restaurant? I should have taken you somewhere nicer. I should have gotten a nice hotel, I know . . . I . . ."

"No. It wasn't that."

"Then what?"

Kelsey shrugged, still not knowing how to tell him. "Everything."

He just blinked. He turned. He paced. Then he walked out of the yard. He walked to the back of the grass and just kept going. Right into the woods, with the bears he had warned her about. "JD!"

But he didn't answer.

Kelsey didn't care if she woke the kids. "JD!"

The neighbors. "J! D!"

But he had disappeared into the night.

The voice on the radio sliced back into her thoughts. "That one was for all of you out there getting it on tonight. And here's another fast one for those of you just looking for a little fun."

She perched on the edge of the table, and waited.

The two-step music ended. Another DJ came on, playing alternative country. She didn't change the station or turn it off. That would mean going inside, and she was sitting right here, waiting for JD until he came back. Even if that was tomorrow.

The only thing that caught her attention was when the man announced one that was getting its last spin. "These guys have moved mainstream on us. Here's Wilder with *Go to Bed Mad*."

Kelsey laughed a harsh sound into the night. She was certain there'd be no waking up glad here. She'd finally fucked it all the way up. But she stayed put.

She had no idea how much later he showed up. She didn't hear him approach.

"What are you still doing out here?"

Her voice wanted to croak, her throat hurt just from stress. "Waiting for you."

She looked up to see him at the edge of the yard, where trees met green grass. "You should have gone inside. You don't know what's out here at night."

"I know you're out here at night, and I know you didn't go far."

JD didn't look at her. "How do you know that? I was gone a long time."

"Because you're you. You wouldn't ever go off and leave us unprotected."

He didn't answer. Didn't nod, didn't concede.

She waited for him. And he waited for her.

Finally, he spoke. "You've had plenty of time to figure out how to say it now. Tell me what made you think you were a road whore." The air seemed to leave him even as he said it. He wasn't expecting anything good here.

"It was my own stupidity, JD. All me."

He still hadn't made any kind of eye contact with her, and he still was exuding a quiet rage. "If you want to salvage anything—anything—of this, you tell me."

"First off, you got stuck with me. I know it and I'm sorry."

"How did I get stuck with you?"

She sucked in a breath. "The guys all disappeared pretty quickly. They had other things to do, and you wound up entertaining me."

JD shook his head. "That's not the way it happened."

"JD! You didn't even hug me when you saw me. Everyone else did, but not you."

"You looked perfect," He sighed, "And I was all sweaty and grimy. I didn't want to mess you up."

"Trust me, I was far from perfect, I'd been dancing in the third row for the whole performance."

"And not getting a hug made you feel like a road whore?"

"No! How about the girl in the black lace underwear?"

"What about her?"

Kelsey couldn't believe he was that callous. She got mad. "How about that she was there? Waiting for you! You went in with her and closed the door! You told her to wait, that you might come back. You told me she'd keep!"

"She was waiting for TJ!" He shot back. "I meant she'd keep for him. That was his room."

"Then why did you go in and close the door?"

He sidestepped her. "That's it?"

"No!" He was waiting and she was pissed, so it spewed. "Craig and TJ went out and got girls. So you took what you had. I was just another girl on the bus."

"There were no other women on the bus. No one ever, except Bridget."

She didn't believe that for a hot second. "Then what was with Craig and TJ disappearing into their rooms so fast? What about the fifteen thousand condoms under your pillow? You were clearly stock-piled for far more than one night!"

He looked at her like she was a fool. Then he told her why. "Kelsey, the bed folds into the wall. They all fell out the next morning. I put them there *after* I opened the bed that night."

That made her mad fizzle like a loosened balloon. But it wasn't happiness that replaced it. "So you just took me along for sex?"

He groaned and put his hands over his face. He didn't say anything for a moment, then he let it all go.

She didn't think he'd looked at her this whole time, but she'd been watching him. She'd seen his posture change. And now it conceded defeat. "When I saw you in the audience, I thought I'd hallucinated you."

"Why?"

"Since the night you showed up at McMinn's, I've been watching for you, hoping you'd show up again. It was such a great surprise to have you come out to watch us. And there you were."

He breathed in and out. "I didn't get stuck with you. *You* got stuck with *me*."

CHAPTER 38

J D sighed and tried again to explain. "The guys disappeared so I could have you to myself. I got the condoms out of TJ's dressing room and put them under the pillow on the off chance that I got so lucky. It turned out so bad that I made you flee a moving bus. I'm sorry that I hurt you. I never meant to.

"I can't go on like this. But I can't lose you as a friend. I just can't. Tell me we'll find some way around it. I just want things to go back to the way they were." He looked at her, finally, "Tell me they can go back to the way they were."

She couldn't find it in her heart to deny him, so she said the words. "Things can go back to the way they were."

He nodded and walked past her, in the graying night, toward the sliding door where he was illuminated by the light from the kitchen.

The weaving of the whole story was clearer now, and for the first time since she'd pulled on her jeans and made the driver stop the bus did she feel that they could find their way back to even ground.

But he didn't have women on the bus or fifteen condoms in

his bed. The guys had left her with him . . . Kelsey rolled the dice.

"JD? I kind of lied to you."

He stopped just shy of opening the door, his hand still resting on the handle. It had been a hard night already. She knew that she might be making it harder, but she admired his willingness to stay and play it out. He answered her volley, but didn't turn. "How do you kind of lie to someone?"

"When I was crying," she didn't have to clarify it more than that, he knew what she was talking about. "You asked me if I missed Andrew, and I said I did. That was true, I miss him every day." She took a fortifying breath and plunged ahead. "But I don't think that's really what you were asking. I think you wanted to know why I was crying, right?"

He nodded, "Yeah, that's about it."

"Andrew wasn't my husband; he was my baby brother."

"I know. I didn't know then, but I know now."

He didn't give her any more opening, so she forged ahead. "I was crying because you jumped up before you even started breathing again. You paced, in like two square feet, you paced, and you did that thing with your hands in your hair that means you're so frustrated you don't know what to do."

He pulled his hands out if his hair and jammed them deep in his pockets. She could see it all from where she sat, too many yards away, and her heart cracked a little more. How her body maintained functioning through all this was beyond her knowledge, but she heard him so she must still be alive.

"I'm sorry that I hurt you. I'm going to go inside now."

He moved to open the door, but she pulled the thread again. "Why? So you can watch me out the window? You won't leave me out here by myself. You're too good of a man, JD. Stay, finish it."

He turned and looked at her, even though she couldn't see

his eyes through the growing dark, where the moon had abandoned them.

She pushed, "Tell me what frustrated you so much that night."

He shrugged, but his words were solid. "I promised myself that I would talk to you before anything happened between us. That we wouldn't be in that position where we were naked and didn't know who wanted something big and who wanted something casual. And I screwed it up."

Kelsey stopped for a minute. She dug deep, but couldn't quite find the bravery to pull that thread anymore. She could interpret what he'd said either way. And she knew she'd collapse into nothing if he told her that he'd wanted to be sure she knew it was just casual, that he'd just wanted sex. But she found a little bit of push, and she used it. "Then tell me what you really want *now*. Do you truly want things to go back the way they were? I can do that," She took a breath, "But I'm open to suggestions."

"Suggestions?" He took a few aggressive steps toward her, and she nodded.

"Okay, how's this?" He took another step. "I want you in my house. At my dinner table. Every day. Saying that you love me."

"Done."

She'd already told him that she loved him. That was what she wanted, too.

But he wasn't done. He let out a sound of exasperation that bordered on laughter, "No, that's not all. I want you in my arms, in my bed, every night, screaming my name."

Her mouth fell open, and her body flooded with heat. Her ears rang and her heart thudded.

She was too slow, and he shook his head and turned away. "Since that's not ever going to hap—"

"Done."

He stopped cold. For a beat he didn't say anything, then she heard it. "What?"

She couldn't run to him, and throw herself into his arms like she wanted to. She couldn't make her muscles respond. But she got her mouth moving.

"I said, 'done', but I should have said 'please'."

The dark clouds above her took that moment to let go of what they'd been saving all day. The water that soaked her barely registered, except that she was surprised it didn't sizzle and evaporate the second it hit her hot skin.

JD faced her again through sheets of rain, only the light radiating from the kitchen giving either of them anything to go by. "Kelse?"

"Please."

He closed the distance to where she sat on top of the picnic table. Stepping between her legs, his fingers found her hips and pulled her to him. He was hard as a rock, and it was almost as though he were testing her. She pressed tighter against him even as she grabbed his neck and pulled his mouth to her.

She led this one, devouring him, gripping his wet shirt in fistfuls, determined not to let him get away this time. She kissed him like the rain was nuclear, and there was no tomorrow. Like nothing else in the world mattered, because right now it didn't. She wrapped her legs around his waist, pulling him closer still.

Kelsey reached for him again and again, enjoying how he felt so solid beneath his skin, enjoying his skin beneath his t-shirt. The way he had them grinding together, she couldn't help rubbing back against him. There were practically sparks flying from where they touched. Without knowing how she got there, she found herself flat on her back across the picnic table, with JD still firmly anchored by her legs around him.

The rain came down colder, but JD was protecting her from the worst of it. It was a beautiful night to be making love on the picnic table, the real storm had passed, and his hand belonged on her breast. She was right to strain against him, wanting his touch, and to pull his mouth back down to hers.

She was tugging at his shirt, trying to pull it off of him when he stepped back shaking his head. Kelsey would have been scared, except for the heat in his eyes. Except for the way his every muscle was focused on her. "We have to go inside."

She shook her head. "No. Stay."

But he stepped away, tugging her up with his hand, the rain coming down on her now. "You're shivering."

"Not from cold." She tugged against him.

But he won. He was simply bigger. "I am not letting you get sick on me. Besides a bear could be two feet from me right now and I wouldn't even know it."

She smiled. He wouldn't. He was only looking at her.

She gave in and allowed him to tug her along the lawn, open the door for her and usher her inside. The air conditioning hit her in an icy blast until his eyes found hers and the cold air was forgotten. He barely had the door closed before he was kissing her up against the refrigerator. His breathing was as heavy as hers, and he made sure he maintained full contact with her, fitting them together perfectly.

Until she pushed him off.

He looked startled and then wary, until Kelsey pushed him against the counter, enjoying being in control of the kiss. She used the space to slide her hands under his shirt again, enjoying how the play of his muscles told her that he wanted this as much as she did.

He tired of the kitchen and scooped her up, carrying her into the living room, where he draped her over the cushioned arm of the couch.

He was unbuttoning her shirt and chasing the exposed skin with his mouth when a door clicked. "Mom?"

They scrambled. Sitting upright, Kelsey grabbed for her shirt. The cabin was small and she had barely a second to tug it closed, she didn't even try to button it. JD was busy pulling her legs across his lap to hide the bulge at the front of his jeans.

Daniel padded out in his t-shirt and underwear, rubbing his eyes. "I have to go potty."

Kelsey found her voice. "Okay, baby. You go back to bed when you're done."

"Okay." He turned around and padded into the bathroom.

They waited, unmoving, until they heard the toilet flush and the sink run, and then Daniel's voice calling out a soft 'good-night' before they breathed.

Kelsey just sucked in a breath.

JD found words. "We just almost traumatized that kid."

She had to laugh. It was that or cry.

JD shook his head. "He doesn't usually get up in the middle of the night, does he?"

"Never."

"Tonight of all nights." He sighed.

Kelsey curled into him, but much of the frenzy she'd felt earlier had dissipated into near guilt. "We're on vacation. I don't sleep well in a strange bed, neither do they." She sighed, as she felt his hand in her hair.

JD's voice was soft and resigned. "We can't do this tonight, can we? We don't have anywhere to go."

Kelsey shook her head, but didn't move from her spot. She wasn't ready to just let him go off to his own room and be confident that things would be okay in the morning.

His words reflected exactly that. "You're not going to jump off the bus tonight, are you?"

"No." She laughed.

"Then you have to get up. I can't stay out here with you without running the risk of screwing up one of those kids for life." He pushed her legs off his lap and stood.

She would have felt rejected except for the fact that standing was obviously awkward for him. JD tugged her to her feet, and pointed her toward her own room. "You'd better get some sleep, because you won't get any tomorrow night."

Again, just like that, heat flooded every piece of her. She wanted to brace a chair under each door and take him there in the hallway. But she couldn't do that to the kids. They'd be petrified if they woke up and couldn't get the door open. But still she was disappointed. "Tomorrow night?"

"Trust me. I'm going to be awake all night, figuring out how early we can put the kids to bed."

She laughed and gave him a quick peck on the cheek before slipping through her own door. She couldn't afford to touch him more or she wouldn't stop. She couldn't even make herself move until she heard his footsteps walking away from her down the hall.

Kelsey worked by the nightlight, stripping quickly out of wet clothes and finding a towel to dry her hair. She slipped on a rib-knit cotton gown and tucked herself between the covers.

Exhausted, she fell right asleep, only to jerk awake a few moments later. Reassuring herself that he wanted her, she would fall back asleep and wake again, her body running hot, her brain replaying his words. *In my arms, in my bed, every night, screaming my name.* She had to gasp for oxygen, even as she lay there by herself.

The third time it happened, she gave up. Throwing back the covers she decided to go drink some of the cranberry juice that was in the fridge. Kelsey quietly pulled the door open, being careful to not wake Daniel or Allie. On soft feet she found the refrigerator and she blinked in the bright light, looking in and trying to find the juice she'd wanted.

Pulling the glass out, she drained it, set it in the sink, and made her way into the living room. She stopped dead when she spotted JD watching her from the couch. He grinned. "Couldn't sleep?"

She shook her head. "You?"

"I can't share a room with my daughter while I'm thinking of you."

She walked over to stand in front of the couch. "So we can't sleep and we can't do anything."

"That about sums it up." He propped one jeans clad leg along the back of the seat cushions and planted the other foot on the floor then motioned for her to sit in the space between. "Watch TV. No hanky panky now."

"Yes, sir." Kelsey settled herself against his bare chest, finding a stillness in his arms that she didn't know she was capable of. She didn't care what was on TV. JD was holding her, and she could feel his cheek against her head. She snuggled in deeper.

She knew that he would take care of her, yet all she wanted was to take care of him. Even now, he was thinking of her children before himself. She turned her head against his chest, enjoying the feel of his skin on hers.

"Stop that!"

"What?" She demanded.

"That squirming."

"Like this?" She couldn't help herself. At least that's what her brain tried to make her believe. But she wiggled her butt against him, and enjoyed the groan he made.

"You know," His arms tightened around her. "Two can play at that game."

He bit at her neck and kissed behind her ear, his tongue hot and searching. His hands trailed down her belly and across her thighs, the material of her nightgown preventing what they both really wanted. In seconds they had picked up where they left off, it was all she could do to keep from exploding and she writhed in his hands as they found her breasts, and made her gasp for air.

His mouth found her other ear, and he stopped kissing her for just long enough to whisper heated words. "I cannot believe you let me touch you like this."

She froze at his voice, her eyes blinking as her hands grabbed his. She pressed his fingers flat and still against her stomach, covering them with her own, "Let me make this clear: I do not *let* you touch me. I love you touching me, I live for you touching me."

Kelsey let go of his hands, and instantly they went further than they had before, unbuttoning the tiny white shell buttons that held the top of her gown together. One hand slipped inside, cupping her breast, making her strain against him. She got revenge by trailing her fingers up his thighs until they met at his zipper. She deftly undid it and plunged her hands inside, feeling his skin hot and tight against hers.

JD growled in her ear, and she would have laughed if she wasn't so out of control herself. His hips moved against her hands, and his fingers pulled the bottom hem of her nightgown up until he reached her hip. She felt his whole body freeze. "You're not wearing any underwear."

His fingers found motion and clenched at her bare skin. Kelsey moved against the hands that touched her. "I don't usually sleep in it."

He pulled her leg up and dove his fingers into her, tearing a loud moan out of her throat.

They both heard a door click, and again scrambled for composure. JD yanked her gown down and his hand out from under her top. Kelsey reclaimed her own hands, and waited. But no small child appeared.

They waited.

Nothing.

JD let out a jagged breath. "What do we do? This obviously won't keep until tomorrow. We can't go get a hotel room. Can we lock ourselves in a closet?"

Kelsey sat up straight, breaking skin contact with him. "I'm going to move Andie into my room."

JD volunteered to move her, but Kelsey insisted. "Let me."

She didn't wait for him to answer. She needed him, and this was the only solution she could figure. So she went into the room, making her way by a nightlight that was identical to the one in the other room. Scooping Andie up, sleeping bag and all, she whispered soft words. "You're going to have a slumber party tonight, with Daniel and Allie. You'll wake up in their room."

Andie murmured a little right then, but Kelsey kept talking to her. JD's daughter was partially awake when she was arranged in the only open floor space in the master bedroom. Kelsey stroked her head and told her to go back to sleep.

She emerged to JD's open arms, but she refused them. "We need to wait about half an hour to be sure she's really back to sleep."

JD looked at her like she was tormenting him.

"I don't want to be interrupted."

He conceded to that, and quietly went into the kitchen where he poured her another glass of juice. It was about the only thing in the fridge now that the fish were out. Kelsey drank it down enjoying the feel of the cold liquid in her throat. She'd spent so much of this night happily overheated.

He turned to her after leaving his own glass in the sink, "It's a good thing you moved Andie, and not the other way around. The condoms are in there."

"You brought condoms on this trip?"

He shook his head, a tiny smile played across his lips. "No. I never imagined this in my wildest dreams." Almost immediately he rescinded. "No, I did imagine this—never this well, mind you —but I didn't believe it would really happen."

Kelsey could feel the flush creeping up her neck and staining her cheeks. It was heady hearing those words from an insanely attractive man, wearing only unzipped jeans, in the middle of the night. That it was JD made it a thousand-fold stronger. She tried changing the topic. "So you *found* the condoms?" She scrunched her nose.

"Here, I'll show you how I found them."

He tugged on her hand, pulling her along into his room,

353

casual now that they had paused, now that they knew what was coming. He lifted his suitcase lid and pulled out a generic red gift bag from under his socks.

Kelsey frowned at it.

With a wry look on his face, JD pulled a huge combo pack of condoms out of the bag.

She laughed. "What is that? The fraternity house pack?" According to the box there were almost fifty condoms of various flavors and textures in there.

"Probably. It also came with these." He produced what looked like two greeting cards.

Her eyebrows went up. Someone made greeting cards to send with a huge box of condoms? One said 'JD' across the front, the other said 'K'.

The 'JD' card was already split open, and he pulled it out of the envelope, handing it over to her. "Here's what mine said."

She flipped open what was originally a blank card. Each of the guys had written in it.

JD—Just tell her how you feel.
    You'll feel better when you do.—Alex
    Yeah, we'll ALL feel better when you do.—Craig
    Hey, Moron, Andrew was her brother.—TJ

JD raised his eyebrows as he watched her read it. "I haven't read yours but I wanted you to have an idea what might be in it." He handed her the unopened envelope and waited while she ripped into it.

It was from only one person, and it made her heart slow.

You should see the way he looks at you when you aren't

watching.

It had to be Bridget. None of the guys had that script. Just that one line. She showed him the card.

JD simply nodded. "That's true."

Kelsey flipped the cards into a corner, not watching where they landed. Then she grabbed the box of condoms out of his hand. "You don't need those. I'm on the pill."

At his grin, she tossed the box of condoms out of the way.

She decided she hadn't heard a peep out of Andie and they'd waited long enough. She tugged at his jeans, and his hands covered hers, but he wasn't helping her. In fact, he was stopping her.

Confused, Kelsey met his gaze.

JD reached behind her and locked the door, then lifted his hands to frame her face. "I messed this up last time. Not again."

Her hands found his lean arms and held on, the rest of her reveled in the feel of his calloused fingertips against her smooth skin.

"Kelsey Conklin, I love you. I am crazy in love with you. This is not casual in the slightest way. And don't you dare leave this bed without notifying me first."

She would have laughed at that last line, but his mouth closed over hers. He had kissed her into such a frenzy for him, that a minute later, when he broke the contact to pull her gown over her head she was crazy without him for even those few seconds.

He just looked at her for a minute, standing naked before him, wearing only the locket he had given her for Christmas. She found her voice. "I love you, JD."

He let her help him slip out of the jeans he was still in, then he laid her backwards onto the comforter and drove into her.

She screamed out his name.

CHAPTER 39

JD cringed when Kelsey punched him in the arm. "What?"

"Don't you dare apologize for that!"

"It was too fast."

Kelsey heaved a sigh at him.

He reminded himself that he was okay. He was naked. She was naked. It was pitch black beyond the window and she was still here.

She pinned him in her sights. "Was I wet?"

God, she made him boil. "Yes."

"Did I come?"

Forget boiling, he went up in flames. It was all he could do to push that one small word out. He was already reaching for her. "Yes."

But she pushed his hands away.

He blinked and started to get worried. But he only managed to get started. She rolled over him and pinned his hands down. "Was it bad for you?"

How could she think that? "Oh, God, Kelse, I've never had anything like you." The words gushed out of him in a river of want.

"Then you will do it again, and you may take as much time as you want, but afterward you will just say how wonderful it was."

She started kissing him, even as he was laughing. "You think you can boss me around just because you're older than me?"

Immediately Kelsey sat back on her heels, bothered. Just bothered, not hot and bothered like he wanted her to be. "Is it a problem that I'm older than you?"

He pushed her hair back away from her beautiful, worried face. He shook his head 'no'. "It doesn't bother me that you're smarter than me, either. Does it bother you that I'm bigger? Stronger? Right now, I'm wealthier."

She stretched out beside him, naked and warm, and kissed his shoulder. "I like that you're bigger than me, and stronger." She shrugged sending a shiver of friction all along the side of his body, and lighting his fire a little brighter, if that was possible. "Wealthier comes and goes."

"I think it's sexy that you're older. Do I act too immature for you?"

She made a face and turned away. "I'm going to admit that I kept expecting you to. But you never did."

He smiled at her, reached for her, but she wasn't finished.

"I underestimated you, and I'm sorry. I've known a lot of 'men' who thought they deserved the title simply because of their gender and some age they'd reached. But you earn it, every day."

How she had the power to undo him like that was beyond him. She thought too much of him, but the last thing he ever wanted to do was lose that. He pulled her close, maybe so she couldn't see how much she'd shaken him. He wanted to find comfort in her. But he was ready for more, too, and he wanted her. He grinned into her hair, content even as he burned that she wanted him, too. He'd implode if he waited in this vacuum where she thought so highly of him. His fingers found his way into her hair, and he exposed one delicious ear. He whispered,

"Aren't women supposed to be hitting their sexual peak at thirty-five?"

She pretended to be offended, her mouth hanging open. "Is that what this is about? You know, *you* are way past your sexual prime, old man." She rolled away, playing with him. "I'll just have to find some seventeen-year-old who can keep up with me."

Because it was simply a joke, JD wasn't prepared for the jolt of deep jealousy that speared him in the gut. He grabbed her before she even made it to the edge of the bed, and kissed them both senseless. "I'll keep up."

He was hard as a rock again, and certain that, with her around, he was about to re-enter his late teens. When she looked up at him, breathless, he found a few words. "No one else, only me. Ever."

He proceeded to show her why.

There was light, too much of it. And a pounding in his head.

But, as tired as he was, JD was enjoying the feeling of being sated and content for the first time in what felt like forever. The pounding continued, and it wasn't in his head, it was on the bedroom door. He rolled to see how Kelsey was managing to sleep through this, since she hadn't moved at all, and he discovered that she wasn't there.

JD bolted from the bed, hollered at whoever was at the door to wait a minute, and slid into clean underwear and jeans. He was zipping them as he reached for the handle, and just put together when he pulled back the noisy door to see his daughter standing there asking if she could go swimming.

Jesus, swimming was so far out of his scope right now. "Baby, we'll decide later, in a little bit. Where's Kelsey?"

"I'm right here." The words were muffled, but it was her voice coming from the open bathroom door.

JD stood there and offered her the courtesy of letting her finish brushing her teeth. His heart slowed its racing as he saw the smile in her eyes. But then he gave her the what for. "Which part of 'you don't dare leave this bed without notifying me' did you have trouble with?"

"You looked so sweet and yummy all worn out, so I decided to let you sleep in."

He shook his head at her, monitoring what he said because three small pairs of eyes and ears were on the two of them. "And I woke up, alone in my bed, *again*."

"Did you have a slumber party, too?" Allie's eyes lit up.

God bless her for giving him something he could work with. He got down to Allie's level. "Yes, we did." He couldn't help the way his eyes lit at the thought, or that they automatically went to Kelsey, who was chewing her lip and making him think things that shouldn't be in his brain with children in the room.

Daniel said he was hungry then, and JD ushered them all off to the living room. "Daniel, why don't you find a cartoon to watch and Kelsey and I will decide what we're doing today."

The kids shuffled off, and JD waited for a moment until he heard the voices coming from the screen. Kelsey must have been waiting for it, too, because she chose that moment to launch herself into his arms, and kiss him senseless. She tasted of mint and rightness.

He pressed her against the wall in the bathroom while the kids watched TV just out of sight. No, she wouldn't have to worry about him keeping up with her. He would more likely have to worry about being presentable in public.

Knowing it wasn't the right time for this, he pried himself away from her and started talking anyway. "I had this idea for what to do our last day out."

"Yeah?" She picked up her hairbrush and started working it through her hair. She made a face; he'd tangled it something fierce last night. He made a face, too, but his was one of arrogance.

"Let me do that." He reached out for the brush, and stood behind her, both of them facing the bathroom mirror in the tiny space. "So I was thinking we might ditch the cabin tonight, and head back to Vegas early."

"There's nothing really for the kids to do there."

He worked through another tangle, starting at the bottom. "They can go shopping with us."

She bit. "What are we shopping for?"

"Depends." He gently pulled through another tangle. "How long do I have you for, Kelse?"

Her eyes met his in the mirror. "As long as you want me."

"Then we're going engagement ring shopping."

Her eyes widened to take up her whole head. "Are you serious?"

"All you have to do is say *yes*." Trying to look like his heart wasn't racing, he casually pulled the brush through her hair again.

She leaned into it. "You're trying to sway me by asking while you brush my hair. You know I love this. But it isn't going to work."

Shit. "Whenever you want."

Her eyes, which had fallen closed again, opened and locked on his. "Yes. We can go today, if you want."

He grinned, and kissed her neck. "Women seem to think men are all commitmentphobes. But that just isn't so. You just need the right woman. For example, I'll marry you in Vegas tonight if you want."

This time she turned to face him. "You're serious."

He held his breath, not knowing why he'd pushed it, she'd

already said 'yes.' JD nodded. She didn't say anything, and his stupid mouth rambled to fill the space. "Again, whenever you want. But I was thinking that we have a best man and a maid of honor and a flower girl sitting in the living room. We could have a big reception later, invite everyone, but I really want this to just be about us."

He stopped. 'This' wasn't written in stone yet. He was pushing her. And pushing a woman was a bad idea most of the time. He didn't know why he'd started it—

Her mouth sealed over his. She pressed herself to him. But there wasn't any passion to it. Just that calm feeling that the world was right. That he was safe where he was. That she loved him. *Him*. Not some image or idea she had of him.

"That sounds like a really good idea." Her eyes were over-bright.

She stepped past him, and into the living room. The TV was on a commercial and Kelsey just quietly flipped it off getting the kids attention. "All right guys. Here's the plan for today: We're going to go to Vegas and get married."

From the breathy quality to her voice, she was still adjusting to the idea.

"Who's getting married?" Andie looked at them.

"All of us." JD crouched down in front of the couch where the three kids sat. "We're all going to be one family." He hugged Andie, then Daniel and Allie joined in as well.

Only Allie looked disappointed.

JD tilted his head to catch her frown. "What's wrong, baby?"

She sniffed. "I want to go swimming."

Daniel looked him in the eye, too mature for his age. Kelsey was right, something had to be done about that. "Can we do both?"

"That sounds like a plan." Kelsey grinned at JD. "Half an hour of swimming then we pack up and go get married."

Allie jumped up, and JD couldn't stifle the laugh. What a weird day it was turning out to be. "Last one in their suit is a rotten egg."

The kids scattered screaming, and he stole one quick kiss from a still-stunned Kelsey before he went to change.

CHAPTER 40

They'd changed their flights and gotten back into Nashville later than they planned. The one-night honeymoon was hardly enough, and hardly a honeymoon. The kids had slept in the other bedroom in the suite, and were so keyed up that they hadn't wanted to sleep until Kelsey took a magazine in and lorded over them, making sure they stayed quiet. Once they calmed down they went right to sleep, and Kelsey emerged with her magazine tucked under her arm.

JD took it away. She didn't need *This month's man without his shirt*.

They did manage to put the whirlpool tub to good use. And later the bed. They didn't get much sleep, that was for certain. And JD had begun to wonder when he ever would rest again. He'd gotten far more sleep as a single parent than he was getting with Kelsey in his bed. Still, he had no complaints.

He let himself into the studio knowing that he was late. "Sorry guys, our flight was delayed."

They had a long practice set this morning, because the guys had all scattered for the last eight days, and they had two shows in the coming week. The others all looked up from various tunings and warm-up exercises.

TJ looked him up and down, and JD waited for it. But it didn't come the way he expected. His face got a better inspection than his hand. They hadn't noticed.

TJ let loose a wicked grin. "You look like you haven't slept, but you look darn happy. You got our present."

"Yes." JD still didn't know what to make of all that.

"How many did you use?"

JD pasted a pained expression on his face. "Not a single one."

"No way!" Craig joined in the conversation vehemently. And JD thought his friend deserved whatever he got for that "We'll ALL feel better" comment.

"Then why do you look happy?" TJ unfurled a microphone cord but didn't take his eyes off his brother.

"We worked something out. It's settled."

"That's it? Settled? Dude, she's head over heels in love with you."

"Oh." JD turned back to his baby brother and laid it on thick. "And that's why I found you wrapped around her in the kitchen that night?"

JD almost laughed as he turned away. Craig and Alex went after TJ like vultures. "You scoped your brother's woman?" and "If you go near Bridget I will kill you."

TJ shot him a burning look, and JD fought for a straight face. "I did *not* go after her. She was upset, and she couldn't turn to you. I was just a stand in."

JD conceded. "Well, we found a truce. Let's just play."

They started up with the guys still shaking their heads and JD fighting not to laugh. They went through the play-list for the next several shows. They had different amounts of time on stage each night, and they adjusted accordingly. *I am* got played in both sets, but didn't twist any knives in him now.

Kelsey showed up with lunch. She brought stacks of deli

sandwiches, and barrels of sodas. She had one of those drink holders with two cokes, a diet coke, a root beer and a lemonade. It was stupid, but he liked that she paid attention to what each of them preferred. She didn't lean in to kiss him, just said 'hi'.

He'd told her he was going to let the guys figure it out for themselves, and when they still hadn't assaulted her about the rock she wore on her left hand after a few minutes she leaned over to JD. "Are they blind?"

"Apparently." Out loud he told her that Brenda had left her some photo information on Straight Up in the office, figuring that he could deliver it to her.

"Oh!" She hopped up and followed him into the office, anxious to see what Brenda had left.

JD just locked the door and kissed her. "You wore that skirt. I can't help myself when you're showing that much leg. Can I?"

"MmmmmHmmmm." She growled at him. Kissed him, bit him, then yelped. "No!"

"What!?"

"I forgot my pill this morning. With getting the kids back to school and being so worn out . . . I just . . ."

"I don't care." He started kissing her again.

Again, she stopped him. "Are you just in the moment or do you really want to try and have a baby?"

"I've got three kids, and I never had a baby. I have lost all phobias about fatherhood. I want your baby. If you do."

She didn't answer him, just launched herself at him in that way she had that told him *yes, yes, yes*. He didn't think he'd ever get enough of that.

He turned her around and placed her hands flat on the wall. He used that short skirt to his advantage and made her bite her lip to keep from screaming out. When they finished, he stood over her breathing heavily, never having thought that the possibility of getting her pregnant would be such an aphrodisiac.

His hands covered hers, and for a moment he just liked the look of those two solid gold bands, side by side, hers stacked with the rock he had spent too much money on. He still didn't care about that though.

He helped her put herself back together, and enjoyed the half shy, half sly smile on her face. And he caught her looking at her ring again.

"Yeah, I like mine, too."

"Most men think it's a shackle."

"Nah." He kissed her ear as he said it. "I like that when I wake up and you're not there, or when I'm here and I think it all isn't quite real yet, I can see I didn't hallucinate the whole thing. You shouldn't have left me on that bus. You gave me a complex."

She wrinkled her nose at him. "Yeah, I'm sorry about that."

"It's my fault. I could have made it all go differently."

Her head tilted, shy and sweet, she was hardly the vixen of a few moments ago. "I married you because it all went wrong."

"You're going to have to explain that one."

"As bad as it was, you didn't walk away. You never let me down, no matter how hurt either of us was. You could have easily disappeared and never spoken to me again. But you picked up the phone and called me and kept coming back and working to fix it."

As usual, she gave him too much credit. "TJ shoved the phone in my face and made me call you."

"Every day?"

"The first two."

She nodded. "Yeah, TJ wasn't there for most of it. It was you."

JD breathed her in and kissed her hair. "I love you. But we'd better get out there before we get missed." He pulled the photos off the desk and put them in her hands before she left empty handed.

TJ looked up the second the door was opened. "You two

were gone quite a little while there, and she's got a serious flush going. I figured it out."

Kelsey blushed an even deeper shade at TJ's proclamation, but JD wanted to hear this. "So?"

TJ looked proud. "You didn't like the brand or something and bought your own. That's how you didn't use any. Because you sure look like you fixed your problems the good way."

Alex looked at JD but spoke to his brother. "TJ, you've missed the most important thing. Look at her hand."

"You're engaged!" TJ shreiked that.

And gave JD the ultimate joy of saying "Nope, wrong again."

"But she's wearing that rock."

JD waited, but none of them got it. Finally, it was Kelsey who heaved a sigh and solved all the puzzled looks. She held up his hand and showed off his wedding band.

EPILOGUE

C hristmas

Kelsey covered her eyes like JD had told her. She was surprised when he slipped her jacket around her shoulders. It was still too big, but not for long. She was getting bigger every day. They had all gotten dressed to see her new present, and she had no idea what it was. All she knew now was that it was outside.

There was a chattering in a little row behind her, "What is it, Daddy?"

Allie had started calling him Daddy even while she'd hopped down the hallways in Vegas, skipping and telling everyone that she'd just gotten married. Everyone had smiled at the little girl because she'd been trailing JD in his tux carrying Kelsey in her white gown.

Daniel still said 'JD' when he addressed his step-father. But he more than accepted JD as his father. Even now, he was getting a little pushy, "What *is* it? Why didn't you tell me? You know I can keep a secret."

"So can I." JD told her son behind her back. She still had her eyes closed, and the kids insisted that she actually cover them.

JD took her arm and led her outside, the cold turning her cheeks a sharp red, she was sure. That was one of those side effects of the pregnancy. But he was a good husband and told her he thought it was cute. He whispered in her ear, "In a little while it's not going to fit, but after the baby it will."

That made her think it was clothes, but she couldn't fathom why he'd bring her outside to give her clothes. She heard little shoes on the porch steps behind her, and thought of one more set of little feet running around.

For a moment she breathed in the harshly cold air, and was content. She wasn't scared. She hadn't felt alone in what felt like forever. Her photography business was doing better and better. She still had all three kids to herself when Wilder went out on tour. But those tours were paying all the bills, and there was nothing like hearing them on the radio.

Brenda had released *I am* just prior to Christmas, thinking that women would want it and men would want to give it. Kelsey knew it was hers. She didn't care if she ever opened her eyes, it was all good already.

But the kids were getting fussy, and JD was shushing them, and it *was* cold.

"Can I look?"

"Go ahead, baby."

She blinked in the bright light, not believing that the antique Mustang convertible was sitting in the driveway. She blinked again, taking in the fresh teal paint job that had been buffed to a waxy shine.

JD was nervous. He started talking a mile a minute. "I got this bonus when the album went platinum, and I didn't tell you. I just knew what I wanted to spend it on. And it was finally ready last week, so it was perfect. I had it delivered last night."

She put her hand on his arm, and smiled at him, knowing it

would calm him down to know that she was okay with it. But still she blinked. "I can't believe you remembered. I . . . I didn't know you were paying attention."

He gave her a wicked grin that stopped her breath. "Baby, I was always paying attention."

AFTERWORD

Dear Reader,

I hope Kelsey and JD moved you as much as they did me. This was one of the first romance novels I wrote, and when I started, this book was a stand-alone novel. Their story spoke to me: an epic boy-next-door classic about finding real love when you'd given up. While I writing their romance, I realized all the guys in *Wilder* needed their stories told. I want to say to them what JD says to Kelsey: I was always paying attention.

If you loved *Our Song*, I'd be honored if you'd leave a review!

PREVIEW OF HEARTSTRINGS
(WILDER - BOOK 2)

Every wedding had that point. The pictures were taken, the reception was over, even the bride and groom were gone. A bridesmaid's job was done. She'd had just enough fun and just enough champagne to find herself standing in the low surf and having big thoughts as the tide rolled in.

Shay was drunk enough to make the effort to hold up the hem on the gown she'd spent painstaking hours on, and sober enough to understand it wasn't working.

"You're going to ruin that dress." The voice came from behind her. From back on dry sand, it rolled over her, deep, masculine, and maybe a little concerned.

"I'll just hem it. That's what you're supposed to do with a bridesmaid's dress anyway, right?" In fact, she'd designed it to be hemmed and worn again. Not that she believed any of the other four bridesmaids would do that. Even if she hemmed it, even if it were shorter, flirtier, less formal, she still wouldn't have anywhere to wear it. So she let go of the wad of taffeta in her clenched fist, allowing the beautiful gauzy fabric to swish with the waves at her feet.

She was officially on vacation now.

Ten minutes down. Two more days to go.

"Are you okay to be standing in the waves? I'm afraid one might knock you over." Definitely concerned.

She smiled and still didn't turn around. It was good this way. A man talking to her, worried about her well-being. It was probably only a clerk who didn't want her to get swept out to sea and create negative publicity for a hot Miami Beach hotel that had just hosted the wedding of country star Hailey Watkins. "Oh yes, I'm really good."

The slightly off answer probably only proved that she wasn't all there. *Oh well.*

"You want some company?" The voice was closer behind her now. He was already standing in the waves.

Shay hoped for his sake he'd taken off his shoes. She knew what salt water did to clothes, shoes, more. "Sure. If you want."

Then he was beside her, though she still didn't look. She just got a glimpse of a sleek suit, worn well, but she wasn't ready to give up the fantasy just yet. His hands went in his pockets. "That dress is amazing, but it doesn't do you justice."

She laughed. "I'm not *that* drunk."

She hadn't been that drunk in a long time, and she wouldn't ever be again. Truth be told, there had been a time when a man hadn't even needed to get her drunk. Just a compliment would do it. Anything she could latch onto and pretend.

Not anymore.

"Good." He chuckled. "But the dress is amazing."

"Thank you. Are you saying that because you know I made it?" She turned and caught his surprise at that.

Hailey had always been really good about talking up Shay and her skills, but never about making her seem like the help. Maybe because Hailey had been the help, too, once upon a time.

They'd grown up next door, fed each other when pantries went empty, waited tables together, partied together, and then Hailey left, taking her guitar and heading to Nashville. When she made it, she'd done as much as she could for Shay. Having Shay as her maid of honor was a touching gesture. Shay's heart had warmed, knowing that Hailey really did still consider her a friend and equal.

She couldn't say the same of the man beside her.

Craig Hibbets. Bass and backup vocals for Wilder. Despite a few rocket-hot, smash singles off their first album, they hadn't faded away. Their new stuff was climbing the charts even faster.

She gave a small smile, glad the fantasy held up. Craig Hibbets was a pleasure to look at.

She knew him intimately. The breadth of his shoulders. The length of his leg. The taper of his waist. The distance from elbow to fingertip. Where his tattoos were. He didn't know her at all.

Shay blinked. She'd made the tie he was wearing. Hailey had requested them as presents for the guys for Christmas. When she'd first been signed, her friend had shared a tour with Wilder, alternating tour dates and allowing each music group occasional breaks. They'd become friends, working under the same label.

Hailey had given her handler at the label Shay's name for costuming. The handler had given it to other groups. It kept Shay employed. For that she was grateful. But the tie was also a reminder of the distance between them.

"Did you make all the bridesmaids' dresses?" He asked, still not realizing who she was. That some of the things he'd worn on stage were things she'd sewed for him.

"Yes."

Shay didn't offer more. It was nice having a stunningly good-looking man standing next to her, while warm water licked at her feet and the hem of the nicest dress she'd ever owned. But she didn't want him to talk, didn't want him to ruin it with reality.

He waited a moment, looking at the last of the light on the

water as the sun set behind them. Then he spoke again. "You were pretty busy back there. Did you get anything to eat?"

"Sure. About an hour ago." She smiled as she turned and felt the world tip a little. "What time is it?"

"Almost eight."

"Shit." She regretted the word as soon as it flew out of her mouth. "I had probably one of the appetizers?"

"That was not an hour ago." He grinned, his eyes lighting up. "Let's get you some food."

She shook her head to protest right as a wave hit her shins. The water had gotten higher while she'd watched the ocean. That wasn't as much of a problem as the fact that the whole lower third of her gown was soaked and wafting with the tide, pushing her to land then pulling her out to sea.

She stumbled, grabbing onto his arm as he caught her. So when she righted herself and stood on her own, Shay agreed. "Okay. I do need food."

He took her hand firmly, probably just to keep her upright and they began the slow trudge of getting her gown out of the water. Finally on dry sand, he leaned over and picked up both their pairs of shoes, not handing her the sandals that were so gorgeous she'd never have a place to wear them again either.

"I'm good."

He didn't let go. "Let's get something to eat." He gestured to the restaurant tables on the patio looking out over the ocean.

Shay could not afford to eat there or anywhere near the posh hotel. But Hailey had booked the room for her as long as she wanted. Covered all the bills, including anything she charged to the room. Even encouraged her to get her sister to babysit so she could stay a few extra days and have a real vacation while Hailey and Adam went off on their honeymoon. Still, Shay refused.

"I have to change. I have sand on my feet. My dress is wet."

He shook his head. "It's a beach-front hotel. You're supposed have sand on your feet when you eat on the terrace. You look stunning. Join me."

He didn't let go of her hand.

"Okay." It was a small concession. One she hadn't made in a very long time.

Shay didn't know if the hostess recognized him, but they were seated quickly at the railing, putting each of them parallel to the beach. The light had disappeared, and though the night was warm, her dress made her chilly.

At the first sign of a shiver, Craig peeled his suit jacket and draped it around her shoulders. She was pulling it up when the server came by, offering wine.

"Maybe just water for us." Craig said, then had her choose appetizers.

"I'm not a lush." She commented. *Who was he to order for her?*

"You didn't eat." He shrugged. "You can order what you want. You want a glass of wine, a margarita, get it." He grinned at her, redeeming an action that had seemed heavy-handed. "But I want to ask you something later, and I'll only ask if you're sober."

"What is that?" She frowned at him.

"Not until later." He became evasive, hiding behind the water glass as it was filled.

He asked her how she knew Hailey, and she explained that the two had grown up together. She didn't tell that their 'houses' had been trailers. Or that Hailey had finally saved enough to get out of town. She answered as evasively as he did, then turned the tables and asked him about Wilder, about touring, about playing on stage.

"You recognized me?" He tipped his head.

Of course she did. She had a file on each of the four guys. Measurements, favorite color, fabric preferences. She didn't say it, just let him talk about what it was like to become a star. Shay compared it to Hailey's story, finding some similarities, some differences.

They ate appetizers while he talked. Then they dug into beautifully plated entrees that couldn't have been enough food for him.

Shay commented.

"I ate at the wedding. You didn't. I'm good." He cleaned the plate with gusto, a second dinner not beyond him.

When she finally sat back, sated, she sighed. On the tail end of her breath came his question.

"Do you want to come up to my room with me?"

Startled, she looked at him.

Craig held the glass of water casually, his big hand drawing her attention. He looked at her through surfer-blond hair that kept creeping over his eyes.

"Was that your 'later' question?"

He nodded, but didn't ask again.

She was completely sober now. She'd heard him.

He waited for nearly a full minute, then asked a follow-up. "Is it that hard to answer?"

She laughed. He wasn't mean or pushy about it. He seemed sincerely interested in having her up to his room. Instead of yes or no she tested the waters.

"You just looking to snag a bridesmaid?"

Despite the catch in her voice, he managed to keep the mood light with a charming grin. "Nope. There were other bridesmaids and single guests that would have been easier to catch."

That was true. The champagne had flowed, the bar had been open, and after the bouquet had been thrown more than one single lady had tried hard to not be single for the night. Shay had not been one of them.

She really hadn't considered this. "And tomorrow?"

"We each fly home. You go your way, I go mine." He was open about it at least. Not leading her on.

They'd only had a few hours together. Could she trust him?

He seemed to catch on and held his arms out to his side openly. "Ask me anything."

She didn't. "Yes. Let's."

Thank you for reading! I love romances with real love and believable characters, and I hope you found all that in these pages. I want to fall in love right along with the characters, and I do, while I'm writing it.

About Savannah

I started writing when I was eight--I hand wrote an 80-page novella that I believed to be (adult) romantic suspense. I'm proud to say, I've gotten a lot better since then. I've grown up to be a nerd at heart! I love neuroscience and people watching, and if you look, you'll find some of that in each Savannah Kade book. Most days you'll find me in my office, looking out my window at a handful of the neighbor's cows, or watching my dogs or my cat roam the backyard.

Follow me, find me, ask me questions! I would love to hear from you.
www.SavannahKade.com
Savannah@SavannahKade.com